THE
BOOK
OF
EXODUS

പുറപ്പാടിന്റെ പുസ്തകം

THE BOOK OF EXODUS

പുറപ്പാടിന്റെ പുസ്തകം

V.J. James

Translated from the Malayalam by
Ministhy S.

VINTAGE
An imprint of Penguin Random House

VINTAGE

Vintage is an imprint of the Penguin Random House group of companies
whose addresses can be found at global.penguinrandomhouse.com

Published by Penguin Random House India Pvt. Ltd
4th Floor, Capital Tower 1, MG Road,
Gurugram 122 002, Haryana, India

Penguin
Random House
India

First published in Vintage by Penguin Random House India 2024

Copyright © V.J. James 2024
Translation copyright © Ministhy S. 2024

All rights reserved

10 9 8 7 6 5 4 3 2 1

This is a work of fiction. Names, characters, places and incidents are either the
product of the author's imagination or are used fictitiously and any resemblance
to any actual person, living or dead, events or locales is entirely coincidental.

Please note that no part of this book may be used or reproduced in any manner
for the purpose of training artifi cial intelligence technologies or systems.

ISBN 9780670096534

Typeset in Adobe Caslon Pro by Manipal Technologies Limited, Manipal
Printed at Replika Press Pvt. Ltd, India

www.penguin.co.in

MIX
Paper | Supporting
responsible forestry
FSC™ C016779

To my loving parents in heaven,
Antony Joseph (Vavachan) and Marykutty Joseph

—V.J. James

In memory of two beloved souls: R. Shankaran Nair, my Kappal
Valiyachan (Ship Uncle), and R. Sreekantan Nair, my father

—Ministhy S.

But when they measured it with an omer,
those who gathered much had nothing over, and those
who gathered little had no shortage

—*Exodus 16:18*

Contents

Author's Note

The Story behind Exodus

It was two years after joining the Vikram Sarabhai Space Centre that I began writing *The Book of Exodus*. However, as I was tied up with official assignments and other commitments, it took me more than twelve years to complete the novel. During that period, I must have edited and rewritten the 430-page-long manuscript, in my own handwriting, nearly ten times. My desire was to get the novel published, as a series, in any reputed literary magazine of Kerala. For someone with no godfathers in literature, a credulous novice who had no acquaintances in the field, it was not an easy task. One day, gathering courage, I shot off a letter to M.T. Vasudevan Nair, the famous writer, who was then the editor of the weekly *Mathrubhumi*. When I received his reply asking me to submit my manuscript, my delight knew no bounds. I was very confident that once he read the novel, it would get published in *Mathrubhumi*. It might have been my misfortune, but MT resigned from his post soon after. Thus ended my dream of publishing *Exodus* as a serialized novel in the best Malayalam literary magazine.

In my second attempt to see the novel in print, I approached *Kala Kaumudi*, another leading magazine. After evaluating the script in a mere fortnight, they informed that it was an excellent novel, assuring publication in a short while. Of course, I was thrilled. However, at that juncture, *Kala Kaumudi* received a novel from the famous writer Madhavikutty, and I was relegated to the sidelines, destined to wait for months. When two more novels became serialized in succession, I endured the agony of a rookie yet again, with nobody to look out for him.

During a phase of depression, since my novel was not getting published due to reasons beyond my control, I unexpectedly ended up reading a discarded newspaper page during a train journey. There was an advertisement about the DC Books Award, about a competition for novelists, in connection with their silver jubilee celebrations. Since I had faced many rejections on various fronts, I did not even inform my family about entering the competition. Under the assumption that a lot of behind-the-scenes games went on while determining winners in any literary event, I had convinced myself not to expect anything from the venture. However, when *The Book of Exodus* was declared the best novel among 161 entries, I realized that the path of the book had been decided much earlier. Thus, after one 'Vana Vasa' and yet another year's 'Ajnata Vasa', *The Book of Exodus* saw the light of day. By that time, the one who had begun writing had transformed into someone totally different.

I believe that words have an unassailable power; and if the writing is robust, the book shall find its own way. Every book shall seek out the person destined to read it. My debut novel was published during the grand function celebrating the silver jubilee of DC Books. And the award sculpture was the creation of O.V. Vijayan, someone whom I had silently revered as my guru in literature. I received the award from the literary star Arundhati Roy, and many of the stalwarts of Malayalam literature, art and culture—O.N.V. Kurup, T. Padmanabhan, Madhavikutty, Zakaria, Punathil Kunjabdulla, M. Mukundan, Adoor Gopalakrishnan, M.V. Devan, Asha Menon, C.V. Balakrishnan, Mundoor Krishnankutty, M. Thomas Mathew et al.—graced the august venue. When my beloved author Madhavikutty handed over the award citation, she blessed me by placing her hand on my head—an unforgettable moment that I shall always cherish.

Thus, ending the long years of waiting and interminable refusals, *Akshara Shakti*, or the perpetual power of words, kindly ushered me in, with all the grandeur that a beginner could ever dream of, and I was offered a seat in the middle of Malayalam literature's glorious courtyard! On that day, I understood that the Akshara can never be inferior to anything. That's why the wise called it Akshara, the non-perishable, indestructible.

While studying in Mar Athanasius Engineering College in Kothamangalam, I had inadvertently visited an isle in the neighbourhood of Kochi, to attend the wedding of my friend Patris's sister. I had no idea that the isle had been waiting for the writer, with a cast of intriguing characters and a haunting ambience. From that vantage point, one could glimpse the sparkling hauteur of Kochi's city lights. But no development had crossed over the river to reach that isolated isle. For a drop of drinking water, the pitiable natives had to row to the opposite riverbank and wait for hours at the water pipe. If that remote isle and its fascinating atmosphere had not stirred me awake, I would never have been a writer.

Unable to resist that siren call, I returned many times to seek the soul of the isle. I made myself an inseparable part of it, trying to comprehend the strange dialect, the fascinating rural customs and the innumerable, mysterious myths. It helped that I had spent my childhood in Kuttanadu and was familiar with lands surrounded by water. Like an inveterate explorer, I travelled for years through the stories of Chemmeen Kettu, Pachu Vanchi, Bhimanattam, local arrack, crab curry and their ilk . . . These had all come together, to invoke *The Book of Exodus*.

A lot of people asked me why *The Book of Exodus* became a book of death and melancholy. There was a time, as the novel evolved, when I could not afford even the luxury of a writing table. It was a time when I recognized that man loved pain and death, even as he pretended to hate them.

Even today, I have among my prized possessions the letters written by many readers—written in the exquisite language of the heart, addressed to someone dear. One reader wrote that no book had ever made him cry until *The Book of Exodus*, and he was writing to testify that poignant fact. Another wrote to me narrating how he had ignored the unknown writer's book for six months in the lending library and unwittingly picked it up one day, since no other option was available. He expressed his deep regret in keeping himself away from *Exodus* for such a long time. The countless letters, from serious readers, including Sathyan Anthikkadu, the brilliant director, who wrote to me while in thrall of the book; the ensuing friendships with many famous and ordinary people—these were among the few gifts *The Book of Exodus* showered on me.

The unexpected death of my friend Patris, who was instrumental in guiding me to the isle where *Exodus* was born, was devastating. Afterwards, though I visited the region where the seed of *Exodus* had germinated and sprouted, I never ventured to the isle, preferring to look at it from the opposite shore. Now it is an isle of pain for me: many characters having chosen it for their eternal rest. As of today, Koppan, Anita, Murali, Parutty provoke grief in many hearts, including mine.

There were many who wished and prayed that *The Book of Exodus* would cross over the frontiers of the Malayalam language. On the silver jubilee year of publication of the original, as if it was destined, that dream stands fulfilled, and one feels joyous at watching a book graciously enduring over time. It gives me much happiness that Penguin Random House India, which has published my four novels: *Chorashastra*, *Anti-Clock*, *Nireeswaran* and *Dattapaharam*, is bringing out *The Book of Exodus*. Much gratitude to Elizabeth Kuruvilla who commissioned all the five books and remained a steady and enthusiastic presence during the publication journey. A big salute to Ministhy S. for her untiring efforts in beautifully translating this book and carefully retaining its essence. Let me sincerely thank Saloni Mital and Vineet Gill of Penguin for their exemplary efforts in making this book a success. Also, my gratitude to Shadab Khan of Penguin's design team.

When I look back, the effort put into *The Book of Exodus* seems very intimidating. In an era when laptops, computers or Malayalam software were inaccessible, I can only reflect with wonder at the endurance which was generously granted to me, to write down every single line and polish it further. If I had known the magnitude of the physical and mental ordeal awaiting me, I might not have dared to write a single line of

Exodus! All I know is that, for more than twelve years, I worked with one hundred percent commitment on this book, unsure of anyone reading it ever. The time period spent or the hard work put in needn't be the measure of a book's quality. That is decided by time and the readers. When the book continues with new editions and reaches new readers even after twenty-five years, I gratefully accept it as the benediction of the letters.

I humbly submit this book to every single reader who has made his or her way through the space–time realms of *The Book of Exodus* till now, and to those who are destined to make their way through it in the future.

Thiruvananthapuram   V.J. James

Translator's Note

Whenever I visit Trivandrum, a trip to my favourite bookstore is part of the homecoming. Back in early 2017, a book almost leapt out of the shelf and reached my hands: *Purappadinte Pustakam,* or *The Book of Exodus*. I was intrigued by the Biblical title and the blurb. It was the debut novel of V.J. James, a scientist and engineer at Vikram Sarabhai Space Centre, and had won the DC Books Award in 1999. It had taken him thirteen years to see his dream come to life.

When I read the novel, I was charmed by many features, the most alluring being the lyrical simplicity of the prose, the author's deep knowledge of various scriptures, the stories of an era when human beings and nature lived in harmony with each another and the philosophical perspective about life. I emailed James and expressed my wish to translate the book.

Today, James and I have translated six books together. Penguin Random House India has published *Anti-Clock* (2021), *Nireeswaran* (2022) and *Dattapaharam* (2023). The first book by James that I translated, back in October 2018, *The Book of Exodus*, decided its own destiny, similar to the original work in Malayalam.

I feel this narrative is similar to the nameless river it speaks about. It flows silently, pondering about human life and its vicissitudes, often throwing up a dark surprise or two, deeply sympathetic to our flawed lives, forgiving, always moving forward . . .

My challenge as a translator was to stay faithful to the rural, ancient ethos of Potta Thuruthu, yet make it accessible to a non-Malayali reader, who might be a stranger to its fables and songs. The Biblical references strewn graciously through the text, the Hanuman Mantras that are abstruse and not easily comprehensible, the solid philosophical interventions which required a loyal translation effort, were rather formidable obstacles. But the author was always there to clarify any doubt and support me in my work. I wish to thank James, Elizabeth Kuruvila, Vineet Gill, Saloni Mital, Shadab Khan and the design team for being part of this wonderful journey.

Lucknow   Ministhy S.

Prologue

Before the Beginning

'Long, it was very long ago . . .' Valiyammachi started narrating the saga of the exodus thus.

'In those times, many fire birds had made their residence in the land of clouds. They were denied permission to alight from the clouds onto this world. Yet, one bird, defying her destiny of flying eternally, gave up the cloud palaces and succumbed to the temptation of the earth. She had a body shimmering with gorgeous colours, poignant eyes and attractive legs that were long and slender. Although many groves, farmlands and water lily ponds in full bloom beckoned her below, it was her destiny to land on a Chama Potta, the resting place of the accursed souls.'

'Oh, why did she land there?'

'Who knows indeed? Poor thing, she should never have done that.'

'Why?'

'She was unaware that there was a crippled tree infested with horrid vultures in the Chama Potta. They were corpse eaters with scalpel-like beaks, bloodied claws and eyes of the dead. The little fire bird landed when they were savagely attacking one another. They were stunned by her luminous beauty and their fights broke off. The predators gawked at her. Soon, they became deadly jealous.'

'What happened then, Valiyammachi?'

With a deep sigh, Valiyammachi cast a look at the smoke-tainted attic above. There, amid the thousands of formless figures that lay intricately entwined therein, the shadow of the fire bird would be present too. Inadvertently, it occurred to the old woman that she was undertaking the Sacrament of Penance now.

'A bloodthirsty vulture poked the fire bird on its head. The rest of the corpse eaters got excited and joined in the fun. The little fire bird was terrified. She hardly knew how to resist. Spreading her wings, she tried to return to the sky. But she could not.'

'Couldn't she fly away?'

The old winds were furiously chasing her from behind, snatching her words as they blew away. Winds that had been haunting her like malignant ghosts from birth.

'A thousand sharp beaks mauled the fire bird's wings. As she flailed around, they attacked her legs. They blinded her, shutting the light from her eyes. That day, that day . . . a death came calling at the Chama Potta, my dearest! Darkness gathered like night and nothing could be seen. In the wailing wind that spread in the eight directions, a few feathers could be seen floating around. The earth was drenched with droplets of blood.'

The little grandchild's heart and eyes were moistened by the memory of the fire bird. As the child lay exhausted, his forehead warming against Valiyammachi's breast, inhaling the fragrances of the ksheerabala oil and dhanwantaram salve emanating from her chaplet, Valiyammachi gently, gently pushed open the crystal door of the story's secret core.

'Afterwards, the Chama Potta dried up, and looked parched and desiccated. Even when it rained all around, not a single drop would grace the area. Only the wind would blow, howling in agony. In it, the feathers, weeping endlessly while trying to float towards the sky. Those could never reach their destination. Since then, no fire bird has ever stepped on earth again.'

'Will they never come again?'

'I do not know, my little one.'

He never understood why his Valiyammachi's words broke, and her eyes got moist while speaking. And he did not know that she was the remnant of a dark exile.

Valiyammachi had not forgotten anything. How many impressions of pain were indelibly imprinted on her ancient, gnarled self!

Almost three decades ago, a night of screams and death stood drenched and hunched up. A cursed night when a mob holding blazing flambeaus had surrounded the house, searching for the betrayer. Not realizing they had hunted down an innocent man, they kicked open the doors and set fire to the roof.

On that day, Valiyammachi became a widow. On that day, her exile began.

She could not even cry out on seeing her beloved—her very life—thrashing about inside the tongues of fire.

'Run, Annamma, escape with our son!'

She had run, her child clutched to her chest, stumbling and screaming in mindless terror. After a while, she had grown tired. Then she had fallen among the wild jack trees.

Valiyammachi wept upon remembering the night.

'Valiyammachi!' her little grandson called out, his arms tightly embracing her.

'Yes, little one!'

'Are you crying?'

'No,' she said, holding him close to her heart, 'now you go to sleep.'

But he did not sleep. It was impossible to sleep.

Staring at the dark desolation in the distance, he stubbornly asked, 'Where is Chama Potta?'

'Far, far away . . .'

'Away means . . . where?'

That was a question riddled with misery. *He did not realize that his own flight of exile had started with that query.* Neither could he comprehend then that a seemingly frivolous fable of a bird could rewrite the plight of many lives.

Valiyammachi wondered how to deal with the curiosity of her grandchild. The furrowed remains of the Chama Potta were far beyond the land where his Valiappachan had breathed his last. How could she quench his growing awareness?

Finally, she left her bed and stepped out with him into the star-filled night. Scattered on the river's breast were stars that had fallen off their stalks. Without the smallest disturbance of an undulating wave, its mind under control, the river was in deep meditation then.

'Look, little one!'

Valiyammachi pointed to the horizon where the planet Venus could be seen vanishing slowly.

'Beyond the mountains lies the Chama Potta.'

The child saw an overcast sky that resembled a canopy. The cloudy haze could not assuage his curiosity.

'Let us go there . . .'

'No one can go there.'

'Why?'

Having nothing to hide any more, Valiyammachi started narrating the story of Ramban, with his filariasis-ridden left leg, and Pakeeri, with his blind left eye. They were rebels who had ventured out, disregarding warnings and taboos, to reach the Chama Potta, conquering mountains in their quest. No one had ever seen them again.

'Those who depart shall never return, little one.'

As she whispered those words with a deep sigh, Valiyammachi became teary eyed, probably remembering the departed ones.

Though not comprehending anything, the little boy scribbled it all down in his mind faithfully. Letting go of his obstinacy, he cuddled next to his Valiyammachi, and started dreaming about the feathers of the fire bird.

The boy slept serenely, not knowing that in a day yet to arrive, he would script the journeys of those who had walked ahead of him on the pages of a book that was stitched together unevenly with the memories of his bloodline. Or that, on its cover page, he would write the title: *The Book of Exodus*.

One day, amid the repetitive patterns of awakening and sleeping, partaking of a deep sleep, Valiyammachi also took off on a journey. Without answering any calls, between the holy gallows of the Betrayed One and the sandalwood agarbattis, Valiyammachi lay with hands folded in prayer, meditating on flights of exile. Leaving behind the requiem, the bier and the dried flowers, Valiyammachi sprouted as a black cross on a mound.

It was a Friday.

The line from the Upanishads engraved on the coffin never vanished from the mind of the grandson, even after he became an adult.

Twenty-one years later, lost in the mystifying dreams of another deep sleep, he recollected that message: *Innu Njan, Nale Nee—Today, it is I. Tomorrow it will be You.*

1

Ghastly Nightmares

Twenty-one years later, inside a narrow room of the shelter home, Kunjootty was losing his way, caught up in ghastly nightmares.

There was only darkness everywhere.

It had been four days since Kunjootty had lost his moorings.

All these days, with a mind heavy with moist pain and eyes swollen with lack of sleep, Eli had been keeping watch at her son's side, gazing intently at his face. Expecting Kunjootty to wake up at any moment, hoping desperately that even in his stupor he might call out, 'Amma', Eli intermittently swabbed at her streaming eyes with the edge of her *kavani* and mopped up the sweat on her son's forehead and neck. Eli did not budge from her seat to change the kavani draped around her torso, which had become a soggy receptacle of tears and perspiration.

Oblivious of the surroundings, Kunjootty lay stretched out, the very embodiment of an impassivity bereft of responsibilities and obligations. He was enchained amid a tangle of tubes like an unbecoming ghost. A face reminiscent of an overgrown wilderness—dried lips that trembled occasionally, blackened eyelids with feeble signs of life. As she watched, a sob emerged from her anguished heart.

'Kunjootty, my son!'

But the calls left Kunjootty untouched. Eli's sobs did not have the vigour to overcome the formidable distance between them and reach her son. Leaving behind the musty corridors of the shelter home, casting aside his appan and amma, Kunjootty had gone journeying far off. There had been many visions during that sojourn. Half-way across, there were formless beings who had befriended him. The secrets that he had shared with them were mistaken by his mother as the crazed outpourings of his feverish self.

The formless beings took Kunjootty in a black skiff, rowing against the wind, to the mysterious depths of the *kayal*, the backwaters. He could see, far away on the shore, a lone gooseberry tree, shivering and shrunken. It had hollowed branches, the trunk rotting in the salt-laden wind, the body strewn with desolate holes discarded by birds . . . almost like an impoverished spirit denied of its sacrificial rites. Kunjootty did not have the heart to watch that piteous sight. To the sounds of a low groan, his body shuddered once.

'Am . . . ma . . .!'

The mother who was counting each of her son's breaths gathered close to hear the vague mutterings rising from his scorched lips. Eagerly expecting more words, keen not to miss even a single syllable, as she stared at her son's lips, Eli heard this:

'A real fruit bearer that gooseberry tree was . . . eh, Amma?'

With intense grief, she replied, 'Do not worry about it, my son!' Eli unwittingly muttered: '*A real fruit bearer that gooseberry tree was!*'

Over the years, Eli herself had wizened, like the shrunken gooseberry tree.

* * *

Twenty-one years earlier, as if the seeds of the celestial stars themselves had been scattered all over, gooseberry pits lay strewn on the courtyard of Edappadathu House. The children of Potta Thuruthu—the isle of potta plants—gathered them up in their little fists, tried to blow life into them and hurled them up into the skies. Even though he tried relentlessly, Kunjootty could never achieve the sowing of those star-seeds in the skies. Neither could Susanna, Kanaran, Vareeth or any other child of that isle. When the gooseberry pits somersaulted many times in the air, sparkling in the sunlight, and inevitably fell on the ground, the kids gathered and counted them assiduously. That was the lone gooseberry tree in their land. It was not usual for such trees to take root in the isle of Potta, which was full of dark, brackish mud. Consequently, the children fell in love with that magical tree, cherishing it with absolute adoration. They watered it in the summers and chased away the pesky birds that disturbed its tender flowers.

After many years, a chameleon with a flower-like crown on its head became a resident of the gooseberry tree. Kunjootty could not recollect exactly when that jester first made its appearance. Either on a dawn ushered in by the chirping of the magpie-robins, or on a lazy afternoon, or on an evening when he stood staring out of the window, the chameleon had leapt from the southern branch to the main trunk.

Kunjootty disliked it immensely.

'Tche! Such a dirty creature.'

Perhaps, the chameleon took offence at that statement; it opened its eyes wide, jerked its head arrogantly and slid down to hide among the mangroves. There, in the mangroves and the potta plants, many water birds had built their nests. Surrounding the area were the prawn farms, with lots of radishes, and the winds combing their way through. And then there was the naval command of potta plants that thrived lushly on the shore, fighting the waves of the river.

The chameleon came back.

This time, Kunjootty did not feel the same animosity towards the creature. Clutching the bars of the window, he stared at it keenly. Caught in a fleeting sense of wonder, he hailed the creature, 'Good day!'

The chameleon seemed to like the formality. It responded by shaking its head. The colour of its body was that of pale sunshine then. A tentative friendship started between two incompatible creatures that day.

Kunjootty had been simply fooling around. However, the greeting ritual between the boy and the chameleon soon assumed a regularity. The chameleon started appearing on the north branch the moment Kunjootty opened his window. Jerking its head, its eyes rolling, it would attempt to converse with the boy.

After some time, Kunjootty started to feel he was able to comprehend the chameleon's language. It was not a mere thought but almost a palpable experience. People would have called him stupid! So Kunjootty had to continue the teaching and learning process without being noticed by anyone. The adventure exhilarated him like a bizarre form of meditation.

When he mastered the language and the friendship deepened, Kunjootty discovered that his friend was an enlightened seer who knew the past, the present and the future. Soon, the secret of its birth was revealed—cursed dinosaurs were reborn as chameleons! Arrogant human beings would also shrink to become ants in the course of time.

Kunjootty could not help opening his own heart to the creature. One evening ripe with auguries, he confessed:

'Do you know, I have given a name to this gooseberry tree.'

'Yes, I know.'

'Lies! No chameleon should be as vain as you!'

'What if I were to tell you the name?'

'Then, I shall crown you an emperor!'

'You named the gooseberry tree on a moonlit night, didn't you?'

'Yes, how did you know that?'

'You scratched the name on the trunk using a shell you picked up from the shore.'

'Oh my God! Yes, indeed.'

'It was a girl's name. Let me . . .'

'You brute! Stop right now! Don't shame me by saying anything more.'

That day, amid the whispers of the wind and the hymns of the birds, Kunjootty granted the possession of his gooseberry tree, free of tax, to the chameleon who had mastered time, and crowned it as the emperor.

* * *

All around was a choked silence. Nurses came and went with medicine-filled syringes, which they routinely injected in various parts of Kunjootty' s body. As her son received the jabs without even a meek groan, Eli stared at the hospital veranda. Seeing Eli's pleading face, seeking an answer or perhaps a consolation, Zavarias became agitated. In their twenty-seven years of living together, he had never faced such a look before. The memory of an ancient flight of escape, dragged by two skinny bullocks, came back to him with all the past helplessness. It felt as if the traumatic journey of yore and their present pathos enmeshed with each other, wiping away the five decades that stood in between. Every exodus has a mystifying effect, causing a disorientation in one's sense of time. Zavarias seemed to be discerning disparate events as a singular one.

The doctor did not discuss any details of Kunjootty's disease with either Zavarias or Eli. All the secret discussions took place with Isaac. The parents consoled themselves with the thought that they were perhaps talking about the name of some newfangled disease unknown to the older generation. They had, much earlier, accepted Kunjootty's state as being stricken with high fever.

The doctor was a fair, lean middle-aged man, with a penetrating look in his eyes, tousled hair and the stethoscope curling around his neck like Shiva's snake ornament. Whenever he dropped in for a visit, he would open Kunjootty's closed eyelids and measure the beats of that frail heart. He always made it a point to reassure Eli with a pat on her shoulder as she stood bewildered and scared during the check-ups.

'Nothing to worry about, Amma! Everything will be fine!'

Recollecting that the doctor was saying the same words ever since they arrived, Eli ended up more worried. She had already indebted herself to all the holy churches known to her by promising innumerable candles and human figurines of silver. Had she known whether the disease belonged to hand, leg or head, she would have offered separate silver figurines of those parts too.

Whenever she felt anxious and confused, Eli would eagerly ask Isaac: 'Son, what did the doctor say?'

'Amma, don't get scared! Everything will be all right!' Isaac would comfort her.

Isaac knew very well that he was uttering those words more to console himself than Eli. His mind was stretched taut. All the omens seemed stacked against them. It had been four days since Isaac enjoyed a proper meal.

Meanwhile, the police officers who visited often, with the air of authority of those conducting investigations, were in a hurry to ascertain whether Kunjootty had regained consciousness. The last who arrived incognito, without the khaki uniform or the cop's cap, had many questions for Isaac.

'Kunjootty got admitted here on a Friday, right?'

'Yes.'

'And Susanna went missing on the same day, didn't she?'

'I have no clue.'

The policeman had the look of someone who had discovered a cryptic secret. Puffing smoke from his cigarette, he commented roughly, 'We have come to know that Susanna and this fellow were more than ordinary acquaintances.'

Isaac felt a rising anger and contempt for the man. In that situation, he had no choice but to control his emotions. He was determined to stop the constant visits by the cops. Both needed peace of mind—the one who was unconscious and the ones who were awake.

Kunjootty was unaware of the predicaments of the mortal world. As he lay immured in deep sleep, suspended between life and death, time ticked past without respite.

At the shelter home, it was time for the evening prayer.

Seated by her son's feet, Eli made the sign of the Holy Cross. Then, she drew another cross on Kunjootty's forehead with her thumb, and prayed with all her heart:

'In the light of the Holy Cross, protect us from our enemies. In the name of the Father, the Son and the Holy Ghost, Amen.'

The mother remembered sadly that it had been quite a while since her son had drawn a cross on his own forehead.

The lack of prayers was the reason for everything.

2

The Isle of Refugees

Zavarias's childhood was haunted by nights of exile. Behind his sleepy eyelids, the sight of a burning hut flamed bright, casting shadows forever, and the howl of an agonizing death rang loud. Then there were the pains of an exodus in a cart, dragged along by skinny bullocks. Those bulls had carried on their shoulders a mother, her son and their endless sufferings. A languid path, a humid day and a freezing night with nightmares as companions.

It was Chonachu, his father's field hand, who had driven the bullock cart all the way to Potta Thuruthu. The mother and son had found refuge inside his hut, on a floor smoothened with cow dung. Zavarias had grown up in that strange land, moistened by the briny winds, puddles of clay and relentless tears. Too young to resist anything, he ate the stale rice gruel his mother served and slept in the leaking hovel. He counted each scab cast by sunlight, seeping in through the roof riddled with holes, on the cow-dung-plastered floor.

Many years later, at an age when he was confident of
conquering the river side, with the help of Chonachu, Zavarias
cordoned off a portion of the shore to build a hut for his mother
and himself. Eventually, his efforts added up and he set up a
small shop too. The edifice of all his further ventures was built
on that.

From far off, on rafts made of logs, bamboo stalks came
floating through the multitudinous rivers slithering down the
hills, parking at Zavarias's ferry. Many skiffs marked with
Zavarias's name snuggled next to one another on the side of
the river. The boat men who ferried goods and passengers, and
those who transported the river sand rented these from him.
As the days went by, all the residents of Potta Thuruthu agreed
unanimously: 'Zavarias is growing big!' Soon, bidders for his
bamboos and skiffs came from far away—Pinadi, Ponjikkara
and Thanthonni Thuruthu. The next monsoon left sheepishly,
not being able to leak its way through the roof of Zavarias's
house.

It was during one of those days that Zavarias proposed
to Eli, who often frequented his shop to purchase pounds of
tapioca and jaggery-hued coir rope. At the altar, in front of her
relatives and the local parish priest—a missionary reverentially
called Arnosacchan—Eli stood with her head bowed and in a
trembling voice whispered, 'I do.'

Eli was sixteen years old at that time.

She gave birth before she turned seventeen.

On the seventh day of the week, with an unending shriek,
the representative of the next generation opened his eyes to the
vulnerabilities of Potta Thuruthu.

'The child is a like a tiny key, very small, a *kunju kutty*,' said
the visitors.

Valiyammachi named the key-like *kunju kutty* Kunjootty.

It rained incessantly the day he was born. It did not abate either on that day or the next. It was rain that Kunjootty first experienced and fell in love with.

'Little one, see how it rains!' Valiyammachi cuddled him next to her breasts. His mother's milk sweetened his tender lips. Zavarias peeped into the room intermittently. On rare occasions, he would hold the baby or play with him. Even from his infant son, Zavarias could not help keeping a wilful distance. Consequently, Kunjootty found himself at a loss, right from childhood, when it came to responding to his father's truculent, unapproachable demeanour.

It was after Kunjootty's birth that Zavarias purchased some land across the river and ambitiously set up a grocery shop. It was located next to the temple of Kavilottamma. There was only a pathway made of red soil in those days. Later, a few small-time kiosks sprouted nearby. In course of time, the place transformed into a bustling junction; stray animals and peddlers of daily ware becoming a common sight.

Starting off for his shop early in the morning and returning very late became Zavarias's daily routine. He hardly had any time to interact with his son. Somewhere between the tenderness that was denied to Kunjootty, and all the love that could not be offered, lay the silent contract of acceptance— that they were father and son. The endearment 'Appan' rusted away, due to disuse, from the memory of the son. It happened that the father too rarely got to address his child as 'Kunjootty'. With the passage of time, the threads of conversation between the father and son slackened and started hanging loose.

* * *

Neither full-moon nor new-moon nights existed in Zavarias's almanac. His calendar consisted of the mundane repetition of market days. Chonachu's son, Koppan, helped him with his trade during these days.

It was another market day.

The usual hailing was heard, from the boat dock, next to Edappadathu House.

'Zavariachha, Zavariaccha!'

As if he was lying in wait for the call, Zavarias opened his eyes. His sleep had broken off much earlier, but he was content to lie in bed with his eyes closed.

Counting out the money to an exact amount, Zavarias opened the latch of the front door and walked to the dock.

'Got a bit late today, eh, Koppan?'

'Yes . . . went to sleep very late.'

'Take the list.'

'How is Kunjootty?' Koppan inquired solicitously, as he received the list of items to be procured and the money.

'He is back home from the hospital. But he is not fit to attend office yet.'

'Bad luck, what else to say? The girl's family is shattered. Not a place left to search! If she has died, where is the corpse?'

Zavarias had grown immune to such conjectures. With a blank mind, he stared at the early-morning mist covering the river. Even when his innards churned, he was not the sort to carelessly expose the turmoil. He did not deign to share with anyone the grievances wrought by Kunjootty's illness or the unyielding losses that hid behind it. No one discussed anything with him either. The darkened past had encroached invidiously into Zavarias's present too.

The skiffs transporting coir pith were lazily moving on the backwaters towards the local companies at Alleppey. The boatmen dipped their poles into the depths of the water, the sounds unbroken and rhythmic. From the insides of the dome-like enclosure built on each *kevu vallam*—the local name given for such skiffs—thick fumes of smoke rose and as if hesitating to spread out, accumulated above the boats. The labourers in the boat were cooking their meals. For them, life was a boat journey between two destinations.

During this journey, many sought mid-way resting places. When night arrived, they would anchor their boats on the riverside and get drunk on the local toddy that set their veins on fire. To quell that heat, they would knock at the thatched doors of the village prostitutes.

Koppan saw that a few boats were moving towards the market from the side of the jetty. Keeping an extra pole for a boat hand he hoped to get from the isle on the other side, Koppan started off after the boats. The isle was the mother to many famous establishments. Koppan had a favourite toddy shop there. The attractions of the woman, Kali, who ran the shop, were notable. All of Koppan's journeys started and ended there.

Unlike his expectations, Koppan could not get a henchman from the isle. It did not worry him. Having ingested enough to have the physical prowess of two men and having flirted with Kali, Koppan dipped his pole in the direction of Kochi. He wanted to hum an old song but felt irritated due to the loneliness.

'Pffa! Damn it all!'

The river was wide but shallow in those parts. Those digging the river sand, and the divers who gathered clams, chatted with him.

'Where are you going, Koppan? Kochi?'

'Yes . . . market day!'

The men dived into the depths causing fissures and rose with their hands full of their catch, resembling the big fish that caused bubbles to break out on the river surface.

Leaving them behind, Koppan reached Kochi before the hot afternoon set in. He pulled his boat ashore and tied it to a wooden stub on the dock. Then he gazed for a while at the goats grazing on the couch grass by the fringes of the river.

Beyond the goats, a young man could be seen seated, his arms around his raised knees, his head bent, looking lost to the surroundings.

Koppan reached his side and asked: 'Will you be around for a while?'

The youth raised his head and looked at the man who had pulled him out of his reverie. He looked bedraggled. Springs of thick, curly hair spread undisciplined on a forehead that was furrowed with worry lines. There were prominent dark circles under his eyes. Yet he looked radiant, as if some limpid light had spilled over his face.

'Am not sure . . . Why?'

'I have left my boat tied up here. Thought I will ask someone to keep an eye on it.'

'As long as I stay here, I shall watch it.'

Koppan felt that the young man's look had an intriguing impassivity. He wondered what he was doing there; he looked so out of place. Then, shrugging off his concerns, Koppan walked towards the market.

Crossing the peddlers who had encroached on the pathways, leaving behind the hubbub of the fishmongers and the vegetable sellers, Koppan moved forward through the shameless hustling taking place around him. He had to manoeuvre around the cycles and hand carts crowding that dirty road. Koppan rented a hand cart from Pappu's shop. After negotiating fiercely with various traders, he loaded the cart with all the items in Zavarias's list.

By the time Koppan reached the dock with his hand cart, the goats had moved far away, still gnawing at the couch grass. But the young man was sitting there, like a statue in the city square, baking in the sun.

'I thought that you might have gone!' Koppan spoke out of courtesy.

The man did not reply.

Observing the lifeless posture and the soiled clothes, Koppan asked:

'Are you from somewhere far off?'

Maybe the young man wanted to respond; that was all that could be surmised. His facial expressions changed quickly and, pressing both his hands on his forehead, the man slid to the ground, panting a bit. His body shuddered and the breathing became rapid.

It was totally unexpected. Koppan stood thunderstruck. Then, overcoming his shock, he raced to the river, and, filling his cupped hands with water, returned to sprinkle it on the young man's face. The man's bewildered eyes gazed alternately at Koppan and the sky that was heavy with rain clouds. His eyelashes were smattered with the powdery salt from the lagoon waters. His gaze was weighed down by many inner burdens: anxiety, inferiority and those of that ilk.

'Come on, get up!'

Koppan supported him and helped him to rise. Then he ushered him on to a bench with a loose leg that belonged to an unnamed roadside tea shop. The shop offered its visitors cold puttu and hot tea. The young man stared anxiously at Koppan.

'Don't hesitate, eat! Consider me like a brother. Where are you from?'

'Cherpulassery.'

'Why did you come here?'

The troubled look on the man's face showed that he had no answers to that query. But there were more questions in the fray.

Name?

Near and dear?

Name, name . . . Chathutty.

Home?

When the stomach burns with hunger, pride is not a virtue. The only son and heir of Valiya Namboodiri—the owner of Karangady Mana, with its Pathinarukettu (a palatial home with four inner courtyards) and prosperous enough to take care of ten generations—had shrunk into a howling stomach, settled on a bench at a roadside shop.

'I have nobody back home. Started off when I felt lonely . . . wandered around a lot. Ended up here. I have no money left with me. Need a job . . . menial work will do too . . .'

Koppan intuitively sensed some anomaly in that narrative. Then there was a break in the conversation, an interval replete with silence and ruminations. Until the young man finished the food, Koppan sat there doing his own mental calculations. He knew that there was no need to attribute any importance to that coincidental meeting. Yet beyond that knowledge, compassion lingered, stubbornly refusing to let go. Whether for better or for worse, Koppan had inherited that lone wealth from his forefathers: a deep compassion.

'I get by with such menial jobs . . . odds and ends, here and there! I came to the market to purchase groceries. Will you be fine with such work, Chathutty?'

A moist sea breeze blew around them.

Chathutty felt reassured after a long time. Carry some packages, navigate a skiff?

'Sure, that will do.'

'Then come along. Do you know how to manoeuvre a bamboo pole?'

'Yes, I guess.'

Chathutty looked towards the faraway isle and endeavoured to bring up a few faces in his memory. He sensed failure. As he took the pole in his hands and thrust it into the soul of the lagoon, he imagined he was pushing away the dark memories of his past. While he made his way across the unruly waves of the brackish backwaters, the irregular undulations, the Gayatri Mantra and the hymns of Agnistoma were slipping away from him.

The Supreme Being—the sun—climbed to the middle of the sky and recited aloud for him:

Om Bhur Bhuvah Swahah

Chathutty felt that everything was back to normal. As the pole dipped into the water, as the lagoon waters rushed into the iron rings at the bottom of the boat, as the pole thrust deep into the depths, the sounds emerging were the first lessons from the Vedas.

Bhur Bhuvah Swahah

As he moved a long distance down that strange waterway, Chathutty found himself in consonance with the rhythm of the bamboo pole.

'Look! We are approaching the toddy shop! Do you drink?' Koppan asked him.

'No.'

'Then I will not insist. I shall be back in a jiffy.'

Tying his *thorthu* around his head, Koppan soon disappeared inside the shop. Chathutty sat on the boat, with his legs immersed in the lagoon's waters. Many small skiffs went past, ignoring him totally. They looked like beasts of burden, labouring under the weight of memories.

After a long time, when Koppan returned, he had a folk song on his lips and a puppy in his arms. That tiny creature was nestling close to Koppan's chest, slurping over his face and arms.

'The little scoundrel has started frequenting toddy shops! It is a male. We shall take him along, eh?' Koppan spoke, as if addressing Chathutty.

Koppan deposited the mewling creature inside the boat, consoling it with gentle caresses. It gazed in wonder at its new surroundings and then sniffed around a bit. Then it curled up at a corner, with utter servitude.

The presence of two lives seemingly dawning on him suddenly, Koppan decided to sing loudly.

'*Kali tricked me, adding water to the toddy*
I tricked her too, by giving false coins shoddy!'

'Do you know Kali?' Koppan asked facetiously.

'No.'

'She manages the shop. Smart woman! We get together at times,' Koppan said with a smug smile.

Chathutty's focus was on the sights at a distance. Marsh barbels flowered all over the bright green mangroves. The potta plants, like welcome groups of hosts, stood on the fringes of the isle, dancing without restraint in the flow of the backwaters. Majestic coconut trees could be seen on the shore abounding with laterite stones. The Chinese nets, *cheenavala*, were extending into the lagoon. He observed the worn-out boulders, *pulimuttu*, where the waves of the lake fought among themselves, the wooden pegs, *oonikutti*, that stood erect in the waters and the wind that ensconced everything.

'We have reached our destination, Chathutty! Try to pull over to the next dock,' Koppan quipped.

There, on the shore, was a withered and shrunken gooseberry tree. Its branches were rotten and on the verge of collapse. The body was full of holes left behind by erstwhile nesting birds. Looking at the man who sat leaning against the tree and gazing at the lake, Koppan called out:

'Hey, son!'

Kunjootty did not respond. The strong medicines that he had been taking had probably weakened his natural impulses. His face was pale, a remnant of his excruciating and ceaseless travels through many Amavasyas.

Koppan did not feel like calling out again.

'He was sick and in the hospital for a very long time,' Koppan told Chathutty.

'What sort of sickness?'

'High fever! He lay there spouting crazy nonsense for quite a while.' Then Koppan whispered, 'Looks like he has lost his mental balance. His sweetheart has gone missing. That is the reason . . . at least that is what people say!'

Unexpectedly Kunjootty turned his head and looked at Koppan.

Koppan grinned almost apologetically.

'We are coming back from the market. Thought we will drop off the purchases before crossing the river. This is Chathutty. He is new to this place.'

Koppan unloaded the items on to the veranda of the house. Kunjootty sat there, gazing passively. Koppan guessed that Eli would be busy in the kitchen.

'Shall we leave, child?'

'Hmm . . .'

'You are free from all sickness now, aren't you?'

Kunjootty's expression was devoid of both life and vitality. Exhaustion was the only prevailing truth. In its acme, all the reasons that had led to that fatigue seemed to have faded away. Staring at the boat, which was now making its way across the lake, Kunjootty continued to sit there, bone-weary.

Both Koppan's house and Zavarias's grocery shop were on the other side of the lagoon. There were no fixed routes in those areas. People travelled as they liked, crossing over the courtyards of houses, freely stepping across the available paths. No one contemplated efficacious ways of travel. Consequently, the pulses of development in the city of Kochi did not enter the dark boundaries of Potta Thuruthu. All around were secluded isles and minds.

After ages, Chathutty slept tranquilly, in the dilapidated back porch of a hut in one of the isles. In the same porch where Muniandi, the poison healer, who had come searching for Chonachu had slept, another refugee, representing the next generation, was seeking sanctuary.

3

The Three Nomads

The first to read the inauspicious auguries was one of the three nomads who had arrived from the mountains. This had happened many years ago. Trudging across many a land, laden with their umpteen bundles, the three nomads named Velandi, Muniandi and Murukandi arrived in Potta Thuruthu. They spoke a pidgin language tinged with Tamil. In their bundles were many curiosities that they had handpicked from the mountain forests.

Mavericks like these were rarely glimpsed in the staid desolation of Potta Thuruthu. Yet, the trio's arrival seemed preordained. In one of the barren fields on that isle, they pitched three camps and deposited their belongings.

True to his name, Velandi was adept at *vela* or tricks. He had a pet monkey who tagged along devotedly. The onlookers quipped that the monkey had more tricks up its sleeve than its master. Clad in dazzling clothes, dancing wildly, walking on its hands and cheekily scratching its bum on being teased, the monkey conquered the heart of Potta Thuruthu. His master used an ancient pellet drum resembling the *damaru*. The itinerant musician referred to his instrument as 'Damarika'. He also claimed that it was a living creature like the monkey.

The second nomad, Muniandi, was reclusive by nature. He caught poisonous serpents and carried them in wicker baskets. He had mastered the art of poisons and could prescribe rare herbal antidotes to the most venomous of bites. Snakes, the villagers believed, were enslaved by him and waited for his command.

The third, Murukandi, was a Siddha, who had conquered the three time zones. He had anointed himself with the name of Lord Muruga who was the master of Vaana Sastra—the science of astronomy. Spreading out the sparkling, divinely powerful white pebbles gathered from the river Sauparnika, he foresaw the future.

The residents of Potta Thuruthu had great anxieties about the future. They crowded around Murukandi, resting in his tent, eager to hear about their fate lines. By reading both the face and the palm, Murukandi would reveal mysterious secrets about the seeker's future.

Kunjootty was four years old then. Koppan was ten. Being the oldest among the kids around, Koppan seized Kunjootty's palm and extended it towards Murukandi for a prophecy.

Murukandi took only one look! Reading the portents on the lines of the child's palm, he unwittingly gasped:

'Oh, God! The lines are so bizarre on this child's hand! Why is it so?'

Both the children and the grown-ups stared at Kunjootty as if he were a grotesque creature. It was then that Eli came rushing in and gathered her child close to herself.

'Stay away from these unholy places! Satan's lot, all of them! For true Christians, such places are forbidden.'

That evening, dipping his hand in the lagoon's clay, the little boy pressed his palm multiple times on the back wall of his house. Zavarias got mad at him for making the wall dirty and gave him a sound hiding. Eli scolded him bitterly. Untouched by any whitewashing, the fate lines lay indelibly imprinted on the wall, like leading evidence.

Sitting beneath the malgova tree behind their school, Kunjootty narrated the mesmerizing tales of the monkey, the white pebbles and the magic serpents to his friend. He shared with her the tidbits kept in the pocket of his suspender knickers—the stem of the pepper elder plant and a raw berry—and both swore that they would never share those with anyone else. He whispered a secret into her ears and strengthened their friendship. He promised to bring the fruits of the gooseberry tree in front of his house only for her. He also boasted that when he grew up, he too would venture into the forest like Velandi and catch a monkey.

It was a woman called Bhangi who was most attracted by the tricks of Velandi and his monkey. She would often visit the nomad's camp with a soft-boiled egg and tobacco. She alone came to realize that it was Velandi, and not his monkey, who knew the maximum tricks! But their secret rendezvous was brought to light rather soon. The residents of Potta Thuruthu surrounded the tent and caught them red-handed. After heated discussions, it was decided to hitch Bhangi and Velandi in matrimony. That was how the nomad from the mountain ended up marrying Bhangi of Potta Thuruthu.

The monkey, however, did not take to this unexpected wedding! The creature, who used to sleep with Velandi, was unceremoniously removed from the house on the very first night. He was chained around the waist and left outside on the back porch, where the chill was bitter. That was more than what the creature's pride could bear. He started on a spree of destruction, shattering everything in sight and snarling viciously at Bhangi whenever she was around. The woman of the house too started hitting back, using every opportunity to hurt the wretched animal. She would gripe about the monkey to Velandi and cause tension between the master and pet.

Once the monkey chanced on Bhangi in a vulnerable state. Using the chance, he tore at the back of her thighs, wounding her badly. Bhangi ran screaming for her life. Velandi chased after the monkey with a cane and whipped it severely. That dumb creature, not understanding the logic of the punishment, shrieked pathetically. The god of the monkeys must have felt pity. As the creature twisted around in agony, the belt on his waist slipped off. In one leap, he jumped on the branch of a mango tree in the vicinity. Velandi screamed at it: 'Come down, you fool!'

For the first time in his life, the monkey disobeyed its master. He did not descend to the ground. He jumped to a coconut tree instead, and safe on his perch, started licking at the multiple lacerations on its body.

That night, a high fever gripped Velandi. He cried in anguish that his head was splitting into two! By the time the local healer arrived, the inevitable had occurred. Apparently, a vein in the patient's brain had burst.

The monkey roamed for many days, like a quintessential rebel, through the vastness of Potta Thuruthu. He chewed up the tender coconut flowers, broke the pots used for tapping toddy, listened to scathing abuses and escaped every attempt at catching it. Bhangi alone pined, thinking about the hapless creature. She remembered Velandi's face whenever she caught sight of the monkey. When she offered him some food, he ignored the gesture with gravity, as if unwilling to accept the hospitality of a woman who had once hurt him badly. Perhaps he had tired of living among the uncivilized human beings. One day, the monkey swam across the lagoon and disappeared. He was never to be seen again.

After Velandi's demise, Murukandi spread out his divine white pebbles and read the auguries. After a moment's deep silence, he told Muniandi, 'We have to leave this land tonight.'

'Why? For what?'

'It is not appropriate to stay here any more.'

'I refuse to leave this land for any other place.'

Murukandi knew that Muniandi would not accompany him. He had asked the question, cognizant of the answer. The white pebbles would never lie. Aware that his destiny was to be alone from that moment, Murukandi left the camp that very night, not bidding goodbye to anyone. In this manner, the three nomads who had descended the hills, went in three different ways.

There was one person in Potta Thuruthu who was fascinated by Muniandi's snakes and herbs—Chonachu. One day, he entered his tent and established a deep friendship by sharing a drink with Muniandi. They started meeting for their drinking sessions regularly, sometimes at Chonachu's home. Having received his *guru dakshina* from Chonachu in the form of liquor, Muniandi started teaching him the secrets of the poisons and the various antidotes. As time passed, Muniandi spent most nights at Chonachu's house. Whenever he dropped in, Muniandi never forgot to bring sweets for Chonachu's son, Koppan.

Chonachu's wife, Cherutheyi, also liked Muniandi's snakes. One twilight, when no one else was around, Muniandi opened his basket and brought out his most venomous serpent. He showed it to the woman.

'Tell me your opinion about this one!'

'Hmm. A real winner! Where did you catch this one?'

'From a dense forest. A beautiful snake, isn't it? Do you want to keep him?'

'God, no! I'm afraid of snakes!'

As the snake hissed at her, Cherutheyi screamed in terror and clutched at Muniandi.

'Hey, naughty one! You should not scare her!'

A serpent emerged from Muniandi's heart and coiled itself tightly around Cherutheyi. Thus bitten, Cherutheyi fainted amid the wicker baskets, looking like a snake herself.

Later one day, when Chonachu opened his eyes in the morning, he found his wife missing. Muniandi, who had been sleeping on the back porch, was missing too. Only his snakes remained in the house. For a long time, Chonachu and Koppan fed the snakes by catching frogs and rats. Then, when the food became scarce and ceased altogether, many emaciated snakes died in their baskets, cursing bitterly. Chonachu freed the last snake, on the verge of death, in Ezhuthassan's snake grove. It slithered away under the serpentine roots of trees next to the statutes of the snake deities.

It was on that same back porch where the itinerant master of poisons had made love to Cherutheyi that Chathutty, another outsider, found refuge.

4

The Shore Marked with Footprints

Kunjootty sat on the seashore, gazing at the revolving beacon from the lighthouse situated at Vypin Island. The same lighthouse had an eye that stared at Potta Thuruthu too.

When darkness fell, through the open window of the west-facing room, one could see the revolving light afar. It was an ancient structure that continued to perform its ritual duty without fail every single day. Sea hawks perched on its pinnacle. After the fourth rotation, almost as if taking a break, the fifth round of the circling beacon light would slow down.

Kunjootty's sleep cycles were intertwined with the lethargy of that fifth round. Listening to the periodic twittering of the night birds and counting the flashing rounds of the beacon, he would deceive sleep. Usually, he slipped off to sleep somewhere between the counts of fifty and hundred, and was never able to pin down the exact number despite trying.

The sandy beach, the sea breeze and the luminescent circles cast by the lighthouse . . . As he sat gazing intently, a few things from the past were tracing their paths back to Kunjootty. Those included scattered conch shells, shimmering cowrie shells, broken turret shells and then a sunset shared by two.

* * *

Susanna had never seen the lighthouse from such proximity before. That was another reason why Kunjootty cajoled her to forgo the tailoring classes and visit the beach.

'How come the fifth round is not in harmony with the rest?' Susanna asked, pointing at the light house.

'The lighthouse's quintessence happens to be the fifth rotation.' Kunjootty poured smooth flowing sand on Susanna's long, slender fingers that had mastered the beautiful art of embroidery. 'When ships get lost in the far-off seas, they will calculate the distance to the land by observing the speed of the fifth circling.'

'Really? That is news to me!'

'There is much more if you want to know!'

'Tell me . . .'

That was how Susanna listened to the tale of the dishonourable captain of a ship that was caught in the stormy sea. Counting the rotations of the lighthouse beacon, he discerned the shore and started steering the ship towards it. After a tumultuous voyage, when the ship was nearing the shore, carrying with it the sins of the immoral captain, a huge wave rose and hid the lighthouse from the line of sight. The waves mercilessly tossed aside the red buoys that marked the boundaries for the ships, and crossing the forbidden frontiers, the ship got stuck in the sand.

Susanna stared for a long time at the inauspicious direction chosen by the doomed ship. Some snooty crabs were hard at work around them on the beach, busy digging up holes, royally ignoring them. It was then that Susanna retrieved a childhood fascination.

'I want a Valampiri *shanku.*'

'Hmm . . . Why?'

'To keep in my house. If one can get it, all the bad luck will flee . . .'

They searched high and low for the Valampiri shankhu, a rare, right-spiralled conch shell anointed with the magical gift for driving away ill luck. Although she had scoured the shore with intense desire, Susanna was not destined to find one. She was unable to rekindle the dying spirit of Vastu Purusha— the cosmic god who ensured health and happiness via perfect architecture—languishing on the pockmarked, cow-dung floor of her hut. Perhaps her fate was to vanish into oblivion in the form of a missing person report.

* * *

By the time he remembered all that, Kunjootty felt enervated. He wanted to fight the thoughts by shutting down all the doors of his mind. The six weeks of his debilitation had weakened his body greatly. He was loath to revisit that *papa kanda*, that canto of sin, which had been meshed by dim days and dark nights.

From a short distance away, amid the chattering of the sea crows, a whining little voice reached his side to rob him of his ruminations. When Kunjootty looked up, a small dark girl, aged around five or six, was standing next to him. Snot was dripping from her nostrils. The child seemed to be exhausted, drooping from the harsh sun.

How and from where had she sprouted suddenly?

Though he saw her standing there pleadingly with her little hand stretched out, Kunjootty continued to sit impassively. She stood staring at his remote posture for a moment. Perhaps she understood that nothing was forthcoming from him. She then clambered up the boulders stacked to safeguard the shore from the ferocious waves. The little girl gazed at the sun's impending departure. Below her, the sea was roaring. Yet, without the least hesitation, she moved towards the rocky edge. The string of her skirt broke, and the cloth slipped down to her knees. The child hastily pulled it up, shame and pain writ large on her face. The shabby skirt was hardly equipped to cover her frail body decently.

Kunjootty was gripped by the fear that she would slip off the rocks. That malnourished little body did not have the wherewithal to survive the sea. The rabid storm and relentless waves would certainly toss her high and slap her against the rocks to shatter her into a million pieces. Besides, there were deadly whirlpools nearby.

Due to that fearful apprehension, Kunjootty had the urge to call out to the child.

'Hey, you!'

Even before he could finish, the child had dived into the sea.

Oh Lord! Kunjootty was scalded for a moment. He raced to the edge of the rocks and peeped below at the roiling sea.

Waves . . . more waves!

Then he saw a dark head bobbing among the warring waves. She was swimming like a sea creature in the raging sea. Her moves were effortless. It was obvious she had had ample practice.

Sheepish at having panicked unnecessarily, Kunjootty seated himself on the rocks. Afterwards, he climbed down to the shore.

Those who had come to enjoy the beach watched the new sea creature curiously. Some children were throwing empty ice cream cups and rolls of paper in her direction. Perhaps thinking that if the kids were appeased, she might get some food, the child swam to retrieve all the trash thrown into the waters. As more discarded objects were tossed into the sea, the girl could be seen floating amid them, as if she herself was another discarded object.

Vengeful, huge waves kept hurling her afar. Yet, bearing her forlorn destiny, she was emerging from her secret hideaways. After some time, tired out, she started for the shore. Leaving the children who were still throwing trash at her, she managed— half swimming, half pushed by the waves—to end up in the sand shore beyond the seawall made of boulders.

The poor child was shivering all over. As she approached with begging hands, some people fixed their gaze at the sea as though they had not seen her. Some others tried to avoid her presence, pretending they did not have any money to give.

Meanwhile, a child, grown plump by eating too many ice creams, offered her half a cup of the cold dessert. As she eagerly stretched out her hand, he tossed the ice cream into the waves, asking her to retrieve it. No one saw the little eyes getting wet, since she was dripping water all over.

As she stood panting near him, Kunjootty's first impulse was to scold the little girl. 'Why did you do that? Want to kill yourself so fast?'

She bowed her head as if she had committed some mortal sin. Anxiety filled her face, and her frail body was coated all over with sugary white sand. The little girl's limbs were extremely malnourished. Like an absurd picture of excruciating poverty, her ribs jutted out like arched bows. She struggled to keep the sliding skirt in place. Kunjootty could only wonder at how she had managed to salvage that lone bit of clothing in her fight with the waves. The skirt had a smattering of tears and holes, and her dark nakedness grinned obscenely through the gaps.

'The kid is mute.' The comment was made by someone who lived near the shore. 'Her mother lies bedridden in one of those shanties. She survives on this girl's earnings.'

So the child was not wrestling with the sea but with her own painful wretchedness. Her father, who had gone fishing in a catamaran one day, had never returned. The people had seen him row away with his fishing nets. The catamaran had hidden itself in some secret cavern of the sea. The Araya woman, having waited in vain for her husband, with rice gruel salted by her tears, had finally fallen unconscious.

As her mother had lain half-dead beside the cold brick chulha, ridden with dripping rainwater, the dead father had beckoned the little child from the sea.

'Parutty, come on . . .'

That was how she had leapt into the sea for the first time.

'Aren't you scared to jump into the sea, dear?' Kunjootty lay an affectionate hand on her frail shoulder.

She could not answer. Yet, he could guess the reply. He took out a hundred-rupee note and proffered it to her. The little girl looked stunned at the amount offered, and then reluctantly accepted it. Carrying the weight of the first hundred-rupee note that she had held, the child sped away in the direction of the decrepit shanties on the darkening seashore. She kept turning back to look at Kunjootty, as if she could not believe her eyes. He sat on the sand, gazing after her, until she disappeared from his view.

By the side of a catamaran, there came another face-to-face interview with the sea.

Kunjootty felt apprehensive that what had been temporarily forgotten would come rushing back. While empathizing with the pain of the little child, he had been oblivious to his own inner turmoil. To heal one wound, nature had tenderly opened another, thus balancing the ecosystem.

To console oneself, a person just had to acknowledge a wound bigger than his own.

Kunjootty listened to the dirge sung by sea crows for the lifeless Chinese nets cast into the sea. The sky lost its smouldering ember, the surroundings filled with shadows cast by dusk, the mind stayed lost somewhere on the outliers of the sea . . . Kunjootty found his existence akin to an aimless, floating object.

His body was in the throes of exhaustion—a legacy of the disease. He sat leaning against a catamaran. Once, he used to walk blithely on the blistering sands, enjoying both the sunshine and the strong breeze. Many footprints were imprinted deeply on that shore.

Kunjootty dipped his fingers into the soft sand and filled his fist. Had he dug up a fistful of footprints? Maybe Susanna's footprints would also be there somewhere. However much he insisted otherwise, the memories refused to listen and would lead him to that point. It followed him like a curse sworn on the sand, the pledge to never let go of him.

The footprints were a mere figment of the imagination. Only the sand was a reality. The footprint was a passing dream. A breeze came whistling by and blew the footprints away. The shape changed; the sand remained. The sand was eternal.

Kunjootty lay on his back on the sand, meditating on the primeval cause that brought into existence everything out of its imagination. Slowly his senses shut down. The goddesses guarding sight, touch and sound started to rest a bit.

He lay languidly by the catamaran for a long time. It was into a blinding darkness that he opened his eyes. There was a surge of panic on checking his watch. It was time for the last bus to arrive. Kunjootty struggled to stand, and then started running, his feet sinking in the white sand. The lights of the bus could be sighted at a distance.

After running for a while, he stopped, fatigued. The red light had started moving away, without waiting for him.

Kunjootty breathed heavily. He felt devastated. This sort of grave mistake should have been avoided. The final bus had departed. Now for the night ahead, all alone, in a beach notorious for pickpockets and prostitutes. There was no way to get to that remote village called Potta Thuruthu. There was not even a taxi for hire at such a late hour.

Kunjootty stood there for a while, waiting for any vehicle that might pass that way by chance.

Nothing came.

Slowly, he made peace with the situation.

Perhaps it was preordained that he spend one night from the Book of Life on the seashore. In the never-ending flow of time, where a human birth itself was inconsequential, why worry about an insignificant night? Thinking thus and gathering the strength to trust the seashore, he decided to return to the vastness of the beach.

From across the span of twenty-five centuries, the Tathagatha—the one who has thus come and has thus gone—came to Kunjootty's aid with his philosophy: *Do not fight anything. Let things transpire as they are. When you force a change, of course, you invite sorrow. All unhappiness originates from desires.*

Kunjootty walked in that faint moonlight along the line of the catamarans pulled up on the shore. Still one part of his mind—yet to reconcile itself to the Tathagata's philosophy— sought anxiously for refuge in the night.

Where would that shelter be?

He heard a chorus of strange sounds made by night creatures. The blind drumming of the wind reverberated around.

Kunjootty stopped short at one of the catamarans. Seeing twinned black shadows writhing on the sand, he regretted his mistake and changed his course. A woman and a man were exchanging their desires with scant regard for the surroundings.

Kunjootty realized then that desire was nothing but *agni*, the fire. It might have been the woman's *jadaragni*—the fire of her ravenous hunger—and the man's *kamagni*—fire of his sexual desire—that had kindled the conflagration. And fire obviously could not pass by without annihilation. Pranam to the Tathagatha!

Wishing desperately for a rest place where no one would intrude, he sat down exhausted by a boat, his hands on the sand for support. Unwittingly he remembered the guardian angel to whom his Valiyammachi had always entrusted him in his childhood. After a rebellious youth that had mockingly viewed that belief, this was the first time he was revisiting that memory.

As if from the angel's lamp, a streak of light was seen afar, and Kunjootty concentrated his mind on that brightness, trying to whittle away time. Then he lay supine on the sand and gazed at the sky. The dark sky entered his eyes drop by drop, weighing down the eyelids.

Kunjootty closed his eyes.

His sleep was not deigned to last long. Kunjootty opened his eyes warily on sensing another's presence. There was a sharp note of cheap fragrance and strands of long hair tickling his face.

He struggled to a sitting position.

'Who . . . who is it?'

'Me . . . it is just me. Were you asleep, Sir?'

As if she had known him all her life, the woman knelt close to him and pressed her hands on his shoulders. The cold touch of a corpse.

'Tcche!' Flicking away that nauseating touch, Kunjootty got up in a hurry.

'Nothing to worry about, Sir!'

Ignoring her seductive murmur, Kunjootty hurried on. The jingle of her anklets followed him.

'Sir, going away?'

He did not cast a backward glance. A shrill whistle rose from behind. By the time Kunjootty recognized the danger signal, many shadows started moving towards him from blurred origins. Keen to escape, Kunjootty forgot his exhaustion and walked faster.

The revelation of peril had been a bit late.

Vulgarly decked-up prostitutes, vicious with diabolical curiosity, encircled him from all sides.

'Edi, Sir is leaving. Sir does not want anything!'

'What sort of a deal is that? How can Sir leave like that?'

'Ah, it seems we are not good enough for him!'

'Really? Then who is good enough, tell me!'

'Even if Sir does not want us, can we easily let go of him?'

'Shall we all try together then?

'Aha . . . Hahaha . . .'

'Koooey!'

Amid the menacing mockery and the abhorrent, ear-piercing whistles, Kunjootty found himself stranded and desperately searched for some succour. At that critical moment, the guardian angel that his Valiyammachi had anointed to be his constant companion in childhood, metamorphosed from a blind faith to something else altogether.

5

Red Tape

The taxi moved over the desolate Venduruthy bridge, carrying two humans and their heavy thoughts. There were no other vehicles plying on the national highway. The lights in the nooks of the seashore and in the various isles interweaved with one another, evocative of another galaxy. The illuminations emanating from the ships seemed to rise and shatter among the stars. There was a bright light atop the monstrous crane in the shipyard too.

Kunjootty sat against the car seat, indifferent to everything around him. After a while, Isaac's silence became unendurable to him. They were like two strangers travelling together for many days at a stretch. The hired vehicle behaved like an unnecessarily mature entity, possessing the tact to respond after assessing the situation, and kept moving silently forward, carrying the weighed down souls within.

Isaac raised the car window, obstructing the bitter cold sea breeze from assailing them.

'Kunjootty!' Isaac called out.

'Yes.'

'Do you think it was wise?'

Silence reigned.

'That is no answer, keeping quiet!'

Yet there was no response.

'If I had not arrived in the nick of time, those foul creatures would have mauled you to bits! This place is infamous for headless corpses that bleach on the shore. Yours too would have floated tomorrow!'

'I missed the last bus,' Kunjootty spoke with regret.

'There is a limit to justifications! I will not bother you with any grievances. But what about your parents?' Isaac paused, recollecting a decision taken earlier, and said, 'Let us forget it now.'

If Kunjootty had to forget, a whole lifetime was due to be forgotten. Most of it was full of forbidden memories.

Yet something inexplicable remained: from where had help come? How had Isaac been prompted to comb the beach in search of his friend? He did not ask Isaac anything. Perhaps it was a hunch based on past experiences. But Kunjootty somehow preferred to believe that it was Valiyammachi's guardian angel who had protected him miraculously.

He had escaped from so many places. Or rather, some beings, seated at unseen places, had often helped him escape. The life he was living was a debt, a veritable debt.

Kunjootty observed that Isaac was deep in thought and hoped he would slip off to sleep in that posture.

But Isaac could hardly catch a wink.

* * *

Isaac was the owner of a decently successful lumber mill on the outskirts of the city. He had reached that position after many years of relentless effort. Isaac had mortgaged whatever meagre property he had when he ventured into the lumber business. The fuel burning within him was a mixture of wily common sense and a good deal of self-assurance. His capital multiplied as he started successfully bidding for the decaying timber in the forests. Though on the face of it, he had traded in hollowed-out logs, in reality, sturdy logs had reached his mill. To ensure that sleight of hand, Isaac had established some tainted relations with the forest officials.

Isaac knew perfectly well that his chosen way was perilous. Yet, with his inherent fortitude, especially while facing adversity, he worked hard to expand his business. Isaac had lost his father in a drowning accident even before his birth. His father had saved the lives of four and was trying to save the fifth from a capsized boat when he had got caught in a whirlpool. Isaac was resting inside his mother's womb, unaware of these happenings. As the devastation of his father's unexpected demise sent shockwaves through his mother, in a sudden push, Isaac had prematurely made his appearance in the world. It was the same child, whose survival was a topic of concern for all, who was now leaning against the car seat as a grown man.

The vehicle carrying the passengers and their obdurate silences reached the reddish clay road and stopped. From there they had to walk, moving around Ezhuthassan's compound and traversing the path behind Koppan's hut, to reach the river side.

The dock was bereft of light.

On the opposite shore of the lagoon, a single house stood out with its lights ablaze. Kunjootty worried about confronting the anxious souls within. Isaac was the one who rowed the boat.

As they neared the lights, Kunjootty felt a growing numbness. They could see the restless man, walking to and fro in the front yard, even from far.

As soon as they embarked on the shore, Zavarias's shout reached them.

'Where the hell were you?'

Kunjootty did not even feel a pang. Though he had known about that impending question, he hadn't bothered to find a suitable answer. He stood still for a moment, forgetting the way ahead, in the thrall of a contemptible apathy that hurried to his aid. Then, seeing his father control his temper with an obvious effort, Kunjootty felt mildly curious.

'Go inside . . . Maybe we are fated to die of worry in this house!'

Isaac started to placate Zavarias with his explanations. Kunjootty walked in, disregarding them. However, it was not easy for him to face his mother. Her look reached him, moist with tears. He felt flustered with his inability to put words to what he was feeling. There was a trace of destiny in all his dealings that day.

'Won't you have dinner?' Eli asked quietly.

'No, I am not hungry.'

After changing his clothes, Kunjootty lay on the cot. He could see the revolving beacon flash of the lighthouse through the western window. It was continuing with the ceaseless circles of life.

Eli stepped inside the room, became part of the melancholic ambience and stood like a scarecrow. She stood motionless for a long time.

'Amma, why don't you take some rest?' Kunjootty murmured guiltily.

Eli did not answer him. Slowly, she stepped out and moved towards the eastern room. When the rustle of her clothes retreated, Kunjootty switched off the light and sought refuge in his bed.

The night stretched out in a bout of denied sleep. From light years away, the stars were conveying messages to Potta Thuruthu. How many years ago must those missives have been sent? One, two, ten? Perhaps they had come from lifetimes away. Still, the messages had reached their destination only now . . . very, very late. The star from which these messages originated must have died years ago. Still, from such a vast distance away, Kunjootty was seeing something that probably might be extinct that moment . . . it was sheer illusion, Maya.

* * *

After resting for a few more days, on the first Monday of the month, Kunjootty started for office. The office functioned in the third storey of a huge building situated in the middle of the hullaballoo and conflicts of the city. There were many buildings nearby, with the arrogant majesty of the forts of yore. Nearby was a junction where four roads intersected one another. Speeding vehicles became modest and deferential when they reached that fork. The emperor of the golden past—having lost his powerful sceptre and crown—stood there in the form of yet another ordinary, undistinguished statue, observing the quotidian happenings.

Owing to his long leave of absence, Kunjootty felt a lethargy creeping all over his body. He felt irritated at the thought of morbidly curious acquaintances hovering over him, making casual small talk. They might dig deeper: a thousand queries, well wishes for health, advice galore. He noted in his mind a few cryptic answers that might need reiteration in their midst.

As usual, the first person to greet him was Diwakar Menon. His seat was next to Kunjootty's. Menon had a serene face with a high forehead and sparkling eyes. He was aware of the important events in Kunjootty's life.

'Hello Kunjootty. Did you take enough rest?'

'Yes.'

'So, you managed to write down another chapter, did you?'

'What do you mean?'

'Another chapter in your *Book of Exodus*! Not all chapters can be filled with good experiences.'

While sharing anecdotes on experiences and setbacks, Kunjootty had once expressed his desire to write such a book.

Seeing his friend flustered, Menon said, 'No, don't brood too much. And there is no need to get stressed. A government clerk need not strive beyond a point.'

A mound of files greeted Kunjootty's eyes; they were tangled in the symbolic red tape. Grievances that were yet to be redressed, typewriters croaking wearily all around, tedious hours stretching out. Usually, his mind would slip past these and reach the pages of the book he planned to write.

'Kunjootty! I was just thinking of a story you once told me.' As Kunjootty stared at him in wonder, Diwakar Menon continued, 'Two classmates were walking under a single umbrella in the pouring rain—a little boy in belted knickers and a little girl who lived in the neighbourhood. They were clutching their slates and books close to their chests. Their homework was scribbled on the slates.

'The umbrella had star-like holes. They walked while counting the raindrops dripping down the stars. They were unaware of that fatso Kadir, their classmate, who came creeping up on them from behind. He sneaked inside their umbrella, shut it down unexpectedly and ran away, laughing uproariously. The rain enveloped them from all sides and their clothes were splashed with muddy water. Their books got drenched and the homework on the slates was washed away in that downpour. But what hurt those tender children the most was the mocking laughter of their friends on seeing Kadir's malicious act.

'When they reached their school, they were punished by their teacher, Karunan Sir, who accused them of not doing the homework! Their palms were imprinted with blue-black swellings caused from his merciless caning. I was just recollecting that anecdote to waken you a bit, my friend!'

When Diwakar Menon ended the story, Kunjootty suddenly remembered, with intense sadness, the curses that the children had rained on their teacher afterwards.

'Wicked man! May his hands become useless!'

The effect of that naïve curse was severe. Karunan Sir ended up paralysed on a cot, his limbs and tongue ceasing to function.

Then, what had happened to the rest of that tale? Two souls had showered that curse unanimously. Where had one ended?

Kunjootty's desk was covered with the accumulated dust of six or seven weeks. It looked as if soiled by a lifetime's dirt.

6

The Eyes of the Night

Kunjootty had written about the first resident of Potta Thuruthu in one of the pages of the *Book of Exodus*. He was a dark-skinned man who had fled from the temptations of sin. When he came to the isle, he had a tender reed in his hand; that was what his descendants believed. He planted it on a virgin corner of the isle and breathed life into it. The reed took root in that dark, wet earth. The leaves started sprouting. That fertile reed was renowned as the potta plant. Overcoming both the mangroves and the screw pines, the reeds flourished on the fringes of the isle and soon the name of that place became Potta Thuruthu: The Isle of Reeds.

The potta plants were assiduous keepers of moral values. They had a streak of inherent resilience in them, helping them overcome any kind of harm. Even if you cut off the mother stem to weave a basket or a mat, new lives would sprout from the wounds and lushly thrive once more.

All those who sought sanctuary in that isle had to first make acquaintance with the unpretentious potta plant.

It was no different for Chathutty.

He soon became familiar with the way of life in the isle of reeds—the fun-loving breeze, the misty lagoon and the serene child-like sleep in the nights. In that compassionate isle that had generously taken him in, Chathutty did not face any shortage of work. On Koppan's recommendation, he became another of Zavarias's handymen. He firmed up the clay borders of the compound and dived into the water to mine the river sand.

Chathutty intentionally refused to follow the cadence of his earlier habits. It was also his way of paying back an old debt. He observed that the distance wasn't too great between the palatial Karangadi Mana, where his forebears had reigned supreme, and the cow dung-plastered floor in Potta Thuruthu.

'Still not up? It is very late . . .' Koppan's wife would wake up Chathutty with karuppetti kaappi, a milkless coffee made of palm jaggery. Every day, his first sight would be the intricate designs made in the air by the swirling steam from the kaappi cup held in Unnicheera's hand. He sought a place for his ablutions by the rushes of pine screws in the western end of the isle, before sunlight started foraging the skies. The residents of Potta Thuruthu would attend the call of nature under such natural coverings. The river would obligingly flow into the screw pine clusters and help them out with the necessities.

Initially, Chathutty had felt grossly embarrassed to answer the call of nature thus. Slowly, he accustomed himself to the morning ritual. Eventually, he started liking the privacy offered by the leaves of the screw pines that beckoned like giant spiders waving their legs. As he squatted, the river filled with pearl spots, cat fishes and tiger panchax. The lone heir of the famous

Karangadi Mana, seated in his leafy lair, experienced the elation evoked by self-inflicted suffering.

The son, devastated by the mysterious death of his mother, who had fought with the Valiya Namboodiri, was now far away from the soiled innards of the Mana, the great ancestral home. The journey had begun after offering obeisance and seeking forgiveness at the Tulsithara, the sacred spot with basil clusters, where the holy ashes of his mother were safeguarded.

'Forgive me, Amma. I am moving away from the path you laid out for me.'

He was certain that his mother would forgive him. Halfway through the journey, when Chathutty had broken the sacred thread and tossed it away, the same faith had come to his aid.

* * *

With dark vengeance, pushed by an obstinacy shorn of reason, Chathutty ate fish for the first time in his life. When his innards churned and bile rose in his throat, Koppan queried:

'What happened?'

'Nothing, just feel like puking.'

'Must be a worm infection.'

Slowly, Chathutty found himself freed from the worm infection. While giving up the austere purity of his Brahminical upbringing and familiarizing himself with fish and meat, he imagined the ending of the sinful clan to which he belonged, and gained a venal pleasure.

Yet, as time passed, Chathutty bemusedly realized that the laws of Ajnatavasa—the years of hiding—were not too simple. Unnicheera's presence was reminiscent of a karmic debt from

the past haunting him wilfully, even as he tried to escape.
Whenever he went to take a dip in the backwaters or spread his
clothes on the clothesline, Unnicheera would walk past casually,
with the lingering eyes of a predator, pretending to gather the
dried coconut leaves.

One morning, after a bath, when Chathutty was trying
to read himself in a broken mirror, Unnicheera's reflection
filled up the cracks. Watching the scorching eyes where a
dozen candles flamed in unison, Chathutty lost his composure
and averted his gaze towards the fissures on the cow-dung-
plastered floor.

One, two, three . . . the moments ticked by.

That day, until Koppan woke up, Chathutty strolled through
the northern yard. He stopped to nibble absent-mindedly at the
hanging leaf of a tender coconut tree, and then picked up stones
to toss into the lagoon. The fishing boats skimmed over the
lagoon, the hoots of the boatmen accompanying them. In their
own unique rhythm, with drumming calls, intermittent visits
to the riverbank, haggling and negotiations, the boats moved
away; the netted fishes that hadn't lived their fill stared glassily
at the sky above.

For breakfast there was warm rice gruel and boiled
chickpeas.

As he sat down on the mat with Koppan, Chathutty's
broodings were unfurling a long way backwards.

Unnicheera served food in two plates. Then, leaning
against a wall that was untouched by a coat of lime, she spoke
nonchalantly.

'The pond water has become very bitter.'

'What happened?' Koppan asked.

'Just started a few days before.'

'The bitter gourd creeper must have fallen and festered perhaps?'

'Not that . . .'

'Then?'

'The ant eater, *eenampechi*, is taking a dip. That's what everyone is saying!' Unnicheera uttered those words cautiously.

Chathutty looked at the mud-filled wall. Above Unnicheera's head dangled a spider web where the remnants of a male spider were visible, consumed after a bout of frantic mating.

'Then you should use the water from the pipe for a few days!'

Unnicheera expressed her vexation at Koppan's solution. 'I cannot walk all that way and carry the pots back.'

'What else can we do?'

'It is a full-moon night!' Unnicheera slyly reminded Koppan.

'Huh?'

'Why can't you both run a bit? Three rounds should suffice. The eenampechi will go away if the men run . . .'

Koppan got so flustered by that suggestion that he choked on his food.

It was not a mere three rounds of running. The rites included a full-moon night and a male body devoid of even a loin cloth or waist chain! The eenampechi would supposedly leave the precincts on seeing masculine nakedness.

Koppan felt that Unnicheera should not have dared to be so outspoken in front of another man. Anyway, he himself hardly believed in such superstitions.

'You must have imagined the bitterness.' Koppan tried to evade the situation.

'No, I am very sure of it!'

'How can you be sure that eenampechi is responsible, eh?'

'All the neighbours agree!'

'All these are made-up tales.'

'I knew you would say this . . . you are good only for getting stone drunk!' Unnicheera lost her patience with Koppan.

Koppan gave up, not having any other weapon to fight with his wife.

'Let me see! The full moon is tonight, eh?'

Kunjootty could not make any sense of the goings-on.

It felt like a film in an alien tongue. Strange queries, bewildering answers and an unwarranted tension in the air!

Koppan and Chathutty started for the next isle in the boat. Koppan had an understanding with Gopala Kaniyan that they would fill up three boatsful of river sand for him that day. The man wanted to build a house by the river front, encroaching on the shore. With the relentless riverbed mining, the flow was running thin.

A traditional astrologer, Gopala Kaniyan was never able to predict when he spread out his cowrie shells to prophesize the future that his own son would steal his mother's mangalsutra and cross the sea to settle in the Gulf. Now his stars were bright. And the father regretted punishing his son for his minor pilfering ventures in his adolescence.

As they pushed at the bamboo poles, Koppan saw Kunjootty on the opposite shore. He was scribbling something, seated in an armchair under the tamarind tree.

'He is writing . . . has been doing that for a very long time,' Koppan informed Chathutty.

'What is he writing?'

'Who knows? Maybe stories.'

Kunjootty did not see them. Koppan did not hail him either.

As they neared the next isle, Koppan said, 'Let us anchor the boat here.'

'Sure.'

They stuck the poles deep into the clayey mud and tied up the boat. Wrapping their thorthu around their waists, they picked up the hand spades and entered the river.

'The flow is getting stronger . . . dig fast!'

They disappeared beneath the water, dug up pitch-black river mud from the bed and emerged like water elephants. Until the edge of the boat lowered itself to the river's level, they continued to fill it up with sand. Before the river's tempestuous mood made it difficult, they emptied out the skiff at Kaniyan's place, finishing the first round. The exercise was repeated twice before twilight set in.

That evening, when he got paid, Koppan emptied half the cash into Chathutty's hands.

'Take it, my boy!'

'No need. I stay in your house, right?'

'But you cannot stay there forever, can you?'

Only temporary resting places existed for a solitary traveller. Journeys, unceasing journeys. There was nothing that Chathutty could think of, between all those wanderings, to save up for. Not even a square foothold worth of land.

That evening, Chathutty took his first drink seated by Koppan's side in the dark recess of the toddy shop. He ate the shredded crab meat on his plate with the reverence of one consuming an offering from a temple. As the intoxication took hold of him, the one who had pondered about a foothold, became the master of the endless universe. Thoughts disappeared into thin air and a feeling of ease and lightness spread over Chathutty.

Like ghosts whose feet never touched the ground, they made their way back through the farm ridges over which the moonlight streamed like liquid. It was when a croaking frog, stopping the recitation of its prayer 'Pekrrom, Pekkrom', leapt into a water hole that Koppan suddenly remembered something.

'Chathutty, we are supposed to run tonight!'

'Run where?'

'Around the pond . . . That will scare the eenampechi! The water will clear up then. Do you have any problem with running?'

'Not at all!'

Chathutty had enough fuel in his veins to run 300 rounds if necessary.

'But,' Koppan grinned conspiratorially, albeit with embarrassment, 'we will do it when everyone goes to sleep. Not that there is anything to be ashamed of.'

'Even if it is daytime, what is there to be ashamed of?'

'Actually, one has to run without any clothes . . . stark naked.'

'What?'

Chathutty felt the fuel in his veins leaking away.

'How can that be? What if someone sees?'

'That is why we should run at midnight, when everyone sleeps! This is the only way to stop the eenampechi from bathing in the pond!'

'Tche! Still!'

'Don't worry, my boy! I will be there too. Once Unnicheera sleeps, I shall wake you up. We will finish the rounds without anyone knowing!'

Chathutty was almost on the verge of returning to the toddy shop. If the evening could be repeated—consuming the same amount of intoxication once more—perhaps he might be able to run without a sense of shame.

He found it difficult to slip into sleep on the porch that night. Whenever his eyelids closed, he felt as if a strange creature was slithering towards him. After some time, he heard Koppan's hushed voice calling out to him. Chathutty pretended to be asleep but Koppan shook him awake.

'Get up! Unnicheera has gone to sleep.'

Realizing that there was no way to avoid the situation, Chathutty prepared himself for the new experience. He walked behind Koppan with soft footsteps.

It was a clear night. The guardian of the skies smiled benignly at them.

The wind murmured and caressed the banana leaves in the backyard; Chathutty wondered whether the ant eater had started its luxurious midnight soak.

'At the count of three, throw off your clothes and run!'

On hearing Koppan's words, all his strength seemed to evaporate, and Chathutty felt his resolve weakening. In the shadows cast by the moonlight, he felt that even the non-living objects had taken on a life of their own.

Koppan, meanwhile, had started counting.

'One, two, three!'

Koppan took off. Not having any time to reflect, Chathutty too followed suit, throwing off his clothes. Koppan started yelling loudly to attract the attention of the mysterious eenampechi.

'Poohoooeyyyy!'

It was not known if the ant eater heard the inviting call.

Chathutty became agitated and wished that Koppan had not created that ruckus. What if someone heard that yell and peeped outside? As the thought passed through his mind, Chathutty found himself racing at a superhuman pace.

In their frantic state, neither of the men noticed that the window of the kitchen was opened wide.

7

The Opportune Time at Dusk

It was after two months of Chathutty's arrival that Potta Thuruthu celebrated Kettu Kalakku, the fishing jamboree.

It was one of the unique occasions when the isle was filled with boisterous energy. After the fish harvesting, where they herded, confined and caught fish in bulk within the embankments, the clayey fish farms, still abounding with prawn and shrimps, were thrown open to the villagers for their ravishment. Anyone could be part of the fishing rite. Most of the isle residents would enter the harvesting arena with an *ottal*, a conical bamboo basket to trap fishes. Expert hands would ferret out the grey mullet fish and the crabs from the deepest crevices.

The islanders believed that to catch fish in their baskets, they needed to appease the reigning deity of the dykes, Chira Mallan. He was an impish ghost who guarded their shrimp-filled water channels. Though he belonged to the lower pantheon of spirits that they worshipped, he was not malicious; even helpful if satiated. Probably because of the geniality and fairness of his ways, the natives adored Chira Mallan. First, the natives would stoke a roaring fire in the middle of the slush-filled dyke. Fried catfish and sweet toddy, tapped at dusk, would be placed as offerings. When the villagers clapped invitingly, gazing at the southern direction, the Chira Mallan, the demi-god, was supposed to make his regal appearance. However, if anyone looked him straight in the eyes, he would be blinded. So, the devotees turned their backs to the food and retraced their steps.

The residents of Potta Thuruthu believed that if Chira Mallan was pleased, they would reap a rich harvest of shrimps during their annual jamboree. As per folklore, there was a pact between the king of the fishes and Chira Mallan. Except that they reached an accord at the end of a long and horrible battle, about which even the most ancient of the islanders had no memory.

The children and women of Potta Thuruthu would try to conciliate Chira Mallan with kallappam made with toddy, fermented rice flour and coconut. The grateful ghost, hungry for that mouthwatering offering would order his minions to fill the slushy clay with the choicest of fishes.

The ghost apparently had a thousand eyes to catch the liars and fibbers! Everyone quoted as evidence the story of the unlucky Chongan, who watched over the fish farms that belonged to the Nedumbath family.

It was a time when shrimp thieves were rife in the isle. They would forcefully open the closed portion of the canal and cast their nets in the running water to snare the rushing shrimps. When the overnight thefts became a nuisance, Chongan was appointed to guard the canal, and an elevated watch tower was constructed. There was no respite from the thefts even after that. No one knew that the fence was eating the crop: Chongan was hand in glove with the petty thieves. On a new-moon night, the rite for Chira Mallan's pacification was proffered by the Nedungath family. They left some toddy inside a hollowed bottle gourd and fried yellow catfish on a tender plantain leaf. That night, Chongan climbed down from his perch and had his belly full of the fish and drink. The next day, the residents of Potta Thuruthu saw him lying dead, his eyes ruptured, next to the canal's mouth.

Koppan, like a consummate raconteur, narrated the story to Chathutty during the jamboree.

'Do you think there is any truth in that?' Chathutty was sceptical.

'Of course! The islanders still light the fire for Chira Mallan, don't they?'

'These are mere superstitions!'

'Until one sees and knows for oneself, it is common to scoff!'

'Even if my eyes burst, I would still like to catch sight of that ghost!'

'For that you will have to wait till they light the fire! Today I will show you another marvel!'

'What marvel?'

'We are going to launch our Pachuvanchi tonight, in the most opportune time at dusk!'

'Pachuvanchi?'

'Hmm. You can see for yourself in the evening. The magic of a skiff filling up with plentiful shrimps! I am going to offer Chira Mallan three fried catfishes and a half-coconut shell filled with toddy for his abundant blessings!'

Koppan beckoned the puppy, seated by the eastern side of the hut. With lightning speed, the creature raced to his master's side and stood whining, its tail wagging ceaselessly.

'Ah, there he is, the smart one!' Koppan caressed the puppy and it moved closer, whimpering. Koppan stroked its ears and chucked it under its chin. The puppy grew excited with the affection showered on it and turned on its left, to lift up the legs. Koppan laughingly tickled its white underbelly. Then an inexplicable thought flashing in his mind, the man's fingers stilled.

'Oh, he will grow up so fast. Then one won't be able to catch sight of him. He will go sniffing after the stray bitches!'

Chathutty just smiled.

A furtive smile came over Koppan's face.

'But there is one way, Chathutty!' Koppan retrieved the folded knife tucked inside his waist band and checked the sharpness of the edge.

'What is this for?' Chathutty asked, confused.

'To prevent him from wandering away. Just watch!' Koppan said.

As Koppan sharpened the knife edge against the washing stone, Chathutty felt the forebodings of an imminent evil and the pangs of an agony yet to come.

After checking the glistening edge of the knife to his satisfaction, Koppan said, 'Chathutty, just hold on firmly to its hind legs!'

'For what?'

'You just hold!'

Chathutty obliged halfheartedly. The puppy, still lying on its side, did not even see the sharp knife moving closer to its stomach.

Everything happened with the speed of lightning.

As Koppan's hand moved, the puppy shuddered in unbearable pain. On its scrotum, a long deep wound was visible, welling up with blood. Quickly, Koppan whisked away a vibrant substance from within the lesion. The puppy was released after Koppan slathered a fistful of ash on to the bruise to allow it to heal. Unaware of what had transpired, the tiny creature rushed frantically through the backyard, moaning in agony and terror. Even as it ran, not knowing where to go or what to do, it kept wagging its tail.

'Now he will not go after the bitches. When it grows, he won't have the urge at all!'

As Koppan replaced the knife in his waist band, Chathutty stood shell-shocked. He was deeply tortured by the puppy's cries. The culled creature would never ever get aroused. The one robbed of vital bloody fluids was still expressing love by wagging its tail.

Chathutty felt that the brutality was unpardonable. Why had the man behaved in such a manner?

A boisterous shout from the fish farms where the Kettu Kalakku was on, snuffed out those ruminations. Villagers might be chasing after a monstrous fish! Or maybe, they were trying to pull out a gigantic crab hidden by Chira Mallan! Their attention turned to the sounds of mirth emanating from the shrimp farms.

Koppan suddenly remembered another Kettu Kalakku—an old memory, but an invigorating one.

The saga had begun on the riverbank.

Janaki had come from the nearby isle to participate in the jamboree. On the reed basket on her head, a multitude of crabs lay clinging to one another. Years later, Koppan remembered Janaki's yellow blouse and her white *mundu*.

'Have you been bitten by a crab ever?' Koppan asked Chathutty.

'No.'

'Ooh. It can be nasty, damned crabs simply do not let go!'

Chathutty was still watching the puppy. It was curled up in a corner, licking its wound dry.

'A crab bit Janaki during one jamboree. She started screaming like hell. Then I had to help her! By the screw pine bushes, I had to bite hard at the leg of the villain! Do you know where the crab's pincers had grabbed Janaki?'

'Where?'

'In her inner thigh! That was when our little affair began! She's a canny woman!' Koppan burst into a belly laugh, thoroughly enjoying himself.

Chathutty felt immured to that gaiety. It seemed like the uncontrollable, theatrical laughter of a puranic character in the movies. No doubt, Koppan must have snatched the crab with the broken claw, inching its way to the screw pines and deposited it inside Janaki's basket.

The sun was going down. Koppan observed the changing moods of the western wind and foresaw a few good portents. Today, if he launched his boat during the opportune time of dusk, the harvest would be plenty. The tides were ebbing and the time of Ashtami, the eighth auspicious time zone, was also approaching. The Pachuvanchi would not betray him. Koppan bubbled with enthusiasm.

'Come, my boy! The time has arrived for getting the Pachuvanchi ready!'

The Pachuvanchi was to be readied by tying two skiffs together. A wooden plank was affixed over the boards near the transom stern, where the two sides of the hull came together, tethering them with a rope. A bamboo pole was fixed in the middle of the skiffs, separating the front ends. Now the boats inclined inwards, one end conjoined, the other wide, resembling a coconut spathe split in the middle, its end point intact.

The shrimps would come bouncing up the gap between the skiffs. Since bunches of coconut flowers, kulanjil, would be spread on the inner steps of the boats, on leaping inside, the shrimps would not be able to escape the trap.

> *'Chem, chem, chemmeenee . . .*
> *How will you flee now, my smart little prawn?'*

Koppan hummed to himself and then dragged an iron chain from the hut.

'What's that for?' Chathutty asked.

'That my boy, is the real secret of the Pachuvanchi. The ends of the chain will be fixed to both the boats and the middle portion will drag in the water as the boats move. The shrimps will get agitated and swim up to the surface. Soon they will get attracted to the light from this blazing lamp and jump inside the skiffs!'

The lamp was placed inside a square-shaped iron enclosure. One side of the contraption was left uncovered, for the light to stream outwards. The side that emitted the light would be turned away from the lagoon, so that the shrimps, tantalized by the glimmer, would leap right inside the boats.

'The Pachuvanchi is ready now,' Koppan said, 'let us ask Kunjootty to join us. We have gone on so many trips together! He is crazy about such adventures.'

'But he is recovering from a serious illness. Will he come in this blustery, gusty night?'

'Let us try. He won't refuse. It has been a while since he recovered.'

They picked up their bamboo poles and steered their way to the opposite shore. Darkness had started taking over the surroundings. As they reached the ferry near Edapaddathu House, all lit up from within, Koppan called out, 'Hey there!'

'Who is it?'

'It is me, Koppan! Going to launch the Pachuvanchi soon in the lagoon. Would you like to join us?'

Pachuvanchi, the lagoon . . .

It had been nearly three months since Kunjootty had broken away from such excitements. He was still in the throes of the lassitude and enervating after-effects of his sickness. Returning to his normal routine was still a challenge. Nonetheless, Kunjootty ached to cool his inner churning and looked forward to a change. Perhaps the smell of the backwaters would wipe clean his ennui.

As Kunjootty walked towards the boat, Eli called out anxiously from behind him, 'Where are you off to, in this night?'

'I will come back soon . . .'

'What if you catch a cold?' The mother stood there worrying. In that house, over whom did she possess the authority to reprimand? Zavarias was yet to return from the shop. Had his father been at home, Kunjootty would not have joined the boat trip.

There were three of them in the Pachuvanchi now. A few flickering lights in the distance were their only companions. A poignant and heavy silence pervaded the seemingly serene surroundings.

Koppan lifted the iron chain and dropped it into the backwaters. Then he lighted up the clay lamp and placed it on the wooden board that linked both the boats together.

Not a single starlight was visible. Darkness enveloped them like a flowing liquid. In that plateau of darkness, only the light from the lamp spread out like a dream. Their boat moved very slowly. All three passengers were caught in an eclipse of silence. Beneath that silence, in the water churned by the pull and push of the boat's movement, a troupe of shrimps lay hiding. Their quietude must have been disturbed by the iron chain transgressing into the depths. Alarmed, the shrimps moved to the surface of the lagoon and were attracted by the light radiating from the lamp.

Suddenly, over the calm surface of backwaters, a shrimp took a giant leap. It landed face down on the boat filled with coconut flowers. It was accompanied by another. A little shrimp joined the melee. Yet another, and soon, thousands of shrimps seemed to follow their track, soaring in the air like the whooshing, luminous sprays from a firecracker. They kept piling up in the boat.

Chathutty gazed unbelievingly at that magic! Without any effort from their side, the shrimps were jumping inside the boat.

'Told you, didn't I? If the Chira Mallan is appeased by fried catfish and toddy, he will grant a bounty!'

'Yes indeed! What a miracle!'

The shrimps' jumping show continued for quite a while. Slowly the movements subsided and the surface became tranquil. Observing the signs, Koppan suggested, 'Let us go back the same way we came!'

As they turned the boat around, the light from the lamp started flowing in the opposite direction. Any onlooker would have felt that the light had vanished mysteriously! The phenomenon of the light's sudden appearance and disappearance as the boats swiveled away had been the source of much trepidation among the naive islanders. A few, suspecting ghouls of the backwaters as a reason behind the chimera, had turned feverish in their terror and even lost lives.

Again, the shrimps started catapulting in the air.

Kunjootty flicked on his torch and scanned the river.

As the circle of light skimmed the surface, the folds of water woven by the wind gleamed bright.

Kunjootty's wandering gaze followed the brightness and then suddenly stopped in rapt attention at one spot. A creepy feeling, that he was witnessing a forbidden sight, swept over him.

He shone his torch yet again at that spot to remove his doubt. This time, Kunjootty saw it clearly. Recognizing what it was, he stopped breathing and a freezing terror seized him.

A human head!

It was floating without causing any ripples in the water. No indication of any limbs at all!

Struck dumb, Kunjootty clutched Chathutty's arm desperately. He silently pointed out the bizarre spectacle to him.

'Koppan chetta! Look over there!' Chathutty cried in panic.

Koppan caught a glimpse too. Even as the trio remained stunned and speechless, the head continued to move away from their boat.

'Sshhh! Don't make a sound!' Koppan cautioned in a whisper, 'Kayal Pottan, the mute who is the terror of the lagoon, is on the prowl!'

'Kayal Pottan?' Chathutty asked aloud, forgetting the warning.

By then the head had turned direction to face them! Kunjootty watched the bald head, shining like a mirror, eyes dense with a feral look, moving rapidly in the direction of their boat.

'Oh help, Muthappa!' Koppan hailed his gods in desperation. 'Hurry, Chathutty! Row fast, else he will sink our boat!'

Hardly had the words sounded when Chathutty furiously pushed the bamboo pole into the depths. Koppan put his full strength in steering the boat towards the tideway coursing to Potta Thuruthu.

Trying to catch up with the swift Pachuvanchi, the hairless head raced at a madly feverish pace.

8

The Marvels Within the Water

'Oww! The Muthappan of Neendakara came to our aid!' Koppan released his breath in utter relief as their boat reached a safe distance.

The three were drenched in sweat even though a moist wind was blowing. It was an inscrutable experience. The isle of Potta Thuruthu slumbered in the dark at a short distance from the boat, which carried the troubled men.

'Chathutty, have you heard of Kayal Pottan?'

'No!'

'There are so many stories about him.'

Koppan cast a look at Kunjootty.

Kunjootty was aware of a confusing haziness. The backwaters were the hideout of infinite mysteries. The lagoon existed without any origin, middle or end. Now a lagoon traveller with a bald head, feral eyes and a monstrous face had shown up from the desolate darkness!

'Very few people have actually seen Kayal Pottan!' Koppan told them.

The boats of the unfortunate lot who encountered him lay orphaned and capsized on the lagoon. The next day, the bloated corpses, whatever was left of those after the fish had their fill, would be found on the outer frontiers of the lagoon. The rare ones who survived brought with them tales of mortal terror.

'There are seven of them; we saw just one! Each has the strength of ten men! But all are mute! Their strength is unmatched!'

'Where do they live?' Chathutty inquired curiously.

'Who knows? In some far-off isle, it is said. They travel in the night. No signs of hands or legs while swimming! The head bobs as if someone is walking through the water. Even in the deepest ends of the lagoon, that is how they move!'

'Are they deaf too?'

'Well, some say yes, some say no. But deaf-mute or whatever, they howl horrendously in the nights at times! You will piss your clothes on hearing it!'

At certain times, Kayal Pottan's ominous howl emanated from the secret depths of the backwaters. It also emerged from the acme of the coconut trees that were ripe for toddy tapping. Many nights of Potta Thuruthu were rendered sleepless as a result. Still some preferred to consider the story of the lagoon monster as a figment of imagination. Yet even they could not give any explanation about those who went mysteriously missing in the lagoon.

'Does the monster venture out in the day?' Chathutty queried.

'No! He travels only by night. He swims from one isle to another. The cretin sniffs out the toddy as he journeys forth. Then he clambers up the coconut trees, binges on the toddy and starts howling! You can see the toddy pots lying broken on the ground the next day. Still some fellows insist that the wind must have pushed those down, huh!'

Koppan's loquacity ceased for some time. The sound of the pole pushing into the water was all that interrupted the night's silence. Koppan's memories had drawn him to a time years and years ago.

It was on a similar night that Koppan's father, Chonachu, had launched the Pachuvanchi. The man who had stepped into the light drizzle had never returned. The islanders firmly believed that it was the lagoon monster that had sunk his boat. That death had caused much grief all around the isle. They had lost a great *vaidyan* that day, someone who had an antidote to any venomous bite! Fate had not allowed Chonachu enough time to pass on the great mantra—which the nomadic healer Muniandi had taught him—to the next generation.

Yet Koppan had picked up a few basic lessons from his father and mastered the cures hidden in the aromatic naruneendi roots, the Indian sarsaparilla, and the powerful sirikuranchan roots, or gumnema sylvestre, used by traditional Tamil healers to cure victims bitten by snakes and scorpions. That was how he had developed the confidence of conjuring up a few tricks occasionally.

As the boat neared his house, Kunjootty requested Koppan, 'Do not mention Kayal Pottan at home!'

'Why?'

'Then you won't be allowed to launch your Pachuvanchi any more.'

'True! What about the shrimps? Not taking them?'

'It is too late now. Bring some over tomorrow.'

'All right then.'

As Kunjootty stepped down from the boat, the house, its inmates and the surroundings were all submerged in sleep. He ignored the cold supper laid out for him on the dining table. No hunger.

Under the circle of light cast by the table lamp, Kunjootty opened his incomplete book. He drew some lines and figures, trying to create a picture. Perhaps one day, all these unclear signs would transform themselves into coherent lines in the *Book of Exodus*. He had to be part of this world again to complete the book. Now his mind was in tatters. Much was left to clear up: his eyes, ears, heart . . .

Shutting the book and switching off the light, Kunjootty hit the bed. As he lay there staring at the flashing beacon lights circling afar, he yearned for a deep sleep. Then a thought came into his mind: it was Sunday tomorrow.

Numerous Holy Mass confessions to pay back.

One had always stayed behind at church, pondering over many thoughts, far away from the Lord. Tonight, Kunjootty realized it was no coincidence that he had enacted the role of Lucifer, that no one else was ready to take on, in the Bible play staged on the church grounds all those years ago. Though it was a malicious prank for him at that juncture, later, Lucifer had entered his own life.

Many sins seeking forgiveness were lamenting at the feet of the Good Shepherd. He opened up his five Holy wounds, accepted the sins and then hanged those on the wooden cross.

Kunjootty's thoughts became entangled. Was he asleep or awake?

He tried to move his little finger, trying to prove to himself he was not dreaming.

A strong wind soughed by just then. The windowpanes banged shut; flashes of lightning and thunder descended on earth.

Everything was obscure outside.

The first harbingers of the monsoon had dropped on Potta Thuruthu.

A lagoon traveller was continuing his sojourn even then. One of the strong western tempests gathered strength near his path. The waves, which were embraced by that natural force, rose sky high. The traveller, growing exhausted on being tossed up and down, started swimming in the direction of Potta Thuruthu. The wings of the night met each other at the sacred Ishan Kon, the northeastern spot, igniting fire! A thunder broke, with its ear-splitting sound reverberating around. As the fire spears from the sky plunged furiously into the water, for the very first time, the lagoon traveller found himself struck down into the depths, to witness its spectacular marvels. He lay motionless inside the palace of the Sea Queen and her mermaids, watching the crystalline splendours around.

9

The Festival Begins

Every year, on the anointed day, at an auspicious time, Lord Shiva, the deity Thekkambara Thevar, would arrive in grandeur to visit his wife, the gorgeous Parvati, Kavilottamma. The journey would be through the skies, in the guise of fire.

When her husband arrived, accompanied by his entourage of *bhoots* who carried star lights to illuminate the paths, Kavilottamma would be waiting impatiently at the doorsteps of her temple's sanctum sanctorum, having bathed in the river and coloured her lips red with sweet betel juice. That day, the temple festival would begin with the Kodiyettam, where the flag symbolizing the start of the festival would be hoisted high. The Thevar would return to his abode only after nine days. Meanwhile, the temple at Thekkambara would remain closed.

For the procession, the majestic tusker was a must. He moved forward through the rustic village paths, proudly carrying the golden deity of the Devi on his head, accompanied by kids who were allured by the chance of pulling out a hair from his tail for

71

making a ring! All the adults around were once children who had squealed in excitement on seeing the elephant. Kunjootty, too, had such a vibrant memory.

Along the pathways, squares would be slathered with cow manure and tender banana leaves would be placed over them. On the leaves would be the offering of nirapara: freshly harvested rice grains heaped in brass vessels, with sprigs of coconut flowers at the top. Next to it, the *nilavilakku*, the gleaming, golden-hued lamp, lighted up welcomingly with seven wicks, added to the glory. Adjacent to the lamp, jaggery, popped rice and bunches of bananas. It was the traditional way of welcoming the ceremonial procession of the Mother Goddess.

Kunjootty watched with curiosity as the temple minions took away the grains from the vessels and offered the jaggery balls to the elephant. The bananas, first tucked inside the elephant's mouth, would be retrieved and proffered to the devotees as 'prasad'.

Isaac felt that it was a strange custom.

'All these devotional rites are fraught with craziness. Look at the rush to get a banana soiled inside an elephant's mouth!'

Four months earlier, Isaac had never expected Kunjootty to regain normalcy. He had been extremely cautious about guiding Kunjootty back to life, his friend veering on the edge of a mental breakdown, or perhaps death itself, at that point of time. Trying to provoke Kunjootty, and coax him to talk, was part of Isaac's strategy.

Kunjootty just stood there grinning.

'It is all relative, is it not? From their perspective, the devotees might call your actions crazy!'

'What then is the border line between sanity and craziness? To appease someone never seen, walking across embers, piercing spears through cheeks, hurling boiling water. Makes no sense at all!' Isaac was shaking his head.

Kunjootty smiled again. 'Will you be able to pierce your mouth with some spear based on an ardent faith?'

'As if I am going to try out such stupid stuff!' Isaac retorted sharply.

'Admit that you will never be able to. But they get the fortitude from somewhere within. Definitely it is based on some deep inner belief. While they express their internal strength through devotional rites, we express ours through some other means, even malicious acts! To each his own way of madness. To insist that one's craziness is exclusively correct is the ultimate stupidity.'

Isaac got vexed at that argument.

The wind was trying its strength against the flagpole of Kavilottamma's temple.

'These are mere word games—picking up a stone from somewhere, polishing it and declaring it God! Does not make sense to me. Much better to worship a human being instead.'

Kshetra devata, adored as the deity of temple, kept herself concealed in the idol, symbolizing 'Gatra tatva', a simulacrum of the human body. Her feet became the spires. The boundary walls were the curves of her waist and the flagpole her spine. Atop the spinal cord, a Garuda had landed, after circumnavigating the temple. He was observing the surroundings like a divine spectator, a sight which no one else noticed.

'It is actually a philosophy,' Kunjootty responded. 'A ritual wherein one steps inside the temple of the body to realize the spirit within. It can be argued that we try to limit an infinite power within an idol. Yet, it follows a natural law of symbolism. We all exist through symbols. Your name "Isaac" and the letters forming your name are symbolic of your existence. Humans find value even in a lifeless silver coin. We worship it as a measure of wealth too. If an idol is a symbol, so is one's name and a coin. To tell the truth, we are idolators and superstitious folk who worship many symbols.'

'We ascribe a value to a silver coin for commercial purposes. Due to that our physical needs are met. But what sort of needs are met when you worship a stone?' Isaac asked sarcastically.

The Garuda ascended and circled the temple yet again. As if satisfied by his review of the various arrangements, he again returned to roost on the flagpole. Kunjootty keenly observed its body resembling a saffron cloth and the whiteness of the neck, akin to a pure white handkerchief knotted around it.

Then he said, 'Isaac, a coin might help in the commercial exchange of physical entities. But there are many others that are immeasurable by coins: love, peace, goodness! For those, some other measuring tool needs to be developed. A silver coin is a valid symbol of exchange in a specific human society. Yet, in another country that follows another system of exchange, it might be rendered totally useless. If you offer a silver coin in exchange of food there, they might ridicule you. They will call you a fool, just like you mock those who see God in a stone. To assuage your hunger in that land, you will have to use the coin that is in vogue there.'

'Hey! That is why exchange rates are fixed for currencies across the world. If I exchange my silver coins for dollars, I will still get my daily bread in America!' Isaac snapped.

'You said that because of your awareness about various currencies and their exchange rates. But you do not know the value of the stone's symbolism. For that, one needs to become a part of the Universal Mind.

'First, our own minds entrap us. Hunger, shame, these are all problems of the human mind. To overcome those, we have to worship the silver coin—the symbolism decided by society's mind. However, it is only by rising above the limitations of the societal mind and reaching the Universal Mind that one achieves complete freedom, sans boundaries. Only then can we recognize the unity underlying all diverse symbols.

'We are all un-evolved beings, struggling inside the limitations of our own mind, mindlessly following the urges of the body. How can we rise to be part of the Universal Mind? Perhaps, by worshipping those stones, which you claim are lifeless, one might be able to join a bigger societal mind. Anything will do: a crucifix, a trishul, a swastika or a sickle, hammer and star! And if you can still climb higher, one might even reach the Universal Mind! And just like you know the values of various currencies, perhaps then, you might master the symbolism behind different beliefs and religions. And when you realize the single truth behind everything, that becomes Mukti. But we are so deficient when it comes to comprehending the truth. One cannot realize the heat in the word "fire" merely by uttering it,' Kunjootty elucidated.

'That sounds cool! Then come on, let us go and bow before the goddess carved out of stone,' Isaac teased.

'If one feels fulfilled on paying obeisance thus, I cannot find any fault with it,' Kunjootty retorted, 'If one can find something with a non-ephemeral nature to fill the hollow within—it could be anything at all, money, status, sexual satisfaction—one might deign to call it God! But tell me, what is there of such permanent nature in this fleeting world of ours?'

'Hey, you renegade! Can I assume that you speak from the heart?'

'To speak from the heart warrants a minimum purity within. And that's what I lack.'

'There, you have spoken the truth now!'

At that instant, Kunjootty saw that there was another Garuda seated above the golden dome of the temple. Two scintillating presences on the flagpole and the pinnacle! One was the Goddess Kavilottamma and the other, Lord Thekkambara Thevar, Kunjootty imagined. But he preferred to keep his thoughts to himself since he did not want them sullied by Isaac's derision.

The children of Potta Thuruthu were thronging the balloon sellers. On sighting a familiar face, Kunjootty reminisced, 'Once, like these children, who stand salivating at the sight of balloons, I too yearned for an apple balloon. But today, a balloon tied to a stick cannot charm my mind. From balloons the attraction changed to sweetmeats, then to new clothes and youthful lusts! The mind roamed after many such enchantments but never found satiation in any.'

Kunjootty saw a child in his mind's canvas.

* * *

It was the time of the church festivities. With an old coin, crusted with verdigris, which his mother had given, a child purchased an apple-shaped balloon. With the euphoria of having conquered the world, holding his precious possession in his right hand, he raced home, only to be stopped by his nemesis, that fat Kadir. 'Lord! Please don't let Kadir see my balloon,' the boy prayed fervently. But God's decision was far beyond his reckonings. All attempts to hide his balloon from Kadir's sharp eyes were futile.

'C'mon, show me that balloon!'

'No way . . . It is mine!'

'Come here, you brat!'

The child fled. Crossing farms and side roads, he sought refuge from the bully huffing behind him. It was to no avail! That fatso Kadir grabbed his balloon.

'Please give my balloon back! Please . . .' the child begged.

Kadir, caught in the intoxication of hitting the balloon up to the skies, ignored his pleas. Every time the balloon descended and the boy reached out, Kadir hit the balloon away to greater heights, far beyond the child's hands. The boy kept on trying, hoping that at some point the balloon would drop right back into his open hands.

Ttthhupp!

The sound of the bursting balloon shattered the boy's tender heart. As if gathering the bits and pieces of his own heart, the child scooped up the scattered balloon pieces from the ground. Kadir was guffawing maliciously, taunting him all the while. The possibility of another coin, coated with a green patina, was next to impossible.

* * *

'Come to think of that now, I can shrug it off as a childhood prank. But at that moment, it was the palpitating truth. The obsession for a balloon in childhood has now metamorphosed into an obsession for life. At every age and time, one will chase after something or the other. The object that one desires will appear as the only truth at that moment. The human mind tantalizes one with a balloon, money, pride. The same mind shall return to point out the fallacies of the desire at a later stage. It was because I was ecstatic on getting the balloon that I felt devastated on losing it. Both were immature reactions. Isaac, if I were to purchase some balloons now, you who mocked the devotees receiving the offerings, will be the first to call me mad!' Kunjootty said.

'Is that so? Then come with me!' Isaac started retracing his steps to the temple's festival grounds.

'Why?'

'One should not dismiss childhood yearnings so causally. Let us fill our minds with balloons today!'

The balloons were dangling from the seller's stand.

'Can you give us the common green snake?' Isaac asked with a childlike lisp.

'Green snake?' The seller was flustered.

'Those ones! The green balloons that are all coiled round like snakes!'

The balloon seller's lips drew into a wide grin coloured by both tobacco juice and mischief. His crooked teeth were exposed as he smiled at them. Uncoiling the *kundalini*-like balloons from his stand, the man offered them to Isaac. Isaac promptly twisted one around his neck and then adorned Kunjootty's neck with another.

'Now all I require is a bit of ash and a tiger skin!' Isaac quipped naughtily.

'What are you doing?' Kunjootty was astounded.

'Listen, if we dress up like that, Goddess Kavilottamma might mistake us as her husband, Thekkambara Thevar himself!'

'Thekkambara Thevar is a Digambara! He has made all the *dik*—the directions—his *ambara*, the dress! Digambara can be interpreted as the state of being naked. No dress allowed.'

'God! Then I am not for the plan!'

'Fear not! It is just another theory unyielding to a tainted human mind.'

Isaac started negotiating over the prices of various balloons. Finally, he ended up like a seller's stand: holding on to balloons shaped like apes and apples, a hydrogen balloon crying for the sky, a toy gun and a kid's long whistle! A very buffoonish figure . . .

'You said that bhakti was total craziness. If those devotees could see you now, imagine what they would be thinking!' Kunjootty laughed.

'Of course, they will think I have gone totally loony! Let the world be filled with more mad men! Then we will have some fun. But then, I do not want to stay mad all alone. Come on, take over your share of the craziness.'

By the time they returned from the temple, the sun was setting. They stopped on seeing a cycle rickshaw make its way through the clay road. It was a rather unique sight in that area. Who could it be, they wondered.

A thin man was riding the cycle rickshaw, putting in an effort to control it as the vehicle precariously careened on the winding path.

A child's ball, probably purchased from the temple fair, could be seen rolling unexpectedly into the rickshaw's path. A little girl ran out from the nearby house, chasing after it. Kunjootty found himself thinking that new inmates had come to occupy the empty house after a long time.

Before he could complete his thought, he saw the rickshaw reach dangerously close to the girl.

'Oh, God!' Kunjootty leapt forward instinctively and pushed the child away. He found himself tossed to the side, as the rickshaw collided with him.

A few frozen moments . . . followed by the child's horrified shout and Isaac's panic. Along with these, Kunjootty experienced a mélange of thoughts . . . *God, Amma, Death* . . . yet many more undecipherable ruminations.

The balloons, which were weeping for the sky, now floated overhead. In the thrill of escaping from captivity, they reduced to dots of green, red and yellow. Then, overcoming the limitations of the visible horizon, they rose further and merged with the endless skies.

10

The Reunion

Another Sunday slipped quietly away.

Sunday, that took birth amid a hazy sleep, grew up in utter lassitude and ended up incomplete.

Kunjootty had been forced into bed rest, owing to the bruises sustained in the accident involving the cycle rickshaw. He had woken up with a sense of desolation, which continued through the afternoon and the evening.

Having no other choice, Kunjootty lay in bed, his outer eyes closed and inner eyes opened.

At sundown, he heard someone knocking on the door.

'Who is it? Do come inside!'

The remnants of mild sunlight lay scattered across the door's threshold. Kunjootty stared in wonder at those who were trying to make their way amid the shimmering light: the child whom he had saved the evening before, her mother and a young man, presumedly the girl's father. The girl was holding on to her father's arm.

As he stared at the man, Kunjootty felt a keen sense of bewilderment take over him. The curly hair, dark physique, that gleaming, sharp look in the eyes . . .

Unwittingly, the words poured forth.

'Murali?'

'Kunjootty!'

Murali sat on the edge of the cot, leaned forward and clasped his friend's hand to his own.

'What a surprise! How come you are here, Murali?'

Kunjootty sat with his left arm around Murali's shoulder, as if jolted awake from a dream. Many years seemed to be coalescing in that single moment, overwhelming him.

'Never thought to find you again. Though I knew you were living somewhere around here. Really, this is so fortuitous!' Murali spoke with extreme emotion.

'But you did not tell me how you ended up here!'

'Transfer! I am in charge of block development here. It is miraculous that we have met again in this way. I was thinking of searching for you after settling down.'

'Didn't you have my address?'

'Ashamed to say that I lost it. Didn't you have mine?'

'No, I lost it!'

As the emotional turmoil evoked by their unexpected meeting lessened slightly, Murali spoke.

'I always remembered you . . .'

'Same here.'

A college campus that was far removed from the chaos of the city; a gulmohar tree that flowered so abundantly that even the leaves were hidden from sight; a hostel, the three precious years that had left memories behind in room number twenty-one. Life's future courses had been set during that period.

'In the excitement of meeting you, I almost forgot to ask. How is your health, Kunjootty?' Murali asked anxiously.

'You can see for yourself! Besides, my mind is brimming over with joy on seeing you. What is the name of your daughter?'

'Nandini.'

Kunjootty hugged Nandini lovingly and asked, 'You got so scared yesterday, didn't you, Nandini?'

'No . . .'

'Then why did you cry?'

'Mm . . . Just like that . . .'

'Nandinikutty weeps just like that! You have inherited all your father's naughtiness!'

Nandini was curiously observing the new relationship blossoming before her eyes. The sparkling dew-like look in her four-year-old eyes brought to life a faded memory in Kunjootty.

Hearing the little girl cough intermittently, he asked, 'What is wrong with you, dear?'

'A niggling cough, started a few days before. Must be due to bathing in unfamiliar water.'

'Have you not given her medication?'

'Her mother is giving her some herbal medicine.' Murali looked at his wife, Savitry. 'See, both mother and daughter insisted that we search for your house. They wanted to express their gratitude! You remember Savitry, don't you? I had waxed eloquent about my Brahmin sweetheart in those student days!'

* * *

Nights filled with the screech of the cicadas.

Heavy sighs emanated from a weary soul.

There was a prophecy that on a rainy night the son of a low-caste servant would steal the daughter of a Brahmin landlord. That turned out to be true. Soaked to their skins, the young couple had escaped in a little skiff and crossed the Kurumali River. The couple had started their new life on that river shore. They had left behind a fast-deteriorating Tharavadu that had once held sovereignty over the lives of many like Murali. Nothing prevented the members of the ancient household from conducting the rite of death for the living young woman—the infamous rite of Irikkapindam—as their response to her rebellion, which had humiliated the pride of their clan.

Kunjootty looked with deep compassion at the face of the young woman, who had been offered that last ball of rice and the appeasing mantra for the dead, by her family members from afar. He found himself slipping into the depths of another old memory.

The cultural festival on the college campus and a stage, where the competition for instrumental music was being held. Many students were showcasing their mastery over large and shining musical instruments. A dark young man walked to the stage empty-handed. Then, retrieving a bamboo flute tucked inside his shirt, he raised it to his lips. Someone cracked a cheap joke at his expense, triggering a mocking burst of laughter around.

'He is a scheduled caste fellow! Half a song would suffice!'

The youth was defeated at that very moment. However, with the determination of a runner who completes the race even after others have crossed the finishing line, he concentrated on filling the holes of the flute with his exquisite music.

The wounds of the bamboo effortlessly translated the language emanating from the deep lacerations of his soul. In a matter of a few seconds, the audience had become utterly still. The listeners were mesmerized by the perfect rhapsody. The denouement was met with hearty applause. But the young man did not stay behind to receive the adulation.

Murali withdrew into his lair in room number twenty-one and shared his bitter pain with his roommate.

'Today is my father's third death anniversary. It was Acchan who had cut and shaped the bamboo into this flute and taught me all the lessons. When I stood humiliated on that stage, I endured it only for his sake. He used to tell me that in his previous life, he must have been a Gandharva who was cursed for disrespecting music. That was why he could never learn music in this lifetime, despite his deep yearning!

'Acchan wanted me to learn music but when he approached a musician, the man taunted him by asking what a Pulaya boy, an outcaste, wanted to do with music! My father, hugging me close, had broken into tears while narrating that story. Today, I am sure my father cried again, when I was mocked on that stage. Now I feel that my father's surmise was correct—about being cursed. Perhaps to repay that debt, I must suffer all this shaming too. I have to continue serving the cause of music despite the ridicule!' Kunjootty could still recollect how, as Murali had finished his sentence, like an inauspicious augury, the bells tolling death had sounded from the nearby church.

* * *

'Do you still have that flute with you?' Kunjootty asked Murali.

'Yes, I do. I still play it, until my wife begs me to stop!'

'I would love to listen to it again. It has been such a long time!'

'A very, very long time indeed.'

'Murali, do you remember our room number?'

'Twenty-one! Why did you ask?'

'Merely checking your memory!'

Kunjootty turned to Savitry.

'I apologize that there is no one at home to welcome you. Everyone has left for a wedding. I am all alone here.'

'What about your food then?'

'My kind neighbours provide me with food!'

Time passed by as they indulged in superfluous conversation once more. A woodpecker flew past the room, singing the Raga Mukhari. Murali became cognizant of the silences that started stretching into longer intervals and got up.

'We need to cross to the other side before the sun sets . . .'

'What is the hurry?'

'I am not sure of the way. We walked across many people's compounds on our way to your home. Oh, I need to tell you something else,' Murali paused. 'We need to find a decent place to stay. Savitry does not like the present house. We need your help.'

'In this dark continent, it is a miracle that you managed to get a place to stay!'

'Do search for a house!'

As Kunjootty searched the neighbourhood's geography in his mind, looking out for an empty house, as unexpectedly as an afternoon shower, a picture emerged in his mind. A poor family that had set off in a boat with their vessels, cane cot and pets. The house they had sold off in desperation had been locked up for years. It must be run over with rodents and spiders now. Bereft of sunlight, the insides would be infested with layers of dust.

'Would you mind shifting to this side of the lagoon?' Kunjootty inquired.

'I would be very interested!'

'The water will be a barrier. You would be cut off from the mainland.'

'Hardly matters! Much before Savitry, I had fallen in love with the river!'

'There is a small house, Vadakke Veedu, over to the north. My father purchased it from the family when they left it. With a little work, it should be a decent place for you to stay.'

'Great news!'

A house by the river, near the farms, lush with breeze and the presence of a sensitive neighbour! Murali was immensely pleased with the idea.

'It is too late to visit the place now. We shall come another day.'

Even after the family bid farewell and stepped into the light of the setting sun, Kunjootty continued to brood about the house situated towards the north. Fatigue seeped in, when whatever he was loath to recollect resurrected in the shadow of unpleasant omens. In the ensuing hours, Kunjootty bitterly regretted speaking about the house to Murali.

Zavarias and Eli were not against renting out the house. They thought it was a good thing to get some money from a decaying place. With help from Koppan and Chathutty, Kunjootty undertook the efforts of getting the house in order. Koppan killed off all the spider families that had taken over the inner rooms. The holes on the floor were filled and levelled. Chathutty liberally used the water from the lagoon to wash the floors clean.

The following Sunday, carrying all his moveable possessions in a boat, Murali shifted to Vadakke Veedu—without knowing the history of that little house. That night, a lightning flash lost its way and landed on the coconut tree in front of Vadakke Veedu, where a family of weaver birds had made a nest. A burnt nest and the charred remains of a fledgling could be seen lying orphaned on the grounds the next morning.

11

The Murmurs of Leaves

'Where does the river go?'

Nandini asked the question, dipping her fingers into the river's mystery.

Kunjootty was observing the bubbles that were being dragged by the waves. The sea breeze was dancing majestically all around. The gushing water was creating paintings around the stone boulders.

'All the rivers flow to the sea, Nandini. Our river too.'

'Where is the sea, uncle?'

'Over there, look! Can't you see the green of the land at the distance? There, the river vanishes.'

Nandini stared at the horizon clouded with the mist. There the river disappeared suddenly! She had an inexhaustible treasury of questions in her mind.

'What is the name of the river, uncle?'

That unforeseen question perplexed Kunjootty. What was the river's name? Had it existed as a nameless river all these ages? Though he had known the river from birth, how come he never recognized that secret of water?

'This river has no name, Nandini,' Kunjootty said, 'Perhaps every river loses her name as she nears the bay. As far as I know, this river is nameless. Maybe we can call her a tributary of the Periyar. Or we can name her the river of Potta Thuruthu!'

'Oh! How can we name her now? The river must be very old!'

'So what?' Kunjootty grinned.

'Won't she die due to old age? All the names will be wasted then!'

This time Kunjootty could not laugh it off. It was true that the Periyar and her tributaries had lost their purity. Wasn't pollution the equivalent of a river's death? The auspicious Shivaratri and the rituals for the forbearers had long lost their glory. The river did not breathe anymore. The liquid chemicals that flowed out like the karmic sins of factories were filled with the carcasses of fishes that had died cursing.

'You are right, Nandini. No point in naming this river now. Let us call her the Nameless One.'

Nandini found that comment acceptable. She threw a fistful of water in the direction of the sun and created tidbits of the rainbow.

'Shall we get inside this boat and row to the sea, uncle?'

'The sea can overturn our little boat and lock us in the sea castle deep under!'

'Is she bad, this sea?'

'Hmm . . . at times! Haven't you seen the sea, Nandini?'

'Only in pictures!'

'I will take you to see the sea one day, okay?'

Kunjootty sensed the 'one day' being carefully tucked away with childlike curiosity in Nandini's memory.

'Are you sure of that, uncle?' she insisted.

'Very sure.'

'Swear on your mother's name?'

'We should never swear by anyone's name!'

'What if we do?'

'That is the habit of wicked children. Those who lack confidence in themselves make others swear oaths and take oaths themselves!'

Nandini fell silent. She did not insist further on taking an oath.

'Would you like to get inside the boat?'

'Oh, yes!'

'Let us row till that river-bend and return!'

As he seated the child safely in the small boat, Kunjootty stared at the newly rented house. Neither Murali nor Savitry was seen on the porch. Maybe they were still working on settling in. The house, which they had expected to stay closed forever, was coming alive again. If only there was no repetition of the disasters of the past.

'Uncle! Who builds these boats? You?' Nandini asked.

'Not me, there are famed builders of boats called Thachhans. Their clan is now dwindling. Nowadays, it is very difficult to discover someone who can craft a perfect boat!'

'Back home, we had lots of boats on our river too!'

'Did your river have a name, Nandini?'

'Yes, Karumali River!'

'You are a smart child!'

'My father says that too!'

Nandini became engrossed in narrating various stories.

Above the serene river, a pickerel flicked into the air and an alert kingfisher swooped to catch it, before disappearing in the mangroves. It had a cosy nest on the farm ridge nearby.

Koppan and Chathutty were approaching from the opposite direction, their boat filled with river sand.

'How is your new friend?' Koppan asked warmly.

'Bright girl! We should take her along for the next Pachuvanchi expedition!'

'What if the Kayal Pottan tries to capsize our boat again?' Chathutty smiled.

'That is a point! We have to go now. The sand is for Gopala Kanian! He wants us to finish the levelling before his son comes from the Gulf!'

They went by, their poles pushing into the waters.

The sound of a motorboat could be heard humming from afar, beyond the coconut groves. Over the calm river that was seemingly devoid of emotions, Kunjootty kept rowing, as if he was undertaking a duty.

'Do you like your new house, Nandini?'

'Oh, yes, I love it! Now I can go boating with you any day. Uncle, I saw something special in our new house!'

'What is that special thing?'

'In the back room, the walls are full of pictures! There are names scribbled there too. Do you want to know whose names, uncle?'

Pictures that remained unfaded, even when one pretended they were forgotten. The wretched family that was forced to leave their house as repayment of their debt. The pathos as they left unwillingly, with tears streaming endlessly. The mother's disease that refused to budge even a bit, even after they had sold off everything in the singular quest of healing her. When she had been lifted into the boat, lying on her cane cot, it had been Susanna who had held the old, hole-ridden umbrella, shading her from the hot sun.

When his best friend had left with a last look, leaving behind a house whose walls were filled with their names and pictures, the seven-year-old Kunjootty had been devastated.

Kunjootty no longer wished to continue that boat journey.

'Let us go back, Nandini,' he said.

'Uncle, please let us go a little more . . .'

'Your father might scold you for getting late!'

'Not at all, since I am with you. My father is very nice. He tells me so many stories. Do you know stories, uncle?'

'I am useless in that subject, Nandini.'

'You are fibbing! Don't you know even one story?'

Don't you know? Kunjootty searched within. A story emerged from his memory, having been indelibly imprinted in his mind, along with early thoughts as a child.

'Have you heard the story of the fire bird, Nandini?'

'No. Acchan probably does not know that one.'

That story could come only from the warmth of a grandmother's breast. His Valiyammachi was returning to fill the losses of the new generation. After the separation of many years, hugging her grandchild close with her thin arm, she lovingly queried, 'My little one, have you forgotten the story that Valiyammachi told you?'

The grandson felt a yearning to convince his grandmother that he had not forgotten that particular lesson of his childhood.

'A long, long time ago, there were many fire birds that lived in the cloud world.'

'Uncle, where is the cloud world?'

'On top of the sky! The fire birds laid their eggs on the clouds. As they fell, the eggs cracked open and the fledglings emerged. The little bird opened its eyes and flew upwards to reach its mother's side! But once, there was a problem . . .'

'What happened?'

'A little fire fledgling felt like seeing the earth. It came flying down in search of flower-filled meadows, groves and delicious fruits. However, it landed on a Chama Potta, the resting place of ghoulish spirits, in the middle of a lonely farm. There was a single-legged tree there, and on it lived a lot of wicked vultures, constantly bickering among themselves. The vultures felt greatly jealous of the beauty of the fire bird and surrounded it.'

'And then?'

'The innocent little one, unaware of the evils of this earth, was aghast! Then one vulture attacked its head. The others joined in the fun. The terror-struck fire bird tried to fly back to the skies. But she couldn't! The corpse eaters pecked at her mercilessly with their scalpel like beaks and destroyed her tender wings. As it hopped around in desperation, they hewed off her tiny legs. They blinded the light of her eyes. Finally, only drops of blood and a few feathers remained on the Chama Potta.'

'Wicked vultures!' Nandini cursed, her eyes welling up with tears.

'After that, not a single drop of rain ever fell on Chama Potta. It stayed accursed and desiccated. Even today, one can see the feathers of the little fire bird floating around, crying for its cloud home! The mother bird is still waiting for its little one, weeping forever.'

Nandini fell silent, in some deep thought.

Kunjootty was silent too.

After a while, he asked, 'Do you know who that vulture is, Nandini?'

'No.'

'There are those who called it "fate". Others named it "the mind". And some recognized that the fire bird and the vulture were one and the same.'

Seeing that the child could not understand the depth of what he was explaining, Kunjootty stopped abruptly.

'Let us return,' he said.

Nandini nodded, half-heartedly.

Kunjootty regretted he had introduced the fire bird in her tender mind as a source of painful turbulence. But one part of his mind whispered that the narration was predestined. If the story lay throbbing in Nandini's memories, at some point of time, yet another generation would listen to the story of the little fire bird.

Kunjootty was silent as he rowed back. Nandini, used to chattering without end, was unusually quiet too.

The only rhythm that accompanied them till the ferry was the stroke of oars. As he anchored the boat and lifted Nandini out of the skiff, Kunjootty gently caressed her gloomy face.

'What happened to my little Nandini?'

A melancholy breeze blew over the nameless river of Potta Thuruthu. The flower-like water bubbles, bereft of any fragrance, floated far away on the river.

'Poor, poor, fire bird!' Nandini sobbed.

Sensing a connection across many births, Kunjootty hugged Nandini close and planted a kiss on her little forehead. As he struggled in vain to console her, Kunjootty felt tears welling up in his eyes too.

12

The Words of Solomon

The hitherto silent Vadakke Veedu becoming redolent with sounds and brightness caused Kunjootty joy and sadness in equal measure. It seemed as if some space in one's mind, evocative of a graveyard, was undergoing a purification ritual.

He sought out the cheerful atmosphere there, to while away his time after office hours. The dark past seemed to slowly fade away as Kunjootty pandered to Nandini's childish inquisitiveness. A sense of assurance that everything would be all right once again!

Three months passed by in this manner.

Migrant birds started arriving in Potta Thuruthu to prepare for their autumn songs.

A very strange incident happened to Kunjootty in the office around that time. It was a dry afternoon. Since it was a Friday before the designated holiday on the second Saturday of the month, many had left around noon, after offering flimsy excuses. Having no places to go, only Kunjootty, Diwakar

Menon and the files ridden by red tape remained in the office. They had been sharing experiences, when most unexpectedly, a pigeon flew in through the open window, and, perching on the file cabinet at the southern corner of the room, started cooing some ancient mantra from the Pakshi Sastra, the Subtle Science of Birds.

The pigeon flitted to a desk, then hopped on to the arm of a chair and continued its recital. Then it took a short flight and landed near Kunjootty's chair.

The pigeon was the colour of a pure, white dream. As he wondered at the unforeseen arrival of the bird, Kunjootty felt that the repayment of another of life's debts was due.

The repayment of a debt: flesh equivalent to a pigeon's weight.

Here was the legendary King Shibi's dove, searching across many accursed centuries for his master. Would the red-eyed hawk make an appearance soon? If Lord Agni had arrived to test him, then let it not fly away now! Thinking thus, Kunjootty stretched his arm towards the pigeon.

Not only did the pigeon remain unflustered, it also docilely settled down. Kunjootty had never touched a pigeon before in his life. All he had cuddled, ever, was a little parrot fledgling that Koppan had once retrieved from the hollow in a coconut tree. It had died three days later.

Now, picking up the submissive visitor carefully and then cuddling it close to his chest, Kunjootty murmured: 'Who are you? Why have you come?'

The bird did not make a sound. Neither did it ask for refuge. Its poignant look seemed to reflect its heart's feelings.

'This is a miracle!' Diwakar Menon quipped, astounded by the happenings. 'In my knowledge, no pigeon has ever come searching for anyone till now.'

'Neither in my knowledge,' smiled Kunjootty.

'Surely, there is a purpose behind this visit!'

'What would that be?'

'In your Holy Bible, isn't there someone, the keeper of the royal granary, who interprets omens and dreams? Someone called Joseph? I consider him as one of my gurus! I shall attempt to interpret this sign.'

'Go ahead!'

Diwakar Menon examined the pigeon at close quarters. Assembling all possible life debts in his inner eye, he started the calculations. Then he took the bird from Kunjootty's hands, went near the open window and pointed in the direction of the sky. The pigeon took a look all around, then rose in a sudden flight and disappeared somewhere amid the obscure skyscrapers. Kunjootty felt it had merged with the surroundings inexplicably. What then was the purpose of its dream-like arrival, followed by the vanishing into nothingness?

'That was a special bird. It was assigned the task of opening a forgotten chapter,' Diwakar Menon said.

'What chapter?'

'The one you are yet to pen down in your *Book of Exodus*. We can laugh this visit off as a mere coincidence. However, in nature, every move has a specific undercurrent triggering it. A cause-and-effect relationship. Haven't you felt like that?'

'Sometimes . . .'

'If so, the message for you is this: An Adam's rib lies discarded somewhere! The time has arrived to find it and grant her a deserving place in your home! The Grihasta Ashrama, the phase of the householder, is imminent!'

That was a shocking interpretation. The bird, with the colour of memory, had swooped in to rest on a dark secret, yet unshared. The rib, which was supposed to grace his home, had gone missing much earlier. An erstwhile prophecy was coming true. The nomad's Lakshana Sastra, the science of omens, had proven true. The lines of his hand had not lied either.

'My God, the lines on this child's hand are so bizarre! Why is it so?'

Memories pushed into oblivion were sprouting anew like innate compulsions; and Kunjootty struggled ineffectually to overcome the turbulence.

'You too had set up a home, didn't you?' he asked Diwakar Menon sharply.

The pigeon had arrived to open every forgotten wound. Staring at the wake of the bird's flight, Diwakar Menon became silent. Birds of omen seemed to be pecking around a series of unfortunate experiences and a useless, tattered life.

'At least, from my experiences, it's all futile!' Menon replied.

The ink in the pen, uncapped and resting on the table, had dried up by then. Diwakar Menon did not feel like putting its cap back on. His mind was on a journey, moving from one isle to another, travelling across the rippling waves of the lagoon on a boat, to reach an unfinished house with a garden in the front yard. The plants were dried up, orphaned for lack of care. An empty house, the steps of stones longing for human feet, where the rooms designed for unborn children were still left incomplete. Like the ruins of an ancient temple, after the Shakti had vanished, the man and the house remained, bereft of any radiance. What was the result of the experiment that nature had conducted on him?

Kunjootty felt a stab of regret on seeing the wounded expression on Menon's face.

'I did not mean to remind you of anything. Just heard a smattering of news.'

'I can guess what you heard,' Menon's face clouded over, 'to put it in local lingo, the woman of the house eloped with someone!'

Kunjootty said nothing.

Menon continued: 'None knew the truth behind it. I never shared it with anyone either. How strange it was . . . like a fantastic tale with no basis in reality. Oh God! That pigeon's pecking around the stories of Adam's ribs today!'

Menon had known that it was inevitable to tell the truth one day. Now, the time had arrived. The secret, which had been crushing his heart, was seeking a way out. When the dusty pages, stained with the pains of an exodus, were re-opened, Kunjootty listened keenly.

* * *

Seventeen years before, when he was in the thrall of the Vedas, Upanishads and philosophical texts, Diwakar Menon had not imagined that he would be securing his master's degree in philosophy. Neither did he know that he would end up supervising clerks in a government office, or that Sarojam would one day become his life partner. However, the seeds of the devastation yet to come had already been sowed by then.

In his relentless quest for mastering the subject, Diwakar Menon had gained an extremely charismatic mentor, Dr Chandrasekhar. He was a famous researcher in Indian philosophy. Menon was enchanted by his deep baritone, as the erudite man elucidated the depths of various perspectives. Dr Chandrasekhar could hypnotize any audience with his magnetic persona. Menon called him 'Chandran Master'. When he was granted permission to use his guide's precious library, Menon had been overwhelmed with joy, unable to think of a better boon.

The mentor told the young man, who was revelling in the magnificence of the philosophical views, ignoring food and rest, one day:

'These are not multiplication tables to be learnt by heart, Diwakar. Rather, a path for attaining Moksha! This doctorate degree that I carry around ostentatiously is similar to the thirty pieces of silver that I got by betraying Indian philosophy— by dissecting the topic to the point of ugliness. My life is the veritable proof of that. If only I could put into practice a bit of what I have learnt, my life would not have been like a disjointed book, with pages all loose. On one side, the learning of Brahmavidya, and on the other, warring against it, my never-ending obsessions of lust! It is like the war between *devas* and *asuras*. This confession is my only truth.'

Chandran Master was not willing to denounce or curtail the demonic yearnings within himself. He freed the wild horses of his fiery bodily desires, allowing them to graze about in every available pasture. Alongside endless fame, limitless money and a personality that was magnetic, his passion for women kept on flaming intensely and relentlessly. That journey did not last very long. Time ushered him down its steps, not allowing him to balance the incongruities. But before his departure, Dr Chandrasekhar had delivered another mysterious missive:

'Time is a mystifying concept. In a single lifetime, one can have infinite parallel lives. During a day, one can live the eighty years of another existence and then die. When he dies, he could very well be enjoying the twentieth year of a different life! "I" exist on multiple planes, as multiple personalities. Even when "I" die, the same "I" might be existing in another time dimension. Yes, even after my death, I shall continue to exist. I shall be here. At an opportune time, I shall demand my guru dakshina from you, Diwakar!'

His mentor's intriguing perspective had not yielded itself to Menon's understanding. He had continued his explorations of the hefty books bequeathed to him.

That was the story that had occurred seventeen years before. Eventually, Diwakar Menon got his master's degree in philosophy. The bookish knowledge remained merely an intellectual pleasure. It could do nothing to help him face real-life experiences. By the time he yearned for a wisdom beyond that hidden in the books, his role had changed to that of a government clerk. Soon, Sarojam arrived to enact her own designated part in his life. In the third life phase, Grihasta Ashrama, all the erstwhile views of philosophy became lifeless. His intimate relationship with his wife was like a simple, straight line, clothed in serenity.

But unexpectedly, one day in the busy streets of Cochin, Diwakar Menon stood shell-shocked on seeing Chandran Master's face. It was the same face, the same physique: a man who was exactly like his former guide. As if a charioteer had returned to his chariot, cutting across time and space, to take over the reins once more! Diwakar Menon had introduced himself to that stranger, unable to control his anxiety.

The stranger's name was Balu, and he was working as a sales executive in a private firm. The young man was appalled on hearing about the similarities between himself and Menon's erstwhile teacher. Balu was a Brahmin lad, unfamiliar with

Dr Chandrasekhar's ways of life. That serendipitous meeting transformed into a deep friendship, and Balu became a frequent visitor to Menon's home.

'One day Balu became deeply inquisitive about Chandran Master. About his way of dress, his favourite food, his mannerisms and the like. When I teased him, asking him if he was possessed by Dr Chandrasekhar's spirit, his face fell. Then, in a sombre tone, Balu confessed that he felt that a hungry soul, still desirous and covetous, was lurking around him; and that he felt the pangs of its yearnings on solitary nights! I thought it was a joke.

'But beyond all jokes, Chandran Master's behaviour started manifesting in that young man. Or else, Balu was trying to be like him! I saw a cigarette case in his pocket that was Master's favourite brand! One day he came home stone drunk and started reciting mantras from Brihadaranyaka Upanishad! That war between devas and asuras must have restarted. But I failed in being wary, Kunjootty! Balu had regained that hypnotizing glance by then. I could never have imagined that he would seduce my wife, Sarojam, and separate her from me with his mesmerizing charms!'

By the time Menon finished his narrative, he was exhausted. Then, as if he was picking up the remains of whatever remained, he muttered, as if to himself: 'But now I understand! These are all the entanglements of karma. They have been handed over to us in measured amounts. One can magnify an internal hurt to gigantic proportions or reduce it to mustard-like proportions. At the end of it all, these remain as mere thoughts!'

Diwakar Menon started laughing. 'Do come to my incomplete house one day!'

'Of course, I shall,' Kunjootty accepted the invitation. 'Why don't you get it completed?'

'Oh, is there need for an adventure any more? Who needs the protection of a wall? If I had the gift of writing, I would have penned down a dozen *Book of Exodus* by now! But listening is what I have true proclivity for. On dark and silent nights, by listening ardently, I finally found a companion. The murmur of my table fan! I have become so accustomed to that murmur that I cannot fall asleep without that friend by my side. Even on freezing nights, Kunjootty, believe me, I still switch it on. I turn it around, facing the wall, but continue to listen to its familiar sound. Else, how can one survive in a dark chamber, without sound or touch? Tchhe! Why am I revealing all my peccadilloes? No one will understand this eccentricity of mine.'

'I understand, Menon Sir!' Kunjootty said softly.

Menon was touched by that reply. He sat staring silently at Kunjootty.

'I know you have an active volcano in your heart too, though I am unaware of the reasons. But Kunjootty, this world has confounded us in a way! If you think deeply, we will be bemused by the vagueness of it all. Remember what Solomon said? *"Whatever my eyes desired, I obtained! Whatever my heart wanted, I had!"* Still at the sunset of his life that wise soul too cried, *"Vanity of vanities! All is vanity."* That is all. One is fortunate if one can see beyond this vanity during one's life. Home, wife, relatives—all these cannot console us in the end.'

Kunjootty felt that the pigeon was returning with its flapping wings. As a reminder of its unexpected visit, it had left behind a tender feather on the office table. The key that had the power to unlock the inner secrets. Kunjootty kept it close to his ear and listened intently for the sound of the bird's flight.

That day, Kunjootty returned home with the pigeon's feather and Diwakar Memon's words resounding in his ears. Opening the diary with the blue cover, strewn with innumerable corrections and incomplete notes, he gently stroked the feather against a page. A book that was continuing across years, with scribblings and edits. Inside it was the history of an exile.

The tainted history had started with the sacrifice of a little fire bird. If one retraced the paths of the mother-clan beyond the Chama Potta, desiccated drylands came in view. There was also Valiyammachi's love, linking the fire fledgling to the present day.

And then, a red kite fluttering upwards in the sky, over the sea . . .

March 21:

Lots of children were competing with one another while flying kites on the seashore. A red kite had reached the top. A slim lad held the ownership of the kite string firmly in his fist.

'That boy won! See, his kite is above all others!'

Susanna used to be thrilled by such silly events. Perhaps that was her strategy of tackling a very arduous life: by accumulating all simple joys together! That might have been the reason why she entangled her own aspirations and mind in that high-flying red kite.

But in a last-minute jerk, the kite had escaped the boy's control and flown away, finally to descend in the uncertainties of the sea.

'How sad!' Susanna had been emotional.

* * *

Kunjootty closed the diary, unable to continue any more. He felt drained. An endless shore and a kite losing its moorings, not knowing the path of its ultimate fall! Were all these illusions? If he reminded himself that all was vanity, would the corporeal world vanish into nothingness? Lord, when could he unveil the covering?

The night was cold. Switching off the table lamp, Kunjootty slipped beneath the bed sheets.

Nandini's stubborn cry rose from the Vadakke Veedu. Savitry was scolding her for some childish prank.

'You are acting too smart nowadays, Nandini!'

'The child is unwell . . .'

Murali was trying for a compromise.

'That is why I am asking her to take her medicines! And she is refusing!'

Nandini's coughs could be heard intermittently amidst her wails. Her discomfort had increased in the heavy downpour.

After some time, a folk song could be heard; Savitry was trying to make Nandini sleep. Soon, the lullaby too relapsed into silence.

Beyond the child's disturbed sleep, the blisteringly cold wind touched the leaves awake.

Silence. Darkness.

In that sleepless night, in some odd hour of the night, Kunjootty got up, like a child upset at being denied a lullaby.

As if fulfilling a mandate, he switched on the table fan and made it face the wall opposite.

The murmur of the fan's leaves. The lullaby of the breeze. Companionship.

Outside, the night waited in vigil among the leaves of the majestic pillar-like trees. Solomon's words dropped down slowly in their midst. Gathering those and shutting his eyes tight, Kunjootty repeated as if praying for salvation: 'Vanity of vanities! All is vanity.'

13

Yet Another Journey

All the coconut trees, ripe for toddy tapping, were petrified of Chupran. No tree flowered after his shadow passed them by. He slashed away mercilessly, mutilating the buds yearning to bloom. As he continued with his compulsory anti-fertilization drives, maybe owing to the curses of the trees, Chupran's own health started deteriorating. A debilitating cough took hold of him. The strangulating hold of the cough worsened and the speed of his ascent on the coconut trees decreased. Even then, Chupran refused to let go of the traditionally anointed task of his clan.

Tucking his sharp knife inside the waistband, Chupran staggered across the nooks and corners of Potta Thuruthu, with the unnerving dry cough. The islanders were scared that he might burst apart in another fit of that villainous cough or slip to his death from a coconut tree; but none of these transpired. Even in his sleep, like an inseparable organ, Chupran kept his knife close to his body. The village astrologer, Gopala Kanian,

108

started spreading the canard that it was a hint of Chupran's impending death.

Then Chupran went missing for a long time.

Those were the days of relentless rains.

The skies of Potta Thuruthu looked dark and brooding always. Wherever one gazed, rains met the eyes; and even while shutting them, the image of the rains prevailed.

Rains affected the mobility of the isle's residents to a great extent. Even Kunjootty, who had grown up loving the rain, started feeling uncomfortable. The daily journey to his office became extremely difficult. The farmlands and roads were flooded, and no one could distinguish between the potholes and the proper road. One had to swim through all that water to reach a dry place and catch the bus to town. If he had no office to attend, Kunjootty might have curled up somewhere, relishing the rains and the infinite vastness of the water around.

Koppan and Chathutty would launch the skiff in the tempestuous river, made more lush by the rains. They religiously rowed Kunjootty to and fro daily.

'Be careful, you might encounter some slithery creature floating along in the rain waters!' Koppan warned Kunjootty.

'I shall be cautious!' Kunjootty promised.

Even after reaching the other shore, Chathutty accompanied Kunjootty to the bus stop.

'Why do you take so much trouble?' Kunjootty asked.

'Just like that,' Chathutty smiled.

Kunjootty felt that the reason was not that simple.

'I heard that you write,' Chathutty said.

Kunjootty smiled vacuously, thinking of the unfinished book languishing behind.

How come a daily labourer had such curiosity?

'How much did you study?' Kunjootty queried.

For a second, Chathutty hesitated. Then giving up before his inherent nature that resisted lies, he spoke, 'I was studying for my final year BA degree. It was then that . . .' Then he paused. 'I am in some sort of Ajnatavasa, a phase of hiding. Haven't told anyone yet. I have a story inside me that you might find worthy of writing about. Shall tell you sometime!'

A private bus came racing, splashing water all over.

Another ferocious rain was on the verge of bursting forth. Chathutty retraced his steps.

Slowly, the intensity of the rain started abating. The clouds started wandering away, in search of new places. That year's monsoon season was slowly coming to an end.

As the rain ceased and the land cleared up, a young coconut tapper, healthy and with no signs of cough, came to Potta Thuruthu. Koppan and Chathutty were fast asleep then. They had worked hard till afternoon and had enjoyed some liquor along with their lunch.

Unnicheera heard the familiar knock of the toddy tapping in the yard. But when she did not hear the omnipresent cough, she grew slightly worried. Had that old man's cough suddenly disappeared?

As she stepped into the backwaters to wash the vessels, she cast a look upwards. A new toddy tapper was descending, using his circular climbing aid, from a tall coconut tree. The waistband had a knife tucked in, and a bottle gourd container was dangling from it.

As soon as he stepped on the soil, the young man threw a look at the next coconut treetop, retrieved a beedi from his waistband and puffed a circle of smoke in the air. The pictures cast by the spirals of smoke vanished slowly. The coconut climber smiled at Unnicheera and spoke jokingly.

'I am not a toddy thief, okay?'

'Where is Chupran?' Unnicheera asked.

'My father is not well. I thought I would cover this shore too, today.'

Unnicheera was busy recollecting an old memory. When she had come to the isle as a new bride from Painady, there was a malnourished boy, who had tailed Chupran, struggling with a heavy pot of toddy on his head. He had now become manly, vital and sturdy. Much time had passed, indeed.

Unnicheera felt herself scalded with sinful desire. The young toddy tapper was busy climbing the next tree. He still had the lit beedi between his lips. Unnicheera watched through a haze of smoke: the sweat drops glistening on his taut muscles and the sharp edges of the knives, grating against one another, inside the knife sheath at his waist.

The man took his *chettukathi*, the special knife used for tapping, from his pouch. He made a slash across a tender coconut and circled it with a splint of fresh coconut leaf. As he tapped against a liquid-filled tender coconut with his tool, his gaze slipped down to the lagoon side. Sail boats were afloat, romantically whispering to one another in the Mithuna winds. The small waves were shattering on touching Unnicheera's exposed, fair shins.

Sweet liquid was gathering near the moist slash on the tender coconut. As he prepared the coconut for tapping, using traditional salve, the man's mind wandered to another place. He emptied the toddy carefully into his gourd container and hitched it to his waistband.

As he descended, the toddy tapper found himself perspiring more than usual.

When he emptied his gourd container into his main vessel, the young man spoke to Unnicheera.

'I feel very thirsty.'

'Lots of toddy in your vessel. Can't you quench your thirst?'

'It will be highly intoxicating. Do you want some?'

'Nnnoo . . .'

'What is your name?'

'Unnicheera. And what's yours?'

'Toddy tapper.'

'Ha! Funny man, aren't you?'

'Not just a funny man!'

'What else?' The look he cast in response bruised her body. Like a statue with a beating heart, Unnicheera stood stunned for a few moments.

The toddy tapper continued to hurt her with his smouldering look as he lifted the toddy vessel. Then, in a soft tone, he bid goodbye.

'Shall see you then.'

The smell of the beedi smoke refused to leave the surroundings even after a breeze blew. Unnicheera prayed fervently that Chupran's illness would linger on.

The young toddy tapper walked away slowly.

The glimpses of the toddy vessel and the beedi smoke could be caught, weaving in and out of the coconut grove, before receding from sight. Yet, Unnicheera continued to stand on the riverbank for no reason.

Twilight was setting in.

As she sat near the stone stove, pushing the wooden splinters in and staring at the blazing fire, Unnicheera felt drenched in sinful desires again. Enticing words, temptations of sights and a lustily stirring mind . . . Unnicheera gave up fighting her natural urges. Nothing was under her control anymore.

Under the grip of an instinct that was overwhelming, Unnicheera got up and shading the flicker of the kerosene lamp with the cup of her hand, made her way towards the eastern room where Chathutty slept. She gazed at the young man by the light of the lamp. He was asleep. A lazy posture, the right leg tucked under his body, as he lay on his stomach.

When the mind starts sinning, the body feels enervated.

She sat down heavily on the floor smoothened with cow dung.

Unnicheera did not realize that a wind had blown in and the flame was flickering. She was beyond all consciousness.

She came back to her senses when Chathutty shouted.

'Hey, you! Aren't you ashamed of yourself?'

Unnicheera got up in shock and stood aghast, her body shivering. Even in that half-darkness, she could see the contemptuous look on Chathutty's face. She could read the signals of loathing.

'Tcche! Horrible!'

Unnicheera desired death intensely. She cursed herself, mortified to her core. The memory of a dream that had come crashing down, haunted her yet again.

Years before, a nomadic healer had stayed the night in that foyer. It was here that he had shown Chonachu's wife the poisonous snake when nobody was around. That serpent might still have been around, slithering in an invisible form. Even though he knew nothing about those stories, Chathutty felt a deep sense of disgust. He stepped out, wanting to flee from the ancient vulnerabilities of the place.

However, Chathutty could not make his escape.

Seeing Koppan in front of him, he panicked. Though Chathutty tried to pretend that nothing was amiss, he failed miserably. His words were stuck in unknown crevices inside his throat.

At that moment, a flock of birds, screeching in misery, flew over the hovel. An uneasy silence prevailed for a long time. And at the end, Chathutty heard Koppan's limp voice.

'You should have done it, Chathutty. What I could not do, at least you should have done.'

After sharing that final secret, Koppan moved away from his home with unsteady steps.

Chathutty stared at that stranger who was trembling as he walked. He was sure that Koppan would be found stone drunk at Kali's toddy shop that night. Was it all a lot of fictitious tales? All that braggadocio about Koppan's secret liaisons with Janaki and spending nights with Kali?

Chathutty no longer felt loathing towards Unnicheera, who stood with her head bowed, shrouded in regret. She had fought against the heat within herself for more than sixteen years!

However, that was not Chathutty's path.

There was a path, clothed in darkness, outside. It had dried flowers on either side, unwanted by anyone.

Without a backward glance at Unnicheera, uttering not even a goodbye, as he stepped into the path stretching forward indefinitely, Chathutty realized a truth.

It was the time for another change of name.

14

The Karkidaka Vavu: The Auspicious New Moon of Cancer

Kunjootty could not fathom the reason behind Chathutty's sudden disappearance.

'He left, just like that . . . was a good lad!' Koppan sounded deeply fatigued.

Kunjootty hoped he might once again meet the man who had left before telling a promised story. Perhaps in the midst of the town's bustle, or near a bus stop, may be as a helper in a roadside shop?

It did not happen.

Yet Kunjootty devoted some space, in the throbbing book of his heart, for Chathutty.

It was the second half of the month of Karkidaka; the auspicious time for the ancestral sacrificial rites was drawing close. After the sorrows and tribulations of the year-long gap, it was the time for the revered souls of the ancestors to return to Potta Thuruthu, on the new-moon day of Cancer.

The paths of the skies were filled with fluttering black wings.

The islanders clapped their wet hands to invite the ancestors after offering sesame and rice on banana leaves. The souls of the ancestors, in the guise of *bali kakka*, the Indian jungle crow, descended to partake of the feast of appeasement.

Rice on a sliver of banana leaf, toddy in a coconut half-shell: the ancestors were hurrying towards these life seeds.

The atmosphere was redolent of the familial rites.

Whenever the cawing became intense, the residents of the isle remembered their obstinate ancestors! Those were the ones who would create such a ruckus . . . total drunkards in their time. There were men who had sold off the grains from the sacred granaries to buy liquor. Their sons were not too bad either. Having sneakily observed their forebearers merrily boozing around, they had followed suit. Keenly eyeing the keys dangling from their fathers' waistbands, as well as the locked-up stores, these men had surreptitiously manoeuvred the loosening of the planks guarding the grains, and gathering those dropping down through the tiny gaps, managed to procure a drink or two. Today, they had all returned from the land of death, in search of the ancestral food and drink offerings!

Koppan lay awake, like an ancient head of the family, listening to the ceaseless caws of the crows. A lot of memories were unfolding chaotically around him, disturbing his peace of mind. Even his awakening seemed to be the continuation of a deep turbulence. It had become a habit after Chathutty's departure. The young man had left behind a long and grave silence suspended between Koppan and his wife.

Unnicheera had been a young girl of thirteen when Koppan had brought her from Painady as his bride. She had landed at Potta Thuruthu with an iron box filled with her meagre possessions, a lot of apprehensions and a few curiosities. However, all her blooming curiosities were left unfulfilled. In the beginning it was a sense of sheer bewilderment, then it became a niggling concern and then grew into a gnawing bitterness. The wooden almirah that her father had got specially made in anticipation of her first childbirth, got eaten by termites back home at Painady.

After sixteen long years, that thirteen-year-old bride demanded her dues harshly from Koppan. Whenever he recollected that truth, Koppan felt like drinking himself senseless. There was no other way to inveigle his way out of memories meticulously filed away. In an imagined freedom from every connection, he wandered around meaninglessly in Potta Thuruthu, and slept on the wet, clayey mud of farmlands and lagoon shores. Waking up at unearthly hours, he would proceed home with heavy steps. And then, his courage failing him from knocking on the closed door, Koppan would curl up in distress to doze under a coconut tree in the yard. His pet dog would give him company during those nights.

Koppan lay reminiscing for a long time. Unwittingly, the thread of his rumination broke off.

'Koppan, Koppan!'

Someone was calling his name. As Koppan jumped to his feet, he saw a frantic Chinnan rushing towards him.

'Chinnan, what happened?'

'She has been bitten by a snake!'

'Who?'

'My daughter, Chirutha!'

'Where is she?'

'Near the river.'

Chinnan was panting heavily as he spoke. His daughter was to be married off in the imminent harvest season. If some mishap occurred . . . God! He could not bring himself to imagine it.

The men raced towards the riverside. Chirutha was sitting on the grassy shore, sobbing desperately.

It must have been some snake that had come floating along with the floodwaters and bitten her.

Koppan, the son of the poison healer Chonachu, knelt near the crying girl and examined her shin. Looking at the bitten spot, Koppan tried to deduce the particulars of the slithering attacker. Then, meditating on his late father, he bent to suck out the venomous blood from the wound. He spat out the blood four or five times.

The beautiful girl, with her dusky complexion, seemed to have taken over a darker hue in her deadly fear.

Her father's face was aghast in terror.

'Neendakara Muthappa! This child that you gave me after praying to you, please protect her!'

'I need some herbs for preparing a cure!' Koppan spoke.

'What do you need?' Chinnan asked.

'Tamilzhaveru, naruneendi, neelayamari . . . vetiver, Indian sarpasarilla, indigo.'

Chinnan raced against time, keeping the list in his agonized heart.

Koppan remembered the precious remedy that his father had bequeathed to him. It was an *ottamooli*, a traditional, obscure single medicine therapy, that Chonachu had been taught by the nomadic healer. The herbs had to be picked fresh and then mixed with a few secret ingredients to concoct that one-stop cure. It was a dangerous proposition that involved the cure of poison with yet another poison! Even the guru, the vagrant healer, had not been ready to explain the consequences if the fates decided otherwise!

Chonachu had never had the opportunity to try it out. The cure was supposed to be used only in the eventuality when no other option was left between the life and death of the patient. He had carried the secret knowledge within him with intense discomfort, like a treasure box left unopened. Finally, he decided to try it on himself, having no control over his intense yearning. He waited till his child, abandoned by his mother, grew up to take care of himself. Chonachu had continued that wait till Koppan turned eighteen years old.

And then, one day, Chonachu had climbed the prickly fence guarding Ezhuthassan's lush compound and wandered in the snake grove situated to the south, searching for the serpent kings. He had extended his hands inside the termite mounds, under the serpentine roots, into all the holes of the silent snakes, wishing to be bitten. But they had not acquiesced. Chonachu had grown angry and frustrated. His fingers itched to smash the statues of the serpent gods drowsing in the enchanted darkness around. Then he had noticed the sparkling fire in two small eyes close by. Chonachu remembered the perfect specimen that he had released into Ezhuthassan's snake grove all those years ago, freeing it from the nomadic healer's basket. He begged for his *dakshina*, return gift, from the beautiful serpent that swayed in front of him with its splayed hood.

Chonachu had almost collapsed when he had turned home with his gift. Lying thus in his deathbed, he had taught his young son the secret antidote. He warned him that until the last stage occurred, he was to ignore all pleas and lamentations, and not try out the medicine. As the throes of the body stilled,

Koppan had to ensure that three drops of the cure were emptied into each of the eyes, and then he had to massage a few drops into the insides of the feet and warm them up. Last, he had to pour nine droplets under the tongue.

That night, as his father had lain dying, grief-stricken and crying, Koppan had tried his hand at his first healing. Having followed the instructions meticulously, he had waited with great anxiety by his father's motionless body. After a while, Chonachu had woken up and cried in joy, hugging his son close. However, after that remarkable and courageous endeavour that went undocumented in medical history, Chonachu had not lived for a long time. He had left, solitary and detached, in his Pachuvanchi, to disappear into the depths of the lagoon. The residents of Potta Thuruthu firmly believed that it was the Kayal Pottan who had sunk the boat of the great poison healer.

As he tried to heal Chirutha, Koppan thought of his father. He had the firm faith that if he meditated even for a second, Chonachu would aid him from the invisible world beyond. In that confidence, Koppan made his antidote from the herbs that Chinnan had gathered frantically.

Koppan was busy tending to the young woman the whole day. Finally, when Chirutha got up, healthy and radiant, a smiling Chinnan offered a wad of cash to Koppan.

'What is it?'

'For my happiness . . .' Chinnan became embarrassed.

'My father made me promise that I would never take money for curing a poisonous bite. If I do so, I shall lose my healing powers.'

Koppan left the house.

He felt exhausted and extremely thirsty. Koppan thought of a new moon day when he too would be returning to Potta

Thuruthu along with the drink-crazy ancestors. He felt amused by that deliberation.

A huge fracas was taking place on the riverside. Men were rushing with huge sticks in their hands. A magnificent black cobra swayed with a raised hood in their midst, frantically trying to protect itself.

People were pushing against one another, trying to reach the snake. Koppan ran towards the serpent.

'Stop, don't kill it!' Koppan screamed.

A poor creature that had lost its dwelling place in the flood waters! It would never hurt anyone except in fear.

Koppan ran to his hut and returned with a clay pot. Placing the pot on its side and staring at the agitated snake's eyes firmly, he commanded, 'Come on, get inside!'

The snake obeyed. The splayed-out hood shrunk and it slithered inside the offered refuge. Ignoring the wondering faces around, Koppan tightly bound the mouth of the pot with his thorthu, and lifted it atop his head.

Reaching the snake grove situated inside Ezhuthassan's compound, Koppan untied the pot's mouth.

The serpent raised its head from within, and then, smelling the earth, it glided sinuously, and soon vanished inside the mélange of roots.

Koppan realized that a pattern was repeating itself. The snake that his father, Chonachu, had freed from the nomad's basket might be still dwelling in that place. Let the 'land of serpents' flourish!

He walked towards the toddy shop.

A high tide was filling the backwaters then. Swirls were visible in the heart of the boundless waters that flowed over. The farmlands were soon inundated.

Unnicheera saw that nature was in an overtly lusty mood. The new moon of Cancer, the Karkidaka Vavu, was casting its magnetic spell over everything.

In that desolate dusk, as the fresh spoor of toddy emanated near her, Unnicheera felt herself overwhelmed with another high tide. She listened to the soft footsteps entering the kitchen and the door being latched. The young toddy tapper could see, in spite of the darkness, the drop of sweat trickling down from Unnicheera's forehead and falling into her heaving bosom like holy water. Hurriedly he removed the knife rack from his waistband and threw it on the kitchen floor.

The time had arrived for a hungry ancestor, searching in vain for his feast of appeasement, to be born again into the wretchedness and woes of Potta Thuruthu.

15

The Onam Festivities

In front of the Edappadath House was an old Chinese net cast into the river. Due to continuous disuse over decades, its body had been rigged with holes. The sides had started decaying. Zavarias contemplated about giving it a new life, with a few stitches here and thither, and strengthening it further with another netting.

After the new householders took over the Vadakke Veedu, his determination was firmed up. In case it was needed, Murali could help in pulling the net. In fact, Murali was more than enthusiastic on hearing about the idea. To possess a Chinese net was pretty nifty. It would mean a lush catch of freshwater fish! Murali agreed that the festival time of Onam was appropriate for the efforts.

Koppan was to be the main priest in the rite. Thus, the auspicious time for the restoration of the Chinese net was decided.

'If only Chathutty was here with me!' Koppan sighed wearily. The mere presence of that youth would have reduced Koppan's efforts by half.

Koppan started working on the net, with the help of Murali, Kunjootty and a few other young men from the neighbourhood. They transported logs of teak in huge freight boats. After pulling up the rotten wooden poles, new ones were hammered in; and a new net was purchased.

Nandini frequented the workplace, often busy with her childish pranks. She also took on a new proprietary right.

'All the fish caught in the first attempt belongs to me!'

'Agreed.' Koppan grinned with amusement.

'What all fishes are likely to be caught?'

'Reef cod, prawns, and . . .'

'And?'

'Do you like crabs?'

'Yuck! I hate to see those!'

'Hate to see, love to eat!'

Having fixed the stumps, they were getting ready to install the new net when the need came up for a gum to dip the net with. The gum had to be made by boiling bits of bark of the kalisha tree, the Indian laurel.

'Now where do we find a kalisha tree?' Kunjootty inquired.

'In Ezhuthassan's compound, near his snake grove, I have seen one!' Koppan answered readily.

'But will he help?' Zavarias was apprehensive.

'Who is bothered with asking him? I shall just climb the tree and break off a bit of the bark!'

'What if Ezhuthassan catches you? He is half crazy!'

'If he is half crazy, Koppan happens to be fully crazy too!' Koppan quipped.

Koppan had boasted for the fun of it. As he sneaked into Ezhuthassan's compound, he felt a niggling fear inside. His ankle was injured by the thorns of the prickly plants used to fence the compound. The agony aggravated the paronychia he was already suffering from! Ignoring the pain, Koppan reached the kalisha tree furtively and cast a wary look around. He took his hand axe and diligently started chipping away the barks. Every few moments, Koppan would be alert and watch out for Ezhuthassan.

It was when the collection of barks grew large that he regretted not bringing a basket with him. He hitched the hand axe to his waistband, gathered the barks into the upper portion of his mundu and tucked it in.

As he turned to walk towards the thorny fence, he heard a sound behind him.

'Who is that?' An angry growl. It was Ezhuthassan!

Koppan started to run with his treasure.

'Stop right there!'

The command stopped Koppan dead in his tracks. Even if he had wished, he couldn't have moved.

Ezhuthassan stared long at the intruder.

'Stealing, eh? That is not proper!'

Koppan stood there sheepishly. There was not much space between them. Koppan started stammering out his explanation.

'Making a gum mix for the China net . . . belonging to Edappadath House!'

Edappadathu House. Net. Gum mix.

All these made no difference to the enraged man before him. Govindan Kutty Asan, known popularly as Ezhuthassan, burnt Koppan with his fiery gaze.

'Dared to encroach into the sacred serpent grove. Your face is disgusting with all those sores and pus! Leave immediately!'

Koppan was not scared of snakes. But he always had an uncanny terror of Ezhuthassan. He left without a backward glance.

Koppan narrated the terrifying encounter only to Kunjootty. Neither could comprehend why Ezhuthassan would point out the sores and pus on Koppan's face. Except for a few moles, and one wart under his eye, his face was quite normal!

Koppan did not deign to dig deep and worry himself over that observation.

One day before Thiru Onam, on the day of Uthradam, the Chinese net was granted a rebirth.

On the first scoop, copious amounts of fat reef-cods were hauled in!

'Look at those fatsos!' Nandini squealed in delight.

Then on seeing them thrashing around for life breath, she started grieving. 'Koppan chetta! Please let them return to the river!'

That evening, when sundown was due, youngsters gathered on the open ground near the backwaters. They were going to announce the arrival of Onam. They danced together in a circle, rhythmically, and the perimeter of the circle increased as they stepped backwards. Moving backwards and forwards, the circles changed in sizes. Amidst the roaring crowd, a white-haired man made a sudden appearance.

'Who is that man, uncle?' Nandini pointed at the man who stood out in the throng. Kunjootty easily recognized the old man, wearing a mundu reaching till his knees, among the rambunctious children.

'We call him Ezhuthassan! He is also known as Kutty Asan.'

'Is he a kutty? A little boy?'

Kunjootty laughed. 'There is a little child inside everyone!'

Though Onam had arrived, Potta Thuruthu continued to be devoid of colours. In its bracken mud, plants and trees struggled to thrive. The Indian tulip tree, the cotton trees and the mangroves could be seen on the isle. An occasional tamarind tree, a few coconuts and the screw-pine completed the major description of flora of the place. Flowers were few and far between. The ones which bloomed were short-lived.

There was a lad wearing a crown made of jack fruit leaves amongst the dancing boys. Ezhuthassan lifted him high in the air.

'Listen to the Kummatti song, children!' he cried.

The children started dancing around him, following the tune.

'Here comes the Kummatti!
He has reached your threshold,
Milk and fruits, if not offered,
He shall steal the raw tamarinds!'

The sounds were multifarious; the vitality and energy were infectious! Then suddenly another song rose from the screw pine bushes!

'Milk and fruits, if not offered,
He shall poop at your doorsteps!'

The laughing young lads turned to the new teacher. Koppan appeared from the dense bushes. His feet were staggering in his drunkenness. His singing sounded like a wild animal's howling. The toddy was fermenting within this particular wild animal's stomach. The money he had got from Zavarias for working on the Chinese net had obviously been transferred to Kali's toddy shop.

'How funny, Kutty Asan's dance!' Nandini expressed her admiration openly for the interesting sights on the opposite shore.

'When I was your age, he taught me my letters,' Kunjootty told her.

'Is that true?'

A, Aa, E, Ee . . . a precocious little child immersed in writing the Malayalam alphabet on the loamy soil in the village school . . .

At that time, Govindan Kutty Asan, popularly known as Ezhuthassan, was sane and normal. Later, his mother and sister were diagnosed with mental illness and passed away. He led a solitary life in his house fenced in by prickly plants all round. Ezhuthassan never requested the companionship of anyone in his lonely sojourn. As time passed, he seemed to have forgotten the alphabet of language and instead sought meaning in the alphabet of silence.

The elementary school he ran soon closed down and people stopped visiting him altogether.

The reason behind Ezhuthassan's mysterious silence remained unknown. The man relegated himself to the darkness of the decrepit Tharavadu situated in the middle of the vast compound. Rats and bats kept him company. He hardly knew when the rats started nibbling at his toes. Incongruities and eccentricities started creeping into his looks, words and actions.

People started gossiping about him. Some discovered that Ezhuthassan frequented the compound in the middle of the night and spent his time at the serpent grove. Some caught wisps of strange chants and spells that Ezhuthassan murmured as he wandered around. The news spread that Ezhuthassan was doing Hanuman Seva, the propitiation of the Monkey Lord. Many peeped from the prickly fence, trying to gauge the acts of the mysterious resident of the house. People started poking fun at Ezhuthassan by calling him Hanuman Kutty instead of

Govindan Kutty. Ezhuthassan remained oblivious to all these canards spreading about him in another world.

Kunjootty failed to understand the exact nature of the boon that had been granted to Ezhuthassan. To frolic around with little children required a vestige of purity and innocence within one's heart.

'Nandini . . .' Murali called from his house. Carrying a bottle of medicine in his hand, he soon reached their side.

'Time to have your medicine, child.'

It was as if the bitterness of the medicine spread over Nandini's face.

'I don't want to drink it.' She pouted in rebellion.

'What is the medicine for?' Kunjootty asked.

'Nothing special. But that cough is persisting . . . she is growing weak.'

As the father and daughter walked away, Kunjootty sat down by the river, his back against a coconut tree. The sounds of festive jubilations had long died down and the shore was serene. The river flowed quietly, her heart apparently untouched by the ripples of emotions.

As he sat there with his eyes closed, Kunjootty felt that a long-forgotten dream, half complete, might step back into his vision.

16

Memories of the Clan

Chirutha's wedding was fixed on a Monday in the Malayalam month of Kanni. On the day before her marriage, the windows of the sky-castle opened wide. Rain and thunderstorm escaped, to descend on Potta Thuruthu in full glory. The yard where the wedding was to be solemnized filled up with rainwater. The brick stoves got wet and the fire was put out. The pandal, with a grass-thatched roof, was wrecked.

'What an inauspicious tiding! This unseasonal rain, Devi!' Chinnan Pulayan could not help his outpourings.

'Been a long time since you worshipped the Shovvas! See, how they are obstructing the auspicious function!' The older lot started scolding Chinnan.

The dead forefathers had been installed as Shovvas in the southern corner of the house. They had been languishing there like border stones, abandoned and neglected. The ancestors were sending out signs of their unappeased hunger and thirst to the generation that had forsaken them.

Chinnan Pulayan immediately promised the belated offerings to the Shovvas that year. He did not want any warning cry from the past to wreak havoc during his daughter's wedding. It was true, the idols had been left untended till now. Not only that, a few shameless villagers had been urinating over the stones in the middle of the night! Did anyone need another reason for the unexpected augury of the ferocious thunderstorm? Yes, he should clean up the place; soothe the frayed tempers of the ancestors with toddy and fried catfish!

It appeared that the Shovvas were mollified after Chinnan's assurances. The obstinacy of the storm subsided and the arrogance of the rain becalmed itself. The morning bloomed, fresh with the scent of moistness.

The drum beaters were ready by the riverside to welcome the bridegroom and his relatives. The procession arrived in a raft created by hitching multiple skiffs together. When the raft, draped with decorative trimmings of tender green coconut leaves, approached, the peppy drumbeats reached a crescendo.

Chirutha's mother poured water from the traditional bronze pitcher over her future son-in-law's feet and ushered him to the house.

The wedding itself was a simple affair.

Kandan reverentially tied the 'thali', sanctified with 1008 prayers by the priest, around Chirutha's neck, with the islanders and Shovvas as witnesses. Thus, Chirutha became Kandan's 'Pulakalli' and he became her 'Pulayan'.

However, as per tradition, they were forbidden from sleeping together for the next four nights.

As the twilight came, the celebrations started in full throttle. The physical hardships of preparing the feast could be washed away only by gulping copious amounts of toddy. That had to be accompanied by Bhimanattam, the ancient form of dance, with its rhythmic steps, based on stories of the Mahabharata.

The whole of Potta Thuruthu seemed to have arrived to witness the Bhimanattam at Chinnan's place that night.

Kunjootty felt happy about such unique dusks. His friend Isaac was no different in his approach. However, he had gone away to some jungle to chase after his unscrupulous logging business. Isaac might be prowling around the depths of some forest like an animal now, Kunjootty reflected somberly. It seemed as if the human species was evolving backwards.

Kunjootty arrived at Chinnan's place with Murali, Nandini and Savitry.

From Vasumathy's riverside shack, bottles filled with the colourless liquid intoxicant started flowing to Chinnan's place, under the cover of darkness. Bottles of arrack, hidden under the slushy clay of the farms and riverside, were retrieved surreptitiously.

Kandan and Chirutha sat next to each other on a bench, the mainstays of the function. Behind the loud crowd thronging around them, those with bottles of toddy and coconut shells were making a ruckus. Kara Mooppan stood up and started addressing everyone. He was the village elder and leader of the clan.

'Tonight is dedicated to our beloved bride and bridegroom!'

Kara Mooppan had hair resembling white fluffs of cotton. There was a huge wart on the left of his forehead. Even in old age, his muscles were toned and firm. A fierce look darted from his eyes.

Offering toddy in an earthen vessel to the 'Adikaranavar' or the 'first village elder' of Potta Thuruthu, Kara Mooppan stood still for a moment. Then he poured that drink into two coconut half-shells for the newlywed couple.

'Drink, my children!'

Kandan received his cup with a sheepish grin. An intoxicated Koppan laughed lasciviously at the sight.

'Yo, Kanda! You are a smart one!'

Chirutha, however, desisted from accepting the proffered drink. After a while, cajoled by Kara Mooppan and her relatives, she had no alternative but to accept it.

Kara Mooppan reached Kunjootty and Murali with two earthen cups. 'If you partake of this, we will feel very happy!'

'No, Mooppa! Some observers are also needed in the scene!' Kunjootty politely declined. But Murali had taken his cup from Mooppan's hand by then. Kunjootty found that gesture rather strange. Murali looked a changed man; his face was disturbed and an attitude of stubborn defiance was palpable in him.

Suddenly many hands reached out greedily for the earthen cups and coconut shells wobbling over with the drink. The cups greeted one another in glee. As the first village elder watched over the scene, invisible to all, the younger generation was retrieving the memories of their clan.

'Arrey . . .' an old man called out in great enthusiasm, his heart warmed by the toddy in his belly.

'The women in the kitchen are supposed to do Poli . . . only then shall the men dance!'

A round of adulatory applause supported the justifiable demand.

A plate appeared from the direction of the kitchen. Relayed through many hands, it reached the main dancers.

Nandini asked curiously, 'What is it, uncle?'

'The Poli plate, dear! Only when money is offered in that plate, the dance acquires vigour and energy!'

Kara Mooppan took over the plate as if it was his legal right and cried, 'Arrey!'

The crowd chanted in reply, 'Arrey!'

Then the cries, the repetitions, and the vibrant shouts filled the throbbing air.

'Our beloved bridegroom!'

'Our beloved bridegroom!'

'Our precious bride!'

'Our precious bride . . .!'

'All their relatives!'

'All their relatives!'

'Is there no one to fill the Poli plate?'

'No one?'

Though the question went as a challenge for the women's row, the older women, dark-skinned and experienced, ignored it smugly.

'Let them dance awhile! If we fill the Poli at the first go, the dance won't reach its peak!' It was Chirutha's grandmother, who had seen many a Bhimanattam in her life, who spoke thus. A half-finished shell of toddy was in her hands.

'Very right! Very right!' The women around her supported her stance.

Kara Mooppan, who had finished two full cups of toddy by now, started on his third and yelled, 'Where is Kunti?'

Everyone paused poignantly with a mild curiosity. Then Kunti appeared on the scene.

Chirutha's oldest uncle came forward with feminine gait, his chest covered with a thorthu, the cynosure of all eyes. His name was Cheethan. He had satiated Potta Thuruthu's heart with hundreds of his Bhimanattam performances across the years.

A woman named Neeli had been fascinated by his song and
dance and had sneaked inside his shack one night. And it was
on his nineteenth year, as he lay guarding the prawn farms,
that Cheethan first got to know a woman. The nights, when
the Kalyana Saugandigam flower of the Bhimanattam folk lores
blossomed fragrantly, repeated many a time. But, one night,
as Neeli returned dazed with joy after their nightly encounter,
she was bitten by a venomous snake and died. That incident
devastated Cheethan. Songs and dance steps fled from him.
He started drinking heavily. It took many long years before he
gained control over his life. When he returned to Bhimanattam,
as a prayerful ritual, his steps had gained more sharpness.

The same dance steps were being repeated today. The
same fire that had burnt down the 'Arakkillam' or the palace of
wax—the fake palace constructed out of combustible sap by the
Kauravas for trapping Queen Kunti and her five sons—flared
up in Cheethan's heart too, lighting up the sky-like emptiness
inside him. Kunti's grief was also Cheethan's grief.

Cheethan sang his song of lamentation of a mother ruing
the fate of her sons, who were destined to wander around in
dense jungles while their cousins stole their rightful kingdom.

'Enthente thaiviyekkaatteelivarinnu
Thendithiriyanu durkathiyay . . .'

'Devi, how come my children wander lost, accursed,
In these dark forests;
These five, who should be ruling the kingdom,
Have no succor, ah, woe betide me!'

With anxiety and helplessness writ large on his face, Cheethan
had undergone a metamorphosis to become Queen Kunti. The

minds of the onlookers were pinned to the rhythm of Kunti's footsteps. They knew her intense pain. And they also knew the destiny awaiting. As the five mighty warriors, enthused by the exhilaration of the liquor, came dancing near their mother, Nandini nestled closer to Kunjootty.

'So nice, isn't it, uncle?'

As Kunjootty smilingly gathered her close, he cast a look at Murali again. A human being was sitting, unaware of what was happening around him, not relishing anything. Whatever had happened to Murali?

'No one ready to put Poli even now?' As Kara Mooppan raised his accusation yet again, a small rustle rose through the women's section of the crowd. Chirutha's grandmother was the first to respond. She searched inside her pouch, gathered the coins and deposited them into the Poli plate.

'How come the dance is not gathering speed? Where has the vigour gone?' Chirutha's grandmother protested vehemently.

In the enthusiasm of the first round of Poli, Kara Mooppan started hollering loudly, 'Arrey!'

'Arrey!'

'Our beloved bride's!'

'Our beloved bride's!'

'Our beloved grandmother's Poli!'

'Our beloved grandmother's Poli!'

'Indian rupees ten!'

'Indian rupees ten!'

The vessels drumming the manic sing-song beats resounded fiercely and a deafening applause rose high in the air.

Kunjootty watched as the hitherto melancholic eyes of Kunti flashed and smoldered! Now more Poli would be offered. The women would start competing with one another to offer it. It was a matter of pride for them to enthuse the dancer with their Poli.

One soul was dancing between two incarnations at that moment. The Kunti from the past life stared covetously at the plate of Poli offerings through the eyes of Cheethan, the present avatar. In an instant Kunti turned into Cheethan, and, at another, he changed into Kunti. Then they merged, and no one could make out who was who. Like a common life, where fantasies and dreams weave their artifice over the harsh realities.

Ignoring all these happenings, the Sindhu flowed furiously. Kunti and her sons stood stoically and sadly, unable to cross the river.

'How do we cross this river today?
Oh, I wonder!
How will my children reach the other side,
What shall I do, Devi?'

The sons stepped around the audience, asking for ways to cross the churning river. In front of them, carrying the plate for Poli offerings, Kara Mooppan moved gracefully with his dance steps. The women moved forward enthusiastically, and coins started piling up on the plate. The repetitive chants reverberated yet again:

'Our beloved bride's!'
'Our beloved aunt's Poli!'
'Beloved aunt's Poli!'
'Indian rupees twenty!'
'Rupees twenty!'
'Arrey . . . Arrey . . . Arrey!'

Nandini, thrilled with the mesmerizing ambience, asked her father, 'Accha, are you not seeing this?'

Murali lifted her into his lap and planted a warm kiss on her tender forehead.

A boatman had arrived by then on the main stage. Koppan, who was heavily drunk, did his dance steps as if he was rowing a boat.

> *'Give me my boat fees, and I shall row you across,*
> *Or you stand and while away your time, what else!'*

The queen mother of five sons, who had once dared to experiment with the Aditya Mantra, became utterly helpless.

> *'Please take pity on us, good soul!*
> *We have no money to offer you!'*

Kunti took over the Poli plate from Kara Mooppan and wandered around the crowd. Many helping hands reached out to her plate this time. Kunjootty deposited hundred rupees on the Poli plate too.

'Arrey . . . all villagers! Listen, our beloved Kunjootty has given hundred rupees for Poli!' Kara Mooppan announced loudly.

The boatman insisted that one son of Kunti be mortgaged as a guarantee of future payment. Once the money was paid, he could leave.

Bhima consoled his shocked mother and readied himself to become an object of mortgage.

> *'Why hesitate, dear mother?*
> *Please cross the Sindhu before dusk!'*

'Should we not give Poli, Accha?' Nandini asked Murali. Her father, starting on his third round of drinking, retrieved a hundred rupee note from his pocket and gave it to her.

'Go ahead, you offer Poli yourself, my child!'

Koppan came near Nandini with the Poli plate and then lifted her high in the air. The followers danced around them with great zeal. As the crowd grew more joyous, Murali pressed his hands against his eyelids. Kunjootty watched somberly.

'What happened to you?' Kunjootty asked Murali anxiously.

'Nothing at all!' Murali had the expression of someone who was blatantly denying the existence of a truth.

The river Sindhu was flowing with great pride and majesty. The boatman leaned against the skiff lazily, as the new slave took over his oars. Then Bhimasena began to narrate a tale. It was that of a queen and her five sons. The boatman sat up in shock and the skiff swayed heavily. Bhima could not bring himself to forgive the greedy man who had asked for a prince in mortgage.

On observing the newly married couple looking drowsy, Kara Mooppan suggested, 'Let them sleep now! We will continue with our story, what?'

Kandan, the bridegroom, laboriously opened his sleepy eyes and looked around warily.

'They sleep in two different rooms tonight. That is the custom, is it not?' Kara Mooppan asked.

Koppan intervened. 'They know each other. Why force them apart for three days?'

Kandan looked up eagerly. It was evident that all his lethargy had vanished! As the onlookers tittered meaningfully, Chirutha blushed crimson. They moved towards the house and the relatives made way for them. Inside the room, when they were left to themselves by the light of the earthen lamp, after shutting the back door, without leaving even a moment for gazing at each other, Kandan took Chirutha into his loving arms.

'Our Poli plate is full now! Who volunteers to go to Vasumathy's place to buy more drinks?' Kara Mooppan asked with a grin.

'I shall go!' Many willing hands were raised. However, it was Koppan, with his praiseworthy experience in that particular field, who was selected for the task.

Koppan disappeared in the darkness and walked towards Vasumathy's house. There, she dived into the secretive hollows of clay and slush near the farms to emerge with more toddy bottles. The holy secret behind that magic was known only to Vasumathy! Many drunkards of Potta Thuruthu had made themselves total fools by frantically searching the slush at midnight.

The festivities were acquiring new rhythms. The dancers encouraged Nandini to join in. She danced elegantly, mimicking the classical steps that her mother had been teaching her in her free time. Murali was devastated at that sight. Hiding something within his heart, he walked away into the darkness outside the lighted pandal.

Bhima's lonely journey had reached the heart of the forest by now. The spoor of wild animals was strong in the virgin forest. There was no way to guess the direction. And he had no idea where to go.

'How do I make my way through this dark forest?
How do I make . . .?'

Perhaps the God of Directions might have listened to that heartfelt prayer!

'Murali!' Kunjootty called, reaching his side.

'Yes?'

'What happened to you?'

'All is lost, Kunjootty!'

Murali stopped short. He covered his streaming eyes with his hands. A nocturnal bird flapped noisily and flew above their heads. It might have been a frantic creature which had lost its way home.

'Please tell me!'

'My child! When I see her so happy!'

'What is wrong with Nandini?'

'She is not well, Kunjootty! Her days are numbered . . . her lungs!'

How do I make my way through this dark forest?

The dance and music had reached a crescendo. Even as she laughed, Nandini kept coughing intermittently.

In Ekachakra, where men were given as sacrificial offerings in front of Asura Baka's cave, a new sacrificial animal was waiting—Bhimasena! Four eyes stared wildly at one another.

'Though she was continuing to suffer from cough and shortness of breath, I never knew that it was so serious!' Murali rued. 'All the treatments were in vain. After a detailed check-up, the expert has asked me to have trust in God! I never trusted that word till now, Kunjootty! But now I am willing! Willing to climb any mountain with my Cross, offer anything, take up any penance . . . anything!'

Kunjootty was totally bewildered. Murali kept on blabbering, as if he had lost his mind. Kunjootty sensed something ineffable burning into cinders within.

An indifferent observer, across light years, transcending time. One that did not have a beginning, middle or end. Neither days nor nights, sins or goodness, happiness nor grief, touched Him. The infinite sky was His head. The earth was His body. The huge trees were akin to His hairs and the men were merely worms and insects. If one of those insects died of a disease, what did it matter to Him?

Look, even a boastful Baka, so full of strength and vitality, lay dead, his neck broken by Bhima. Even in Syamantaka Panchaka, as Bhima shattered the thighs of his nemesis, what had he achieved? The fulfilling of an oath? But during his final journey, the Maha Prasthana, he too was destined to fall.

Bhima's victory had electrified the crowd. The wild tribal tunes were at the pinnacle. A human mind, attuned to that music, suddenly started resonating at a high vibrational level. Chirutha's aunt sat down on the floor all of a sudden, and, spreading her hair all over her face, started shaking and heaving. Forgetting the surroundings, as if commanded by an invisible entity, she threw her hands to the skies and howled ferociously.

'Death is arriving, death is arriving! In the house where Poli has fallen, death is arriving!'

Nandini ran in terror towards her mother and nestled close to her chest.

A black raiment seemed to descend from the skies and ensconce the house celebrating the wedding. Silence and anxiety started taking root therein like an anthill. Meanwhile, the possessed woman collapsed on the ground heavily.

The bridegroom, Kandan, who was winning a war inside, and Murali, who was enduring the agonies of life outside, were the only ones oblivious to that new development.

Kunjootty was discovering with more clarity that in a single moment of existence, both realities and illusions could mesh together inextricably. Wherever the mind got entangled, that appeared true to the viewer. The same truth, due to varying perspectives, was being interpreted as a multitude of truths.

If so, dear God, what was the truth?

17

After the Rain

The next day too, the rain continued without respite. The north-east monsoon, Thulavarsha, was showcasing its strength, much like sending an emissary before war.

Kunjootty's love affair with the rain had started from his childhood. The intensity had not been affected by the passage of years. But his mind was heavy with gloom. Occasionally a few sound bites reached him from Vadakke Veedu to interrupt the roar of the rain—in the form of Nandini's cough or the sliver of a song. Unwittingly, his attention was drawn to the disturbing cough.

He tried to coax his mind away by focusing on his usual research topic. An endeavour to discover the syllables of the rain! On silencing the mind and sharpening his ears, Kunjootty could hear the unique note emanating from the pitter-patter. As he listened to that secret music and stared at the rain drumming on the river, Kunjootty saw shadows moving on the opposite shore. They were strangers, else he would have found some signs to identify them even in the heaviest of outpourings. A shrill whistle came from the other shore, requesting a boat. Kunjootty wondered about the wayfarers who, instead of going to the panchayat ferry, were whistling for a skiff from the opposite shore.

Kunjootty walked towards the riverbank, wearing a *thoppi-kuda*, the traditional waterproof hat that flowered out like an umbrella.

'Are you crazy, trying to launch a skiff in this rain?' Eli discouraged him.

'There are people waiting on that shore!'

'Who are they?' His mother couldn't identify them either. 'The river's flow is so strong! Why don't you wait for the rain to lessen a bit?'

The strangers on the other shore were drenched thoroughly. Bubbles were being born with every rain drop that hit the river surface unceasingly. Kunjootty launched his boat, crossing the threads of rain ahead of him, maneuvering his way across the roiling river. The wind whipped up the waves into a frenzy. The omens were not good.

Kunjootty could not recognize the visitors who had dropped in at such a time.

As he neared the shore, he heard the question:

'Is that Kunjootty?'

'Yes!'

'Don't you recognize me?'

As he hesitated to answer in the negative and searched deeply for a flicker of a memory, it struck him!

'Oh, Chiriyankan! Sorry, David!'

'Call me by the first name . . . Chiriyankan!'

Kunjootty smiled, trying to hide his discomfiture. Along with the dark-skinned Chiriyankan, also known as David, stood a fair, rose-complexioned foreign girl. She was of six or seven years of age though her build was of someone older. Her blue eyes sparkled like sapphires. The child was enjoying the mischievous antics of the rain to the hilt. The rain had diminished a bit by then.

Kunjootty helped them both into the boat. He took off his hat and put it on the girl's head.

She smiled and thanked him, '*Je vous remercie!*'

Kunjootty smiled. He had learnt French as his second language in the university.

'My daughter! She is thrilled about her first visit to her father's land!' Chiriyankan introduced her.

The child smiled politely in response to Kunjootty's own welcoming grin.

'Does she understand Malayalam?' Kunjootty inquired.

'No! She was born and brought up in France.'

'*Quel est votre nom?*' Kunjootty queried.

'Anita . . . Anita David!' The little girl looked wonderingly and respectfully at the villager who spoke French.

Then she asked, '*Oncle, votre nom?*'

'Kunjootty!'

'Kun Chutty! Hai! *Quel nom!*'

Both her father and Kunjootty couldn't stop their laughter. By the time they reached the isle, they were drenched to their bones. They had to cross the backyard of the Vadakke Veedu and then trudge over the farmland ridges to reach Chinnan's home.

'Is Chinnanvappan doing well?'

Chiriyankan's voice was timid, affected by an unspoken pain.

'Yes . . . it was Chirutha's wedding yesterday!' Kunjootty informed him.

'Good news! Wonder how they will treat me! I have been away for more than a decade!'

Why on earth had this man returned to the house where a death had been foretold the night before?

* * *

Chiriyankan had left Potta Thuruthu and boarded a ship for France almost fourteen years ago. Seven years before that happened, his father, Chennan, had passed away. He had been the youngest in a family of six brothers, including Chinnan and a sister.

While the rest survived on manual labour, it was Chriyankan's father, Chennan, who attempted to educate himself. On the path of the alphabet, the man befriended revolutionary ideas and atheism. He started uttering holy hymns not yet heard in Potta Thuruthu! Chennan was adamant on implementing whatever he preached. He refused to compromise with the exploitative feudal system around.

It reached a stage of encroaching into the lands of the upper-caste landlords and hacking off their heads. The duration of that revolutionary life was, however, short-lived. Sir C.P. Ramaswamy Iyer's army caught Chennan and took him into custody. He was tortured to death and became the first martyr of Potta Thuruthu. Chennan was respectfully buried in a vault situated south of his brother Chinnan's hut. While alive, he had issued instructions that no rites of death should be conducted for him and that he should never be venerated as a Shovva. His thoughts, rooted in dialectical materialism, could not make terms with the 'ridiculous strategy' of installing a soul in a stone. Yet he desired that his lifeless body should be covered by a bright red wrapping. Thus, someone who disliked being installed as a stone ended up buried in a vault.

Chinnan never bore any resentment that while all ancestors occupied merely a stone's space in his yard measuring five cents, his youngest brother had taken over the space of a vault and a flagpole.

Chiriyankan was all of eleven years during the incident. He was sharper than his father when it came to studies. His uncle had sent him to a far-off missionary school, persuaded by the advice of many well-wishers. The priests of the school, impressed by the young lad's brilliance, arranged for his higher education in the university. Neither Chinnan nor anyone else recognized that the boy was undergoing a transformation in the company of the missionaries and the church. On a holy day, Chiriyankan underwent baptism of both fire and water and became a Christian, and took on a new name, David.

For his uncle Chinnan, who had constructed a vault for his revolutionary brother, the news of his nephew turning Christian was not very shocking. He merely wished that the boy would be able to attain higher educational qualifications. Of course, there was no way of helping him out from their limited means but the new religion offered hope in that aspect.

Chiriyankan had calculated that adopting a new religion would free him from the burden of humiliation thrust on him by society, and also accord him a higher status. However, the man who relinquished his religion to be reborn as David, found that he had no place in either religion. The Pulayas refused to consider him as one of their kind and the Christians never respected him as a fellow believer. Caught betwixt the two, he became a 'Pulaya-Christian' and was known as 'David Chiriyankan'; he lived a mortified existence. The pastors who had taken the initiative to convert Chiriyankan could not help him either. The man felt trapped.

It was during that time that the 'Awakening Faith' gospel preacher from France, Dimitri Terriel, came to propagate faith in the parish where David was a member. David was an active member in the organizing committee of those prayer sessions. The preacher became impressed by the dark young man with a fascinating past of conversion. David accompanied him during the rest of the assemblies conducted across the Malayalam-speaking land. The servant of God listened for a revelation. The preacher, while returning after completing his assignment, took David with him to France, as if obeying a godly decree.

Chiriyankan, who had caught a ship to France fourteen years before, had now returned to Potta Thuruthu with a fair-skinned, blue-eyed little daughter. He had not attempted to reach out, not even through a letter, during the fourteen-year-long desolation. Fourteen years, what a long time period it was!

* * *

On seeing his nephew, Chinnan burst into tears. He was his brother Chennan's replica, the only difference was the coat and trousers that David wore. Chinnan found himself overwhelmed by the emotional climax of that encounter. Many villagers milled around Chinnan's house—mostly curious young children and the neighbours who had rushed in on hearing the news. Many relatives, who had arrived for the wedding and were yet to return, also partook of the emotions of that singular homecoming. Chirutha and Kandan too witnessed the scene, unsure of their roles.

'Still, my dear child, you never even bothered to drop us a line,' David's aunt started her usually whining.

'Somehow it happened!' David apologized.

'Who is this foreign child?'

'My daughter, Anita!'

Every eye turned to stare unblinkingly at the beautiful, fair-skinned child of the dark man.

'Where is her mother?'

For a moment, David bowed his head. Muttering that 'she could not come along', trying to distract everyone from the topic, he turned to Anita and spoke in French.

'*Enfant, voici ta famille* (Child, this is your family!)'

The listeners could not comprehend what Chiriyankan had spoken to his daughter. But when Anita smiled, they started to guess the meaning. It was the moist smile of having recognized blood relations.

Chiryankan, who had turned David, gazed mournfully at the red-coloured stone vault wherein his dead father rested. Did a martyr's soul weep from inside that grave, decorated all over with the revolution's insignia? Beyond the grave, perhaps the eyes of many forebearers, enshrined as the stone Shovvas, might have become wet too.

'I shall take your leave now,' Kunjootty spoke, addressing David. He had accompanied them till Chinnan's home. The homecoming had been intriguing. Kunjootty stepped on the farm road, away from the spot of the reunion. The rain was pattering on. He looked up when he reached the coconut tree where weaver birds had woven their nests. The tree, which had been struck by lightning, had new nests dangling from it, thoroughly drenched. Only the birds knew the secret of why they made nests in a tree that had been once struck by disaster.

The window of the Vadakke Veedu opened. Beyond the windowpanes—under which the names 'Susanna' and 'Kunjootty' were scribbled—Nandini's young face could be seen.

'Uncle, who has arrived?'

'People from far off. From France.'

'That *chechi* looks so pretty. Hope she will play with me!'

'Why not? Uncle will tell her about you.'

'Shall I come out now?'

'No! Your cough will worsen if you get wet in this rain!'

'Bad rain! No one is allowing me to get out of the house!'

Kunjootty became unhappy at Nandini's griping. He tried to make himself believe that it was the cold weather that had aggravated her cough. The cough had wound itself around her like a rope, narrowing her world, limiting her to herself. At her tender age, boundaries and limits were more reprehensible than imprisonment.

That night, David slept soundly on the cow-dung-plastered floor of his family home, a practice of yore. Chinnan had made a delicious dinner, complete with fried shrimps and crab curry. David had indulged himself thoroughly with his favourite dishes.

The next day, with Anita by his side, David stepped into the neighbouring areas. His footsteps retraced forgotten landscapes as he searched for the young Chiriyankan's presence. Pausing by the shrimp farms where he had once fished with a handmade fishing coop, an *ottal*; gazing at the unattainable heights of the coconut tree from which he'd once stolen tender fruits; observing the gentle undulations of the lake's silver waters where he had once thrown fishing nets; listening to the echoes of the traditional folk songs . . . His daughter followed his journey, unaware of his existential angst.

David continued his journeys the next day too. He seemed to be deep in thought. Something troubled his mind and disturbed his sleep.

On the third day, even before dawn broke, David left Potta Thuruthu, leaving little Anita behind.

18

The Backdoor Man

Chinnan was terrified that the prophecy of death had come true! He went running frantically to Kunjootty. Due to the exertion, the old man was panting heavily.

'What happened?' Kunjootty asked.

'He left, he left!'

'Who?'

'Chiriyankan! He is missing since last night!'

'What is there to worry about? He must have gone somewhere nearby!'

'No, he has left. Only the child's bag has been left behind. He has taken his bags.'

The return had been as mysterious as the arrival.

Where must have Chiriyankan gone, leaving behind a little girl who spoke only French? Kunjootty could arrive at no definite conclusion. Even if there was some emergency, Chiriyankan could have easily given the reason.

Anita's state was really pitiful. She could not survive without her papa. The little girl was in unfamiliar surroundings. Anita was not used to the cow-dung-plastered floor or the tattered grass mat. The helpless girl kept sobbing, holding onto the leather bag that her father had left behind. The child refused food, and did not even drink a cup of tea.

Kunjootty tried hard to break down the barrier between Anita and the people around her. He could hardly speak fluent French, but somehow managed to communicate the basic ideas. He had to lie to the child that her father would return soon. To distract her, he took her to the riverside. When Anita met Nandini, her insecurity reduced quite a bit.

Both became friends very fast. Language was not a hindrance to either of them.

Nandini showed Anita the nests of the weaver birds. She took her to the kitchen yard where the hens were clucking around. They threw stones at the bombastic gulls perched on the top of the wooden barriers near the lagoon. Kunjootty observed wonderingly as the two little girls overcame the great language dilemma that had trounced adults. Whatever Nandini asked in Malayalam, Anita answered in French. Neither felt anything was amiss in their communication. Perhaps pure minds, untouched by prejudice, had the same wavelength. Or it was the inexplicable gift of language when the souls knew one another.

Kunjootty knew that Anita could not be appeased for long by these momentary distractions. Even while playing with Nandini, she would raise her head to stare at the distance. The child must believe that one of her glances would fall on her papa, clad in his putative coat and trousers.

That day passed by somehow.

At night, Anita slept in Nandini's house. Neither Murali nor Chinnan wished to separate the two playmates. The playing and waiting continued the next day too. But Chiriyankan did not return. No news came of his whereabouts even after many days.

Murali felt that Anita's presence acted as an elixir for Nandini's health. It was as if the intensity of her cough had abated a bit. He did not dare speak about it, just watched their play from a distance. Even then, he made sure that Nandini did not indulge in any game that might cause physical exertion. Another medical check-up was scheduled shortly. Murali also wanted to visit his family house during that journey.

'Why such a sudden trip?' Kunjootty queried.

'When can I go with my child again? Another check-up is due . . .'

'She will be fine very soon,' Kunjootty reassured Murali. 'When do you plan to return?'

'In two days' time. In case we are late, I shall whistle from the shore. Come with your boat.'

'Oh, sure!'

Hearing that Nandini was going away, Anita insisted on accompanying her. Savitry took pity on her.

'Poor kid! Let her come!'

'What if Chiriyankan comes when we are away?'

'Do not worry about that! If he comes, I shall tell him about it. Take her along if you wish!' Chinnan encouraged them.

That evening, when his family was praying, without participating in it, Kunjootty sat alone in his room and untied the bundle of memories. The melancholy of a hapless childhood transgressed into his mind's desolation, catching him unawares. The poor family that had to sell everything and move away in a

small boat with their wretched belongings . . . The hopelessness
and insecurity in the eyes drooping under the scorching sun.

Just wanted to vex a bit. Merely, merely vex a bit . . .

'Have you stopped praying too?' Eli's accusatory voice woke
him up from the burden of his reverie.

'I prayed while sitting here!'

'All lies! No wonder it is said that you are possessed by
some evil spirit!'

'Who said that?'

'Your father! Who else?'

Kunjootty smiled grimly. He admitted to himself that it was
true. An evil spirit had targeted a young boy who meticulously
followed the rites of Sabbath and all his religious duties. The
ghoul attacked him unexpectedly during his sojourn and added
the lad's name to his own kingdom. That had been inscribed in
the *Book of Exodus*.

When he tried to catch sleep with his unruly mind troubling
him, Kunjootty found himself listening for Murali's whistle.
Though he was sure the family would not return that same
night, he found himself listening relentlessly whenever he woke
from his disturbed sleep. The same pattern repeated itself the
next night too. Proper sleep evaded Kunjootty on both nights.

On the third night, Kunjootty awoke on hearing a shrill
whistle from the opposite shore. Even in the dim moonlight, he
caught a glimmer of white light on the other side of the lagoon.
Presumedly, the travellers who had returned from their journey
were waiting for a boat.

Kunjootty untied his boat. He rowed swiftly, trying
to outwit the cold of the moist breeze. It would be good to

perspire a bit. But on reaching the other shore, following the flicker of light, Kunjootty sat bemused at the desolate shore! An empty riverbank . . . just a fluttering piece of mundu, drying on a clothesline nearby.

Kunjootty felt that some intruder was watching his foolish journey, hiding in the dark. Who had whistled and disturbed his sleep? Kunjootty felt irked by his hearing that had obviously deceived him. He sat in the boat utterly still; the oars silent and unmoving.

Kunjootty was not aware of the time or its passage. The phenomenon of time did not seem to have much significance. On the moonlit expanse of the sky, the glory of the shimmering stars. The sparkling lights of Kochi were glimmering afar. He could see the lights from the anchored ships. Could it be the time when ghouls, the Agnimadan, emerged to enchant wayfarers to their death? He had heard that the ghosts of those who had died due to smallpox, wandering without rest, would entice people at the middle of the night. If so, let him meet an Agnimadan tonight.

The skiff moved by itself, caught in the river's unquenchable thirst for journey. Kunjootty did not bother to steer it in any direction.

As the boat moved past Koppan's house, which seemingly was hiding in the dark night, Kunjootty gazed at it inadvertently. The back door opened at the same time. Kunjootty watched someone stepping into the backyard in the dim moonlight. Behind him was Unnicheera, languorously tying her loose, long hair.

Kunjootty could not recognize the man who had stepped away into the darkness. By that time, Unnicheera had shut the door to the secret of the night, and the Agnimadan was on the prowl.

Kunjootty could no longer let the boat move under its own will. His mind had become heavy with concern, thinking about Koppan. He steered his boat back, aiming at his own shore. By the time Kunjootty reached the other side, he was sweating profusely.

After tying the boat, when he moved towards his house, Zavarias opened the door and stepped outside.

Looking at Kunjootty's awkward stance, his father asked, 'Did you use the boat?'

'No, I just stepped out to piss.'

'Maybe I imagined it!'

Withdrawing into the darkness of his room, Kunjootty pulled open the drawer and retrieved a small pill to defeat the sleep that had been taunting him. In the throes of its ecstasy, Kunjootty did not heed the multiple whistles that arose from the other shore as the travellers returned from their long journey.

The next day was the first anniversary of Susanna's disappearance. Kunjootty crossed the three hundred and sixty fifth day of the holy suffering by sleeping through it.

19

The Wings of Life

Murali returned with a heavy heart. He was seized by an intense anxiety that his daughter's sickness was getting worse. Murali did not fully trust the mollifying platitudes of the doctors. He felt that he could see the germs wandering inside Nandini's tender body, ignoring the medicines that were trying to fight them.

A quote, which he had memorized in the days of voracious reading, started recurring in his ruminations:

'Every dawn, like a skilled huntress, snips off a fragment from the wings of life!'

The huntress hid in the pitch darkness. She sharpened the edge of her deadly weapon, chafing it against the whetstones called human hearts.

Friction.

Heat.

Sleepless nights.

How could he sleep when his daughter was wracked by a paroxysmal cough? In that frail body, which was bent like a bow in the struggle to survive, there was the flailing of a fledgling, whose wings were getting hacked away.

Murali alone was cognizant of that desperate fluttering. He had started wishing desperately for a peaceful night's sleep. An unconditional serenity, devoid of any pride, any hope.

The man had gloated only once in his life. Years before, in the thrill of elopement, after crossing the Kurumali river, flush with breaking off all fetters of inferiority, the low-caste youth had mumbled thus, dazedly staring at the gleaming eyes of his high-born sweetheart: 'I have won it all!'

Today, on the colourless shores of another river, he stood as a mere human being, drained of all vitality. Murali had come to realize the transience of victories hard won in battles. A man could be a king in his dreams. On waking up, he would start begging with his bowl again. What then was the truth? That he had forgotten the fact of his poverty and relished being a king in his fantasy? Maybe while awakening to the truth of death, he would realize that life was but another hallucination!

Murali yearned to soothe Nandini and ensure her an unbroken sleep as she started coughing without respite. Yet the trapped little bird in her lungs kept chirping peevishly. Nandini groaned as she opened her eyes. Recognizing her father in her half-asleep state, she called out to him,

'Achha!'

'Yes, my dear?'

Before she could say anything more, her eyes closed in exhaustion. Nandini embraced her father's arm with both her hands and clasped it close to her heart, for security. Murali kissed his daughter's forehead and found himself praying to a power beyond sensory perceptions. He wondered: *Whom am I praying to?*

A baseless belief that he had never trusted till now?

Savitry woke up and stared at her husband.

'How come you are not sleeping?'

'Just woke up now,' he lied.

'What sort of cough is that? I am scared hearing it!'

'It will be all right! Do not worry!'

'Devi! Why is it not getting cured after all these medicines?'

Murali became defeated and lost both his speech and logic. The man who had always mocked Savitry's Devi, sat forlorn, hapless and stupefied . . .

One should reveal nothing, losing self-control. Even when the huntress sharpened her weapon and the grating sound rang out eerily, one should ignore it totally. Let her chafe one's heart as much as she wished . . .

A morose wind, devoid of any compassion, entered the room through the window. The mysteries of the universe's dictates remained hidden from the sleeping humans.

It was Nandini who shook Murali awake at dawn. He had slept off at some point of time. The colour of the sleep-deprived nights had spread out as dark circles around his eyes.

'Accha! Wake up please! It is getting late.'

Murali struggled to open his eyelids that were heavy with sleep. Feeling the sunshine trickling in through the window, he felt fatigued. A depression enveloped him, making him lose interest in everything.

'You are so lazy, Accha! If you take a shower and freshen up, I shall tell you something special!'

'What?'

'I can't tell you before you take your bath.'

The lethargy had gripped both his body and soul. When he returned after a long time, ready for office, Nandini came running to him.

'Slow down a bit my child,' Murali cautioned, feeling a stab of worry.

Instantly, he felt guilty at rebuking her natural enthusiasm. What sort of fate was this that made one apprehensive even about a child's innate vibrance?

Outside the house, dewdrops nodded from the tips of grass blades. A wind wafted through the mangroves.

'Accha! Are you crying?'

'No, my dear!'

'Shall I tell a secret for crybabies?'

'Sure!'

'Lend me your ears.'

He waited for the secret and it came: a pure whisper, the pristine Veda, dripped into his ear.

'Kuttikurrrrr . . .' Nandini buzzed naughtily.

Murali experienced a holy baptism like the fire arising out of sacred letters. A reality untouched by time and space. The mantric core of a childish prank that had been unexplored until then.

Gathering the vigour of the outlandish language, the father repeated into his child's ears the very same words: 'Kuttikurrr . . .'

Wiping his overflowing eyes, Murali moved away.

Kunjootty was bathing in the river. As he emerged from the water, he saw Murali.

'How come you are so late today?'

'It has become a habit recently. I am planning to apply for a long leave.'

'Why?'

'I need to get my child hospitalized. How shall I tell Savitry?'

'I think you are panicking for no reason . . .'

Without replying, Murali got on the boat. Kunjootty watched the melancholy motion of the boat moving away, creating ripples of pain around.

'Uncle!'

As Kunjootty turned, he saw Nandini, resembling a pale rice sheaf.

She sat cross-legged on the grass nearby and started to throw black shells into the water. Eventually, losing interest in her game, she pouted.

'You did not keep your word, Uncle!'

'How?'

'You promised to show me the sea!'

A promise that was left unfulfilled till now. Observing that the distance between the desires and fulfilment was increasing by leaps and bounds, Kunjootty answered sadly, 'I shall show you the sea.'

'When?'

'This evening, perhaps?'

'Why not in the morning?'

'It is more beautiful in the evening. The heat will be less and you can watch the sunset.'

'Shall we take Anita chechi along?'

'Why not?'

'Wow! That's so great!'

With the exuberance of knowing the sea for the first time, Nandini hurled another shell into the river. A little fish swam up to gobble it up, mistaking the shell as feed. Recognizing the mistake, it embarrassedly dived right back into the lagoon waters.

As the sound of her father's scooter rose from the opposite shore, Nandini waved happily. This was her normal routine. She would not return until her father moved away from her sight, over the curved mud path on the other side. Today, she sat near the riverside, listening to the hum of his vehicle, as it moved further and further away.

As Kunjootty came out of the water, she reminded him, 'Uncle, don't forget the promise!'

'No, I shall not.'

'Let me tell Anita chechi about it. Oh, how am I supposed to make her understand?'

That evening, to keep his word, Kunjootty started back early from his office. He told Diwakar Menon that something urgent had come up. Menon was feverish but had come to office only because he hated to be alone in his home. He did not bother to probe further into Kunjootty's reason.

Kunjootty got down from the bus and hurried to reach home before the sun started setting. As he reached the riverside, he heard the loud wails and horror-filled shouts from the opposite shore and stood stunned.

There was a teeming crowd in front of Murali's house. Bad omens could be seen.

As he saw Koppan with a sharp axe on his shoulder, getting ready to fell wood for a pyre, a dread of death snatched Kunjootty's thoughts and he rushed towards Nandini.

His body losing strength, Kunjootty clutched a nearby poovarasu tree for support.

20

Crossing over the Frontier

As the pyre was readied on the shore, the river lay shrivelled and cold, containing all the wounds and pangs within her own self. The axe fell unremittingly on the trunk of the poovarasu tree whose branches were leaning over the river. Finally, it fell with a heart-rending wail. Koppan struggled to retrieve the branches that had fallen into the river. He started chopping the wood into smaller pieces.

Kunjootty stood still staring at it all. The screams had ceased. Savitry lay numb and unconscious on the floor. A few whimpers emerged frequently, escaping the prison of her chest.

'Dear God!'

Nandini too was exhausted, weeping and crying, not really comprehending the enormity of what had happened. Kunjootty stared once again at the dead body of Murali, draped in white, next to the burning lamp made of a half coconut filled with ghee, looking like an abandoned bundle of clothes. The grunts of a death-bearing vehicle seemed to be inching closer. Having crushed Murali, it was ruthlessly mowing down the beating hearts of the rest.

As the body, mutilated during the post-mortem, was carried into the pyre, gathering the last remnants of their strength, the mother and daughter wailed agonizingly.

Kara Mooppan heaped dried coconut shells near the pyre, scooped in smouldering embers and set fire to the pyre.

Fire.

Fire, that turned everything to ashes.

In the serenity of the pyre, Murali lay alone, awaiting the purification by fire. Black birds kept circling above in the sky, frantic at the sight of ashes and smoke.

There was a crackling sound from the pyre, as if the last relationship was getting broken off too.

'The skull has burst . . .'

Kunjootty heard someone whisper. He felt a tremor pass through him, realizing that he was hearing this about the most beloved friend he had had. Blue whirlpools formed in the sky and started pouring down as a drizzle. Kunjootty, thoroughly drenched, started brooding.

How fast had everything changed! Leaving behind whatever he had gathered yesterday, and abandoning all he had vouchsafed for the future, Murali had gone away. He had arrived from somewhere, just to turn into a mound of ashes in Potta Thuruthu.

Before the pyre burned down completely, a middle-aged man, carrying Nandini, her head on his shoulder, reached Kunjootty's side.

'I am Savitry's elder brother. Could reach only now.'

A sanctuary had arrived very late. Kunjootty found that he had no words, those lay frozen within.

The child, who was resting against the man's shoulder, raised her head, and seeing him, wailed loudly, 'Uncle, my acchan!'

Her voice was weak due to continuous crying. Yet her cries evoked a scalpel-like sharpness. Another child was becoming an heir to the harsh summer of scarcity and deprivation.

Sadness tried to console sadness for a long time. Savitry's brother talked about many issues. Kunjootty felt that all those were conundrums which never met at a common point.

Anita sat all alone, desolate and unhappy. Nandini's pathos had affected her deeply. The French child stood out in that house of death, like an unwanted object that could not fit in anywhere. Everyone ignored her. When twilight arrived, Anita trudged back to Chinnan's house. Kunjootty watched that journey and felt pity welling up within him.

Kunjootty returned after making Nandini have her dinner and putting her to sleep. Savitry was lying weeping all that while. Like a bundle of endless grief.

Kunjootty could not sleep that night. He kept meditating on the banality of human births.

What had happened to Murali? Who was it that he called Murali, so lovingly, all these years?

Was it the body that burnt in the fire? Or the mind's ineffable magnetic field that had always been affectionate and consoling? Or was it a transcendental radiant consciousness, which was eternal?

'Manobuddhyahankara Chittani Naham . . .'
'I am neither the mind, nor the intelligence, or the ego!'

No interpretation of death could become a solace to Kunjootty. The lesson learnt by Tathagatha's female disciple, who was asked to search for mustard seeds from a house into which death had never entered, did not heal him either. As he stumbled like a blind man amid the indecipherable mysteries of natural laws, Kunjootty realized one truth: From the house north to his own, flute music had emanated until last night, lulling him to sleep. The night breeze would be bereft of music from tonight. The bamboo flute would slowly wither away in disuse, dusty and unheeded, in the dark emptiness of life.

Kunjootty felt the night stretching out. Without switching the lights on, he stumbled about searching for a candle and matches. By the flickering candlelight, he saw many cassettes lying in a motley heap on the table, along with a magazine, with the last pages open. Kunjootty searched out one cassette from the medley.

On the outer cover, with black ink, the inscription read thus: *Murali Ganam*. The Song of Murali, also understood as the Flute's Song. The exquisite flute music that he had recorded during an evening of friendship.

He inserted the cassette into the player and switched it on. When the clear note emerged from the bamboo flute, Kunjootty lost his composure. A song left behind by Murali.

Entharo Mahanu Bhavalu . . . the popular *kirtana*, a Telugu composition by the legendary Tyagaraja Bhagavathar.

Seeking more clarity of tone, Kunjootty raised the volume a bit. Then a bit further. Still unsatisfied, he increased it a notch more. Murali sat alongside, with a flute on his lips and an open smile. He was taking Kunjootty on a mesmerizing journey of the ragas. The sensory holes in the flute were thrumming with sweetness. As the song proceeded, some other sound enmeshed with it.

Someone was knocking at his door. Who was it?

Switching off the tape recorder, Kunjootty sat up listening. Knocking incessantly at the other side of the door, a weary intransigence was pleading for entry.

'Accha!'

A flood of emotions overwhelmed Kunjootty.

'Nandini!' He ran to open the door. Nandini stood there, tears streaming down her eyes. Did the child run all the way through the riverside in the night, to reach his door?

'Where is my acchan?'

She started crying. Then a cough shook the fragile frame. Kunjootty hugged Nandini close and tried to calm her down.

'Your father . . .' He stopped, realizing that he did not have the knowledge to go beyond that.

'I heard my acchan playing the music!' the four-year-old insisted.

It was then that Kunjootty realized the enormity of his insensitive act.

'Do you want to listen to your father's song?'

'Yes . . .'

He seated the child on the cot and switched on the tape recorder once again. When the song resurrected from where it had been forcibly stopped, Nandini listened intently.

Suddenly a woman rushed in, with unkempt hair and clothes. She ran to Nandini and embraced her tightly.

'My darling child!' Savitry wept loudly. 'If something happens to you . . .'

Savitry's brother, who was close behind her, anxiously exclaimed, 'Oh, Nandini was here!'

Savitry stared at the origin of the flute music and stood stunned to the core.

The lullabies, the nights, the music lessons . . .
    'This is Sri Raga . . . now I shall play Devadundhubhi.
Would you like to hear that, my high-born lady?'

She would sit listening eagerly to his music, not really understanding the depths of his proficiency.

Weeping, Savitry stepped out with her daughter into the pitch darkness.

Zavarias and Eli had woken up by then. They stood forlorn, not knowing what to do as the events unfolded in front of their eyes.

Kunjootty switched off the music.

All it took was one second or one day . . . for thwarting every plan of life.

The nameless river flowed moodily afterwards. Kunjootty started getting frantic as the days passed by, as if in an undulant rhythm. A warning of a disaster, the heavy secret entrusted to him by Murali, gathered weight within his heart. To whom should he reveal it? How would Nandini's treatment, which Murali had ensured meticulously, continue, if he did not disclose it to someone?

That situation did not continue for long.

One day, most unexpectedly, Savitry's brother met Kunjootty.

'I am taking them with me.'

'Where?'

'To my house. No one else is willing to accept her in our family. How long can she live alone like this?'

What was inevitable had to happen. Unable to look into the man's eyes, Kunjootty fixed his gaze at the river's depths. Then he garnered courage to convey the truth.

'Please be brave. I am going to share another bitter news,' he said.

'What!?'

'Please ensure Nandini's treatment continues without a break . . .'

As the man stood shell-shocked, Kunjootty explained about the child's health, without much preface. As the man gasped, 'Oh God!' and clutched at his head desperately, Kunjootty pleaded, 'Please do not tell this to Savitry!'

The grieving man could not even make a sound in affirmation.

Kunjootty cursed his own fate; only a sinner like himself had the destiny of shoving burning embers into human hearts.

The next afternoon, the family packed up their scarce belongings, having been forced to leave behind what could never be taken with them.

'Uncle, we are going away. When I return, do not forget to take Anita chechi and me to see the sea.'

The sea—will the child ever be able to gauge the depth and spread of it someday? Another promise, which would remain unfulfilled, was being bestowed on her.

'No, I shall not forget.'

Pleased, Nandini turned to Anita. 'The ant lion in the sand . . . we shall tie him up when I return, okay?'

Not understanding the sudden departure of her only playmate, Anita asked Kunjootty,

'*Quand sera-t-elle de retour* (When will she return)?'

'Very soon, my dear!'

Anita hugged her friend, '*Reviens bientôt* (Come back very soon).'

Savitry bid goodbye to Eli. They wept together.

As she handed over the keys to the Vadakke Veedu, accursed with disasters, Savitry asked Kunjootty, 'Can you please give me that cassette?'

Kunjootty felt something shattering within himself. He went to his room and, picking up the cassette, stared at it for some time. Now, leaving behind many long sleepless nights, this too was moving on.

He struggled to be stoic as he handed the cassette over to Savitry.

The family stepped into the boat.

Nandini kept waving her hand until the boat crossed over to the other side. Anita responded by waving back. Even when no shadow remained, as the family moved over the curving road, Anita refused to stop waving her little hand.

Just a canopy of pain remained, in which everything seemed to merge. Bidding farewell to that vagueness of grief, ignoring Anita's palpable sadness, Kunjootty went inside his room and shut the door tight. He wanted back the sleep, which had played truant with many of his nights.

As he took the sleeping pill in his hand, he prayed briefly, 'Lord, may this not turn into a habit!'

He found himself praying intensely and sincerely after a very long time.

21

The Vanquished Warriors

Koppan's pet dog never even bothered to bark once when his master's home was encroached into by sneaky, secretive visitors. The poor creature, whose virility was destroyed when it was a puppy, languidly curled up in the warm ashes or under the coconut trees most of the time. Ignoring the indifferent sentinel, chameleons and rats started crossing over the boundaries. A pregnant black cat came in search of refuge and gave birth to three kittens in Koppan's attic. The smart creature, who had come uninvited, ended up mauling and biting Koppan's dog one day.

It was on the day following the above-mentioned disaster that Unnicheera was seen vomiting copiously near the banana tree in the compound. As her bile dripped over the young plant, Koppan suspected nothing more serious than indigestion. Soon after, the secret got confirmed—Unnicheera's belly was swelling up.

Koppan started burning from within.

Words disappeared into the very origin. He avoided entering his home to escape the sight of Unnicheera's bulging stomach. At night, he slept with his pet dog on the veranda, enduring mosquito bites. And he left early in the morning, even before the dog became aware of it. Days went by lazily, not accountable to anybody for their comings and goings.

One day, Isaac returned to Potta Thuruthu, carrying the exhaustion of his relentless forest sojourns. It had been a while since Kunjootty had met him. As if burnt by sun, Isaac's face had blackened. As an ominous sign of bad times, dark circles had appeared around his eyes. Kunjootty realized at first glance that a lost soul stood before him. For a moment he felt apprehensive that the next name to appear in his 'table of losses' would be that of Isaac.

'What happened to you? You look awful.'

'Bad times! Perhaps it is the dice of destiny that you often mention. I got involved in a police case.'

'How did that happen?' Kunjootty lost his nonchalance.

'Nothing to worry about. In this game, one has to learn to disentangle the knots too. Else, one shouldn't play it at all.'

The coconut trees by the lagoon stood obsequious and still. The river flowed indifferently. Only she remained beyond the touch of time, which was striding along arrogantly.

'What is the problem?' Kunjootty voiced his anxiety.

'You know the manipulations behind the auctions of discarded forest lumber. They are supposed to sell off rotting, hollow logs, destroyed by rain and sun. Instead of the useless wood that is auctioned off, in truth, it is solid lumber that is transported from the forests. But this time . . .'

Isaac stooped to pick up a small, shrivelled coconut kernel and threw it into the river. It started its enthusiastic journey to the sea in the rushing flow.

'I had managed the range officer, the forester, the watchman and their ilk. Still there was a loophole somewhere. Bad luck! Some bad blood between those who received their bribes! One of them stabbed me in the back. A lorry carrying the lumber got caught.'

'Where were you all this while?'

'I was trying to influence the top guys. Somehow, it seemed to be too problematic this time around. If only I get out of this mess! I plan to leave this dangerous business forever. Are you feeling amused, my friend?'

'Why do you say that?'

'You were the only adviser of my royal court who cautioned me against it . . .'

'The adviser or the joker? Nobody would give up that power, to decide one's future, to anyone else.'

'Only one smarter and wiser than an adviser can become the joker. Haven't you seen the clowns in the circus? They are masters of the toughest twists and turns. Their constant focus is on the main guys who perform the most dangerous gymnastics. The clowns stick around closely, while playing the fool always, keenly watching out for every misstep that could turn fatal, ensuring no disaster.'

Isaac tried to grin like a circus clown, even amid impending disaster.

Huge boats carrying coconut fibre could be seen on the river, dipping their long bamboo poles deep into the river's heart, as they moved towards the many coir factories in Alleppey.

The river, though hurt, flowed uncomplainingly. The sharp iron rings, which were affixed at the end of the bamboo poles, dripped tear drops that sparkled in sunlight. The river's core became the receptacle.

'I shall return the day after tomorrow,' Isaac said, staring at the river.

'Where to?'

'To the capital city. I have to meet some top shots.'

'When will you come back?'

'No clue.'

Isaac got up. As he removed the sharp glass blades that had stuck on to his mundu, he continued,

'Wanted to take a swim and cool myself down. The river is not polluted by the sea waters at this time, right? How long since both of us had a swimming competition, eh?'

Perhaps Isaac wanted to soothe his inner burning in the lagoon waters. That was why he was searching for childish delights. There were a lot of childhood memories scattered all over the riverside. A lot of youngsters used to scamper around and leap into the water, a long time ago. Isaac, Kunjootty, Susanna, Kanaran . . . many were there. The children would pray that the sinful sea water stain would disappear from their river so that they could relish their swimming again. And every year, when the monsoons freed the river from the brackishness, they would delightedly leap into the water. The elders, busy catching fish using the China nets near the shore, would cavil at the kids.

'These brats will scare away the fish!'

There would be a luscious harvest of fish during the auspicious dusks. The China nets would rejoice in the still hours where the tides would be balanced.

Everything had passed away.

Kunjootty became emotional while stepping into the river, a thorthu wrapped around his waist.

'I was very lonely too . . . these few days,' he said.

'How come? You have Murali and Nandini for company!' Isaac commented.

'That house is locked up once more.'

'What happened? Murali got a transfer to a new place again?'

'He has moved far beyond us,' Kunjootty found his voice wavering in grief.

Isaac listened to the story of yet another exodus. Both the storyteller and listener slipped into a distressing silence. Striped panchax fish were at play, circling around their shins. Getting no reaction from the human creatures, the fish rubbed against their bodies to verify a semblance of life. They did not get a definite answer.

'What happened to the mother and the child?' Isaac broke the silence.

'After shedding many tears, looking back again and again, they too returned.'

Kunjootty took multiple dips in the river. But despite the number of times he submerged himself, the *janmadosha*, the accumulated sins of life, could not be washed away.

'You wanted to take a swim, did you not?' Kunjootty reminded Isaac.

'No, I am exhausted.'

A small family of bubbles came swimming up to Isaac and having half circumambulated around him, drifted back to the main flow. Isaac contemplated deeply for some time and then muttered aloud.

'I dread to think of what all would happen by the time you finish your book, Kunjootty! *The Book of Exodus*. Why did you have to choose that name, my friend? It is like an ominous warning, which augurs certain unfortunate events . . .'

'I have no idea. I am not even sure that I would ever be able to finish it!'

'You should definitely finish it. Write it all down after calming yourself.'

Even when he resolved to write, Kunjootty found himself robbed of words. There were umpteen notes he had scribbled, outlining the book; nowadays his efforts lacked vitality.

Nature had, long ago, completed all the stories. As the pages flipped, each person experienced it as his or her own life. While watching a movie, oblivious to the fact that it was a mere illusion made by the play of light and shade, one merged emotionally with it, and ensnared by the treachery woven by the eyes and ears, one ended up laughing, crying and succumbing to the passions. If the cinematic experience, provoked by two senses, was so impactful, imagine the power of the life experience, where all five senses played their roles!

Gratitude was due to the great souls of yore who called it 'Maya'. Thankfulness was due to the incarnation of compassion, who advised an alternative path.

If you close your eyes and ears, no movie experience would tempt you. There was no happiness or sadness, nor any play of emotions. If you mastered your five senses, there were no life experiences, not even the universe! Was there ever a state where there was neither happiness nor sorrow, no more dualities, emptiness or completeness?

'Let me return from the city. We need to go somewhere,' Isaac said.

'Where?'

'To the land of the fire bird! You have been wanting to go there for a long time. I have not been to my aunt's place for a long while. Something disastrous has occurred in their lives. We will discuss further after I return. Meanwhile, you write your *Book of Exodus*. Try to write something positive! What if they started happening?'

'Yes, imagination manifests as the universe . . .'

Isaac saw a woman stepping into the river for a bath on the opposite shore. She seemed to be unaware of their presence on the riverbank.

'Isn't that Koppan's wife? She seems to have put on some weight. Looks like she would be willing to play around a bit . . . eh?'

Kunjootty noticed that Isaac had let his lethargic mind wander to Unnicheera's bathing spot. Where the eyes reached, the mind reached soon after. The ambience was such that the body soon followed suit. By what folly did a human being, on the verge of tears a little while before, forget everything in the thrall of the next moment?

Kunjootty remembered the black door of Koppan's house opening during the nights, when the Agnimadan was supposedly on the prowl. However, all insights were not to be shared with others.

In the night, a six-legged insect, with yellow wings and red eyes, attracted by the light emanating from the table lamp, landed on the *Book of Exodus*.

A return journey, through a path cutting across many centuries. The fatigue of sleepless nights spent toiling over the history of exiles. The meditation on holidays, abandoning many temptations. The book alone remained, as a lonely, hopeful yearning to stay connected to life, even as all the moorings were being ripped asunder. Perhaps it was ridiculous that a human life could get obsessed with a pile of papers. Still, Kunjootty accepted that fate. Erasing, correcting, copying . . . how long would this journey last?

No answer.

He did not wish to know it either.

Kunjootty caressed the *Book of Exodus* as if touching a tender memory.

He opened a new page, and wrote the title with a strong new emotion.

The Book of Exodus

It dawned on Kunjootty that he would write profusely that day.

22

Turbulent Times

'Harvesting of virgin fields and indulging in intercourse were the two major weaknesses of the feudal landlords of Potta Thuruthu. They encroached into fields and threshing grounds with their lust-filled eyes. Many secret rooms were strategically constructed beneath the granaries of their homes. The dark-skinned girls who disappeared from the threshing grounds were mercilessly ravaged in these spaces.

'The very appearance of the farmlands changed dramatically after the harvesting season. Shortly, the fields turned into shrimp farms. The lower-caste servants were the guards, spending sleepless nights in the *erumadam*, the elevated watch towers. The feudal lords insisted that certain men stay in such towers on certain nights. The next morning, the betel juice that the feudal lord spat out could be seen in front of the watchman's hovel, along with the tears of his wife.

'The feudal lords slept lazily, feeling not a bit remorseful, making cushions out of bulging money bags.

'However, sleep has a law: when compassion dries up in one's mind, reasons for sleeplessness get churned up. The same happened to the feudal landlords of Potta Thuruthu.

'A new generation, oppressed beyond tolerance by the relentless exploitation, sprouted from the fields and shrimp farms. Their sturdy hands held sharpened work implements. They crossed into the compounds of the landlords. Blood flowed as streams, spreading on the farmlands, the shrimp farms and the whole of Potta Thuruthu.

'Even today, the soil of Potta Thuruthu retained the black hue of dried-up blood. The horrifying smell of blood still emanated from the earth. That was the first and last revolution witnessed by Potta Thuruthu.

'If one sat in the dreariness of the isle and looked up, the growing city of Kochi could be seen—merely a stone's throw away. Caught in the bindings of the boundaries, Potta Thuruthu stayed undeveloped, akin to a mentally disabled child. Not a single drop of drinking water available in the isle was free from germs. The seeds of dreaded diseases transmigrated into the bodies of the islanders who quenched their thirst by drinking the stagnant water of the ponds. Many children died due to diarrhoea and jaundice. The shrivelled nipples of the poor mothers were devoid of milk for assuaging the thirst of the dying infants. There was no flow of blood in their veins either. Nor did their eyes have tears. The tear glands had dried up along with the hopes. The islanders could only gaze with deep despair and helplessness at the piped water project that terminated on the opposite shore. Potta Thuruthu was ruthlessly cut off from its benefits.

'The islanders crossed the river with as many vessels as they could hold, in search of water from the pipes. The public taps on the opposite shore were surrounded by umpteen vessels awaiting precious drinking water.

'Turbulent times were coming for the residents of Potta Thuruthu.

'The islanders learnt to wake up at dawn and reach the other shore before their neighbours could. Their women conceived in those waiting periods. They also suffered the pangs of labour while waiting for water. During the ceaseless waiting, they gave birth to their children. The offspring grew up with that legacy in their blood. They, in turn, lost their childhood, adolescence and youth while waiting for water near the taps. Forgetting what they were waiting for, the islanders became familiar with the process of waiting . . .'

Having written the above lines in the diary with the blue cover, Kunjootty sat brooding for some time. These were the different faces of *Exodus*.

There was a flatland, belonging to his forebears, where it never rained. Kunjootty was aware that the pages of the *Book of Exodus* lay scattered over the plains cursed by the little fire bird, extending till the blood-stained dark mud of Potta Thuruthu. He hoped to gather the loose sheets and stitch them up into a book one day. 'One day' . . . even the words appeared vague, exhausted by incessant waiting.

Kunjootty sensed the presence of someone behind him and woke up from his reverie. The grating footsteps seemed to be intentionally noisy. He saw Zavarias and became perturbed. This was not usual for his father. The distance between them had grown unwittingly, preventing any open conversations. Owing to that, instead of calling Kunjootty, Zavarias was intrusively stepping inside the room.

'You should meet that Ezhuthassan and talk with him,' Zavarias said without any preface.

That was his inherent nature. He could not bring himself to make small talk or express his emotions. Zavarias always spoke to the point and seemed to be bearing an unnecessary burden of gravitas.

Zavarias's colourless and nightmare-ridden childhood might have moulded his nature. The thick moustache, hair cut close to the skull, stubbles of hair emerging from his ears, the red-tinted eyes—all served to give him a rather forbidding demeanour. Kunjootty could not recollect any episode when his father had raised a hand at him. Yet, his father's shadow had always caused discomfiture to Kunjootty.

'I heard that Ezhuthassan is planning to sell his land. He is heavily indebted. It has been accruing for a while now. He has no other way out. I am contemplating purchasing it,' Zavarias announced.

'Do we need that land?' Kunjootty asked with concern.

'It is prime land, no doubt about it! Enough access to both the lagoon and the main road. The vehicles stop near Ezhuthassan's place on the opposite shore. The price will keep escalating. A very profitable deal in my view!'

Eli stepped in with a cup of tea and could not help overhearing that conversation.

'That land is good, I agree! Yet if someone is forced to sell his land because of debt, it is sure to be accursed with his tears and imprecations. Why buy such a place?' Eli asked querulously.

Kunjootty remembered another story. His ancestors had a bit of land in the valley of the Potta Hills. The heirs had to abandon everything and run away for their lives in the middle of the night. Such a story could be repeated at any time. One could hang on to a piece of land for some years. On the day when it's time to leave it all behind, lamentations about its value or size would hardly be of any use.

Why had Ezhuthassan, usually immersed in prayerful rites, confined himself to his house and land all this while? Was it for the trivial purpose of getting rid of the debts?

'One has to be practical in such matters. If you start seeing sin and stuff in all actions, you will not be able to survive in the world,' mocked Zavarias. 'It is not as if we are going to loot anyone's place! There is talk that Ezhuthassan is half-crazy. He is into mantras and all sorts of tantric puja. Before he turns completely insane, we should purchase that land from him. The road reaches his compound. If possible, we should build a house for Kunjootty there. The next generation will benefit from it.'

Next generation!

Kunjootty almost blurted out his thoughts: no one was immune from the world of irrationality. The only partition between sanity and insanity was a transparent membrane in the brain. Owing to external stress, when the membrane fluctuated, any human being would exhibit signs of craziness. If a hole was formed therein, then one could laugh freely or cry without any inhibitions. If needed, as the mind raced, one might even howl in accompaniment!

'Anyway, go and talk with Govindan Kutty Asan. We will decide after that!' Zavarias said with finality.

A silence fell between the father, the mother and the son. Distances crept up unseen between them. Outside the home, the river was unmoving. A few small skiffs passed by, like deep sighs.

Kunjootty decided that he would visit Ezhuthassan the very next day. He was the guru who had taught him the very first alphabet. It had been a long time since they had met each other.

After his parents left the room, Kunjootty heard a sob near the west-facing window.

It was Anita.

The child stood with tears in her eyes, her face pressed against the window bars. Kunjootty felt a stab of guilt that he had ignored her for a few days.

'*Qu'est-il arrivé* (What happened)?' Kunjootty asked the child.

'I am fed up, Uncle! My parents have not come to take me back. Nandini has not returned either. I have nobody in this world!' Anita replied in French.

Kunjootty stood befuddled, unable to comprehend how he could pacify her. Where had Chiriyankan disappeared after leaving this innocent child here? The child was enduring the anguish of being stranded in a remote place. She did not know the language or the customs of the place. The only person she could communicate with was Kunjootty.

Anita had become totally lonely after Nandini's departure. She had started waiting by the riverside, expecting her friend to return from her trip. Slowly, her hopes dwindled.

Abject loneliness.

Anita thought of her father, who had suddenly left her alone in the uncertainty of an isle. She remembered her mother, at a distance beyond her imagination, many skies away, busy with her life. The child also recollected her parents squabbling over something in the middle of the night.

Her country was far beyond her reach now. Inside her home, her pet African macaw would be waiting for her. It used to wake her up in the mornings.

'*Anita! Réveillez-vous* (Anita, wake up)!'

Anita kept worrying whether her busy mother was looking after her pet properly.

She had become a source of ineffable pain for the villagers of Potta Thuruthu. Chinnan hardly knew what food she liked or wanted.

Eli would often cook meat or fry fish for the child. Anita would relish the food with Kunjootty.

Koppan made a makeshift raft out of banana stems and gave it to Anita to play with. She enjoyed floating that on the river. The child tried to learn swimming by holding on to the raft. She played with kakkappoo and kurunji flowers on the lagoon. When they drifted away like the swans of Lilliput, Anita watched for a long time.

The previous Sunday, Kunjootty had taken Anita along when the festival flag was hoisted at the church, celebrating the feast of the Saint. Chinnan hadn't objected. Anita was a child who had been baptized in her native country. Chinnan did not know much about the rights and wrongs of such customs. He had the solemn duty of protecting Anita until Chiriyankan returned to her side. He was sure that his nephew would return one day.

Kunjootty thought that Anita would like a change of scene. 'Would you like to go to the beach?'

He had to fulfil a promise that he had given to Nandini.

Anita's face brightened up a little.

'Shall we go now, Uncle?'

'Of course!'

Kunjootty called out loudly to Chinnan and informed him of their plan.

23

The Sunset

Kunjootty and Anita went to Isaac's lumber mill first. There, surrounded by the various smells of wood dust, Isaac asked, 'Such an unexpected visit?'

'Why not? You will be off tomorrow on your trip!'

'Yes.'

'We are going to the beach. Anita wants to see the sea.'

'I shall join you. Just give me a moment!'

After giving some instructions to the workers around, Isaac set out with them.

By the time the trio reached the beach, the colours of the evening sky had started leaking into the sea. They could see almost twenty-odd China nets cast into the water. They kept dipping and lifting rhythmically. The teak wood scaffoldings of the China nets resembled monstrous spiders from some ancient era.

When they moved further, they saw children staring at the sea. There was an amusing scene playing out for them. A small dark head was bobbing up and down in the forceful waves. It was the mute girl child, Parutty, who would dive into the sea, somehow fastening her loose skirt around her emaciated body!

She fell from the rocks, resembling a flower dropping off its slender stem. Then she swam towards the discarded material thrown by the onlookers. As the waves tossed and hurled her back to the shore, she emerged shivering, soaked in mud and stretched her tiny hand for coins.

Anita stared with great wonder at the little girl who seemed to be an inseparable part of the sea. She became greatly engrossed by that sight. The acute insecurity that had enveloped her was temporarily forgotten in the mélange of curious sights near the seashore.

Three burly youths were busy heaving a heavy net nearby. They were murmuring the mantra of the nets . . .

'Elam, Elelamma, Elam, Elelamma,
Kadalamma valaniraye kadalmeentha Elelam.'

'Mother of the sea, grant us a plentiful scoop!'

The prayer reached the deep recesses of the listeners' hearts like a lovely hymn.

Kunjootty clutched at Anita's hand and soon they were part of a small crowd. The childhoods nourished by the compassion of the seashore, the rebellious youth who smoked away their ennui and frustration of unemployment, the old age's weariness and listlessness when faced with penury, all were part of the crowd.

Negotiations, auctions of the shoals of fishes, women carrying fish baskets like Matsyagandhi of the Puranas . . .

It was all very strange to Anita's young eyes. Her golden hair, extending till her neck, fluttered in the sea breeze.

Kunjootty felt a stirring of adventure in his blood.

'What if we try to win an auction, Isaac?'

'Are you joking? You have a China net at home, don't you?'

'Just for fun! If we happen to win, we can try reselling and make some money!'

'Participate just like that? Want to put in a bid with eyes tightly shut?'

'Yes, that is the spirit!'

Kunjootty went near a China net that was scooping up fish regularly from the sea. He was trying to evaluate the circumstances before jumping in with 'eyes tightly shut'. Else it was easy to make an error. The method, 'eyes tightly shut', involved quoting a price as the net went down into the sea. The very uncertainty triggered the thrill. If the price was accepted for a low amount and the net emerged with a fine catch, it would be great!

'Starting the auction at hundred rupees! A mere hundred, all of you please listen!' a man called out loudly. He started enumerating the various achievements of the net. He had made a loudspeaker out of a newspaper folded into a conical shape. Anita looked unblinkingly at the paper cone speaker.

'What about one hundred and fifty rupees?' someone dared to fiddle with the auction amount.

'Two hundred!' another shouted.

'Three hundred.'

'Four hundred.'

Kunjootty waited with bated breath, observing how much the quotes would get hiked. The men at the net were egging the bystanders on, by provoking bets and exaggerating the potential gains. People got sucked into the game and finally the rate was fixed at six hundred and fifty rupees.

A short, squat man approached the fishermen and handed over the money as per the custom. As soon as the money was handed over, the men heaved away at the ropes and lifted the net. The fish leapt frantically. The curiosity of the spectators turned into a combined shout of appreciation.

'Full tummy!'

'Fortunate man!'

Anita stood open-mouthed as the fish in the net gasped for breath. They were desperate for air, flipping side to side, searching for a space of escape, even as the sea stretched from continent to continent so close. They had not been aware of the net laid for them while boisterously swimming about in the sea, exuberant in their untrammeled freedom, just a few moments before. Perhaps a similar cosmic net must have been cast for the human beings on the shore too. Those who were already trapped were negotiating the price of the fish, getting their dinner ready, preparing homes for their nightly rest.

Like a veteran circus performer, a man manoeuvred his way across the China net. His face, as he scooped out the fish using a hand net, was gloomy. He and his team had lost that round. However, they did not exhibit much emotion and got ready with the next round. Kunjootty was determined to participate in the second auction.

The fish catchers started trading at two hundred and fifty rupees to compensate for the previous loss. The quotes started rising. They rose from three hundred to four hundred to thousand rapidly, exciting Kunjootty.

'Thousand five hundred,' Kunjootty called. He expected nobody to outbid him. However, his calculations failed.

'Two thousand.'

He could not distinguish the person in the crowd. It escaped him that the psychology of auctions lay in the inexplicable human urge to win. Without deliberation, Kunjootty challenged:

'Two thousand five hundred.'

'No, let it go!' Isaac cautioned him warily.

'Not now!'

The embarrassment of stepping back after becoming the cynosure of all eyes: another psychological tactic of the auction!

The audience was fully enthused by the rising bids. Even Anita was thrilled. She was imagining a net full of prize catch by now.

'Three thousand!' The unseen opponent was hell bent on tightening his grip.

'Three thousand three hundred,' Kunjootty raised to the bait again.

'Three thousand five hundred.'

Kunjootty felt a prick of alarm. He tried to convince himself to withdraw at that juncture.

'First call, three thousand five hundred. Second call . . . any other bids?'

Everyone turned to stare at Kunjootty. Pointed looks, as if he was bound by some solemn duty to honour the challenge.

Ignoring Isaac's forebodings, determined that it would be his last venture, Kunjootty called out once again.

'Four thousand.'

No voice outbid him. The catcher did not deign to wait further. With an unnecessary hurry, he hailed loudly, 'Four thousand first call, second call, third call . . . finalized!'

Kunjootty felt the relief of having outwitted his opponent, though at a steep price. Isaac looked disgruntled. Kunjootty felt sure that the king of fishes would usher his citizenry into the waiting net.

Kunjootty gave the money and signalled to raise the net. Seagulls and eagles gathered close, their wings spread and eyes alert; a few perched on the stumps, as the catchers started raising the net.

The heavy stone tied to the rope sunk deep into the sea, and, in conformal rhythm, the net slowly emerged from the depths.

A shout of excitement electrified the crowd.

Kunjootty eagerly looked into the net, waiting for a luscious catch.

But the net was empty. A few small fish struggled here and there. The black birds descended together and rose with the struggling fish in their beaks.

In a matter of seconds, the uproar of the crowd transformed into mocking laughter.

'What a disappointment!'

'Poor guy!'

The atmosphere became taut with pity and ridicule. Kunjootty, now a laughing stock, left the net behind and walked away. Anita accompanied him with the face of one who had witnessed a disaster.

'Happy now?' It was Isaac's turn to pour derision on him now.

But, instead of regret, Kunjootty felt a rising anger. But he did not reply.

'They tricked you properly. It was their men who instigated you by raising the bid!'

Kunjootty stood dumbstruck, feeling like a fool whose intelligence had temporarily become clouded by his mule headedness. Isaac's words were a revelation to him.

'They can easily identify the naïve ones, who can be easily beguiled!'

Kunjootty walked with a stride through the sandy soil, moving against the blowing wind, silently receiving that stinging recrimination too. Isaac felt more irritated at that withdrawal.

'Running away, are we?'

'What else?'

'To run away like a coward after losing? When will you start learning, Kunjootty?'

The little girl who had dived into the sea from the treacherous rocks had not reached the shores till then. Four thousand rupees would have been like a precious treasure to her, Kunjootty thought wanly. To be addicted to the vagaries of the China net was a folly; the lone lesson remained.

Kunjootty felt no interest as the auction calls started behind him. But Isaac had returned with a resolute look on his face. Kunjootty felt astonished to see him participate actively in the third auction. Why had he changed his mind all of a sudden?

There was no spirit in the new round.

Few calls were raised.

Even the catcher's voice was weak, as if bereft of hope. At the end of a bleak bidding war, Kunjootty heard:

'Eighteen first call, second . . . final call . . . fixed!'

Isaac won the auction at five hundred rupees. Kunjootty was flabbergasted and found himself curious as the net started to rise.

He remembered an old fisherman advising to throw the net towards the right of the skiff. The catch was huge and the men had struggled to raise the net filled with the glorious catch.

It was a repetition of the tale.

The harvest of fish was mind-boggling! Kunjootty listened unbelievingly as the audience shouted in jubilation. The catchers became morose, and Kunjootty felt vindicated. The king of fish had been slightly delayed, that was all.

Anita was absolutely delighted. She clapped her little hands and was beaming at everyone. It was amazing how she had forgotten all her travails at that small victory.

Isaac was surrounded by many bidders.

'Shall give you five thousand. Will you accept?'

'Six thousand is my offer!' Another fixed his eyes at the plump reef cods that were leaping about as he made his deal.

'Seven thousand, what do you say?'

Isaac started some quick mental mathematics. Even if four thousand and five hundred were gone, there was a good two thousand five hundred rupees profit overall. Without bargaining for more, he closed the deal at seven thousand rupees.

As he counted out four thousand rupees and offered it to Kunjootty, Isaac quipped, 'There is a saying that unless you are trained, one should not participate in an archery competition. Do not forget it!'

'I do not need the money! Let my loss remain mine. But I am awed at how you managed to clinch this one!'

'There are lessons beyond those grasped by rote repetition. There are lessons of survival requiring observation and introspection. Then you will notice the different faces of the sea and the fishermen. Stay alert, really alert.'

Kunjootty became aware that he was yet to master many lessons. The China net was as unassailable as the human mind. What it would reveal from its depths, at different times, remained a matter of conjecture.

The vibrancy in the beach air started diminishing slowly. Visitors were returning to their homes. Yet there were people watching the little girl who was battling the sea. Anita was entranced at the sight of the girl. Soon, a few foreigners gathered close to encourage the child in the sea. The ones who brought in foreign exchange for the nation. A few of them started throwing foreign coins into the sea. The little girl eagerly dived into the depths to gather them. The foreigners were tempting her by throwing the coins further away in the sea. As he saw the child swimming to dangerous distances, a pained Kunjootty addressed Isaac.

'Do you see that sight, Isaac? People are having fun by torturing a poor, hungry child! She is called Parutty. Her father did not return from the sea one day. Her mother is bedridden in one of those dilapidated shacks over there.'

Isaac looked at the child. He recognized the hunger pangs in that thin and malnourished body fighting the sea. The fire of hunger was not assuaged by the cold and brackish seawater. Perhaps Isaac remembered another child, who had swum in the river, with similar pangs of hunger and hurt. The rain and wind had arrived to beckon his father, inviting him into the fury of the river. He had cried from his mother's womb that day. The only inheritance he had got from his father was the orphan's insecurity.

The profit from the fish sale froze in Isaac's hand. He wished to give the money to the dusky little girl who would emerge from the sea soon.

'You can give the money to the child!' he told Kunjootty.

He had hardly handed over the money when a bizarre hubbub started on the beach.

People were shouting as they pointed at the monstrous waves rising in the sea.

Children were crying out hysterically.

As Kunjootty rushed forward, he discovered that the little girl who had dived into the sea was no longer visible. He searched desperately to catch a glimpse of her black-haired head in the midst of some dark wave or another.

Where was the child?

A few manual labourers, their conscience yet undead, dived into the sea and started searching for the little girl. But she gave the slip to everyone and remained hidden from their sight.

After a long time, setting all worries at bay, a huge wave carried in her body and deposited it on the shore. As she lay, her face deep in the sand, the birds circled on the sky and a crowd hovered near.

The sea had torn away the skirt from her tiny body. The onlookers were aghast and pained by the nakedness. In her little fist, the child held her last earnings. Foreign exchange!

Kunjootty stood thunderstruck, hoping against hope that she would rise and clad herself again with her skirt. But the sense of shame in that little consciousness had long set with the faraway sun.

'My God!' Kunjootty sobbed, feeling shattered.

Seawater burst in a wave and fell on the fist with the coin. An offering of devotion!

Anita was weeping, her face hidden in her hands. Kunjootty hugged her close and struggled to calm her down.

'How horrible!' someone said vehemently from the crowd.

Unable to watch another mad wave rising and covering Parutty's pathetic little body with moist sand, Kunjootty turned his face away from the sea, hating it forever.

24

The Monk in the Bamboo Grove

The holy feast celebration of the Saint was as glorious as that of Kavilottamma's festival. The Thekkambara Thevar and his accomplices usually visited Kavilottamma every year, flying over the church of the Holy Saint. During those journeys, the beautiful spirits of both temple and church met each other, and shared their news. The festivals and feasts thus transcended the common beliefs.

The Holy Saint stood as a mediator during healings and miracles. The believers established their mediator inside a glass cage, placed it on a trolley and wheeled him all over the village. Clad in a shining armour, holding a sharp spear, astride a brawny horse, when the Saint appeared on his feast day, the needy and the suffering became oblivious of the scorching sun and surrounded the glass cage. Some touched the cage and kissed their own fingers. Some others leaned their faces against the cage and attained salvation.

Trained dancers who played the *parichamuttu*, the clash of the shields, stepped rhythmically in front of the trolley. They wore white shirts and white mundus. Around their foreheads and waists were colourful bands. Each dancer held a yellow shining sword in his right hand and in the left, a red and yellow shield. They sang and danced, turning left to clash their shields with one another. Kunjootty stood on the side and listened to the song praising Saint George.

Thanthina thana, thanthina thanana
Thanthina thana, thanthinana
Padachattayanijitte kalurayaninjitte
Theeyalum serpethinte navuthulachukondayathil
Kundamonnu payikkane!

Wearing the armor and body suit
He thrust the spear through the tongue
Of the ferocious dragon!

The shields shone brightly in the sun. Sweat poured down the bodies of the dancers. Their footsteps were very much in tandem. In front of the shield dancers, one could see a dark man pulling a hand cart that in turn carried another dark man. He was filling the gunpowder to make the fire crackers ready. Both men wore dirty thorthu that barely covered their nakedness.

Kunjootty focused on the man atop the hand cart. He seemed unaware of the festivities and happiness around him, and was concentrating on the arduous and dangerous task at hand. Whenever the hand cart puller stopped, drenched with sweat, the deafening sounds of the firecrackers burst from the trolley.

Kunjootty found that he had no prayer to present before the Holy One. What made his heart surge with despair was the sight of the malnourished body of the cart puller and the dark indifference of the man firing the crackers. Kunjootty discarded the festivities with that same indifference and walked away.

His walk had an aim. He wanted to meet Ezhuthassan.

As he neared the compound barricaded against the world with brambles, he hesitated a bit. In the shadows of the ancient mango tree nearby, a dilapidated tiled house could be seen, all hunched up and evoking a mournful memory.

The surroundings were desolate and dark. There was a grove of bamboos towards the western part of the huge compound. It looked almost three decades old. One more spring was left to blossom all over before shrivelling up to die.

Kunjootty was anxious about stepping into the bizarre ambience of that mysterious place. How was he supposed to face Ezhuthassan? He had been forced to become an emissary in a distasteful task. Kunjootty had been sent by his father to negotiate the purchase of Ezhuthassan's land.

Kunjootty, however, was not in favour of his father's avarice. His mind was curious about the adventure fraught with mystery.

Dried leaves fluttered inside the bamboo grove.

A chameleon, resting on the bramble boundary, scampered away in a sudden terror. Two eyes had discovered Kunjootty by then.

'Kutty!' The voice came as if from two decades before. After looking around to ensure that nobody else was near, Ezhuthassan came near the bramble fence.

'Where are you off to?' A whisper.

'Nowhere in particular . . .'

'Come inside . . .' Another whisper.

Kunjootty crossed the gate that was constructed from coconut leaves woven with brambles.

He remembered his young self crossing over the same gate in search of the first letters of knowledge, holding on to his study materials and enveloped by total ignorance. How long had it been since he had offered Ezhuthassan the *dakshina* and had formally become his disciple? There had been a *kudippallikkodam*, a school for beginners, inside the compound, with a makeshift room roofed with a thatch of coconut leaves and its ground full of fine white sand. The sound of chains clanging could be heard from the attic of the tiled house located towards the south-eastern part of the compound. As Ezhuthassan's mother would wail in the captivity of the chains, the young children would be terrified. After a very long time, that unfortunate mother broke off the chains of her misery and departed for her final journey.

'Come, come my boy . . . Wanted to tell you a secret . . .'

Ezhuthassan invited Kunjootty to a room with broken stone walls. In that room, infested with cobwebs, he was offered a shaky stool to sit on. The resident spiders moved away swiftly on seeing the new intruder. It seemed to a bemused Kunjootty that they might even have attacked him for their survival.

Sunlight sneaked in through the broken tiles of the roof and shattered on the bald spots of Ezhuthassan's head. His appearance added a chill to the dark ambience of the old room.

'I am telling it to you, only to you. It is not to be shared with anyone else. Everything will turn fine very soon.'

'What?' Kunjootty was astounded.

'Everything. Don't you believe me?'

Kunjootty sat bewildered, unable to comprehend anything.

Ezhuthassan was speaking in a manner as if narrating the final half of a story that he had started a long time ago.

'If it is Anjaneya's will, what is impossible? Hanuman is the incarnation of might. Do you know the secret behind his unsurpassable strength?'

Without waiting for a response, Ezhuthassan continued breathlessly, 'The unspent manliness, the semen, is the secret behind that indomitable energy. Whoever serves Hanuman has to take the vow of celibacy!'

Was that the reason behind Ezhuthassan's bachelorhood? Kunjootty felt a growing respect for his intractable dedication, albeit verging on the border of insanity.

Suddenly, as if trying to prevent someone from overhearing a great secret, Ezhuthassan jumped up and bolted the door. The bolt was blackened with the grime accumulated across innumerable decades.

Folding his hands, Ezhuthassan became engrossed in meditation. A mud dauber buzzed around his scarce white mane, looking for a nesting place. Kunjootty felt that Anjaneya was growing into life from within the prayers written down in the Shatadruta Samhita and the Bhavishya Purana, to manifest in Ezhuthassan's body.

Kunjootty thought he could hear the Hanuman Stuti, praising the twelve famous names of Lord Hanuman, indicating his great virtues.

'Hanuman anjani sunu vayuputro mahabalaha
Rameshtaha falgun sakhaha pingaksho amitvikramaha
Udadhikramanaha chaiva sitashoka vinashana
Laxman pranadata cha dashagriivashya darpaha'

Many a eons ago, Parvati and Shiva enjoyed their marital life, seeking joys within dense forests. They mated in the form of monkeys, and the goddess became pregnant. But Uma refused to give birth to a monkey child. Lord Shiva used his yogic powers to transfer the foetus to the hands of Marut, the Wind God. Vayu wandered with his precious gift, seeking a suitable mother. Finding Anjani, the virtuous monkey queen, wife of King Kesari, he deposited the divine child in her womb. Thus, Hanuman became Anjaneya, the son of Anjani.

Kunjootty glanced outside, his gaze slipping past the windows with broken bars. On the side of the pond covered with moss, at a corner of the compound, a white crane was waiting for someone. Kunjootty was yet to declare the purpose behind his arrival. How could he discuss the mundane land sale with Ezhuthassan, who seemed to be living in a strange world of his own? He believed that someone had tricked Zavarias into believing that Ezhuthassan was trying to sell his land. It was impossible to conceive that Ezhuthassan would be amenable to materialistic actions like selling and buying of property.

'Asan! Would it be okay if I were to seek clarity on an issue?' Finally, Kunjootty dared to ask the question.

Ezhuthassan woke up from his meditation. 'Why not? Ask me,' he said.

'Forgive me if I speak wrongly. I have heard that Hanuman tries to frighten away those unworthy of his worship. Especially those who are weak of character?'

Ezhuthassan's face became very serene. Then furrows started appearing on his swollen eyelids and forehead. His eyes fixed on Kunjootty unblinkingly.

Kunjootty started feeling apprehensive whether he had committed a blunder! Was it a tactless query?

Ezhuthassan moved closer to Kunjootty, his penetrating gaze still intact.

'You were one of the smartest among my students . . . I remember!'

Kunjootty could not decipher the intention behind the innocuous words. Ezhuthassan came nearer and put his icy cold hands on Kunjootty's shoulders. He then looked deep into his eyes. Kunjootty felt a creeping wariness, an instinctive sense of something dangerous. He could not get up from the stool, due to the strength in the restraining hands. All ways of escape denied, Kunjootty continued to sit benumbed. Then he saw Ezhuthassan's eyes move down and stop at his chest. Ezhuthassan stared, with the wonder of discovery, at the left pocket on Kunjootty's shirt. Slowly, slowly, his hand extended towards his pocket. Calmly retrieving the folded notes of money therein, Ezhuthassan regarded those vigilantly.

'You are employed now, aren't you? Will be having lots of money!'

Ezhuthassan started examining the notes diligently, flipping both sides. Then, replacing the wad of rupees, except one, in Kunjootty's pocket, he remarked, 'I am taking this for myself. Just this currency note.'

'Why don't you take it all?' Kunjootty offered.

Ezhuthassan smiled.

'Under this dilapidated stone wall, there is a hidden treasure. I can dig it out, anytime I wish.'

Kunjootty was perplexed. If that was the case, what was his old teacher's singular quest?

He did not know the answer. The one who knew, did not reveal it either.

Outside, the fierce sunlight dripped through the dense branches of the trees. The memories of the shield dancers and firecrackers had long vanished from Kunjootty's memory like yesterday's forgotten dream. The glass cage of the Saint would lie abandoned at some corner, dusty and neglected, until the next year's feast day.

Kunjootty found himself sinking into a melancholy for some undefinable reason.

Had Ezhuthassan become a recluse from reality due to the darkness of his surroundings and his solitary existence? Or, could it be that his experience was the true reality? If one contemplated, what was life? It sprouted by coincidence and returned as yet another coincidence. In the midst, caught in limited time–space, such an avalanche of illusions, desires . . .

Kunjootty had no clue about where desires started and ended. Somewhere, there was an ineffable underpinning; moving away when you sought it and edging close when you sat still.

No, negotiating the sale of land with Ezhuthassan was beyond his capability.

'I shall leave now, Asan!' Kunjootty sought permission.

'Do come whenever you can!'

'Yes.'

'You have *gurutvam*, the quality of reverence to your teachers. You will do well.'

Gurutvam. Well-being. Kunjootty knew that he possessed neither.

Wondering at the inexplicable curiosities, leaving behind the musty smells fraught with decay, Kunjootty made his way back to the bramble gate.

Ezhuthassan came running behind him.

'Kutty! I forgot to answer your question! You were right. Hanuman would do his best to scare the devotee. He will tempt you, frighten you, trouble you badly . . . If you do not possess the equanimity gained through meditation, you will be totally lost. If you get scared, either death or madness will be yours for sure. I am revealing the secret to you. Keep that in your mind.'

Quick as a flash, Ezhuthassan disappeared into the dark recesses of the compound.

Kunjootty's mind was akin to that of a confused child.

He tried to recollect whatever had happened.

It was with shattered musings that Kunjootty reached home. As soon as she saw him, Eli came rushing.

'Chinnan wanted to meet you. That child is suffering from high fever!'

'Who? Anita?'

The disaster that she had witnessed at the beach the day before had affected Anita severely. She had been silent all through the return journey.

Kunjootty felt wounded on seeing the little girl lying feverish on the manure-plastered floor of Chinnan's hut. Kunjootty tenderly touched her forehead, covered by a wet cloth.

His hand was scalded. Anita, sensing the touch, opened her eyes.

The child did not smile. Neither did she make an effort to speak.

25

Black Crosses

Everything was mere thought. Some occurred in *sushupti* or the stage of deep sleep, some in half wakefulness, yet others during *jagrata* or full consciousness. Whichever state one identified with, one presumed to be the reality.

Kunjootty's thoughts meandered thus as he stood waiting apathetically on the boat jetty in the city. A stink arose from the surroundings and a brackish wind blew about. Diwakar Menon, who was with him, was ensconced in a world of his own.

A mosquito rose from a pile of garbage nearby, and, after circling Kunjootty thrice, descended on his arm. It was hell-bent on stinging him with the needle, not bothered about the bright daylight around.

Kunjootty raised his hand instinctively to crush it. Then he controlled the feeling and stood still. How come a human being did not have the ability to endure a small mosquito's bite? Even that demanded much inner strength!

Like a man becoming fascinated with his own mortal body, the insect too was fascinated with its own. The egoistic 'I' inside a human was radiating with the same intensity from the mosquito too! The natural instinct to survive was equal in both species.

Annam vai pranah!
All life forces spring from food.

Kunjootty recognized that his blood fed the life force of the mosquito. It would be his own blood that would splatter if he crushed the insect. He felt an attachment and a sense of compassion towards the creature. The revelation dawned that he was living inside the mosquito too! At the minutest level, the Rishi Veda, the Vedic darshan of the ancient sages became realized: the self-manifested in all other beings.

Kunjootty did not disturb the rishi, who had taken the guise of a mosquito, to enunciate the Veda. He stared nonchalantly until it finished drinking the *soma rasa* and ecstatically flew off.

The boat had reached the jetty by then; its engine quite noisy. The jetty was divided into two parts by wooden bars. One was meant for those who disembarked from the boat and the other for the passengers who boarded it. Following Diwakar Menon, Kunjootty made his way inside the boat and found a seat.

Menon had returned to office after a week's leave. An unfamiliar silence enveloped him. His hair was dishevelled and his clothes looked untidy. Kunjootty failed to understand how the man, who was never prone to display any emotional turmoil, sat brooding silently at a hand's distance. When the time for leaving office edged close, Diwakar Menon asked casually,

'Are you in a hurry?'

'Why do you ask?'

'If it is not too much trouble, can you come with me?'

'Where?'

'To my unfinished home!'

Diwakar Menon's incomplete house was on the opposite side of the lagoon. That was how the journey came about.

And to witness the journey stood the Holy Cross atop the Vallarpatam church. It was the first Cross seen by the foreigners who travelled by ships. After an uncertain sea journey, when their vessels neared the shores, they saw the Cross and fell in love with it. Filled with gratitude to the Great Fisherman who controlled the sea winds and waves, they paid obeisance by kneeling before the Holy Cross, singing hymns.

Many crosses and churches were reviled due to the gravitas wrought by faith. There were allegations that churches were being built and crosses erected just to garner the attention of the tourists and fill the coffers. Yet, accepting the blame and showering compassion on all the mudslingers, the crosses grew in number. Black crosses, sprouting by waysides, houses and human hearts.

The boat left behind the fishing skiffs that were at rest after the night's work and neared the Vypin beach. They walked across the seashore and moved through some byroads. When they reached the porch of the unfinished home, Diwakar Menon remarked:

'This is the nest of a solitary sparrow. Do not expect great comforts.'

The walls that were bereft of whitewash, the untidy front yard and the shrivelled flower plants in the compound seemed to agree with that statement. They did not heed the arrival of the guest.

Diwakar Menon knocked thrice at the door.

Kunjootty felt astonished on seeing that. Who else was living in the nest of the lone bird?

Then, Diwakar Menon took out his key and opened the door.

'Only one room is of any use, and so, I have anointed it with a soul. I seek permission to enter every time I return. And whenever I leave, I bid farewell.'

As Kunjootty stood dumbfounded, Menon continued:

'You feel shocked, don't you? Then let me tell you another secret. In absolute silence, when even a leaf doesn't rustle, the room's soul comes searching for me. True!'

Kunjootty wondered whether his friend's words were emanating from some chimerical world. Either Menon's mind had undergone an upheaval or he was in communion with some ineffable level of existence beyond anyone's understanding.

'I know it will be difficult for you to comprehend,' Menon read Kunjootty's face and commented. 'But it is a fact, my friend. Unexpectedly waking up one night, I got to know the soul's room for the first time. In that pristine silence, the vibes came flowing towards me. I was able to feel all those sensations. Why are you staring at me like that?'

'I . . . I am listening!'

'You must be wondering why I am blabbering such gibberish. Just that my mind told me that it was time to reveal everything. Nature has a law for all these happenings. My mind was extremely turbulent last night, Kunjootty. I could not sense the vibrations.'

Saying that, Menon listlessly leaned back on the cot. His gaze was fixed on the ceiling and he appeared to have forgotten the basic courtesy of asking his guest to take a seat.

Kunjootty felt unnerved and seated himself on a cane chair nearby, becoming a part of that unkempt room. Inside the almirah were uneven piles of books with cobwebs enwrapping them; remnants of insects were visible nearby. Clothes hung on a clothesline beyond. A blue shirt, tilted to a side, was swaying gently, like someone hanging from a noose.

By the time Kunjootty's gaze turned from those quixotic sights, Menon was entangled in some remote contemplation, seemingly disconnected from the world around.

'Anita is not well,' muttered Kunjootty, desperately trying to clear the intolerable severity in the room.

'Who? The French girl?'

'Yes . . .'

'What happened to her? Poor child!'

'High fever.'

'You feel a great compassion for her, don't you Kunjootty?'

'Compassion? I really do not know . . .'

'Something or other is always there to disturb one's peace of mind. When I took a week's leave, I just wanted to float around aimlessly. But the seeker of serenity ended up losing whatever peace he possessed.'

Kunjootty sat dumbstruck, unable to detect the meaning of this new detour in the conversation, and Menon turned to look at him. The blue veins on his neck pulsated in extreme stress, and his voice emerged wounded.

'I have to confess it . . . at least to you!'

'What?'

Menon seemed to retreat within himself. His mind was stumbling about in the darkness therein.

'I had prayed that it should never happen! But it did. I saw her, Kunjootty! I saw Sarojam!'

Menon had to overcome much inner conflict to reveal the rest.

'One night, I received the premonitions. I wasn't sure of the place I would meet her though. And then I heard the knock on the door of my unfinished home! Kunjootty, it was her, my Sarojam!'

Menon's hard-won control over his emotions seemed to be wavering. He closed his eyes.

'I froze on seeing her . . . she looked awful! Her body was weak and undernourished. Her hair was messy, face was shorn of any vitality . . . that was how she had returned to me . . . I could have never imagined that look. The child with her resembled me strongly. It appeared like a dream, an illusion . . . where the time and place did not have clarity.'

Another poignant interval.

Kunjootty felt a tenuous sadness enveloping his own self. Whose fault was it? When had it happened? Menon's eyes were still shut. Perhaps, he was still travelling through various scenes in his mind. Then he spoke, as if to himself.

'Sarojam should not have come searching for me. She came without any expectations. Just to get a slight relief from that burning guilt within her. I could not respond at all. And now I feel so weighed down . . . Why did God punish me like this? Did he think I would be delighted to see that sight? But I had never hated or cursed her! I watched helplessly when she returned sobbing with her son, not receiving even a kind word from me. I saw a mole on the neck of the boy . . . like mine. Yet, I could not bring myself to call them back or utter a word. I stood there speechlessly. Though on leave, I have been confined to this house for all these days. I waited for an answer in the nights. Perhaps because my mind is not tranquil, I have not received any reply . . . none at all.'

Kunjootty felt miserable as Menon's eyes filled with tears. After sharing this much, Menon had reached the stage where he had nothing more to say. He did not seek any advice from Kunjootty. Even if he sought it, Kunjootty had nothing to offer.

What was the need for the revelation?

The silence deepened in the room. Darkness too.

The wind that blew from the island was filled with the interminable sighs of a sailor whose ship had lost its moorings.

Kunjootty sat there helplessly, waiting for Menon to make a move. Seagulls made a ruckus as they came home to roost. They were sharing the disastrous happenings of the day.

After a long time, hearing the siren from a distant ship that was anchoring, Menon woke up from his deep reverie.

'Time for you to return, eh?'

'Yes.'

'You were the first guest after a long interval. Yet it became a dark welcome. Forgive me.'

'Nothing like that.'

'Let me accompany you to the ferry.'

'No need, please take some rest.'

Before he left, Kunjootty silently sought permission from the throbbing soul of the room. May guidance be provided to Menon. No answer could be sought after. By itself, the answer would arrive compassionately.

It was very late by the time Kunjootty reached Potta Thuruthu. As he got down from the bus and walked down the dark road, he was brooding darkly. He wanted to check on Anita. Kunjootty felt guilty thinking he should have purchased some oranges and a packet of glucose. That was a task for tomorrow.

As he walked immersed in deep thoughts, he heard some strange sounds from Ezhuthassan's compound. It seemed as if someone was forcibly trying to open a locked door. Ezhuthassan's loud scolding could be heard above the ruckus.

'No way! I am not going to free anyone!'

Who on earth was Ezhuthassan speaking to? Could some thieves have entered his house?

As the sounds of the bitter fighting grew louder, Kunjootty crossed the bramble gate and entered the compound.

The uproar emanated not from the house but from the Samadhi Griham, a small room built in the corner of the vast yard as a resting place for the forbearers.

Ezhuthassan was pushing against the locked door of the Samadhi Griham with all his might, to prevent it from opening.

'No, I shall not free anyone!'

It felt as though Ezhuthassan was involved in a battle of strength.

Kunjootty watched with bewildered eyes as the confrontation continued for some time.

Ezhuthassan calmed down eventually. Then he looked around the rapidly darkening surroundings and shouted loudly, 'Who is there?'

Kunjootty, terrified, spoke. 'Asan! It is me, Kunjootty!'

Ezhuthassan beamed at his former student in the half-light. 'Ah, so it was you!'

Kunjootty found his panic subsiding. 'Who were you angry with?' he asked gently.

'Those inside . . . who caused all those curses to rain down on our family . . . still insist on being worshipped. No way they are getting any morsel of rice from me!'

'Who caused the curses?' Kunjootty asked curiously.

'The ancestors! The curse is that everyone will die of madness! When my mother and sister died of craziness, they were appeased. I am the only one remaining. I will not be another idol among them. I will never open that door again! No more puja, no more prayer for their salvation! Blasted souls who caused the curse!'

Ezhuthassan was the last of the line that was doomed with insanity. After him, no person remained to take over the family heirloom.

'Kutty, come on. You should not be standing here. Foul place!'

Clutching Kunjootty's arm, Ezhuthassan walked towards the house.

A stray dog that had managed to sneak into the compound started barking at them furiously.

Ezhuthassan threw a look of great fury at the dog and snarled at it.

'Mad one! Throw a stone at it!'

Kunjootty bent to pick up a stone and aimed it at the creature.

However, the perfect player of marbles had long forgotten his childhood prowess. The watch on his right wrist became loose and accompanied the stone, and dropped somewhere on the dark yard. The dog, eluding the stone, continued to make its stance very clear, by barking more violently.

Kunjootty became apprehensive that the glass case of his watch might have shattered. That apprehension alone was not wrong.

While he searched for his watch, bitterly rueing the habit of tying it on the right wrist, the dog, with the satisfaction of having accomplished its goal, merged in the dark obscurity of the surroundings.

As Kunjootty gathered up the broken pieces of his watch, he was astounded.

Time, in spite of the wreckage, was pulsing, without breaking its rhythm.

26

Holy Wounds

On the completion of ten lunar months, Unnicheera's labour pains began. Supporting her pale, swollen stomach with both hands she started screaming with pain.

'Amma!'

The dog was the only living creature around. After a while, Koppan arrived. On hearing the agonizing cries, he ran. Crossing the river, leaving behind the shrimp farms and farmlands of Potta Thuruthu, he finally reached the point where the river parted ways. To the wizened midwife who emerged from the hovel, he managed to gasp thus:

'Unnicheera is having labour pains!'

The old midwife smiled. She then started calculating some figures on her gnarled fingers, and spat the red juice of the betel leaves mixture she was chewing on the yard.

'This shall be my two hundred and eighty-third delivery. Three and eight and two . . . thirteen! Oh, Devi!'

'What are you mumbling?' Koppan became anxious.

'Nothing much! It adds to thirteen, that is all! A matter of belief!'

'Please come fast!'

Tucking a few betel leaves and tobacco into her waist pouch, the old woman followed Koppan. By the time they reached, Unnicheera was twisting about wretchedly in the throes of excruciating pain, on the hand-woven mattress spread on the floor. The dog was standing guard at the door, as if it had sensed something intriguing was afoot. The midwife shooed away both the man and the dog, and shut the door firmly behind them. Not knowing what to do, Koppan started smoking a beedi while the dog sat on its haunches on the cow-dung-plastered floor.

Before long, the cry of a newborn was heard from within the house. The purity of that sound rained softly into Koppan's heart.

The midwife opened the door and stepped out, exposing her betel-juice-stained teeth.

'It is a boy! All your prayers have been answered.'

A son was born to him. The pleadings and offerings of sixteen years had borne fruit.

Who had pleaded?

Who had offered?

As the child, born from no offerings from him, cried loudly, Koppan felt like weeping himself. He stood there, forgetting the surroundings, his eyes filling with tears.

It was a totally new experience for the man. He had no clue how to respond when women from the neighborhood came to visit the new mother and infant.

The women started showering him with praise.

'Finally, God heard your prayers!'

'To get a male heir in your old age is nothing short of a fortune!'

'He has his father's nose and eyes!'

'The baby is your replica!'

Poor Koppan did not have the capability of enduring all those adulations. Suffocating in the generous commendations, he looked pathetically at Unnicheera. Her eyes were still dazed with exhaustion. By her side, a small rosy being slept quietly. How had he been conceived? What soul connection had ushered him into that hut?

The visitors slowly frittered away.

The midwife got ready to leave too.

'I shall return after taking a bath!'

Koppan offered money, stained with perspiration, to the old woman. In the blink of an eye the money disappeared inside her blouse. As she walked away, spitting betel juice at intervals and leaving red sign marks on the farm ridges of Potta Thuruthu, Koppan was left feeling lonely. Though he was not alone, he felt alone.

Perhaps the child understood his appan's loneliness; he started wailing again. Koppan could read the words in that cry.

'Let me cry a bit, Appa. It is my first day on earth.'

'Son, cry as much as you wish to! Wash away the stains of your birth with those tears!'

He wished to cry out openly too. However, he had lost the purity to burst into innocent tears a very long time ago.

Unnicheera turned to her left and opened her blouse. She steered her nipple into the baby's tender mouth. Koppan got scalded, as if he had witnessed something that he shouldn't have. The golden breasts of his wife were a strange sight to him. Koppan stepped out and tried to pass the time in some frivolous activities. Then he remembered the one-shot medical remedy, for the health of new mothers, that the old vagrant healer had taught. He wandered about the place gathering herbs and pounded them into a ball that was the size of a goose berry.

When he reached Unnicheera's side, she was asleep, laying on her left side, her arm around the child.

The son was asleep too, safe in the warmth of his mother's protection.

Koppan felt a moistening inside his heart.

He turned back, unable to disturb the serenity of their sleep. Meanwhile, Unnicheera awoke and became alert to his presence.

Koppan saw the pupils of her eyes move and her lips open to whisper something. Then the imminent words turned into a weak smile, which seemed ugly. Her arm was stroking the child continuously. Koppan felt apprehensive that her attempt to calm her mind would disturb the child's slumber.

'You are not feeling ill, are you?' Koppan inquired solicitously.

Unnicheera shook her head in negation.

'Please have this medicine. Will ensure good health!'

Unnicheera unquestioningly accepted the medicine. Not a word or syllable escaped her lips.

Koppan stood there, unable to comprehend the next step. The son of the famous poison healer Chonachu found his eyes slipping away from his wife's face to the corner of the dark room.

Then he asked with utmost calmness, 'Whom should I inform?'

'What?' Unnicheera was stunned.

'About the baby. That a son has been born. Whom should I inform?'

Unnicheera started sobbing softly. Koppan knelt on the floor and stopped her.

'No, don't tell me! I won't be able to bear it. He is my son, Koppan's son! The son born to me due to the gods answering my prayers!'

Those words were beyond Unnicheera's fragile tolerance. She burst into tears.

'Won't you forgive me?'

Koppan did not reply. He was wracked with guilt at another thought—the unforgivable cruelty he had meted out to his pet dog.

As unrestrained emotions gathered strength within him, Koppan yearned for toddy.

Koppan reached Kali's shop before sunset. He sat on his usual bench and loudly called out.

'Kali! A special for me! I became a father today!'

Kali stared at Koppan with wonderment.

'Did you add water to toddy today?'

'Hey, don't you dare utter blasphemy here!'

'What will you do if I say so, you green chilli? My son has been born today. My child! If you add water to the drink today, I shall sing about it most definitely!

Kali tricked me, adding water to the toddy
I tricked her too, by giving false coins shoddy!'

Kali started bickering with him.

'What's the matter with you today?'

'Koppan's flag is flying high today, woman!'

The villagers in the toddy shop started wishing Koppan, sharing his joy.

'Oh, after a long wait, he has become a father!'

Koppan drank himself crazy with that joy. As he staggered out of the toddy shack, he offered Kali much more money than usual.

'Keep it! If some drunkard comes in and cannot afford a drink, offer one on my behalf!'

He gambolled away slowly.

As he moved over the farm ridges, clouded over with a gathering darkness, he remembered that Unnicheera and the baby were alone in his house. Koppan felt deeply ashamed about his drinking spree. He hurried to reach home.

When Koppan came near Edappdathu House, he hailed loudly:

'Hey there! Unnicheera has given birth to a baby boy!'

As Kunjootty came out of his house, Koppan smiled.

'A handsome child! Are you not going to visit us?'

'Sure.'

'Then come along!'

'Not now. Maybe tomorrow!'

As if he was spilling a secret into trusted ears, Koppan went near Kunjootty and whispered in his ears, 'He is my son! The answer to sixteen years of prayers!'

Kunjootty could perceive the deep despair underlying that overt pride. Who was the man who had opened the back door of Koppan's house and stepped into that dark night? The great soul who had magnanimously raised Koppan to his new stature of fatherhood?

Koppan did not wait to observe the doubting look on Kunjootty's face.

'I am going. They are alone at home.'

Kunjootty stared after the man who was taking heavy steps, burdened by the weight of his new fatherhood. Over the farm crests, over the prayerful murmurings of the flowing river, through the fingertips of the night breeze, Koppan's humming floated. Then a cloud pulled a veil on the face of the moon.

Koppan walked, loving everything around, caressing the brambles marking Ezhuthassan's compound.

He leaned in and stared at the mesmerizing mystery of the snake grove in the yard. Ezhuthassan was somewhere inside his house.

'Asan! Listen to the news! I have become the father of a boy!'

Perhaps Ezhuthassan heard it. Or maybe he did not.

In the gathering darkness, instinctively, Koppan stopped moving. Two eyes glittered amidst the colour of mud.

It was in front of him, just a step ahead.

Koppan remembered the scripts written on ancient palmyra; the iron nails creating wounds on the leaves. The serpent belonged to the royal clan. A deadly stinger who would attack if hurt.

Even in his extreme state of drunkenness, Koppan could make out that his foot had unwittingly landed on the snake. It was twisting about in agony. Now he should not move an inch. Let it struggle . . . struggle to its death!

'You fool of a snake! What do you think you are going to do to the great Chonachu's son? He was a poison healer, my father!'

Koppan mocked the serpent writhing under his foot.

'Go ahead and bite! On the day my son was born, let me see you bite!'

The snake struggled for its life beneath the shaking foot of the drunken man. Manoeuvring its body out of the fearsome hold, it spread the hood and stung hard.

The fangs sunk into the veins, flooding them with intoxicating venom.

'You bit me, did you? Now I want to see how many times you would dare again!' Koppan howled wildly and stamped the snake with renewed strength. His eyes blazed like fiery embers. Perspiration dotted his nose tip. Staring at the snake as it stung again and again, Koppan started counting.

'One, two, three, four, five, six!'

Six holy wounds!

The snake stopped biting and collapsed. The poison added to Koppan's intoxication. The son of Chonachu, the poison healer, caught the snake in his hands. He stared intently at the sparkling patterns of the slippery form trapped in his firm hold.

'You bit me six times, did you not? Now watch this! I am going to bite you back!'

Gathering all his strength, Koppan brought his face close to the snake.

'One, two, three, four, five, six!'

After returning the exact number of holy wounds to the creature, as he clutched the lifeless snake by its tail and hurled the carcass into the lagoon waters, Koppan felt thirsty enough to drink the river herself.

A frenzy began within. The night entered his eyes.

Even as he dropped down on the wet earth, near a tender coconut tree, Koppan continued to mumble:

'He is my son . . . Koppan's son!'

27

From the Jaws of Death

That night, notes from exquisite wind instruments came floating to befriend Koppan. From the cloud canopies, in the company of the gods, Koppan peered down. Potta Thuruthu seemed as small as the eye of a needle. There, at the corner of that isle, he could see his lifeless body, lying awry near a coconut sapling.

Koppan recognized his own self as a featherlight consciousness. No sense of weight, shape or measure. Far below, his body lay immobile and forlorn. The eyes were half closed, the mouth was twisted, neck turned to a side, no sign of breath, bereft of life . . . a despicable sight. Koppan did not hesitate to start his journey, after denigrating that pathetic body.

He could see Unnicheera as he journeyed forth. She was fatigued, but lay with her eyes open. Her face had the serenity wrought by her atonement. Her hand was caressing the baby who resembled a sparkling, tiny star.

'Unnicheera!' Koppan called out with great feeling.

She did not hear his call; it was not audible to her. He tried in vain to touch her. How could Unnicheera have recognized a consciousness that transcended touch and hearing?

Koppan accepted that he had metamorphosed into something beyond recognition. The rules of the mortal world did not apply to him any more.

There was a tempting light flickering from far off.

Valleys filled with enchanting fragrances invited him over.

Waterfalls, pristine and pure, rushed past at a distance.

Beyond the flow, many known souls raised their hands akin to white handkerchiefs and greeted him warmly.

His learned and wise Appan.

His loving Amma.

Kuncheriya, who had drowned in the river.

Josephine, Chothi, Douglas . . . they all stood together, beckoning him onwards.

'Come now, come to us!'

Koppan yearned to reach their side. He wanted to feel the touch of his parents!

'Oh, my appan, my amma!'

He thrust himself forward. But he could not move an inch. Some invisible forces were pulling him backwards. The light slowly vanished. He found himself dropping backwards, through a dreary, depressing smoke.

Darkness, only darkness all around.

Slowly, the riverside became visible.

The coconut trees stood with a deathlike stillness. There was a lifeless body near the sapling. The insects were clambering all over the man's unmoving limbs. A black crab had its pincers around the right toe.

Koppan was caught in a very strong whirlpool. Tossed about in endless circles, losing consciousness bit by bit.

When he woke up, it was very dark.

His lips were parched and burning. A great ravaging thirst and nerves stretched to the point of bursting. The whole body was in flames of agony. Somehow, Koppan managed to sit up. He kicked away the biting crab. As it crawled away into the night, Koppan bellowed with all his might:

'I have been bitten by a snake!'

No one responded. Koppan felt that it was perhaps for the good.

Ezhuthassan's compound seemed to be in deep sleep. No movement could be discerned from the snake grove either. Was there any other serpent remaining inside?

Koppan swayed as he made his way forward, struggling against the blowing wind. He crossed the lifeless Chinese net and turned into a side path. On reaching the porch of his house, he fell. A deep sleep came to claim Koppan.

He lay like that until the midwife shook him awake.

'Were you sleeping here? Leaving your wife all alone in the house?'

Koppan struggled to open his eyes into the light. His eyelids were heavy, his lips dry and shivering. His body stung all over.

He shuddered on remembering what had happened the previous night.

Seeing his face, the midwife inquired, 'Tell me, what happened to you?'

Koppan stroked his ankle, where telltale signs were visible. It was swollen all around.

'A snake bit me . . .'

'Oh, Devi! When did it happen?'

'Last night . . .'

'What snake was it?'

'Cannot remember. Cobra, I think . . .'

'Yet . . . Neendakara Muthappa!' The midwife bit her tongue. If it had been a black cobra, would he have survived till now?

'How many bites?' The woman stared aghast at his leg.

'Six!' Koppan started counting them. Suddenly he caught a sniff of screw pine flowers. There was clotted black blood near the bites.

'I bit the snake back! Six times!'

'Devi! Is that true?'

'Yes, that is why I did not die.'

The old midwife was overwhelmed by what she had heard. Koppan watched as she frantically rushed inside the house to share the news with Unnicheera.

Koppan stared at his reflection in a half-broken mirror hanging on the wall. Swollen, crimson lips . . . flaming blood-red eyes . . . A lizard tittered nearby.

Koppan felt nauseous. He felt a slimy taste in his mouth.

He stepped into the yard and washed his face. He plucked a tender coconut and treated his blistered mouth with its sweet milk. Then nonchalantly he went to see Unnicheera and the baby.

'Was it a venomous one?' Unnicheera asked anxiously.

'I don't know!'

'Better to take an antidote!'

'Yes.'

The baby looked angelic in his sleep. Looking at him, Koppan murmured his wish to the midwife.

'I want to hold him once.'

'Not now! It would not be good for the infant. Please wait for a few more days.'

Koppan stood staring at the sleeping baby for a long while.

'I feel so thirsty!' he said.

'I will get some kappi,' the midwife answered.

'No, kappi can aggravate the poison.'

Time slipped by. When it was afternoon, Koppan felt that he could taste blood in his mouth. He started yawning uncontrollably. As a terrible tremor seized him, Koppan recollected the basic lessons taught by his father.

He rushed out in a great hurry.

He searched for neelayamari and the root of tamarind. The midwife brewed a potion from these ingredients. That draught could not lessen his fever. Water boiled with karuka and nalpamara barks could not ease his thirst either.

The next day, his fever reached intolerable levels. The burning of his lips was beyond endurance. As he started suffocating, the son of the renowned poison healer started whimpering desperately.

'Appa, great healer, please help!'

Koppan felt an inner call, as if in answer to his plea. He remembered the Ottamooli, the singular cure that his healer father had once tested on his own self. The invaluable secret that his father had procured from the nomadic healer, after appeasing him with toddy. The medicine that could save life if used meticulously and kill mercilessly if anything went amiss! The fates had decreed that like his father, the son should conduct the same experiment on his own body.

Koppan started his search for the ingredients as per his father's lessons. He entered Ezhuthassan's compound, seemingly unseen. He was wrong in his presumption though.

As he struggled forward in the wild undergrowth, he saw Ezhuthassan in front of him. Koppan was taken aback. He felt remorseful that he should have sought permission before trying to collect the herbs.

Somehow he managed to stammer out his explanation.

'I got bitten by a snake . . . was searching for a herb!'

Ezhuthassan stared at him as if he knew everything. Unexpectedly, he stretched his hands forward. Koppan felt a tremor of inexplicable terror as he saw the rare herbs, complete with roots, intact in Ezhuthassan's hands.

Trembling, Koppan received the offering.

As he handed over the medicinal plant, Ezhuthassan's face became taut and intense.

Looking deeply into Koppan's eyes, Ezhuthassan said, 'So monstrous and repellent! Raw ulcers all over! Go now and never return! Do not make my yard impure.'

Koppan could not comprehend what was being uttered. Again, a sliver of horror passed through him. Something foul was sure to happen. Or was it merely his imagination?

When he reached the bramble gate with the free gift, he wanted to turn and look behind his shoulder. But he desisted out of a gnawing fear inside.

Koppan brewed his special medicine.

The unbending rule was that the medicine should not be tried until the last throes of death. It was impossible to follow that, so Koppan started treating himself, meditating on his father all the while.

Two drops of medicine for each eye. A few drops to be rubbed on the inner soles of both feet. Nine drops beneath the tongue. Then Koppan stretched out on the ground.

Exhaustion filled him. He lay like that for one full day.

On the first day, there was no perceptible change.

On the second day, he felt a slow relief creeping over him.

On the third day, Koppan sensed that he was undergoing some transformations.

After a few days, his skin started cracking and blood seeped to the surface. Slowly ulcers formed all over his body. These got infected badly. The ulcers spread to his lips. His teeth started falling off.

As the stink of rotten blood filled his nostrils, Koppan cried out heartbroken:

'Appa! Where did I err?'

Unnicheera was devastated on seeing Koppan's trauma. The terrified midwife declined to continue working in that home. She did not return.

Koppan never stepped into the daylight again.

28

Vidyarambham: Initiation of Learning

Chinnan Pulayan came to meet Kunjootty with a quaint request. One monsoon season and one half of cold weather had passed since Chiriyankan had left the isle. No one was sure of his return. Anita could not be left to such vagaries of fate. Chinnan wanted to start her education. It was time for her Vidyarambham ceremony, the formal initiation of learning with a guru.

Kunjootty agreed with the idea. The child was almost seven. She had started learning French in her land of birth. If she could be introduced to Malayalam, that would be worthwhile for her too. It would serve as a place for her mind to drop anchor, until her father returned.

'What if we request Ezhuthassan to do the honour?' Kunjootty suggested.

'Do you think he will agree?'

'Let me try.'

'All right with me.'

Kunjootty reached Ezhuthassan's house that evening. When he made his request, Asan did not decline. It seemed to Kunjootty that his mind was wandering elsewhere.

'I had stopped it all, a long time before. 'But since you ask . . .' Ezhuthassan murmured.

'When should we have the ceremony?'

'Why not tomorrow?'

'Any particular time . . . auspicious?'

'Auspiciousness is a mere concept. If the mind is pure, the time will also be pure. Doesn't your Bible also say that rules are for those who are above the rules?'

As Kunjootty stood confused, wondering if it might be there in the Bible. Ezhuthassan continued,

'Don't doubt. Go through the holy book when you reach home. The second and third chapters of "The Letter to the Romans" are simply outstanding!'

Kunjootty felt as if his physical self was crumbling. Ezhuthassan assumed proportions of magnificence beyond his intellectual range at times!

He took leave and started back home.

As he crossed the bramble gate and moved forward, he reached Koppan's house. He wondered whether he should pay a visit.

Many days had passed since Koppan had been seen. He no longer came to Kunjootty's house to help Zavarias in purchasing wholesale stationery items from Kochi. His father had struggled to arrange for labourers. He was displeased with them and often urged Kunjootty to check Koppan's whereabouts. However, Kunjootty had not listened to his father. Every time he stepped through that path, he remembered the night when the stranger had sneaked out through the back door and a sense of revulsion overtook him.

There was no movement anywhere on the front yard.

Kunjootty called out half embarrassed, 'Koppan Chetta!'

The dog lying on the veranda lifted its head. Then, indifferently, it snuck its head back between its paws and went back to sleep.

Unnicheera appeared on the doorway with an infant on her hip. She was slimmer than before. Her skin was glowing.

'Where is Koppan Chettan?' Kunjootty asked her.

Her face fell. Before she could answer, Koppan's voice was heard from within the house.

'Tell him that I cannot see him.'

'It is me, Kunjootty!'

'Whoever it is, I cannot meet you.'

As Kunjootty stood hurt by that stubborn resistance, Unnicheera spoke.

'He is not well.'

'What happened? Let me see!'

Without waiting for a reply, Kunjootty stepped into the house. An appalling stink greeted him. Flies were buzzing all around the room, some mating, some hopping around. A loathsome hideousness lay on the wooden cot inside.

As soon as he saw Kunjootty, Koppan rose with a shout and then collapsed on the manure-plastered floor.

Kunjootty could take only one look.

Unable to continue in those surroundings, feeling nauseated, he stepped out. He felt numb and could hardly breathe properly. It seemed as if the outside air was infected too.

'Are you not getting him treated?' he asked Unnicheera.

'Some herbal remedies . . . No use actually . . . The antidote he tried for the snake bite . . . it went wrong!'

Kunjootty gave some money to Unnicheera. He ignored her grateful look that contained some other sparks and left hastily.

He heard the baby cry as he walked away.

Koppan's son. Koppan's beloved son!

That whole day, the sight of the festering ulcers and horrid stench of Koppan's room regurgitated in Kunjootty's memory. He ruminated over the chilling unpredictability of human life. If the body rotted away, even the dearest family members would hate and abandon the person! The body was a mere structure that could be quickly decomposed by germs. Over an accumulation of excrement, urine, pus and germs, Maya or illusion draped a beautiful covering and stirred desires! If one could open the inner eye for a moment to catch a glimpse of the horrors within the 'beautiful exterior', all attachment to the body would end instantly.

Kunjootty could not eat any food that day. He lied to his mother that he had some digestive problems. He drank the mustard-draught that Eli made, and inspired by Ezhuthassan's words, opened the Bible after a long time.

'For a person is not a Jew who is one outwardly, nor is true circumcision something external and physical. Rather, a person is a Jew who is one inwardly, and real circumcision is a matter of the heart—it is spiritual and not literal. Such a person receives praise not from others but from God.'

* * *

Early the next morning, Chinnan, Chirutha and Kandan came along with Anita to meet Kunjootty. They had brought along rice in a small cloth bag, betel leaves, areca nuts, a silver coin and a plate for the ceremony. Kunjootty led the group to Ezhuthassan's home.

When they reached the bramble gate, Chinnan hesitated to move forward.

'We will stay here. You please proceed with the child.'

He seemed to be ridden by unseen terrors as he mentioned Ezhuthassan's name.

'We will all go together!' Kunjootty gave him courage.

He walked ahead, holding Anita's little hand. Still fearful, the rest of them accompanied Kunjootty.

Before they could reach the front door, Ezhuthassan rushed towards them like the wind, screaming loudly. 'Stop right there!'

It was so unexpected that even Kunjootty found himself shaken. Ezhuthassan's mood seemed to have changed overnight. He seemed to have adopted a very aggressive stance.

'Ezhuthassan! How come you are behaving like this? I have brought the child for the learning ceremony.'

Ezhuthassan stared hard at the plate Anita held, which was filled with different items. Then he glanced at her face. His expression changed and turned more intense and twisted.

'Get away from me!' Shouting thus, he seized the plate and hurled it far away.

The plate crashed with a loud sound, and the rice scattered all over the place. Anita gave a cry of terror and hugged Kunjootty tightly.

Kunjootty had no hint about such a bitter possibility. Something had changed drastically overnight. Instead of aggravating Ezhuthassan further, he bent to retrieve the platter and led the group out of the compound. Ezhuthassan rushed inside the house and shut the door with a great sound.

Anita was weeping even after they had reached the road. Chinnan was devastated too. Kunjootty tried to console them by explaining that Ezhuthassan must be going through some mental imbalance. He promised them that on another auspicious day, the ceremony would be completed. Yet, the ruined Vidyarambham imprinted itself like a terrible disaster in all their hearts. Though Kunjootty tried to analyse it with all known logic, he could not find a justification. It should not have happened at all.

The next day, Kunjootty told Diwakar Menon the story of Ezhuthassan's inexplicable rejection.

After listening to the tale, Menon asked, 'But why did you go searching for Ezhuthassan?'

'Who else is there to initiate her into education?'

'You, who else? That child knows only French! You are the only suitable person around to teach her. She will learn two languages, and you will acquire more proficiency in French.'

'Are you sure about that?'

'Why not? Let us have the ceremony on the coming Sunday. I shall come to Potta Thuruthu too. One gets to see all the sights that have become familiar through your stories.'

The very next day, Menon purchased a slate, a French picture book and a Malayalam beginner's book for Anita and handed them all to Kunjootty.

However, the next Sunday, Diwakar Menon did not reach Potta Thuruthu as he had promised. After waiting for a long time, a rather morose Kunjootty lit a lamp and got ready for Anita's Vidyarambham.

Even before the child could write the first letter of the alphabet, a strong breeze blew and snuffed out the lamp.

29

Metamorphosis

Beyond the bamboo grove in Ezhuthassan's compound was an ancient well, hidden by a profusion of weeds. Further, on the south of the yard were the remnants of the *sarpakkavu*, the sacred place reserved for the worship of the snakes, now dilapidated and moss-ridden. Wild undergrowth covered that area, with creepers and roots shaped like slithering serpents. It was surreal and even intimidating. Yet the presence of a lone kalisha tree tempted many people to trespass into the yard. They surreptitiously crossed over the bramble boundary and sneaked away with the barks of the tree for making the glue into which fishing nets were dipped.

Ezhuthassan remained unaware of these activities. In his solitary, dark days, they had long ceased to perturb him. The old man lived on a plane of existence that precluded everything else.

In the enigmatic grove, serpents with sparkling emeralds crowning their hoods hid themselves craftily. Gods made their presence felt in the grass, the dust and the ruptured roof.

Conversing with all these divine entities, Ezhuthassan crossed the boundaries between reality and hallucinations.

It was in such circumstances that Kunjootty had brought Anita for the learning ceremony. Seeing the young child slowly blossoming in her growth, Ezhuthassan's memories had rushed back to a tainted past. His misdemeanours during the time when wild wax apple blossoms grew lushly. The fading memories involving a twelve-year-old girl . . .

As Ezhuthassan struggled to carry on with the memories flooding him, one night, a call exploded like a great blast and woke him up.

'Govinda!'

It was pitch dark all around him.

Unable to see anything, his heart beating fast, Ezhuthassan whispered, 'Bhagwan!'

There were hoots of death from a night bird outside the window and the sound of flapping bat wings above the decrepit roof.

Ezhuthassan affirmed to himself that the damned creatures had arrived to distract him. The sinful remembrances from previous phases of life started heckling him again. Stains that were yet to be washed clean . . .

Ezhuthassan got up vengefully.

Beneath his cot, dried Catalonian jasmines lay scattered along with wrinkled caper tree seeds and copious amounts of sacred ash. He gathered these and threw them afar.

He washed his face and his limbs, and lit the mud lamp before the picture of Lord Hanuman.

The rebellious bird gave another long trill from the night's secret hideaway. A feeling that someone was spying on him gathered force in Ezhuthassan's mind.

'Kuhoo . . . Kooh . . . Kooh!'

Ezhuthassan listened intently.

'Who is that?'

'Kuhoo . . .Kooh . . .Kooh!'

The same sound again! Ah, an effort was on to disturb the focus of his mind and create obstacles in his path!

He could not afford to make the slightest error now. Extreme caution was called for!

By assuming the Astra Mudra, Ezhuthassan bound down the directions and protected himself.

'Sahasrara Hum Phat!'

Immediately he began Anga-Nyaasa, the installation of his god in his own self so that there was no more differentiation between them.

Haum Hridayaya Namah
Husfrom Sirasse Swaha
Sphrom Shikhayai Vashal
Hasphrom Kavachaya Hum
Husfroum Netrabhyam Vashal
Hasaum Hamumathe Namah
Astraya Phat!

He sat in Padma-asana, the lotus position, and took a deep breath. As Ezhuthassan sat with folded hands and eyes closed tight, the beautiful feet of the Lord appeared in his inner eye. His whole being yearned to touch the radiance of one crore suns, embodied by his favourite deity.

Ezhuthassan started reciting the Anjaneya Dhyana mantra:

Vaame jaanuni vaamabaahumaparam jnanatya mudrayutham
Hruddhese kalayanvrutho muniganair naasagra dathekshana
Aasinaha kadalivane manimaye baalaarka koti prabhaha
Dhyayan brahma param karothumanasa suddhim Hanuman namah.

The left hand on left knee, the right near the heart in Gyana Mudra
Surrounded by many sages, seated in the Kadali Vanam,
With the radiance of a crore young suns, look at Lord Hanuman!
Meditating on Him purifies your mind, and helps to attain Para
Brahma.

Thoughts became untangled and slowly vanished. Ezhuthassan's being awoke with a new energy empowered by the rhythm of the mantras. Staring at the incipient image with his inner eye, Ezhuthassan started forgetting the external realities.

Yet there remained some impediment in that inner sojourn. Asan felt as if someone was observing his inner journey from the outside. His mind started wavering. He could not focus on the divine image in the centre of his mind. The yearning to open his eyes and look around increased intensely.

'Hanuman Kutty!'

Was someone calling him or was it his imagination?

'Hanuman Kutty! Kooh, Kooh!'

Ezhuthassan lost his patience and opened his eyes. He grabbed a flambeau and rushed outside. The cold chilled him to the bones even as he glared into the dark night.

'Who is it, I ask you?' he bellowed.

Unexpectedly, something, like a ship sailing on the sky, darted away after brushing against his head.

'Oww!' Asan shuddered in horror. His heartbeats acquired the frenzy of a drum. He raised his light at the creature that was returning towards him.

It was a bat! The creature was on the prowl at night. Having feasted on the nectar of the tender banana flowers, it was intoxicated and fluttering its wings wildly.

After all, who else would be awake at this odd hour in the freezing night? All these were attempts to lead him astray, Asan concluded.

The frozen sky above was dense with dark clouds. Not even a firefly could be seen shimmering around. By the light of his flaming torch, Ezhuthassan wove his way through dense shrubs, aiming for the pond. He wanted to dip his body into the cold depths. That was the only way to regain control over his madly undulating mind.

In the light of the flambeau, the Samadhi Griham, the house of the dead, reared its head like an unhealed old wound. Ezhuthassan could hear the moist whimpering and sighs of his ancestors emerging from within the closed door.

'Govinda, dear child! Please free us!'

Leaving behind his hungry forbearers, languishing due to lack of rituals and sacrifices, Ezhuthassan walked on with determination. As he reached the kalisha tree, he saw that all the barks had been sundered forcefully by someone.

Who had dared to cross the bramble gate?

The serpent grove was one step away.

The stone steps lay decrepit; creepers, cobwebs spread out all around, and everything was draped in an uncanny mystery.

Perhaps a golden-skinned serpent lay in wait amid the dark greenery around. Pointing his light at the secretive grove, Asan stared intently at it. There was an invasion of the devil weed— Communist Pacha plant—which had polluted the sacred grounds. Let alone the emerald carrying serpent king, not even a water snake could be seen anywhere in that vicinity.

Perhaps the serpents had perished within their dark nesting places in the stone ledges. He had not been worshipping them with what they desired: the legendary Noorum Palum ritual—milk and turmeric, tender coconut water and areca nut flowers. This was to appease them and solicit their benign blessings. Maybe they had cursed as they died out, one by one.

Why had the rituals been conducted anyway? What was the need for the knowledge that his grandfather had taught him, that the Naga was the living embodiment of Kundalini Shakti? He could never devote himself to any divinity or incarnation in his life!

Ezhuthassan felt something slithering between his feet. Irritated, he kicked out and walked hurriedly. This too was a testing ground. He should not stand brooding hereabouts.

Asan breathed in relief only after reaching the still pool. He planted the burning torch firmly on the black sand. The reflection of the fiery flames started spreading on the water surface.

He removed his mundu and left it on the first stone step. Only the loin cloth and the black thread looped around his waist remained on his body.

He was aware of many a menacing presence eager to waylay his mind. Most were in the guise of shadows.

The first step was crossed safely.

The pool was lying below.

He carefully crossed the second stone step too.

One by one, his feet traversed the remaining steps. Finally, they touched the cold water. As he stepped down further, the water reached up to his knees. By the next step, it covered his waist. Ezhuthassan felt a searing cold envelop him.

There were no more steps.

If he was not careful, he would be sucked in by the treacherous mud of the deep pond. Ezhuthassan imagined that he had successfully crossed all the tempting barriers of his sensory organs.

Water rose from the waist to the chest. Now only the head stood above the water.

Ezhuthassan forgot all the discomforts wrought by old age.

Controlling his mind that tended to slip away from the boundaries set by the water, his lips recited the Dhyana mantra:

Dahanatapta suvarna samaprabham
Bhayaharam hridaye vihitanjalim
Kanakakundala shobhitambujam
Namatha vanararajamihatbhutam

Like molten gold, his great radiance
Removes fear if you meditate on Him.
Golden earrings on that lotus–like face
I bow before the magnificent King of Monkeys!

Recollecting the precious mantras inscribed on the palmyra leaves, Ezhuthassan started enunciating them with extreme attention. His consciousness was dissolving into something ineffable beyond time and space.

Haum husfrom sphrom hasfrom
Husfroum hasaum Hanumate Namah

Hanuman Kutty! Kooh, kooh!
Hasfrem Sfrem hum saum
Hamsfrem hasaum
Hanuman Kutty! Hanuman Kutty!

Ezhuthassan became frantic to perceive the happenings of the external world. As a frog jumped into the water from its perch on the stone step, his body shuddered heavily; his foot clamped to the mud. When the water rocked wildly and rose to his forehead, Ezhuthassan opened his eyes and screamed!

'Hanuman!!!'

The echoes intermingled in the serpent grove and the pond side, while a colony of terrified bats fled the scene.

Ezhuthassan turned into an incandescent being, inundated with a new knowledge!

A great strength had passed into him, overcoming all the chakras.

His feet, hands, body, head . . . an untrammelled force filled all of his physique.

Youthful energy filled his old limbs!

'Owww!'

His courage was that of the one who could not be harmed with weapons. His ferocity was that of the one who could not be touched by fire. His radiance was that of the one who would never know death.

The magnificent strength of Lord Hanuman.

Hanuman . . . he had transformed into Hanuman himself!

In that recognition, as the last of the threads of sanity connecting him to the real world fell apart, the son of Anjani leapt out of the pool and raced madly through the darkest corners of the yard, weaving his way through the decaying serpent grove.

During that frantic caper, Hanuman discovered his old tail, the great tail that had burnt Lanka down, tangled amid a few banana trees. He plucked the bark of the banana tree ferociously, tied it up with his loin cloth and hung it like a tail. Puffing up his cheeks, with his eyes protruding, Hanuman jumped from side to side before bellowing the proclamation of his victory:

'Poohooey!'

Hearing that shrill invocation, Potta Thuruthu woke up, even before dawn set in.

30

A Journey to the Estuary

Isaac travelled back and forth to the capital city relentlessly. At the end of many journeys filled with tensions and fraught with hopes, having spent lots of money, he managed to escape the police case. By the time Kunjootty met him, his natural enthusiasm, which had abandoned Isaac in between, seemed to have returned. The 'wilderness' that had spread over his face had been shaved off and he looked fresh.

Seated on a patch of abundant couch grass near the riverside, Isaac spoke:

'Now I know one fact! You can get a star from the sky, if you hurl money at it!'

'But then your peace of mind remains at someone's disposal. Can money retrieve that for you?'

'What you say is true. That is why I have decided to stop the lumber deal. I felt like a jungle animal, sneaking in the dark . . . no food, no sleep and no peace at all!'

'I have always been your solitary listener whenever you swore a futile new oath. And I have not seen any fructified till now!'

'This one is going to work out fine! The visit to the capital city had that positive effect. Listen, I have a new project planned out.'

'What is it about?'

'A change from timber to shrimps!'

A siren sounded from a far-off ship harbouring in Kochi, and the sounds merged with Isaac's words. Kunjootty felt that this change of direction from timber to shrimp had an innate incompatibility.

'Why are you looking so unconvinced? I have been planning it for a long time. It is a plan to catch shrimps from the deep end of the lagoon, after building up exclusive embankments. Perhaps I might have to work hard in the beginning . . . that is fine. Why are you staring like this?'

'I am just listening.'

'I plan to get some portion of the lagoon in my name, cordon it off and convert that space to shrimp farms. How does it sound?'

'I have no comments.'

Kunjootty leaned against a tender coconut sapling and looked up at the sky. He could see cracks in the wings of the blue clouds above. Silver sunlight dripped through those fissures and made him blink.

'You have started negating it already?' Isaac was annoyed.

'How does my objection count in your plans, anyway? Yet I find myself incapable of comprehending such grand plans nowadays. What is it that we are all relentlessly searching for? In a short journey entailing at most fifty or sixty years, we are chasing after such grandiose desires. At the end, would all these help us in anyway? I don't know . . .'

'Great Vedanta!' Isaac grinned mockingly. 'This sort of stuff calls for guts and gumption. If everyone remained silent and meek like you, the basket would remain empty!'

'I agree. There are some common habits ruling us. The hunger of a stomach of a few inches' length. The other hunger, stirring a few inches beneath. Like animals, we too live by appeasing these two hungers. If life is merely a hunger that can be fed by eating once and a lust that can be satiated by having intercourse once, why then trump it up as something great?'

'Those are pretty outdated arguments, my friend! When you live in this world, think of the material world. What is the use of muttering meaningless words like death, virtue, moksha and dropping such heavy words as existential dilemma and Maya? It is all a big fraud! That's essentially running away from reality and the challenges of life. The courage lies in facing life. Those who cannot handle life are the ones who seek refuge in Vedanta and Sanyasa, shy away from physical efforts and end up useless to this world!' Isaac was in no mood to concede his viewpoint.

'If the measure of usefulness happens to be the amount of money they handle, you might be right! But even if someone has a crore in his hand but has no peace of mind, what is the use? If a beggar gets a coin and experiences happiness that a rich guy cannot gain while earning his millions, who is the lucky one among them? The beggar is happier than the millionaire! You have built that shrimp farm in your mind. That mind will jump like a mischievous monkey from timber to shrimp! Until you control that monkey, you will be enslaved by it.

'So, I feel that a sanyasi who goes deep into the mind and travels even beyond, is doing a karma that is more evolved.

To judge that as an act of cowardice could be due to a wrong perspective, right? Real guts and gumption are required in taking that path. When we succumb to the pettiness of our own little minds, a true sanyasi stays detached and free! We sit on top of a horse that is dragging us in multiple directions. We brag that we are "facing challenges". And when a yogi controls that wild horse with great mastery, we tend to mock him, saying he does not have the courage to ride it! The real strength is in not allowing that horse to move, is it not?' Kunjootty argued with conviction.

'Oh, great! Why don't you adorn yourself with saffron clothes and staff and begin renunciation? May the world become blessed by the doings of Kunjootty Ananda Swami!'

'Of course, the tendency to taunt anything that cannot be comprehended or that doesn't suit our tastes is endemic to our generation. One doesn't need saffron for it. If only one can embark on a journey with no regrets . . . after untangling all the knots of life. With absolutely no possessions, with no thought for the morrow, just start walking . . . Sleep under a banyan tree, eat the food offered from a place of worship, then again walk onwards . . . no conditions or attachments involved. However, I cannot undertake one. I am a sinner.'

'Do you actually mean all this stuff that you are blabbering?'

'Everyone will have such a desire somewhere in the corner of their mind.'

'Nonsense! A crazy thought emanating from an intense sense of loss. An escape route for cowards!'

'Not at all. Difficulties and losses are all coincidental events pointing the way like a signboard. I have endured so many deaths and disappearances. Very often, I feel that I do not belong to this world. Not just a mere feeling, there is a strong sense of truth in that. Can you tell me that you are a contented man?'

'I have no idea!'

'There is a tinge of disgruntlement in your answer. You are jumping from one thing to another in search of an elusive happiness that you suspect to be hiding somewhere. One loves one's mother or smokes a cigarette—all for one's own satisfaction. You give a blind beggar some coins because you want to calm your own agitated mind. You may call it compassion or kindness towards your brethren. Even that, if you analyze it deeper, happens to be mere selfishness. When you say that one should tackle challenges and live a worthy life, you are simply fibbing.

'Everyone is searching for pleasure. The challenges happen to occur in that singular quest; there is no other way than to face them. So, this much vaunted "challenge" is just a byproduct of selfishness. Real courage is needed to annihilate that selfishness seeking petty pleasures. How can that be termed "running away" or "cowardice"? Only those who have exceptional fortitude would attempt that. The strong, incidentally, never brags about their strength. OK, let us stop this discussion right here!

'So long as one cannot actualize these thoughts, they will remain paper tigers. A trickery with words akin to a clown's dress. The mind is so much attached to this world! But I will cross that stage once. Perhaps in my next birth,' Kunjootty concluded.

'May you cross that stage in this life itself! My hearty wishes for that!' Isaac replied sarcastically.

'Thank you for your kindness! In the middle of my soliloquy, I forgot to inquire about your affairs. Tell me, how do you plan to get access to the outer lagoon?'

'Good that you are being practical now. I might have to negotiate purchases with small shrimp farm owners. Then I will have to get government permission to ensure that the adjoining lagoon area comes under my control. I have managed the necessary deals. All that running around was for that goal.'

'You have been like this always. Only at the last moment do you reveal anything significant.'

'See, that has never been intentional.'

Kunjootty was observing the waves of the river shattering noisily against the stone boulders. More and more waves were hastening to destroy themselves.

'I want to finish this job fast. I plan to go boating tomorrow in the lagoon to survey the area.'

'The project must need quite a bit of capital.'

'Yes, many lakhs of rupees. I might have to mortgage whatever I have right now. But then I am sure to get it all back. Do not stare at me like that! I am getting into a partnership. Might have to borrow considerable money.'

'Is it worth it, Isaac?'

'Of course! Do you think I'll venture into dumping stones inside the lagoon if not for my certainty? After one season of harvesting, you will see my shrimps ruling the foreign markets!'

Kunjootty watched a lone bird sitting all hunched up on a wooden stump emerging from the chest of the river. It was a kingfisher, with a splash of red and blue on its body. After biding its time, the kingfisher swooped into the water and emerged with a small fish in its beak. Again, it started its false meditation on the wooden perch, with half closed eyes.

'Look! A fish, lustily swimming in the safety of the river, is now inside the kingfisher's stomach.' Kunjootty observed.

'You think it is a bad omen, is it so?' Isaac asked.

'I do not have the gift of reading portents.'

The scene of the struggling fish and the bird made a deep impression on Kunjootty's mind. Isaac sat quietly for a while, enveloped in loops of cigarette smoke.

'I need some help in transporting some material from Kochi. Is Koppan around?'

'Yes, but he is very sick.'

'What happened?'

'He was bitten by a poisonous snake. His body is totally covered with ulcers.'

'How pitiful!'

As they returned, Isaac invited Kunjootty. 'Please come with me for that boat trip tomorrow!'

Kunjootty acquiesced.

Snipping the couch grass with his fingers and staring at the flow of the lagoon, Kunjootty sat brooding. Once upon a time there was a lagoon with no beginning or end. Perhaps the wording should change: it had no beginning. Now, stone embankments would come up right in her breast, dividing and separating the waters. Boats filled with rocks and boulders would soon make their way over the river, disturbing her serenity. The artificial partitions within the backwaters would soon shatter the intricate balance of the natural ecosystem. Perhaps the next generation would be left wondering about the 'great ancient wonders': the ritual of shrimp harvesting during Krishna Paksha, and the Pachuvanchi fishing rite during the opportune time at dusk.

Suddenly Kunjootty woke up from his reverie at a loud shout from the opposite shore.

'Hooey!' Movements could be discerned in the broken screw-pine bushes afar. The figures became clear: mostly children, yelling and laughing. They were running towards the river, chasing someone. A man, almost stark naked, was running like a wild animal, fleeing from that rabble.

Kunjootty sat shocked to the core.

A banana bark trailing behind his loin cloth, Ezhuthassan was leaping and jumping crazily into the air.

'Rama! Rama!' Sliding through the furious flow of the river, touching the deep darkness of Potta Thuruthu, Hanuman's voice wandered around . . .

The eyes of the son of the Wind God were popping out from the sockets; his cheeks were puffed up and hands folded together.

'Hanuman Kutty!'

A mocking voice from the crowd rang out. The onlookers laughed raucously, relishing the crass joke, but Ezhuthassan seemed oblivious of it.

Hanuman was in search of Sita. The incomparable monkey army of Lord Rama accompanied him. It was time now for burning Lanka down.

The winds of Treta Yuga blew over the river. Recognizing the Wind God, the leaves of the screw-pine bushes flailed wildly.

Eager to understand what was happening, Kunjootty rushed towards to the jetty and untied the boat. He started rowing hard, desperate to reach the other shore.

Far away, Sita waited with flowing tears, beneath the asoka tree. Hanuman was starting his journey, after accepting the signet ring of Lord Rama, to destroy the clan of Rakshasas.

As the son of the Wind God glared at them, the black birds started flying away frantically. Getting ready for his leap, Hanuman started calculating the distance to Lanka. Today, he would conquer this ocean that protected Lanka. He was the mighty warrior who had once leapt to eat the sun. The one who had threatened to eat Iravat, Indra's white elephant! In one leap, Lanka would be under his feet.

An Indian jungle crow, revered as the incarnation of the ancestor's soul, sat forlornly on a tree branch, cawing inauspiciously. By that time, having thrashed his long tail on the ground, Hanuman had leapt from the peak of Mahendra Giri. Over the sea, through the transparent clouds, leaving the wind behind in his speed, overcoming a hundred *yojanas*!

Hanuman was floating in the air.

Floating, floating . . . Then, a dizzying descent . . .

Losing control, Ezhuthassan sank into the depths of the nameless river of Potta Thuruthu.

In the strong rush of the river, water circles burst and ripples scattered all around.

The river transformed into the accursed Punjikasthala. The woman, who had been doing penance for centuries to conceive Hanuman in her womb, was being granted salvation today.

Entrapped by the ferocious flow of the river, the weak limbs moving weakly, Ezhuthassan's emaciated body surfaced for a few moments. The islanders stood motionless and stunned at that sight.

Kunjootty too watched as Ezhuthassan started drowning, unable to swim any longer. The precious soul connection, forged during his student days in Ezhuthassan's village school, churned up within. Unwilling to forsake that relationship, Kunjootty dived into the river, which was rushing like a mad woman to the estuary. By the time Kunjootty swam up to Ezhuthassan and pulled him up by his hair, the frail body was motionless.

Carrying the heaviest of life's burdens on his back, fighting against the river's forceful flow, Kunjootty reached the shore and collapsed among the reeds. A crowd thronged around him, as people rushed from all sides.

Ezhuthassan's stomach was swollen like that of a fully pregnant woman. Somebody made him lie on his stomach and started pressing his back forcefully, making the old man throw up the ingested river water.

'Govindan Kutty Asan!'

The keen student of the erstwhile village school desperately shook his first guru's prostrate body. Sounds emerged slowly, from the valley of unconsciousness, with the hesitation accompanying a small child's first syllables.

'I . . . am . . . coming! Hanu . . . man! Rama!'

31

Humongous Transformations

The boats filled with granite travelled through the river, like malignant ghosts prowling around to devastate the ancient isle. One by one, they trooped in. Then they unburdened themselves, dumping the stone cargo in the heart of the lagoon. The stones, stacked one upon another, jutted out from the pristine waters like an inadvertent error.

Many manual labourers toiled day and night ceaselessly. They shoved in mud and sand on top of the stones and built dykes. They worked even on Sundays, as if partaking of a holy ritual.

Chaitra, Ashada and Ashwina, all three months passed by in that manner. Cast down by the accumulated sins wearying her heart, the lagoon had lost her true face by then.

No one listened to the lamentations of the lagoon. Rather, busying themselves in setting up the bulwarks and barriers of stone within the river, they ignored the wails. Kunjootty was transcribing that transformation in his blue-covered diary, as illustrative notes for his *Book of Exodus*.

He believed that the lagoon had her own mind. Sighs, grievances and the agonizing footprints of her own exile . . . With sensitivity, one could discern all these.

The Araya people had their God's house—Daiva Pura—by the side of the lagoon. In the past, before the stone walls and the polluting gases, the outcastes were denied permission to worship the deities in the temples belonging to the dominant castes. There were divisions among the outcastes too. The Mannadiyar people considered the Araya as untouchable and denied them entry into their temples.

The Araya in turn ostracized the Pulaya and Paraya castes and forbade them from visiting their Daiva Pura! The Arayas appointed Dwarapalikas—Guardians of the Gate—holding shining swords, at the thresholds of worship. If these gatekeepers saw a child belonging to the Pulaya caste anywhere in the vicinity, they would rush at him ferociously, brandishing their swords.

'You swine! Clear off from here!'

That was the way they protected their clan's gods from getting polluted.

The upper-caste landlords, who created hierarchies among the gods, magnanimously allowed certain monstrous gods to the Parayas and Pulayas. These people started appeasing these subsidiary deities that included 'Marutha', embodying the souls who had met an unnatural death, the single-breasted 'Ottamulachi', supposedly a cannibal, and the hideous demigod, 'Rakshas'.

When the Pulaya women gave birth, the men would stand obsequiously at a distance from the home steads of the upper-caste landlords and call out humbly: 'I have been blessed with a child!'

Only the master could anoint the child with a name. The great one would announce the names soon enough.

Name him Chathan. Or call her Kali.

Burying deep the sweet and charming names that they had dreamed of for their beloved children, the men would return with benumbed minds. Their children grew up as Kali and Chathan. When the boy became a young man, he was enslaved by the master. The dark beauty Kali, on reaching her adolescence, became pregnant in the master's secret hideaway. After nine months of carrying her shameful burden, she too gave birth. The girl was fair in complexion.

'She shall be named Pothi!' the master announced.

Pothi too was sexually abused by the master and his son when she reached puberty. Like animals, these men did not distinguish between daughter or sister. So many Pothis had to carry the bloodline of their own fathers and brothers in their wombs.

Some of them sought refuge in the branches of the kalisha tree or in the secret recesses of the backwaters. Those who could not gather courage for that gave birth to the children of shame.

Many rituals for the ancestors occurred in Potta Thuruthu year after year. Slowly the rituals and customs started mutating and vanishing. Finally, every twilight, a lone light burned before the deity Neendakara Muthan. Those who were denied the power to worship the Lord of Annihilation had to satisfy themselves by placating the leader of his army.

Having acquired the legacy of worship, the head of the *tharavadu*, the main household, would arrive every year wearing a garland of hibiscus flowers, with a sword in hand. There, in front of the Muthan, the oracle would enter into a trance, dancing while uttering the mantras. The human identity being displaced, possessed by the unknown, howling around like a disembodied wild spirit, sacred paste smeared on his forehead, he would quench the hunger and thirst of the Muthan and usher in Potta Thuruthu's prosperity.

The isle, which had thrived under the shielding gaze of the Muthan, now seemed to have shrunk in all ways. The ancient rituals had now been relegated to mere formalities, losing their sheen. When the temples opened to all, many sought the gods belonging to the higher echelons. The circumambulating of the temple flagpole and the worshipping of the ornate architecture of the temples gave them immense satisfaction. Those who could not attain that solace, nurtured in their hearts an intense hatred for the gods.

'We turn our face away from those Gods, who had turned their faces from us all this while!'

Smug in their new stature of wisdom, they ridiculed the superstitious temple worshippers. Yet, on encountering a sudden mishap, they too could not help invoking the Goddess instinctively!

The present generation in Potta Thuruthu hardly remembered any prayer ritual of Muthan. The next generation was destined to totally forget their legacies of Kettuppattu, singing with the accompaniments of drum instruments and the Bhimanattam, the dance based on the Mahabharata. Losing the last threads of their rich native culture, they would become enslaved by a new one.

Kunjootty did not believe that the lagoon would last till then. Only the stone partitions would remain. Today, watching the humongous transformations, some hearts were still pained. Their response on observing the huge concrete jungles and the false grandeur of the fast-growing cities were at least chronicled somewhere.

In such a depiction, a father was holding on to his son's tiny finger and pointing at a flat. He was saying,

'Look at that, my son! The lagoon lies somewhere far beyond that building. I had seen it when I was your age.'

The wounded self-mockery in that anecdote was fast turning into an ugly reality. Isaac too had joined forces with the dominating consumerist culture.

Kunjootty's days limped by as he ruminated on the happenings around and jotted them down in his diary. His listlessness in daily life soon invited criticism. It started off as loving admonishments, which soon assumed the form of reproaches and grave strictures.

It was his mother, Eli, who initiated the process.

Eli started encroaching into the depressing gloominess of Kunjootty's room, the brooding ambience of the riverside, and the unconcern and lethargy he exhibited at the dining table.

'Don't think that you can avoid everything and continue in this manner. How long will you stay unmarried?'

Kunjootty knew that he had run out of excuses. For his ordinary mother, the fact that the lagoon was slowly vanishing or the rituals of the Muthan were getting forgotten were irrelevant. Even so, whenever his mother started with her peeves, he would hurriedly finish his meal, escape to his room or seek the moist solace of the riverside.

One day, when he could not find a way out, Kunjootty muttered, 'I need some more time!'

'It has been a long while since I have been hearing this excuse! There is an age for everything. What impediment is holding you back now?'

Impediment!

Many memories awoke in Kunjootty. A cursed Sunday, a sin that lay heavily in his heart, a wound that no *Exodus* could heal . . . His mother knew nothing. All that had lain quietly within him, sprouted together, waking up from their seed-like sleep. Perhaps he should have confessed everything much earlier. Did he have such a hankering for this worthless life?

In his effort to wriggle out, Kunjootty said, 'Let me pull on, without any trouble to others.'

Eli raised her voice.

'Now what is your intention, tell me! What a bright lad you were! Now, you just sit brooding in your room all the while, scribbling something or the other. You don't talk to anyone either! What happened to you, my child?'

Eli got exhausted after her rather long monologue. Her complaints and vexations, typical of her age, were beginning to irritate Kunjootty. He got up in a miff.

'This cursed place! I do not want to live here any more.'

Eli felt as if she had been slapped. Her son's stubbornness infected her too.

'Okay then! No rice shall be cooked in this house again. For whom should I prepare food?'

Kunjootty could not oppose her any more. Too many offences and mistakes had been committed already. His mind and thoughts were no longer under his control. It was a dangerous situation, leading nowhere.

'Forgive me!' Kunjootty prayed to the food on his plate. Like a prisoner of war, he returned to his seat and started eating.

Apprehensive that her son might leave without eating the food made Eli ingest silence. She tried to retrieve memories in the lull cast between them—scolding the boisterous boy who would always be found swimming and diving in the river; drying his wet hair with her upper cloth; not fully satisfied, how she would try to dry even the unseen water drops; rubbing in the Rasnadi ayurvedic powder used to prevent cold and cough, procured from Sadanand *vaidyan*'s shop on his little head. There was no likelihood of her upper cloth ever getting wet with her son's river-soaked hair again. He had stopped using Rasnadi powder a long time ago.

By the time Kunjootty finished his food and looked up, Eli was leaning against the door, staring unblinkingly at him. As her eyes met his own, she turned her face away—as if afraid of an unforeseen tragedy—and moved forward to pick up the plates. Kunjootty perceived that the stone walls rising in the lagoon could also get replicated in human hearts.

The ancient sages were right: whatever one saw outside was but a reflection of his own inner mirror.

'Yatraisha jagadabhasah darpananthapuram yadha!'

The next day at office, sluggishness gripped Kunjootty. He was not able to take an interest in anything at all. A pile of unresolved files, the humming fan circling above and silence sticking up like a termite mound in the midst.

'What happened to you, Kunjootty?' Diwakar Menon asked. Possibly he had seen the perplexity on his friend's face.

'Nothing at all!' Kunjootty shrugged. Menon returned to his own cocoon of contemplation. He had become utterly silent nowadays. After the first confession, he had not elaborated more on that inadvertent meeting with his ex-wife or its aftermath. Sometimes he was absent from office. Then he would appear unexpectedly. It was as if he marched to a tune that was beyond normal rules and regulations. Many complaints had been filed against him already, accusations of tardiness and indiscipline being prominent. There was a strong likelihood of his transfer too.

Who could guess the upheaval happening within human beings? Each was tangled up in his own problems, unique and self-contradictory at times. Yet Kunjootty found himself yearning for a single measuring technique to assess all conflicts. Some underpinning where all incongruities could merge.

That evening, when Kunjootty returned from office, Isaac was waiting with a boat. Kunjootty was eager for a diversion too. So he clambered inside the boat without intimating his mother or having his cup of tea. As the boat sped away, churning up the waves, Eli, who was watching, sighed deeply from behind a pillar.

The lagoon looked forlorn, as if bereft of hope. To avoid shaking the foundations of the half-completed barricades inside the lagoon, Isaac slowed the boat. The imperceptible colour changes of the sky, a harbinger of the sunset, could be seen reflected on the backwaters. Inside the circular enclosures of stone walls, some men could be seen casting their nets; the poor folk who subsisted on the lagoon for their daily bread. The backwaters in which their small skiffs could go fishing freely was being taken away from them. When the forbidding blockades became complete, the islanders would lose their fishing rights over these areas. The painful question of their livelihood and the cries of their hungry children would haunt the lagoon.

Kunjootty was deeply affected by what he saw.

'Isaac, can't you see these people?' he asked.

'Who? The fishermen?'

'Yes.'

'Let these enclosures get finished. I won't let anyone trespass into these areas!'

'But this is their lagoon. They survive by fishing on these waters.'

'That is an old story! Now it belongs to its new owner, Isaac. Nobody has any right over my property.'

'Why should someone's livelihood be wrested away from him for another to turn rich? Would such riches last, Isaac?'

'I have already told you that I am not in the least interested in Vedanta!'

'Do you not feel a prick of conscience? How will these people live?'

'There is another Vedanta that if God could create a gaping mouth, he would show the way to appease it too!'

'It won't be as easy as you say. These are hungry men you are dealing with! I even apprehend that they might join forces and oppose you!'

'I have planned for that too! Perhaps even police intervention!'

Kunjootty felt that his ancestors and their flight of escape were stepping back into the scene. These were the times when the seeds for multiple exoduses were being sowed. His mind whispered that those would soon ripen in the forms of murderous mobs in boats, brandishing burning torches.

Would that form another black chapter in the *Book of Exodus*?

32

The End of a Journey

Fire serpents were slithering among the clouds. Koppan was hunkering down under a thick blanket when thunderclaps followed.

The baby, asleep in his cradle, woke up startled and began wailing. The crying continued for a long time, yet Unnicheera did not come to console him.

Koppan became worried.

Where had the child's mother gone?

Somehow he struggled up from his mattress. His joints creaked in great agony. Yet he stumbled his way to the room from which the baby's screams rose.

'The child is weeping!' Koppan said, as if to himself. He wished to take the baby from the cloth, cradle and rock him in his arms. But how could he touch him with his lacerated hands? How could he kiss him with his ulcer-stricken lips? Even an infant would loathe him.

Reaching the cradle, Koppan looked at the child.

'Don't cry, child! Your amma will come soon!'

The baby was inconsolable.

The intensity of his cries increased in tandem with the furious rhythm of rain pattering on the roof.

Where had Unnicheera gone in the wretched rain, leaving the baby alone?

When Koppan reached the southern room searching for Unnicheera, he felt as if struck by lightning. He could make out two human forms in the gathering darkness. One of them sprang up, rushed out of the back door and disappeared in the darkness and rain. It was the time when the serpents came out from their holes to savour the freshly scented earth.

'What are you braying for?'

Unnicheera hissed like a disgruntled female snake, interrupted during coitus.

Koppan felt an intense disgust.

'Do you want to give birth once more?'

Unnicheera stood shocked and pale. In a moment she overcame her emotions and answered.

'That is my freedom! Who are you to ask?'

The woman's insolent response was too much for Koppan to bear. He started screaming at her.

'Such women are called whores!'

'What are you good for anyway?' A primitive expression came over Unnicheera's face. 'Look at the useless husband! How many days since you brought home a paisa? How do you think we are surviving?'

Koppan stood panting heavily. He had no more weapons, no more wars to win. Only a dark, ungrateful night awaited him now.

The infant was flailing his little limbs inside the cloth cradle. The pure, innocent child, who did not understand the meaning of sin. He should not cry in this manner. If he cried, he would grow up. What would happen when he would grow up?

Koppan reached the infant's side. The whimpering had now weakened and sounded like the thin notes of the snake worshipper's traditional string instrument. His face had the radiance of innocence. The infant's cries opened the recesses of Koppan's heart.

'Appa!' His son was calling out to him.

'My son!' The father's arms were stretched for an ardent embrace.

Koppan's fingers, swollen with pus, touched the baby's tender skin for the first time. In a sudden impulse, he lifted the infant and embraced him.

'Oh God! My baby!'

Unnicheera came rushing like the wind and stretched her arms. Koppan was determined not to let go of the child. A direct combat was the only way now.

'Let go, I tell you, let go of my baby! Someone please help! He is killing my child!'

Accompanying the loud cries of the mother and son, the rain became intense, and yet another lightning flashed across the skies. Thousands of toadstools sprouted from unseen, moist sanctuaries.

Unnicheera snarled wildly, 'Give me my child! You will infect him with leprosy too!'

The lightning in the sky whizzed through Koppan's heart now. His hands weakened. His mind lost its strength. He slowly plucked the child from his chest and laid him inside the cradle.

No, no . . . the child should never get infected with his sickness.

Unnicheera rushed towards her child.

'Owww . . . My baby stinks! Why don't you get lost, damn you!'

Whatever was simmering within Koppan exploded and shattered into many pieces. An endless thirst and panic filled him.

Without looking back at Unnicheera, ignoring the infant's wails, Koppan stepped into the compassion of the rain. He wrapped himself head to foot with the blanket.

Koppan saw the silent dog lying curled up on the porch. The useless creature, without the potency to guard the house against trespassers.

'Bbhuu!'

Koppan felt like giving it a vicious kick. Then he felt a stab of remorse. He was the one who had mutilated the creature's life.

Losing his sense of direction, he stood stranded in the darkness. The burning thirst was consuming him, and he desperately needed a drink or two of toddy.

Koppan stepped inside the boat that was drenched in the rain and rowed against the wind towards the opposite shore. He made his way through the ridges and reached Edappadathu House.

Light from a room trickled out and mingled with the rain.

A mumble emerged from the huddled form wrapped by the blanket.

'Hey, son!'

The *Book of Exodus* lay open under the circle of light emanating from the table lamp. Kunjootty, caught in the random chapters scattered around, heard the call from his open window.

'Who is it?'

'It is me, Koppan!'

'Koppan Chettan! What are you doing in this heavy rain? Come inside, please.'

'No, I cannot. Can you do me a favour?'

'What?'

'I will not be able to return it . . . but can you please lend me a hundred rupees?'

'Of course! Here, take this.' Kunjootty retrieved two five-hundred-rupee notes from the table drawer and extended it to Koppan.

'I need only a hundred rupees. For toddy.'

'Keep it. The rest you can use for drinking tomorrow.'

'I won't drink tomorrow. I am stopping it tonight.'

The eyes shining from within the blanket withdrew themselves back into the thick protection. Kunjootty stared helplessly at the soaking wet blanket, which was receiving all the bitter incriminations of the rain.

'Why don't you step inside?'

'No, I have to go now . . .'

Koppan sharpened his ears to catch the roar of the sea from afar. Remembrances of past happiness, when he would decipher the sea by listening to the sound from the empty seashells, came welling up in his heart. The nights when he would go fishing— the call of the lagoon, his Pachuvanchi, the opportune time of the dusk.

Almost like a soliloquy, he uttered:

'Everything is over now. I don't think we will go adventuring in the backwaters again, son!'

'Why do you say that, Koppan Chetta?'

'Nothing, let me leave now.'

'Are you feeling better now? The sickness must have reduced.'

'All the diseases will disappear if I take a dip in the lagoon!' Koppan smiled. 'The backwaters will not hate me even if the wounds are infected. It will suffocate me with its love.'

'Koppan Chetta!'

'I will never return this money to you.'

'That is fine.'

Koppan looked at Kunjootty once more. The sky, the river, the shore, all had the same colour now—black.

Koppan made his way back to the boat. Kunjootty watched from his window as the boat moved further and further away.

As Koppan entered the toddy shop, which was lit by a hurricane lamp, he covered himself all over tightly. Seating himself on a bench in an obscure corner, he called out:

'Kali, one bottle of toddy!'

Kali recognized that voice instantly. She lifted the lamp and raised it to shine on the soaking blanket-clad figure.

'Ayyo! Why did you come here?'

'Don't shout, Kali. Please give me a bottle of toddy.'

'Get out fast. No toddy for you.'

'I have money to pay.'

'Who wants money touched by a leper?'

Kali spat contemptuously.

Specks of spittle fell on Koppan's face. Other drinkers stared at Koppan from the benches nearby.

'How you stink! I told you, get out from here!'

'So you won't give me toddy, is it so?'

'I will hit you with my broom if you don't get out!'

'Let me see that!' Koppan fulminated. Throwing away his blanket, he yelled wildly: 'Fill your eyes with my sight. Now you hit me with your broom.'

A body full of stinking lacerations and ulcers! Kali could not take another look. She stood frozen in shock. Then, recovering momentarily from the horror, caught between loathing and panic, she screamed for help: 'Chupra, Chankara! Come running, boys! Get this damned man out!'

When the tall, dark men came running, they too stood helplessly after taking one look at Koppan.

'You sons of a bitch! Hit me if you can!'

The sons of a bitch did not hit Koppan.

As they stood cowering, Koppan turned proudly. Grabbing two bottles of toddy, he threw a five hundred rupee note at Kali.

'Keep the money, even if it is leprosy-ridden! Koppan wants no favours from anyone.'

Seated in front of the frightened onlookers, Koppan finished drinking both the bottles. He felt hugely amused that the people staring at him were frightened of his rotting skeletal body.

He laughed out loudly. At the end of that laugh, tears welled up in his eyes. These mixed with the rain drops on his forehead and flowed downwards.

'Kali . . . I am leaving now!'

As Koppan bid his familiar goodbye without a tinge of malice, Kali stood silently. She could not understand why she felt gloomy on hearing those words today.

Kali wished that Koppan would start singing his sardonic song once again.

'Kali tricked me, adding water to the toddy
I tricked her too, by giving false coins shoddy!'

But Koppan did not sing that night.

Kali felt utterly despondent. If only Koppan would sing that song once more. Just one more time.

Koppan could hear the call of the lagoon. The night belonged to him and nobody else.

It was on a night like tonight that he had vengefully bitten the snake back . . . when he had drunk himself delirious to forget how his manhood had been challenged. All the debts should be repaid at night.

Koppan felt an overwhelming desire to merge with the lagoon.

The heavy clouds congregating in the sky, the shimmying rain and the invigorating warmth flowing in his veins . . . Koppan felt that he was man enough for any action. He could even have forcefully copulated with Unnicheera then. But it was all too late.

Reaching the riverside, Koppan touched the waters. The river kissed his rotting fingers.

'Come Koppan, launch your boat!' the river invited him.

Koppan freed the little boat on the shore and stared as it danced prettily on the waves. In a flare of madness, he lifted the heavy washing stone on the shore and dropped it inside the boat.

No one would see that stone again.

Koppan's pet dog reached his side through the slivers of rain. As if it knew what was happening, it whined softly while wagging its tail. Koppan knew that certain creatures could foresee the future.

Koppan felt an overwhelming love for his dog. Embracing it warmly, he kissed its neck.

'You alone remain without hating me in the end, dear one. Forgive me please! Come with me now. If you remain without me, they will kick you dead.'

The puppy from the toddy shop that he had taken along in his boat a long time ago, again accompanied him tonight. Clutching the oar with his diseased fingers, Koppan rowed against the tide.

The lagoon was calling out to him. Koppan's lagoon. The same lagoon that had always gifted him with a harvest of fish was pleased with his songs.

Theyyakam, theyyakam, theyyakam tharo
Theyyakam, theyyakam, theyyakam tharo
Innenthe pennoruppattu padathu?
Innenthe penninoreenamillathu?'

'How come the girl is not singing today?
How come the tune is not rhythmic today?'

Even when Koppan's eyes overflowed, the river did not answer. She lay unconscious, like a fisherwoman who had lost her beloved.

Darkness encompassed everything.

Koppan untied the rope from the step of the boat. He lassoed the washing stone with the middle portion. Then he made two nooses at each end. He looked awhile at the noose, the stone and the river below. Then he put one noose around his own neck and slipped the other around the dog's head. Even if they suffocated, they would not be able to swim.

He had had enough of this accursed earth. There would be no return from this final journey. This time he would get to touch his healer father and his loving mother.

'Let us go, my son!' Koppan stroked the dog's neck. It lovingly licked Koppan's festering lesions.

Koppan stood erect, holding the heavy washing stone in his hands. This stone, this worthless stone would soon ensure the separation of two souls. Where would they—he and the dog—sprout anew again?

Koppan wept as he looked in the direction of Potta Thuruthu.

No more potta plants.

No more shrimp farms or Chinese nets.

No more harvest songs or Pachuvanchi.

Darkness, only darkness . . .

Along with a sudden rain that came crashing down, the washing stone fell into the breast of the lagoon. Two sacrificial animals followed, sinking deeper and deeper in the backwaters.

A few bubbles rose up to burst near the orphaned boat.

The creatures of the nether regions of the lagoon crowded near the two strangers who had suddenly transgressed into their pristine space. Who were these new inhabitants? A fish, which furtively hovered around till its fears died, kissed Koppan's lips without hurting them.

As Koppan lay still, savouring the tasty kiss, more fish thronged his body. Perhaps they recognized the man who had caught many of their brethren in his deadly fishing nets.

Taking generous bites of his swollen lips, dancing through the lacerations of his body, feasting on his eyes, ears, nose, skin and tongue, they ecstatically rushed towards the canals.

Many of them lay frozen in the fishing boats that came near Potta Thuruthu the next day.

'Pooey!'

Unnicheera clapped her hands together to attract the attention of the fish monger. She haggled over the price of the fish that had tasted a human being.

That afternoon, in the absence of Koppan, when she relished rice and fish curry with the toddy tapper, for the very first time Koppan's blood entered Unnicheera's body.

The infant, however, was too small to eat fish.

33

Unquenched Urges

'He must have left the village! What else?'

'But how will he live, I ask you? His body was rotting all over!'

'He will beg like other vagrants.'

'I don't think so. I have another thought!'

'What thought?'

'Must have died! Who can live like that?'

'Don't be stupid. If Koppan has died, where is his body?'

The conjectures lay unburied in the isle. Kunjootty felt that there was an air of magical uncanniness in the surroundings of Potta Thuruthu. Here, anyone could get lost in a fissure of the universe, without leaving a trace of evidence. If this pattern was going to be repetitive, who would be the next one to go missing? Kunjootty read out many names in his mind. Then, he added his own to the list.

The riverside nights became more sinister and mysterious. Many stories abounded about Ezhuthassan's strange activities.

The islanders gossiped about him in Vasumathy's toddy shack and Kuttappu's barber shop.

'I think he is totally bonkers!' It was Kora who proclaimed so, raising his head from the newspapers. Every evening, he would arrive at the barber shop to read newspapers and engage in political debates.

A scar ran from his left forehead down to the side of his lip. He had obtained this battle scar when he was running a nondescript cloth store and a small tailoring shop in Vaduthala.

Kora had been an expert in stitching men's shirts and women's blouses. Due to his constant companionship with clothes, Kora procured a special prowess. At the mere sight of a woman, he could accurately predict her chest size! One day, he tried his special gift of measurement with a young woman who was visiting his shop. She was the only sister of four sturdy brothers. That was the day when he received the distinguishing mark running from his head to lip, and saw the end of his multiple enterprises. After that incident, he whiled away his time between the alleys frequented by youthful card players and Kuttappu's barber shop.

'No one has seen Ezhuthassan for a long time now!' Kuttappu responded as he sharpened his shaving knife.

'I have often seen him sneaking around the compound, stark naked . . .'

'Is that so? What has happened to that man, I wonder!'

'People say different things! That he is possessed by spirits, that he is mad. Who knows for sure?'

'Really troublesome situation, eh?'

'In his youth, he had sowed many wild oats, didn't he? Was up to no good at all, they say! It seems he changed after his mother and sister died from madness.'

'Even I have heard there are many secrets surrounding that man! That he ravaged many women in his time! If you are cursed, there is no way but to endure the effects!'

'You are very right!'

'Yesterday Velan Pulayan said he saw him snooping around near his hut.'

'Who? Ezhuthassan?'

'Yes! On seeing Velan, Kutty Asan ran away to the riverside frantically and jumped on top of a tree like a monkey!'

'God! On top of a tree?' Kuttappu's grip on his shaving knife was lost momentarily.

'You damn idiot! You have cut my face!'

A lot of bizarre, superhuman stories were amassing around Ezhuthassan. What the keen ears absorbed was exaggerated by the wagging tongues. The residents of Potta Thuruthu plugged the gaps in their windows and strengthened the bolts and latches of their doors to save themselves from an unknown horror. Everyone tried their best to avoid a face-to-face encounter with Ezhuthassan.

These stories reached Kunjootty too. He noted down whatever he heard in the pages of the *Book of Exodus*. He never forgot to meet Ezhuthassan whenever he went near his house. There was a discernible, deepening gravity on Ezhuthassan's face. It was as if someone else was acting and speaking on his behalf. He would crosscheck at times:

'Kutty! Don't you believe me?'

Kunjootty would pretend to believe him.

No one saw Ezhuthassan eat any food. No one saw him purchasing any groceries either. Then how was it that he was thriving so well? Though his body was in this physical plane, could it be that his spirit and consciousness belonged to some other sphere?

After satisfying their lusts, in the evenings when they were together, the toddy tapper would narrate the tales about Ezhuthassan to Unnicheera. She felt that it was a mix of grain and chaff. No one could decipher how much was fact and how much imagination. Unnicheera was increasingly haunted by the memories of Koppan. She felt two watchful eyes unceasingly glaring at her.

Then, one day, Unnicheera, plagued with anxiety, discovered someone amidst the shadows of twilight.

She called out tremblingly: 'Who is it?'

'Sshhh . . .'

She could see the origin of the sound in the feeble light filtering through the waving coconut leaves. As she made out who it was, a panic gripped Unnicheera. A head full of white hair, the sparkling ear stud, a naked hairy body, the loin cloth and the long banana bark trailing behind as a long tail!

'Help, Neendakara Mutha!' Unnicheera cried out in fear.

'Ssshhh . . . don't make a sound!' Ezhuthassan warned her. Without any preface, he added, 'Died . . .'

Unnicheera shuddered.

'Yes, he died!'

'Who?'

'Koppan!'

'Devi!'

As she unexpectedly heard Koppan's name, Unnicheera felt terrified. She held her breath and stared at the obscure figure speechlessly.

Even the sea breeze had stopped blowing.

'There are ghosts prowling around!' As Ezhuthassan looked intently around the house, Unnicheera felt that she would fall in her nervousness. She remembered sensing someone's presence in her sleep and waking up at an unearthly hour. Even if Koppan had returned alive then, Unnicheera would have considered him a ghost.

'Nothing to be afraid of,' Ezhuthassan said. 'I will give you a sacred thread. Tie it around your wrist!'

Those words should have soothed Unnicheera like a reassuring touch. However, the toddy tapper's voice emerged from behind as soon as Ezhuthassan finished speaking.

'No one wants your thread or mantra in this house!'

Four eyes glared furiously at one another in the darkness. If looks could kill, they would have burnt each other into cinders.

While Unnicheera stood watching helplessly as a witness, an old resentment raised its head from the past, encroached into the present and sparked a fight between them.

'Who the hell are you to say that?' Ezhuthassan snarled.

'That does not matter. But what are you doing here? Have you taken over the responsibility of the mother and child? Setting off shamelessly every night! I've heard much about your great deeds.'

'You . . . you . . . wait and watch! You will suffer. The child and its mother too shall suffer!'

'We will all gladly suffer! Wandering around . . . crazy as a loon!'

Without listening to that outburst, like an unleashed cyclone, Ezhuthassan rushed away into the thickets of weeds and banana plants.

Unnicheera started sobbing in apprehension of the future, covering her face.

'Why did you have to say all that to him?' she asked the toddy tapper.

'Consider it my vengeance. Totally mine. Come on, let the old geezer become aware of my madness.'

An ancient vendetta. A stinging vengeance that began during a summer when wild wax apples were blooming lushly. He was stepping from boyhood to adolescence then, perhaps around fourteen or fifteen years old. The son of the tapper, Chupran, had worshipped the image of the pretty Pennu Kunju within the secret chambers of his heart. The girl never even cared to acknowledge his presence.

One summer afternoon, warily observing the surroundings, she sneaked in through the bramble boundary, entering the forbidden compound. Pennu Kunju had returned after a very long time with luscious wax apples in her arms and a flurry of agitation on her face. Why had the twelve-year-old girl become attracted to the corridor of that dilapidated house? Why had the adolescent son of Chupran been unable to sleep for nights, wondering about that mystery? And then, one afternoon, unable to endure it any longer, he had stopped her by the copses of tapioca.

'Hey girl! I know what you are up to!'

'What are you blabbering about?'

'How you daily sneak into Kutty Asan's compound . . . and then!'

'What is your problem with that? Bbhuu!'

Pennu Kunju spat out her utter disgust. And then, chewing a rosy wax apple, she haughtily walked away. He stood there burning up slowly. Humiliation and the shattering of his dreams filled the young lad with vengeance and fury. He kept seeking an opportunity for retribution by hiding in the corners of the snake grove and the ungodly nooks of the dark yard. However, he did not have the wherewithal to accomplish anything then.

Chupran's son had grown up nourished by that thought of revenge. Leaving behind a childhood when he could not even face Ezhuthassan, the toddy tapper was now a formidable opponent.

Unnicheera knew nothing about his story.

A voice inside kept warning her that whatever Ezhuthassan had spoken was true, and that she should not disregard his curse lightly. Ezhuthassan was not just another ordinary mad man. There were some ominous truths hovering around the old man.

One evening, when she could not bear her anxiety any more, Unnicheera made her way to Ezhuthassan's house.

The rats in the corridor scattered in all directions as the stranger stepped inside. The crumbling crannies of the stone walls were getting flooded with the scent of a woman. Ezhuthassan keenly observed the changing undercurrents of the surroundings.

Ezhuthassan gazed with contentment as a deep-rooted regret started vanishing.

A woman's presence after decades in that ramshackle place. Even the old soil was filled with a new vigour at the touch of her feet!

'Asan, forgive him, his ignorance. Protect my baby from harm,' Unnicheera pleaded in a choked voice.

'Who was that man?' The question and the detestation brimming in those words sapped Unnicheera's strength.

'He . . . he is . . .' she stuttered.

'I know!'

Facing the old man's penetrating look, Unnicheera cringed. Piercing her clothes, her flesh and bones, the gaze went deeper!

Unnicheera sensed a mysterious and unbearable spell of attraction being cast on her.

Though the years had eaten away his youthful vigour, Ezhuthassan was still lean and manly in the sunset of his life. His glance could burn a woman even now. Unnicheera felt dizzy, unable to look into his blazing eyes.

'I will give you an amulet. Wear it.'

Unnicheera stood reverentially, with folded hands.

'It will take some time to prepare. Come after two days. But that arrogant fool, he is going to suffer!'

Unnicheera found herself dumbstruck. She stood staring at the broken-down floor, confused and bewildered.

She desperately wished to get away from that place.

'I will come later,' she mumbled.

Unnicheera turned towards the corridor, her heartbeat rising fast.

'Wait!'

As she turned, Unnicheera found Ezhuthassan standing very close to her. She had no time to even catch her startled breath.

Unquenched urges took Ezhuthassan back to his youthful days of morbid hungers. When the wind started blowing with unfinished karmic remnants, the bats and rats in that old building panicked and ran helter-skelter.

A loin cloth tied up with a dried banana bark lay orphaned amidst the din.

34

In the Land of the Fire Bird

Kunjootty was preoccupied with educating Anita. There was discernible progress; the little girl had quickly mastered a few Malayalam letters. She could also enunciate a few words, albeit with some difficulty.

Isaac dropped in during one such teaching session.

'Get ready fast. We need to go somewhere urgently.'

'Where?'

'Cannot disclose that now. Just get ready quickly!'

Kunjootty acquiesced, knowing that there was nothing to be gained by debating with Isaac; he always maintained an air of mystery about the most trivial issues.

Anita became stubborn when she understood that Kunjootty was going on a journey.

'*Je veux venir aussi* (I want to come too)!'

Kunjootty looked at Isaac.

'Maybe the next time, we will take her along.' Isaac was firm.

It took much effort to dissuade Anita. Somehow, Kunjootty managed to pacify her and sent her back home.

Feeling disgruntled, he boarded the bus without even reading the destination. He lethargically stretched himself, disregarding both the direction and the distance the vehicle trundled over. The expedition continued long, over plains and riverbanks. The journey ended in the land of an ancient love.

Kunjootty stood in the valley, filled with gratitude. He even regretted the grudge he felt against Isaac.

The surroundings were pure and peaceful.

Deeply meditating hills. Saffron hued steps, zigzagging up the pinnacles, were embracing them.

They started walking through a clayey pathway in the valley.

'Look there! That huge one seems to be the Potta Mala!' Isaac pointed afar.

As if a light had been kindled inside his heart, Kunjootty felt the continuance of the life-spirit that had pulsated in his forbearers. This was also the place where the umbilical cord of the family legacy had been agonizingly severed. Perhaps each square foot around was a veritable treasure chest of memories!

Kunjootty felt that he could stand there forever, staring at the clouds, that resembled bales of cotton, slithering down the hilltops. He could trace the fire bird, like a holy remembrance of sacrifice, in the shapes formed by the clouds.

'Is it possible to reach there?' he wondered aloud, unable to suppress his thrill.

'No one goes there usually.'

'Beyond that hill lies Chama Potta! Would that be true then? I would like to believe that the feathers of the fire bird are still floating there!'

'Huh! You and your depressing fairy tales!'

Kunjootty put an end to the conversation at that point. He intently started absorbing the geography of the Potta Mala.

The eponymous Potta Hill looked like a compassionate sage, willingly enduring the bitter fruits of someone else's karma. With its head shaven, gazing at the dry sky and the barren clouds, the majestic hill stood like a silent witness. An occasional cloud enveloped the meditating yogi as it passed by.

'We have to hurry up or else it will get dark soon!' Isaac warned.

The breeze wafting from the banana plantations paused to touch the strangers. There, the green leaves were waving as if welcoming them.

Kunjootty felt that the drumbeats that had arisen from a small shack in Potta Thuruthu, at the beginning of the sojourn, were still accompanying him. There was life and vigour in the setting.

Isaac's aunt's house was in the vicinity. Kunjootty remembered that Isaac had mentioned an imminent journey a few weeks back.

'We should have brought Anita along!' Kunjootty said.

'No harm in the idea. But not in this trip. The very purpose might be defeated.'

'What do you mean?'

'Forget it! Now, you hurry up.'

Many stories were hidden in the murmurs of the dried banana barks as they rustled, and in the chirps of the unseen birds around. The road seemed to be moist with the memories of many tearful flights of exile. Kunjootty ruminated that the wheel marks left behind by the cart carrying besieged humans, pulled by emaciated bullocks, would remain indelible. Doomed days when men raised work tools against their own brethren!

His Valiyappachan's blood had been brutally shed on this earth. The mob had stamped the peace maker a betrayer before ruthlessly claiming his life. The debt of the blood, shed decades ago, was lying on the soil around, still unpaid.

Kunjootty felt a deep regret welling within.

A journey to the crossroads of time, never given a backward glance by the exiled generations. If Isaac was not with him, Kunjootty might have knelt down to drop a loving kiss on that earth.

He could hear drumbeats resounding from the sides of the hills. In the sudden flight of the wind, dried leaves twirled and moved in a group, ahead of the path.

After a steep climb down and a turn, they came across a whitewashed house.

Kunjootty looked around.

Could a feather of the legendary fire bird have fallen somewhere in this area too?

Henna plants, trimmed to a certain length, stood like sentinels around the residence. There was no other boundary. On the wall was a crucifix made of lime, with a groove to store the holy Hannan water.

Kunjootty pressed his finger curiously into the furrow. Only dust clung to his fingertip, the water having long dried up. He blew the specks away.

'Who is it?'

There was movement inside the house. A dignified-looking woman of middle age came to the porch, wearing the traditional dress of Christian women, a long blouse and a mundu with pleats. A young girl accompanied her, clad in a half-sari.

'Hey, Isaac! I thought that you had set off for Kashi with your bundles a long time ago!' the woman laughed heartily.

'I was on my way to Kashi! Thought I would drop in and inform you about the trip!' Isaac retorted warmly.

'Sounds wise enough!'

'Well, are you planning to come along then, Ammayi?'

'Where?'

'Kashi!'

'Absolute buffoon!'

Small talk, meaningless banter, innocent peeves . . . Kunjootty stepped into the visiting room with Isaac.

The room was neat and tidy. The figure of the crucified Holy One, bearing the five holy wounds and crown of thorns, was mounted on the wall.

There were cushions with dainty needlework beautifying the chairs. The tablecloth was coloured light green and the hand-embroidered flowers looked lovely.

Kunjootty observed the young girl standing behind Isaac's aunt. She was communicating something to Isaac with her eyes.

'Oh, I forgot to introduce him! This is Kunjootty. His bad habits include writing!'

'Oh, do you write stories?' the girl asked curiously.

Kunjootty presumed that she enjoyed reading.

'Nothing worthwhile. My misadventure was never more than a page in the college magazine!' Kunjootty shrugged.

That had been page number one hundred and thirty-five. The title had been 'The Poem without a Title'.

'Don't be so modest! Over-modesty and vanity are one and the same!' Isaac teased as the women joined in the ensuing laughter.

'He has yet another bad habit. He collects feathers! If you can find some rooster's tail, just give him one! Only tell him that it belongs to the fire bird.'

Kunjootty pretended to partake of the hearty laughter. But his mind was travelling somewhere far beyond. The clay path became smaller and smaller in width and terminated somewhere in the prickly shrubs in the valley overlooking the Potta Hills. There was a church on a nearby hill. His ancestors were at rest there, in the form of black crosses. Kunjootty yearned to visit the sacred sanctuary at least once.

The drumbeats had reached a crescendo at a distance. A silver streak could be seen leaping down from the pinnacle of the hill. A waterfall, which was not bountiful. It fell into the depths, made the soil fertile, merged with the Periyar, reached the nameless river of Potta Thuruthu, before disappearing into the mouth of the sea.

Kunjootty felt a sense of discomfiture that he was not fitting in with the prevailing lighthearted ambience. Meaningless queries, neighbourhood gossip, mocking snippets of conversations . . .

Then, Isaac raised a question casually, 'Where is Teresa?'

All the effulgence seemed to disappear in a moment. There was a perceptible loss of cheer on all faces. All eyes were downcast. Kunjootty guessed from the atmosphere that there were some inauspicious secrets associated with the name 'Teresa'.

'Where is she?'

'In the eastern room. She never comes out . . .'

'Where is David? Did not see him either!'

'Went out. Might be late . . .'

Isaac and Kunjootty went inside the house. Thrusting the curtains apart, they entered a room that seemed denuded of light. The room was cool and gave off the scent of tears. A girl sat in a corner, riveted to the spot like an ancient statue, her face turned towards the wall.

'Teresa! Are you aware of your guests or not?' Isaac called out.

As if the fragile glass weaves of her daydreams were suddenly shattered, the girl slowly turned her head and stared at them, flustered.

Kunjootty observed that the forcibly shut windows prevented the sight of the Potta Hill as well as the bright light from entering the room. Even the breeze seemed to have been forbidden from entering the room.

'Why are you meditating like this, shutting all these windows, eh?'

Isaac freed the bolts and opened the windows wide. As the bright sunshine rushed inside ecstatically, the bells tolled a sacred music, akin to the Pranava mantra, from the church on the nearby hill.

'Om . . . Om . . . Om!'

The signs were returning—Sunday, the Holy Sacrament, the ringing church bells . . .

A small breeze took off on a sharp dive from the top of the Potta Hill and started frolicking in the valley. Beyond the hills, the desiccated Chama Potta lay thirsting bitterly for a drop of water.

'Meet my friend, Kunjootty.'

Teresa nodded her head in a show of courtesy. Her eyes reminded Kunjootty of a rainy season that was yet to empty itself of its woes. The young woman was as piteous as a timid little pigeon. It seemed as if she had been crying all her life.

Suddenly Kunjootty became dumbfounded, sensing that he had seen the likeness of that face before. A very familiar face, which had unexpectedly vanished from his life. A sea breeze enveloped him, emerging from a seashore imprinted with the deep wounds caused by the footprints of the passersby. Kunjootty was stranded amidst the many wet turret shells and one red kite whose string was broken. The macabre pangs of thirst emanating from Chama Potta, the harsh wind, the shadows, then a dark cross . . .

Unable to piece together all those images assaulting his senses, Kunjootty called out in bewilderment, forgetting his surroundings: 'Isaac, let us leave!'

The church bells rang a second time, intimating the devotees about the Holy Qurbana; the sound reverberating through the valley. Kunjootty perceived that yet another debt of Holy Mass was accruing in the *Book of Life*.

* * *

By the time they reached Potta Thuruthu, it was very late. Kunjootty had firmly resisted the offer of the hosts that they should stay overnight. No leave, too much pending work at office, his mother waiting at home—a bevy of reasons.

Silence, loosening its clasp, fell on the pathways gripped by darkness. Kunjootty was quiet during the return trip.

What had been the purpose of that singular journey? Why had all the forbidden memories come rushing back in a deluge?

'Kunjootty!' Isaac called out.

'Yes?'

'I cannot understand you at times.'

'Even I cannot.'

'Why did you behave like that?'

'I do not know.'

'You intentionally did not ask about her, right?'

'Who?'

'Teresa.'

'Is that so? Maybe you are right.'

'Don't you want to hear about it?'

'I do not know.'

'But I want to speak about it.'

'Was that your aim behind planning this trip? The reason why you did not want to bring Anita along?'

There were fireflies hovering around an orangeberry tree. A divine radiance was enveloping the surroundings.

'Death is a strange experience. In a flicker of an eye, to be shoved into a situation of loneliness from a full, wholesome life! Poor Teresa!'

The fireflies scattered suddenly. The night birds of prey had arrived stealthily to catch the little light carriers.

How had Teresa become lonely? An accident, a disease or a snake bite. All those beautiful opportunities for death to step into someone's life!

Kunjootty did not probe further. He did not want to listen either.

'Probably because of her intolerable loneliness, she too tried once. However, she was saved in the nick of time.'

'You really think that you saved her? A soul denied justice! That was exactly what was done to me by injecting all those medicines—forcing me to live on!'

Isaac was probably stunned into silence. Kunjootty could not see his reaction in the prevailing darkness. The time was imminent for the disclosure of all secrets. Was the journey to the land of the fire bird foreshadowing yet another disaster?

As the branches of the roadside trees started swishing and swaying, Kunjootty was jolted awake from his reverie.

Undulating branches, the mysterious murmur of the leaves and a familiar voice . . .

'Poohoey!'

'Ezhuthassan!' Isaac whispered.

The secretive trees stood towering above them. Different branches were oscillating now.

'Parijaata tarumoola vaasinam, bhavayamai pavamaana nandanam
Parijaata tarumoola vaasinam, bhavayamai pavamaana nandanam

'The son of Anjani, the red-faced one with the magnificent golden body,
The one who resides at the base of the parijata tree, son of the Wind God, I bow to thee!'

Out of concern for the dangerous leaping from branch to branch, Kunjootty submitted a prayer before God in the darkness:

'May the grip be firm; may the branches be steady.'

35

Flames of Fire

The trip to the land of the fire bird's sacrifice was unleashing memories possessing powerful destructive capabilities. Although he reached home very late at night, Kunjootty found himself unable to sleep. He opened the *Book of Exodus* and filled many pages. The book was egging him on to hurry up with his task. A vague, but firm belief of time running out washed over him. If he were to work harder, it might get finished sooner.

By the time it was morning, Kunjootty was groggy and exhausted. He started off for office very late. He was dishevelled and untidy. When he was battling fatigue and the tension of reaching office on time, Anita approached him with her unending grievances.

'*Tu ne m'as pas emmené avec toi hier! Pouvez-vous me prendre aujourd'hui oncle?* (You did not take me with you yesterday! Can you take me along today, uncle?)'

'*Peut-être plus tard* (Perhaps later),' Kunjootty said irritably. '*Maintenant il n'y a pas de temps* (Now, there is no time).'

'*Tu dois me prendre avec toi! Je suis tellement fatigué de cet endroit* (You have to take me with you. I am so tired of this place)!'

'*Comment puis-je vous emmener au bureau?* (How can I take you to the office?)' Kunjootty was in a bad mood.

'*Alors laissez-nous aller à un autre endroit aujourd'hui* (Then let us go to some other place today)!' Anita suggested innocently.

'*Pourquoi ne me laisse pas seul* (Why don't you just leave me alone)?'

Kunjootty got fed up and spoke peevishly without much thought.

Whatever he had tried to control with a firm hand within his heart had overcome the barricades and started flowing out. He turned his face away testily and veered the boat to the opposite shore.

As he rowed for a while, he found his temper subsiding. Halfway through, Kunjootty turned to look back at Anita, his heart regretful at his words. The child was walking back home, her head lowered, her enthusiasm totally extinguished. Kunjootty felt bitter at himself. The young child had found refuge in him. That was why she felt free to be stubborn with her demands. There was no one else in that whole isle with whom she could share her thoughts. Poor kid. He decided to console her as soon as he returned in the evening.

Kunjootty became engrossed in his routine work at office. When he was floundering between files and public complaints, the peon, Damu, called out from the door.

'Someone is here to see you, sir!'

'Who is it?'

'Someone called Kandan. He is your neighbour, he says!'

Kunjootty got up in a hurry, his heart full of fearful apprehensions. Something untoward must have occurred. Else, Kandan would never come searching for him this far.

Kandan was waiting for him impatiently outside the office. Seeing the perturbed man, Kunjootty asked anxiously:

'What happened, Kandan? Why are you here?'

'Did you see Anita before you left for work?' Kandan asked.

'Yes, she was standing at the riverside. What happened?'

'She is missing.'

Something fluttered, as if grievously hurt, within Kunjootty's heart, before going still. A deep sense of guilt gathered inside, deepening the turmoil.

'Missing! Is that true?'

'We searched everywhere . . . no place left now!'

'Give me a moment. I will come with you.'

Kunjootty stood silently in front of Diwakar Menon. Looking at his blanched face, Menon could not help asking, 'What is it? Who came to meet you?'

'Someone from the isle. Anita is missing.'

Kunjootty felt increasingly agitated as he spoke.

'I fear something bad has befallen her. I had scolded her in the morning.'

Menon stared at him disbelievingly. But he did not ask about the reasons for Kunjootty's ill temper.

'What is destined to happen, shall happen!' Menon murmured after a few poignant moments.

Kunjootty did not comprehend what he meant.

Chinnan was lying exhausted on the floor. Chirutha and her aunt, frantic with worry, were by his side.

The old man started sobbing on seeing Kunjootty.

'I am feeling so afraid, son!'

'Do not worry. We will search.'

Kunjootty had no idea where to begin, yet he made a search team with Kandan and a few others.

People went searching through the shrimp farms and fields. The slippery spaces, where she could have lost her foothold, were diligently explored. They searched the mangroves and marshes. The search groups called out Anita's name loudly.

Nobody could find any trace of the child.

'What if she has stepped into the river?' Kandan asked hesitantly.

'No way! Let us search further,' Kunjootty reassured them.

They reached the common village ferry at the western end of the isle. The man in the small shop said that he had seen a fair-skinned foreign girl early that day. The boatman told them that a small foreign girl—a Madamma Kutty—had crossed the river on his boat.

Kunjootty felt a slight relief.

* * *

Anita sat on the boat, staring at the frolicking of fish in the water. Everyone was a stranger to her. The passengers stared at the little girl who stood apart like a mistake amongst the dark-skinned natives.

'Little foreign girl, are you on a trip to see the isles?' someone asked her kindly.

Anita was busy dipping her hand in the water. She heard the roar of a boat at a distance. It was beyond her line of sight.

When the boat reached the opposite isle, Anita disembarked with the other passengers. That place too had farms, clayey boundaries, luxuriant trees. Without any worries, Anita walked along, enjoying the sights of the new land. She wandered freely, aimlessly.

As the walk progressed, the sun became hotter. She settled under a tree to rest and wonderingly looked at the man who was climbing a coconut tree so effortlessly.

'Do you want a tender coconut?' the man asked.

She smiled at the climber, a man who belonged to the Vannan community. Happily sipping the tender coconut milk, she refreshed herself.

There was a ferry at the end of that isle too. And there were more isles beyond that, waiting for Anita with their skiffs. She enjoyed all the trips through the backwaters. She kept moving farther and farther from Potta Thuruthu with every boat journey.

Anita became aware of the setting sun and panic gripped her about the return journey. She was hungry and tired. The child had no clue about her location or which boat to take to return home.

Je me suis perdu.'

Anita begged for help.

'What is this child saying?'

'Pouvez-vous m'aider à rentrer chez moi?'

No one understood her language or her pleas. Tears filled her eyes.

Anita walked away from the people who did not understand her. Finally, she reached an isolated farm where pigs were reared. It was desolate except for the dirty animals, who were lolling about in the slushy mud. There was darkness and a harsh stink everywhere.

Anita clambered up a small shack, used as watch tower in the isle shorn of light. She was on the verge of a collapse due to hunger, thirst and rising terror. The cold wind and insects did not spare her either. There were no lights anywhere, not even starlight. It was a kingdom of darkness.

Far off, flickers of light could be seen. Without knowing that people were searching for her, the little child curled up, burning with high fever, on a piece of torn sack-cloth in the corner of the hovel. Anita did not know that the search teams had given up and returned home for the night.

The next evening, Anita's lifeless body was found next to an othalanga plant, near the shack. A few ripe othalanga fruits, deadly poisonous, lay half eaten by her side. Her body was bluish in hue.

* * *

When the corpse reached Chinnan's home, his desperate wails could be heard. Chirutha and her aunt wept while holding each other.

'Remember the prophecy . . . that the house where the Poli fell, death would arrive!'

'What answer will I give Chiriyankan when he returns for his daughter, Devi?'

Chinnan kept on lamenting.

Kunjootty stood without any answers, wracked with guilt, caught in his own turbulent emotions. The damning self-recrimination that an innocent life had ended because of his negligence. The responsibility, albeit unwritten, of the child's welfare had been invisibly assigned to him alone. And then?

'Should we not get on with the burial now?'

The query was addressed to Kunjootty. He did not have another view.

'How will we inform her father?' Kara Mooppan wondered aloud.

Anita's parents were alive somewhere, not knowing of her departure. What was the way to get in touch with them?

There was another grave, uncertain issue at hand.

The child had been baptized. What should be the religious rites during her funeral?

'We should bury her at the cemetery. The child was a Christian soul,' Kora the erstwhile tailor ventured.

Kandan opposed that suggestion. 'How can that be? No church has her name in their rolls. We will cremate her in this house.'

'The child's father was part of the church, wasn't he?'

'Is that so? Then her grandfather's remains are here in this stone grave!'

The arguments quickly turned convoluted and mendacious. The islanders became part of two opposite groups. The argument about burying the body in the church versus cremating it in the house compound reached a vicious crescendo. Kunjootty stood apart from the ruckus, repelled by the antics.

The fight was over a little body bereft of any life.

When the war became heated in the house of the dead, Chinnan got up from the floor. He rushed to the middle of the divisive crowd.

'All of you, get out! Fighting over my little girl's corpse! I will do as I please!'

No one dared to confront him.

That evening, at the southern end of the compound, next to Chennan's stone grave, a small pyre was lit. In the light of the bed of fire, where his granddaughter lay in repose, the grandfather's burial vault blazed a fiery crimson. The souls seemed to have recognized each other.

On the third day after the cremation, Gopala Kanian and the Injakkal Tantric reached Chinnan's hut.

Spreading his cowrie shells, the Kanian discovered the whereabouts of Anita's soul. Seven Samhara Rudras, spirits full of wile and craftiness, stole away the souls of the dead. Gopala Kandan was adamant that Anita's soul was in the confinement of one of the seven Rudras.

If one did not retrieve the soul back and anoint it as a Shovva in one of the sacred stones, the aftermath would be awful, wreaking havoc in the family forever!

The tantric's Karmakanda began after that.

Chinnan and Kandan arranged for all the ritual materials.

Tender coconut leaves were used to decorate the ground for the possessed humans to dance around.

After lighting up seven wicks in a lamp that was placed on the banana leaf, each of the seven Rudras were invited one by one to owe up to its crime. The offerings to tempt them included fresh grains, puffed rice and toddy. There was roasted yellow catfish for appeasing the powerful deity of the Ullada community.

The Tantric drank many draughts of toddy and amassed strength for the ritual. He clanged the iron nail against a metal plate and hollered:

'Itthanumberu theliyatta numberu
Itthanumberu theliyatta numberu!'

'Let the correct number of the Rudras appear!'

The tantric mercilessly interrogated each Rudra spirit . . .

'Who has stolen away our little child's soul?'

'Not me, not me!'

Six of the Rudras denied any wrongdoing. The seventh Rudra of the North admitted it was him.

'What do you want in return for her?'

'Give me whatever I like!'

'Will you be happy with grains?'

'No.'

'Will you be happy with puffed rice?'

'No.'

'Will you be happy with catfish?'

'Yes.'

Four women sat on the ritualistic dance floor with their hair untied—Chirutha, her aunt and two women labourers. The soul that the Samhara Rudra left behind would possess one of the women. Then it had to be lured into a pot of bronze before emptying it on top of the sacred stone.

The Tantric started rushing to and fro among the seated women, with the cane twisted around his neck. Then he started swishing his cane left and right brutally.

'Sshhhhoooey! Let go and leave now!'

It was an atmosphere mired with dark secrets and mysteries. Kunjootty did not wish to interfere. Neither did he feel like staying away. To each, his own. Kunjootty's stance was akin to an aimless boat bobbing around on the dark river.

Meanwhile, one of the women started exhibiting the signs of being possessed by a spirit. The Tantric ran towards her, eager to showcase his prowess.

'Have you come? Have you come?'

He swished his cane energetically and roared.

'*Oui* (Yes)'

'So tell me . . .'

'*Jui viene* (I am here)'

Hearing the familiar voice, Kunjootty stood shocked and horrified.

It was Anita's voice!

To make sure that he was not hallucinating, Kunjootty moved closer to the woman. Anita was making her presence felt through the tongue of an illiterate woman labourer!

The woman leapt from her place and rushed towards Kunjootty.

'*Je me suis perdu* . . . (I lost my way)'

Kunjootty felt as if he had going mad. The trust he had in his own eyes and ears was gone.

'*Je me suis perdu* . . . *pouvez-vous m'aider à rentrer chez moi* (I lost my way! Can you help me reach home?)'

The Tantric reached his side in a jiffy. He held a bronze pot in his hand.

'Can you reside here, child?'

'*Oui.*'

'Then make it fast! Come on . . .'

The woman's dance steps reached a culmination and she collapsed on the floor. The Tantric tied a red cloth over the mouth of the pot quickly. Then he placed a new stone by the boundary where the cotton plants blossomed wild. Chanting mantras, he ritualistically emptied the pot over the stone and housed the lost soul therein.

Kunjootty's eyes welled over with tears.

A tender soul, born thousands of miles away, caught in its circle of karma, was installed as a Shovva inside a stone in a far-off isle.

Je me suis perdu . . . *pouvez-vous m'aider à rentrer chez moi?*

36

Beyond the Body

Diwakar Menon stood with folded hands in front of the temple of Kavilottamma. Watching the deity's luminous eyes and the sparkling sacred weapons in her eight arms in the glow of Arati, he stood lost to himself. Reposing faith in the bountiful gesture of blessings, he prayed for an answer.

'What have you planned for me, Amma?'

The serpents intertwined with Amma's tresses opened their eyes. The horoscope of the universe reflected in their eyes.

'You have piled up many debts across births. Lad, it is now time to set forth.' Amma beckoned.

'I wish to travel too. But I do not know where to go. I have become an orphan with no place to go!'

Amma smiled on hearing that.

'My child, you have forgotten one fact. To be an orphan implies a state where one becomes the owner of everything. Every human being desires it secretly in his heart. When someone has no place to go, he becomes free to go anywhere.

Only such a free soul can put down his burdens in the shade of the Bodhi Tree of Wisdom.

'Know that the royal pleasures of Kapilavastu were all illusionary. That Yashoda and Rahul were nothing but deterring calls from behind, in the path to the Bodhi Tree. So do not let a thatched hut and a penitent woman stop you from your journey!'

Hearing Amma's words, as if he had been gifted with inner sight, Menon felt fulfilled. He prostrated himself in front of her sanctum sanctorum. Diwakar Menon realized that 'peace' was not a meaningless word.

Menon started off from the temple towards Potta Thuruthu. He wished to meet Kunjootty but he was away. Eli hinted that her son might be late in returning. Menon did not wait.

He crossed the shrimp farm and reached Chinnan's hut. He introduced himself as Kunjootty's friend. Menon wished to look at Anita, who was now dwelling as a Shovva.

Chinnan showed him the way to the boundary of the compound. They saw the unsettling sight of many stones lying next to one another. There was a new stone in the group: a dried-up garland made of hibiscus flowers was draped over it.

Desiccated flowers were scattered around. A few petals still clung to the stone. Diwakar Menon stared at it for a while. Then he bid goodbye and left the place.

With a sense of impending urgency, Menon observed the universe of the *Book of Exodus*, a book which he had never read and was never ever likely to read. The nameless river, the Vadakke Veedu, bearing curses and tears, the nest of the weaver bird that had been struck by lightning, the tragic home of Koppan, the beloved son of the great poison healer, the bramble boundary of Ezhuthassan's compound—Menon walked past each of them.

Kunjootty received a letter after one week.

Kunjootty,

In office, you were so close that I could reach out and touch you. It is ironic that despite all that proximity, I am writing this sort of an epistle to you. I came to your house to meet you but failed to do so. But, by the time of return, my mental state was such that I was praying not to meet you on the way. I knew that a meeting would be meaningless, since we would only look silently at each other and then desperately try to avert our gazes.

I travelled leisurely through the geography depicted in the *Book of Exodus*, touching the grass blades that you have spoken about, caressing the trellis-vine plants and feeling the wind. It was like a beast of burden that I reached the sanctorum of Kavilottamma. I needed an answer. Amma very compassionately advised me to travel. She gifted me with a light heart, freed from the heaviness of all worries. I felt as if I was born again: with the holy water, a redeemed soul. My obeisance to Lord Jesus.

You must be wondering why I am writing all this. Let me tell you the truth straightaway. I became a traveller yet again. The woman and child who had knocked at my door pulled me back. I went in search of them. My search took me to a thatched hovel where one could enter only after bowing the head. I bowed mine.

She started sobbing on seeing me. Unceasingly.

I never knew that tear glands could store so many tears. Did I weep too? I do not remember.

Now listen to the law decreed by time: she has yet again become a forsaken woman. Perhaps, at some point of his life journey, Balu dumped Sarojam. She did not know whether he was alive or dead.

Maybe he has died and was reborn again. Or he is still existing in multiple guises, relishing different ages. I hope I never meet him again. If such a contingency occurs, I would be unable to decide whether I should look at him as Chandran Master or Balu or some man who existed long before both these incarnations. I am not sure who came first or whether they all exist in tandem in the same period of time. Who knows, at some inflection point of time, these forms might amalgamate and transform into my own self!

I have no idea when that might happen. Now, I am just an ordinary man whose heart can melt with feelings. In that state, I embraced her son, who had a close resemblance to me, and caressed his hair. His tender body was soiled with so much grime that I could not bring myself to kiss him. He was akin to a dirty, tattered little paper that had been folded and unfolded multiple times. Rather, a scarecrow frayed and torn by the wind and rain . . .

I wish God had given me the strength to let go of them then. He did not do that. Perhaps it is all a part of his great joke—to bring together bitter experiences and a human mind incapable of facing those. Whatever it may be, I am someone who has already humbled himself. I cannot run away from the magical whispers emanating from the nest of the solitary bird. Neither can I discard the fact that my silent house, the termite ridden rooms and the orphaned compound belong to the woman and her child.

Thus, I arrived at a decision.

This letter is also to inform you that my decision has been implemented. If you reach my half-finished home today, you might not get even a whiff of my presence.

I cannot continue in that house anymore, Kunjootty. I have no more rights over it. I have fulfilled all legalities to transfer it to their names.

Now this freedom that I enjoy, how can I even begin to describe it to you? Without leaving behind a photograph, any old clothes, without even a bundle to call mine, I can float freely to any corner of this vast universe. I came alone, I lived alone, why seek an attachment now? Even if a man has umpteen relatives and friends, ultimately, he lives in his own space, in his own company.

My sanctioned leave of absence has ended. I will not be applying to extend it further. Neither have I resigned from the post. Whatever one decides, it necessitates many meaningless procedures. There will be so many queries to be satisfied. I am in no mood for all that now. Many official inquiries are bound to happen. The notices will return unacknowledged. Then the whole process will repeat again. As a last attempt, there will be an advertisement in the inside pages of some newspaper.

'And so, if you do not join work within one month of this notification . . .'

They will terminate me, right? They will cut off my name from the list. But then, do I have a name? Do I have an address? Am I just a skeleton, a few blood vessels and the excretory system?

If so, they could have easily hacked away at me.

But since I cannot be thus defined, who can cut me off?

I have installed in my heart the Avadhoota who accepted the different spirits of nature as his own gurus. I wish I can learn forgiveness from Mother Earth. I wish I can master detachment from the wind that is not bound by any fragrance. If only I can imitate the sky when it comes to freeing oneself of limitations . . .

Should I pen down a separate farewell note? I am leaving, Kunjootty. I have no idea where to. On a snow-clad mountain, the dark insides of a cave, under a banyan tree, I could be anywhere. Perhaps, a dense forest might welcome me. By the time you read these alphabets, I might be in some land that is unknown to me at present. If I could withdraw myself without scribbling these notes, then my return would have been complete. Nobody would have known about my whereabouts then. Even in disappearance, I cannot help leaving behind a sense of incompleteness.

I have shared this secret with you, knowing that it will not spread further. Give me justice by never revealing anything about this letter or my departure to anyone. Let me get annihilated inside the decaying old page of my own name, dusty with disuse.

This might be the very last letter that I write. Even as I set off, allow me to reveal a wish, still unsated. It might sound quite insane. However, I am not hesitant because it is you that I am submitting my request. A trivial wish that remains after shedding everything! Do you remember the pigeon that came to peck around the stories of Adam's ribs? When you discover that, can you do me a foolish favour? Address an invitation card to my name, Diwakar Menon. Wherever I might be at that point of time, I shall perceive the thrill. I will touch and feel the joy. Let that letter stay dumped inside the Dead Letter Office: as a symbol of this life.

Farewell.

Yours, Diwakar Menon

* * *

Dear Menon Sir,

What am I supposed to write back? Yet another stinging secret destined to be carried inside my heart! I was living with my own heavy secret all this while; unable to unburden myself. In a favourable time, I might have confessed to you.

I look at your chosen path with an awestruck admiration. May you be able to discover the truth.

If only I too could embark on such a journey . . . I know I cannot, yet I feel the stir within me. For the one who has lost his very core of existence, a search for serenity would not be written in his fate. Yet something obdurate inside me would like to believe that it might occur one day, and that we would meet again. Till that appropriate time, let me write down my farewell wishes in the *Book of Exodus*.

Yours,
Kunjootty

* * *

Memories of Menon oppressed Kunjootty for a long time afterwards. He tried to convince himself that his friend was on a journey and would return very soon. Yet, even after days and weeks passed, Menon did not return. Knowing everything but pretending otherwise, Kunjootty attended office. He sat like an idiot while gossip abounded about the inexplicable disappearance, and investigations were initiated.

The body had very limited worth, Kunjootty brooded. The truth was somewhere far beyond. Beyond . . . beyond . . . the body.

37

The Last Leaf

When the work on the stone barricades around the shrimp farms started progressing, Isaac ignored all other activities. The rising and setting of his days were in the backwaters. It seemed as though when one eye slept, the other stayed awake. The weeks sidled by, as if focused on chanting a lone mantra. With nobody to talk to, Kunjootty felt trapped, albeit briefly, at a trial-point in time and space. After Anita too went away, the intolerable pain of departure became palpable with all its intensity. He never again opened the books meant for teaching the child. Her picture books were tied up with a piece of coir rope and forsaken in the attic. He was yet to discover anything everlasting. Whatever he had discovered had moved on, leaving him alone.

When he tried to analyse his loneliness, Kunjootty discovered that all movements were relative. The scientific principle, that even time was a relative experience associated with motion, started making sense. Depending on the mind's rate of pulsations, each person experienced a different time zone. Situated in another zone of time, his amma was trying to converse with him, resorting to minimal words and few gestures. His father was in a plane rendered unreachable due to the different speed with which his mind worked, and had become unrecognizable and distant. A few people continued to subsist at some level, analogous to certain ideas that were supposedly in existence.

In the office, time symbolized boredom. No one conversed with an open mind with anyone else. After Diwakar Menon's exit, Kunjootty was deprived of any meaningful friendship.

Kunjootty recorded in his book: '*If you can join many dry journeys, stale seclusion, and fading thoughts together and call it a life, then it defines my condition.*'

He wondered, what had been leached away from his life? Spirit, essence, soul?

If so, shouldn't he be able to recoup all those losses?

But Kunjootty knew that nothing was really lost. All were the delusions of a joker-like mind. It created the circumstances to beguile itself, before rushing into a morass of disappointment.

Many unfortunate incidents started occurring in Potta Thuruthu.

A fracas started between the dark-skinned people and the fair ones. An ancient vendetta was raising its head again. The trigger point was not due to any major issue. Both groups had plenty of idle and hot-blooded youth. One such loser commented tastelessly on a girl belonging to the other group. When someone went to inquire about the complaint, they manhandled him. Everything turned topsy turvy after that. Both groups stood vigilant, with sharp-edged weapons and sticks. The merest spark could have kindled a raging fire.

The night witnessed the worst of fears coming true. Flaming torches could be seen dotting the pitch darkness. The sounds of frantic running could be heard. Following the murderous howls and undistinguishable screams, a posse of police reached Potta Thuruthu. When the sound of marching boots was heard, even the roosting birds woke up startled and scattered afar. The policemen sniffed around like dogs, covering nooks, corners, searching for the suspects. They got drunk at Vasumathy's arrack shop and staggered away to their camps. The blood of a stranger slowly mixed with the soil of Potta Thuruthu that day. The black mud, on receiving the crimson blood, became a tint darker in shade that day.

The next day, a corpse was found in the common area adjoining the compounds of Ezhuthassan and Koppan. The cops tried to talk to Ezhuthassan, but that strange man, clad in loin cloth and a tail of banana bark, scared them away, snarling.

'He is loony!' The policemen fled for their lives.

Searching for clues, the cops reached Koppan's house. They started competing with one another to gather clues from Unnicheera. The islanders could not comprehend the special information that Unnicheera alone was privy to!

The place where the corpse was found was turned into a makeshift postmortem area, barely hidden from public view with a thatch. No one ventured near that area. The whole day, an enraged Ezhuthassan could be seen racing around his yard.

Kunjootty did not go to office that day.

Zavarias did not dare to open his shop either.

The residents of Potta Thuruthu did not step out even for work.

On that forced holiday, having nothing to do, Kunjootty found himself walking towards the ridges in the southern part of the isle. Unexpectedly, he caught sight of the potta plants that were growing at the edges of the shrimp farms. The Adikaranavar, the original clan leader who had arrived in Potta Thuruthu with the sapling of the eponymous reed, made his presence felt as a breeze amidst the plants. Today, one of his descendants had been hunted down in Potta Thuruthu. The potta plant, holder of the isle's legacy, remained a silent witness to the saga.

The isle was named after the wildly abundant potta plants in the bygone eras. The legendary plants were now sparse; a few scraggly reeds peeked out randomly near the backwaters. No one sought the reeds to weave baskets or mats. The times were changing. In the future, children of the isle might hear about the plant only through folklore.

Kunjootty stepped into the shrimp farm and pulled out a few potta plants with their roots. Then he returned home and planted those near the boundaries of the compound. Let the unpretentious plant, brought by the first native, thrive in the yard. When the genus of the potta plants faced an imminent extinction, the quintessence and the very ethos of Potta Thuruthu were at a risk too.

'Have you gone mad? Got nothing else to plant in the yard except that useless weed?' Zavarias's voice rose from behind.

Kunjootty felt a sarcastic laughter rising within him. It had been ages since father and son had spoken face to face. By a twist of fate, Zavarias could not open his shop today. Else, even on Sabbath, his father would not hesitate to indulge in all forbidden activities.

He wished to explain that the potta plant was not a weed but the very essence of the isle's heritage. But he did not speak. After all, if one had to be sensitive about such nuances, the blades of grass or such trivialities, a bit of craziness was needed inside. The 'fortunate ones' who walked untroubled on the earth, untouched by that madness, could never be convinced about such matters.

The few potta plants that remained in his hand, Kunjootty threw near the mangrove swamps. A few water birds flew up from among the brackish waters and flew away chattering in fear.

By the time Kunjootty emerged from the river, after washing his hands and feet, his father was waiting impatiently for him.

'What are you up to? You wish to create bitterness all around?' Zavarias asked grimly.

As Kunjootty looked up baffled, his father continued.

'What about the proposal from the valley? There is no reason to decline that offer. The girl is educated and the family is well off.'

His father was transgressing into the area from which his mother had tactically withdrawn. Kunjootty could understand their goal of getting their only son married. But, a secret crept up to his tongue tip and dithered. As he tried to untangle the vexatious knot, it became more and more garbled.

Kunjootty stood listlessly, with no answers.

Zavarias read that obdurate silence perfectly.

'I heard about the drivel you spoke to your mother! But you will not get away easily from me!'

Still, Kunjootty stood like an idiot, unresponsive. When subjugation was the aim of the combatant, the opponent's logical reasoning had no relevance at all.

'Are you deaf? Acting like a moron, are you?' Zavarias lost his temper.

Deep within the silent recesses of his heart, Kunjootty became conscious of a rebellion sprouting up fast. It grew into a vengeful attitude, still without a clear form or shape.

Silence, deeper silence.

Zavarias found the silent man obnoxious and detestable.

'Eda, tell me now! What are you thinking?' Zavarias's belligerent voice again rang sharp.

In the next moment, losing all control, Kunjootty shouted:

'Do you want to know? Are you so damn sure about it?'

Zavarias was stunned. Yet he did not give up the fight.

'Go on! Don't stop!'

No, it was too late. Could have confessed much earlier. Why was life, so undeserved, stretched till now? Had there been such fascination with this despicable life?

A hapless warrior, bereft of weapons, was an easy victim on the battlefield, easily vanquished by anyone. He had accepted failure through a sin. Mutilated with multiple battle wounds, the warrior himself was reduced to one big, burning wound. Kunjootty did not want to continue as that fighter anymore. One should be equipped with the strategy for attacks and counter-attacks involving sixty-four squares. One should not contemplate who the enemy might be. A chess move for sheer survival.

'I have nothing to say. And I will not be interrogated by anybody!' Kunjootty raised his voice.

'Eda . . . how dare you?'

Zavarias started yelling. Hearing the sharp screams, Eli came running and the neighbours peeped from their yards.

Zavarias spoke, as if addressing Eli:

'Let him get lost! I don't want to see him any more!'

Yet another curse. With gratitude, Kunjootty added it
to the ones received before. He added it to the collection of
aggrieved curses that was his lot to endure in life. Carrying the
sinful bundle of the first rebellion, Kunjootty stood there for
a while.

He did not eat his lunch that afternoon.

No one insisted that he take it either.

* * *

In the morose twilight when a slow rain was drizzling, the
Velichappadu, the temple oracle, clad in red mundu, torso
wrapped with silk, heaved the *pallival*, the scythe-shaped sword,
and screamed uproariously before the deity of Neendakara
Muthan. A shrivelled-up mango tree stood sleepily nearby.
The few leaves remaining on a branch showered themselves
reverentially on the platform of the deity.

The crowd around the oracle could not understand the
gibberish he spouted. For the first time, a defiant young man
had dared to question the ancient custom that was being
practised for ages.

'Tell me, Velichappadu, who resides in this whitewashed
platform?'

The oracle saw red. His pallival gleamed in the dimming
light. His waist bells rang out together. 'Hooey, Hooey!'

'Mocking us, are you? You will suffer!'

'Welcome! We are the youngsters who live around here. And
we have a right to know, who is it that you try to awaken every
year through your dance? Who are the major residents here?'

Suddenly a wind stirred, as if giving an answer. The last leaf
dropped from the tree and fell with a whimper on the earth.

'Neendakara Mutha! They have desecrated your name and your place of worship. For the sake of this devotee who dances every year for your appeasement, for his heirs, for the bleeding lacerations on my forehead, please take revenge on these infidels! Open your fist and hurl the seeds of smallpox on them! Unleash your ten thousand bhoots now! Sow the seeds, sow the seeds!'

Kora, the erstwhile tailor, came running with a piece of news into that tense surroundings.

He shouted, 'Chiriyankan has returned . . . from France . . . the *madamma* is with him!'

'Devi! Is that true?'

'Yes, just saw them!'

The devotees who were thronging the deity's platform rushed towards Chinnan's house. Vellichappadu followed suit, forgetting the ridicule and his special invocation.

Kunjootty saw a horde scurrying through the farm ridges. Curiously, he too stepped out.

The heart-rending wails could be heard even from a distance.

After many months, Chiriyankan had returned with his French wife to Potta Thuruthu, in search of Anita. He was wailing while embracing Chinnan.

'My little one! My precious child!'

Anita's mother was weeping inconsolably by his side. It was clear to everyone from where Anita had inherited her beautiful blue eyes.

Chiriyankan's sorrow knew no bounds.

'Why am I still alive? For whom should I live now? Patricia, we have lost our angel!'

The lovely French woman stood grief-stricken near the boundary of the house where the new stone was lying amid dried flowers. Her little daughter's spirit was residing in the stone, in the form of a Shovva.

Patricia's religion had not taught her that a stone could hold a soul within it. It would be denigrated as a superstition. Yet, caught in the grips of an emotion far beyond beliefs and teachings, the mother lamented unceasingly, hugging the stone close to her heart.

38

Papa Kanda: The Canto of Sin

After he had openly confronted his father, Kunjootty felt extremely dispirited. No one invited him for supper that night. Before breakfast could be denied the next morning, his mind and body drained of strength, Kunjootty left his house.

He decided not to attend office that day and wandered hither and thither, wishing to reach a state untouched by life's benumbing conditionalities. Visiting Chinnan's house would be agonizing. He could not bear to watch the devastation in Chiriyankan and Patricia's eyes. After the trauma subsided a bit, he would meet them, Kunjootty consoled himself.

In the evening, for a brief respite, he accompanied Isaac to the lagoon. As the boat moved forward, dividing the waters, Kunjootty let out a deep sigh.

'I cannot stand it anymore. Everyone despises me.'

The backwaters lay bleak and cold: like a passage that had been brutally used by many trespassers. The heart of the lagoon seemed to reflect many emotions: the detachment of a monk, the skies of an orphan and the withdrawal of a loser.

'Do not insist that everyone should understand only your feelings,' Isaac commented after listening to Kunjootty's narrative. 'There are people who carry disasters in their hearts, clad in the attire of a non-existing agony. You remind me of them sometimes!'

'Non-existing agony . . . now you are using cliches. I hardly know how to show my emotions,' Kunjootty said sadly.

'This discussion will lead nowhere. If I suggest something, will you consider it patiently?' Isaac asked.

'What is it?'

'Do not object to it, before appreciating the possibilities.'

'This sounds like a negotiation!'

'I have been wanting to say this for a long time. I can even guess your response. You will say it is ridiculous!'

Crabs, as dark as the night, hid their faces in the crevices of the stone walls, afraid of being caught. The last barricades were being built, demarcating the forbidden areas. The boats of the local fisher folk could be seen bobbing up hither and thither, in isolation. After staring at them for some time, Isaac commented: 'I know you have an affinity for the place of your ancestors. We had visited the place. Do you remember seeing another agonized soul over there, Teresa?'

Kunjootty recollected two moist eyes, in the valley of Potta Hill, far away from the barren plains of Chama Potta. How did Isaac's long preface connect with those eyes?

'She is one of the living dead. Fated to be alone just a day before her wedding. The young couple were known to each other and the wedding date was fixed. You will sympathize with the depths of that devastating destiny. It is a small village. The bridegroom's family alleged that it was due to her ill-fate that he died. They spread canards that any prospective bridegroom of Teresa would die. That accusation shrouds her life.'

'Why are you recounting all this now?' Kunjootty felt acutely discomfited.

'Don't get annoyed. When the mind searches for a solution, it is bound to traverse quite a distance. Consider that I have reached an intriguing possibility!'

'Stop, let us not discuss any further.'

'No, I have to finish what I have started. You have to listen.'

'I can guess your plan without listening further. But you are aware that I cannot even contemplate such a matter.'

'I never suggested anything, did I? In fact, Teresa would object more strongly than you.'

'Then why are you elaborating?'

Isaac lit another cigarette in accompaniment to the one he had just finished. He threw the burning cigarette butt into the backwaters.

'You said once that the *mangalsutra*, the wedding dress— these are all mere symbols of marriage. What does not occur in the imagination, will never happen in actuality. Right?'

'Perhaps!'

'Not perhaps . . . that is the truth. I am speaking about a farce, which will never occur in imagination, but happens in reality . . .'

'How come you are speaking in such inscrutable language today?' Kunjootty got irritated.

'Listen, I too have to handle the grievances of people I care about. Your parents are lamenting about you. There are some who are worried sick about a girl of marriageable age. If both of you can come to a mutual understanding—a marriage merely in name—for the sake of the world. Both of you can continue to have your respective privacies, without binding each other down!'

'What foolishness you utter sometimes!' Kunjootty lost his patience completely.

'To willingly let oneself be fooled could be a psychologically healthy solution sometimes!'

'Solution! Only someone who knows the cause can find a solution! You know nothing about me! Just because one wears the holy robes does not make him less of a sinner! I was never your true friend, Isaac!' Kunjootty broke down.

Isaac stared at him dumbstruck. He had not expected such a turn of events.

Kunjootty panted heavily, 'A memory is all that is needed to turn everything upside down. Lord, how come I escaped madness?'

Kunjootty pressed his fingers against his forehead, as if trying to forcibly hold back the rush of thoughts.

'What is the matter, Kunjootty?'

'I cannot bear it any more . . . too heavy!'

'What are you blabbering?'

Nothing was under his control anymore. Words, surroundings, memories, everything intertwined inexplicably.

Kunjootty stared at his right palm. The nomad from the hills had looked at the fate lines and predicted accurately.

'Oh, God! The lines are so bizarre on this child's hand! Why is it so?'

Kunjootty's eyes became bloodshot. His facial muscles stretched taut in stress. Veins popped in his neck and forehead, and he started sweating profusely.

'This hand has sinned! Susanna did not vanish, Isaac . . . I killed her!'

'Kunjootty!'
Isaac felt scorched: it felt as if a lightning bolt had hit him.
Kunjootty heard that call. Very clearly.

* * *

Kunjootty felt the wind buffeting around blindly.

The lagoon was dark all over. The waves rose to hide the horizon. Susanna sat in utter fear, clutching tightly at the sides of the heaving skiff.

'Please don't shake the boat! The wind is very strong! I will fall,' Susanna pleaded.

'You should fall into the water, only then will your fear of water go away!'

It was an innocent prank to see her perturbed. He knew every secret nook and corner of the lagoon. He was also confident that the waves and the wind would obey his commands. The more Susanna pleaded, the more Kunjootty had the urge to scare her.

'I will never come with you again!' Susanna pouted.

'Are you sure?'

'Sure!'

'Then let me shake this boat one more time!'

As he laughingly shook the boat, an unexpected strong wind gathered close, waves surged, the unbalanced boat turned on its side and a fountain of water spurted all over. Susanna screamed as she fell into the river. Water rushed inside the lopsided boat.

'Amma!'

When Kunjootty sprang up to dive into the depths where the screams had disappeared, the rope nearby entangled his ankles and tripped him up, and he fell heavily, hitting his forehead hard on the boat's platform, losing consciousness, slipping into oblivion.

Darkness, darkness, darkness . . .

After what seemed ages, when Kunjootty opened his eyes in a blur, there was no wind. No more frothing waves around. He was lying like a corpse, his face pressed on the platform inside the boat brimming over with water. His body was wet and freezing. Drops of blood trickled from his nostrils, made furrows on the boat's wooden platform and threaded their way into the water.

When he sprang up and looked around, there was no evidence of anything having occurred. Only the lagoon lay deceptively silent, after swallowing everything. His heart felt splintered. He tore away at his clothes and howled in agony. Then his limbs lost strength and he fell into the deep caverns of unconsciousness.

The rest was a blur.

The boat must have bobbed around in the desolation of the backwaters, the man inside having almost lost his mind. Somehow it must have neared the shore. In the burning heat within, his mind had been affected. Time zones got mixed up in his consciousness. The bitter odour of medicines, the touch of death, and somewhere, the memories of a dying gooseberry tree . . . haziness all around.

Isaac sat dumbfounded, listening to all of it. The cigarette had been reduced to a small butt, and it burned his fingers. Hearing, Isaac realized for the first time, was also a curse.

A few birds that had flown to the sea were returning homewards then.

39

Worthless Coins

Isaac was busy soothing the festering lesions, and stood for a long time unaware of the flow of time. His thoughts crossed over the river, in search of a doomed, impoverished family's excruciating summer. A father who died bitterly lamenting his missing daughter. A skeletal form, lying on the bed, one half of her body paralyzed, waking up intermittently to ask, 'Is she back?' That woman was Susanna's mother. Six-legged lice roamed around her gummed eyelashes. Her daughter's stitching machine lay rusted, like the mother herself. And the girl, she must have been caught by one of the lagoon's deadly whirlpools and cast far away into the sea. Or she might have been eaten up by fish, surfaced and then got buried somewhere as an orphaned corpse.

An unthinkably cruel eventuality.

Isaac stood staring at the gathering darkness of the lonely night, utterly helpless. He did not know how to handle his bone-weary friend.

Finally, a cold hand was laid on Kunjootty's shoulder. Holding on to it for dear life, Kunjootty wept uninhibitedly.

'Calm yourself, Kunjootty. It is like you often say. As if someone had scripted everything a long time before.'

'I cannot bear this guilt!'

The sea roared afar.

A seabird flew overhead all alone, keening wretchedly.

'Consider it as an unwarranted error. But would it justify the secretiveness? You withheld it even from me all this time.'

'I wanted to . . . many times,' Kunjootty spoke regretfully. 'I wanted to announce it to the whole world and take on whatever punishment it might decree. But I was unconscious for such a long time. And you protected me from every inquiry. A single question would have seen me confess. Just a question from anybody. Then my mind went into some sort of a deep freeze. Nothing seemed to touch me at all in that interval. Exhausted beyond words, I never even felt that I was alive. Slowly, I returned to life. I know these are not acceptable justifications. At least now I should confess. Let everyone know the truth.'

'It is too late now. That admission will do no good to anyone either.' Isaac fell into a contemplative mood. 'You should promise me something!'

'What?'

'That you will not reveal the secret to anyone else!'

As Kunjootty stood helplessly, Isaac spoke.

'The problem does not end there. The sin that accrued because of a woman should be atoned by helping another woman. Can you not free another woman?'

'Why are you giving out such strictures, Isaac?' Kunjootty asked in a poignant tone.

'Assume that the time has arrived to repay your debts. Else, would the circumstances get aligned like this? If what I suggested can be a resolution, why not? It is your decision.'

Kunjootty discerned woefully how Isaac used the opportunity, regardless of the inappropriate time, to push his point through. Here was a man trying to carve out two isles within four walls of a house. Maybe he believed that the two isles would end up discovering each other in a fortuitous future. A rather weak storyline . . .

The lagoon stretched far, languid in the evening. There was no wind now. The gleaming sparkles on the lagoon resembled eyes that shimmered in darkness. The specks were yearning to flow towards the sea.

What's destined will remain so. The one who had scripted the tale should not be affected by the turn of events. He should be able to flip through the chapters indifferently. When one explores either side of the possibilities, it is like touching the subtle thread of life. Surreal experiences might come searching for the one destined. Maybe the time was imminent for a journey to the land imprinted with the ancestor's blood. Once the mind reached there, the portents would ensure that the body was transmitted too. Remain in the flow, offering no resistance, just like a corpse.

The lagoon, which blotted out the existence of Susanna, had also freed her from grievances and worries. What happened after that was unknown to Kunjootty. Perhaps, on becoming dead to the world, the surroundings did not affect one anymore. If only he could reach that state where the ties of the body loosened its hold.

Neither Kunjootty nor Isaac discussed the topic until they returned to Potta Thuruthu. The silence was an unspoken mutual pact. They could not meet each other for a few days after that. Neither inquired about the other. Kunjootty surmised that Isaac must have gone off on one of his trips. Perhaps he was hard at work, trying to get the barricades around the shrimp farms completed before the monsoons started.

It could have been the confession, or because he was trying to evade the ties of the body, but Kunjootty felt lighthearted. A few days passed by in this manner.

When Kunjootty returned from office that Friday, Eli was by the riverbank. His mother did not even wait for him to disembark.

'Is it true what I am hearing?'

Seeing her beaming face, which was unusual, Kunjootty felt bemused.

'Isaac told me that he had gone to his aunt's place to inquire about her daughter!'

Kunjootty wondered how to respond to his mother's genuine innocence. He felt a deep sense of compassion welling within him. In the same kindly spirit, he replied:

'Then it must be true, Amma!'

'Malayatoor Muthappa! I shall follow the way of the Cross and climb your sacred hill!'

Eli had endured all the good and bad tidings in her life by resorting to such prayerful offerings.

When he heard his mother's ecstatic promise, Kunjootty remembered learning the alphabets in his childhood by scrawling them on rice. His amma had promised yet another offering when he mastered his first letter of the alphabet: 'A'. Then, when the lessons progressed, he wrote 'mma' on the loamy sand, and he had read them together with a dawning wonder—'Amma'.

If numerous supplications were gathered together, that would embody Eli's life. Now, yet another promise, connecting her son's wedding to a pilgrimage that followed the way of the Cross.

Kunjootty watched compassionately as his mother's joy overflowed. Eli hailed the Pulaya women fishing in the river.

'If you get a good catch, bring it over!'

'Something special happening today?'

'Oh, yes, Nangeli!'

The women dived under water, dragging the tender coconut leaves tied to a rope. Afraid of the intermittent flashes of the coconut leaves, the fish hid themselves in the slushy riverbed. The women caught them with their bare hands, shoving them inside pots floating on the river surface. Sometimes when they caught more than a handful, the women emerged with fish in their jaws. A story was told about a fisherman of the Chova community, who dived into the water and surfaced with a fish between his teeth. The fish apparently struggled its way into his windpipe and choked him to death. From that time onwards, that particular species was called 'Chovan-Kolli': the killer of Chovans.

Kunjootty spent a long time near the river. He was feeling lethargic again. When he encountered Isaac after the sun set, he was still in that sluggish mood.

'Unpleasant deeds need quick execution, right?'

'It was not too easy a task, by the way. Had to inveigle with some Vedanta too.'

'Good!'

'Why are you so moody?'

'It seems nonsensical to me. As if nothing matters anymore. Ezhuthassan is so fortunate, is he not? Without any obligations, he lives comfortably in a world of his own imagination.'

'That is called madness.'

'Who knows? Who is truly mad?' Then Kunjootty paused before asking, 'Is that true, what you said, Isaac?'

'What?'

'About Teresa's strange destiny. That the bridegroom dies before arriving for the wedding?'

'So what if it is true? Are you feeling afraid?'

'Fear? That remains my only hope now!' Kunjootty laughed mirthlessly.

Isaac was not pleased with that dark humour.

'Do not brood too much and then everything will pass comfortably,' he advised Kunjootty.

'Really?'

'In my case, there is a rising rebellion against my barricaded shrimp farms. The fisher folk are organizing under many multicoloured flags to assail my project! But I will fight back. I will resort to any means!'

As Kunjootty stared unblinkingly at him, Isaac grinned.

'What, are you feeling terrified?'

'Are you drunk?'

'Yes, a bit. If you ask me the reason, well, the writer of the *Book of Exodus* can guess for himself.'

A fisherwoman came up for air, with a fish fluttering between her clenched teeth. A river fish, which was terrified of the shadow of the tender coconut leaf and had hidden itself in the clay hoping to escape, had been caught! The waters were muddy all around.

* * *

Soon afterwards, a small group started off to the valley of Potta Hill from Potta Thuruthu. Not having anything left to convince or be convinced by, Kunjootty stayed away. When the party returned from the land of his forebearers, they informed him that the date of the wedding had been fixed for the second Sunday following Holy Easter: The Sunday of Resurrection.

'Every day is a medley of many pulsing moments,' Kunjootty wrote in the *Book of Exodus* that night.

He imagined the destruction of Potta Thuruthu in an earthquake and a successor discovering his book after a long interval. He realized that he adored the book like a beloved child. After years of effort, the *arani*—the ceremonial wood piece to kindle the first spark in the fire ceremony—had stoked the agni in the form of his book. All forms were the manifest reflections of the One Divine Light.

As he stared long at the *Book of Exodus*, Kunjootty felt that it could breathe, albeit like any other creature. The heart was beating like infinite time, without a beginning or an end.

Kunjootty staggered through the book like a blind man who was lost. He encountered pale blades of grass, dark statues, sharp thorns. He saw death temptingly take along those who had not yet lived to their fill. And those who yearned to let go of life, it dissuaded with a pat on the shoulder. The master-play of the Time Lord!

Kunjootty unexpectedly remembered Diwakar Menon. The man who set off, abandoning his life in a carefree manner, like a nonsensical fairy tale. In which citadel of truth had he reached now? Kunjootty recollected that he had to honour an absurd promise.

Taking up a white paper, he started writing.

'Is our meeting place erroneous or are we are nearing it? No idea. Yes, I am inviting you. If you feel your heart lurch, if the destiny is benevolent . . . I can hope at least . . . even if it is futile.'

Kunjootty folded the paper into four and put it inside an envelope. On top of it he wrote: Shri Diwakar Menon. The address petered out at that instant itself. The pen lay between his fingers, unsure of the next words.

Kunjootty saw the truth now: Even from afar, Menon was teaching him a new lesson. At the end, every human being was like worthless coins, bereft of address. The next day was the Last Supper of the Betrayed One. The day after, on Good Friday, a summer rain dense with sorrow pounded the isle. In the ferocious storm, many trees arched like bows and splintered in the middle. Leaving behind the corpses of trees here and there, the rain and wind returned the same day.

The summer heat was relentless.

40

Recurrences

There was a time when screwpines and marsh barbels were abundant near the river. Water birds nestled amid the dark hollows and fledglings were hatched. The old timers believed that when the white-breasted water hen warbled, the goddess of inauspicious tidings, Jyestha Devi, would be cast out afar. Consequently, they never disturbed the birds or their young.

Their next generation started slashing away at the vayalchulli and screwpines. Building stone walls where once the plants thrived, they demarcated their boundaries. With no place to make their nests, most of the waterhens died away or took flight like refugees. In their place, burning summer and drought came searching for Potta Thuruthu.

In spite of that, no one regretted their ruthlessness against the screwpines or the auspicious birds that had once sheltered amongst the bushes.

Occasionally a grandmother could be heard humming a lullaby to her grandchild about the bird.

'Unjalo, Chakiamma, Kulakozhi Muttayittu
Koodu thatti thottilittu . . .'

'Hey, listen, as the swing flies,
The water hen laid an egg
The nest fell into the canal . . .'

In the course of time, those songs, carrying the ethos of Potta
Thuruthu, languished away too.

The summer was intense that year. Drinking-water sources
dried up and reddish layers of dust coated the surfaces. The
burning wings of the wind fluttered around the isle from morn
to dusk. The farms were desiccated and lay lifeless, like the
witnesses of an ancient wrong.

The only person who remained unaffected by these climatic
changes was Ezhuthassan. He stayed in his own world: of
powerful amulets and mantras.

Inside the sacred space of the amulet, he inscribed the
Bijakshara mantra. The various rites of Tantric rituals and
sorcery—Ashtavajra, Chaturasram, Ashtadalam, Mala Mantra—
and all the intricate steps involved in armouring oneself against
evil were scrupulously conducted by Ezhuthassan.

Om, Aim, Hreem, Hraam . . .

By the time the rites were over, Ezhuthassan felt exhausted
as if he had been on a long journey. He had no premonition
that the creation of the protective amulet would involve such
gruelling effort. It was his first creation.

'Keep guard, Anjaneya!'

Ezhuthassan was eager to know the results. A guilt started
eating him from within. Would the impulse that he hadn't

been able to control stand in the way of this amulet's protecting powers? Had the rites been correct?

He controlled his doubts, and tying the amulet to a thread, waited for dusk. While measuring the length of the thread, he had imagined the curves of the woman's waist.

The owls hooted dejectedly from the treetops at twilight. A faint fragrance of distant evening flowers spread in the breeze.

Unnicheera had reached the bramble boundary by then. Ezhuthassan once again sensed a thrill spread all over the surroundings.

The man's glance fell on the waist that had been playing in his mind. Now the amulet will stick close to that body forever . . .

Another union. Unnicheera had accepted that part of the ritual by now.

With shaking hands, she received the enchanted amulet. Ezhuthassan refused to take the coin that she offered as *dakshina*.

'You keep it.'

'Let me go now.'

'Do not be afraid. Everything will be fine now.'

Unnicheera did not feel any remorse. Her only worry was that the infant was alone in the house. Before he woke up, she intended to return.

As Unnicheera crossed the fence, she met Kunjootty.

A red hue of embarrassment spread over Unnicheera's face. She struggled to smile, tucking away her loose and awry hair.

'How come you are here?' Kunjootty asked.

'Have to rush!'

Her face downcast, Unnicheera hurried away.

Perplexed, Kunjootty stared at the retreating figure of the young woman and then at the eerie darkness of Ezhuthassan's compound, unable to make the connection. He had come to inform Ezhuthassan about his marriage. However, now he did not feel like putting even a single step forward.

As he walked to the ferry, he curiously looked towards the dark path that Unnicheera had taken. He could see a man waiting in the shadows. Aware of his own unhealthy curiosity, Kunjootty paused in the darkness.

As the waiting man shouted, Kunjootty realized who it was.

'Where had you gone?'

Unnicheera was flustered at the toddy tapper's tone. She stuttered as she responded.

'I . . . I . . . just nearby!'

'Leaving the baby all alone! Where? What is in your hand?'

'That . . . a thread!'

'What thread?'

Kunjootty could not see the perturbed woman in the partial darkness.

Her answer came, trying to evade an answer,' Why do you want to know?'

'If not me, who else would ask you?'

The thick lips of the toddy tapper curled into a sneer.

'Oh, I can guess! That must be the gift from the mad old Asan! You went to his place, didn't you?'

'Yes.'

'He tied the thread, did he?'

No response.

The man's face became ugly with wrath.

'Ah, so you slept with him too, did you?'

'Now you stop!' Unnicheera's response was weak, her mind not being in consonance.

Kunjootty listened alertly to know the aftermath.

The toddy tapper spat with utter disgust on the front yard. Then he wrenched away the 'Dharana yantra', the magical amulet, from Unnicheera's hand. Unfurling the metal roll, the man glared at the inscribed letters. Like ancient runes, undecipherable alphabets lay immersed in the delicacy of the metal surface.

> . . . *Mama sarvagriha vinashana*
> *Sarva jwarochhadana*
> *Sarva vishanashana*
> *Sarvapatthinivarana* . . .
> *Ghegheghe* . . . *hahaha* . . . *humhumhum* . . . *bhatbhatbhat* . . .
> *swaha!*

Fury filled the toddy tapper's face.

'His blasted mantras and damned thread! Thbbhu!' As Unnicheera stood thunderstruck, the amulet containing the protective mantras sank deep into the river.

Kunjootty furtively made his way to his boat.

The toddy tapper did not stay afterwards.

From eons past, the memories came to haunt him once more: Pennu Kunju, the beautiful twelve-year-old dream girl, the wild wax apples, the sneaking beneath the bramble boundary. He felt a pernicious churning inside.

Unnicheera stared dumbly at his receding form. Pangs of remorse started troubling her.

'Perhaps tomorrow, or even the day after . . . maybe the next day . . . he will return.' Unnicheera waited.

The windy nights, filled with the chirps of lonely birds, passed away one by one.

The toddy tapper did not return the next day.

Neither the day after, nor the following day.

The salt-laden wind, oppressive with the Chaitra heat, blew forcefully over the dark river shore. Even the coconut trees looked enervated. The river was infested with brackish waters. Rare sea creatures came visiting Potta Thuruthu in the encroaching sea waters. As if to fulfil their destinies, otters could be seen swimming up the estuary into the lagoon, along with the deadly Theechoriyan, the toxic creature whose diabolical touch could burn the skin on a mere touch. There was a malevolent atmosphere prevailing all over the place.

Ezhuthassan was busy in the torrid nights. Intermittently, he searched for mantras among the ancient palmyra manuscripts. Then he would set off on his unceasing walks. He would saunter around aimlessly in all four directions without any rest, crushing the dried leaves under his feet along with the crawling centipedes. One parched night, he ended up in the cremation ground.

The old man squatted near a new pyre that was slowly dying away. Gathering the ashes, Ezhuthassan created the form of his enemy. Next, he wrote the name on the chest. Reciting the mantra from the ancient scripts, he plunged a sharp dagger into the creation's heart.

'Chindibhindi maraya!'

The invocation of an ancient evil spell!

As he bit his lower lip and clapped his hands together, the nocturnal creatures skittered in terror and sought hideaways.

Seven disturbed nights passed by.

The eighth day was a Friday.

The toddy tapper scoured the riverside for a private space to answer nature's call. On the riverbanks from where screwpine bushes had been evicted, stones were waiting for him like Ahalya of the legends. He sat on his heels on one of the cropped-up stones. After some time, he stepped into the river to wash himself. In the blink of an eye, he scrambled up the shore, screaming in horror.

His legs had started swelling and bloating, the colour of his skin turning red.

The islanders identified the culprit: 'Neendakara Mutha! That fatal touch of the Theechoriyan!'

The sores started spreading upwards in a matter of days. Suppurating wounds were visible all over his body. Flies buzzed around the toddy tapper.

The villagers desisted from stepping into the river after that. Theechoriyan, with its mushroom like white body filled with dark spots and long threadlike formations on its backside, thrived and multiplied fast in the lagoon. They swam about leisurely in the polluted backwaters without any encumbrances. Even the sand diggers kept away from the waters, preferring to starve.

'It is all Ezhuthassan's doing. He is the one behind all this!' The news spread fast in Potta Thuruthu.

'What are you saying? As if no one has been hurt by the Theechoriyan before!'

'Whatever you may please! But don't deny that the man had some enmity with Ezhuthassan!'

Kunjootty could not gauge the depth of truth in whatever he heard. Ezhuthassan was his first teacher. Someone who always behaved politely with him. If he did not inform him about the wedding, it would be like denigrating the guru.

Kunjootty went to meet Ezhuthassan once more. The old man was sitting huddled, oddly silent.

On hearing Kunjootty call out his name, Asan recognized him.

'Ah, come inside!'

It was as if the man was waiting for him. Clutching Kunjootty's arm, Asan ushered him inside his house. They crossed a pitch-black corridor and reached a musty room. When the old doors opened, many life forms scattered in terror and vanished in different corners.

From the incongruities around, Asan retrieved an arcane wooden box. Opening its intricate lock with a key, he searched inside and pulled out an old manuscript made of palmyra leaves.

The room was redolent with the smell of a bygone era.

Ezhuthassan lifted the manuscript reverently, touching both eyes with it.

Then he looked at Kunjootty and asked, 'I don't need it anymore. Would you like to have it?'

That was totally unforeseen.

Though he was intrigued about the contents of the manuscript, Kunjootty's words came out strangely.

'I . . . I cannot touch it! I am not pure enough for that!'

Ezhuthassan's face became serene. He gazed compassionately at Kunjootty, as if realizing the secret behind the pain. Then he smiled with great kindness.

Locking the manuscript inside the box once more, Ezhuthassan stepped out with Kunjootty.

When they reached the moss ridden pond, beyond the snake grove where the Naga statues stood languorously, Asan stopped.

He contemplated the pond for a while, or perhaps, he might have been meditating.

Ezhuthassan hurled the key into the pond. It disappeared inside the dark vagueness covered with moss and weeds.

Looking at Kunjootty who stood uncomprehending and nonplussed, Ezhuthassan spoke.

'If you want, you can take this compound for yourself. I only need this tree!'

Ezhuthassan stroked the thanni tree nearby with great affection.

Then he mumbled to himself.

'If you go wrong even once, you continue to repeat it. If you do not rectify, it will recur . . .'

Ezhuthassan's composure slipped suddenly. His cheeks were now puffed up and his eyes popped out. He made a climbing ring out of his hands and started clambering up the tree like a monkey.

Kunjootty gaped at the nest at the top, made of an assortment of creepers, palm leaves and grass stalks. Ezhuthassan crept inside and pulled a thatch of coconut leaves to hide himself from view.

Kunjootty stared at the precarious resting place on the tree.

He waited for a long time. There was no sound, no movement.

As he wondered whether he should turn back, the permission came from the skies. Or was it a farewell?

'Kutty, you may leave now! Do not come here again!'

Kunjootty had forgotten about the wedding invitation.

That night, Unnicheera, sleepless and tense, heard an insistent knocking at her door. She clutched the baby to her breast and called out frantically:

'Who is it?'

'It is me. Please open the door.'

The voice was familiar, yet Unnicheera felt a tremor passing through her.

As she hesitatingly opened the door, Unnicheera saw the toddy tapper and suppressed an urge to scream. The once handsome body was rotting, and the pus-filled sores were a loathsome sight.

Unnicheera shut her eyes with her hands and wept.

'Why did you come here? Go away . . . go!'

The toddy tapper begged pitifully: 'I am starving. Can you please give me some rice gruel?'

Unnicheera could not bear it any more. Shutting the door with a bang and bolting the latch, she stood sobbing her heart out until dawn.

41

The Verdict

Migratory birds, hitherto unseen in the area, swooped down on Potta Thuruthu and surrounding isles. They perched on the mango trees, coconut trees and the thanni tree. Pecking around the slender diamond flowers in the yard and swaying on the abundant neyunni climbers in the serpent grove, the birds seemed to be joyous. These visitors had longer wings and were larger than the native birds.

Ezhuthassan, who was jumping from branch to branch, enjoyed the presence of birds the most. They communicated with each other with no limitation of language. As the birds hopped over his thatched makeshift residence on the thanni tree, he reached out and touched them. He moved from one branch to another, seeking them out. It was amidst this boisterous sky walking adventure that Ezhuthassan sighted the bird sitting grandly at the pinnacle. It was majestic, with kingly stature.

'Now, I will touch you too, smart one!'

Grinning to himself, Ezhuthassan made a leap. His hand did not reach the target and he lost his footing. Slipping through the branches, the old man fell on the hard ground below.

'Ramaaaa!' The scream echoed in the surroundings and the birds scattered in terror. Afterwards, only their cries resounded for a long time—as if they were wailing about the tragic incident, in their own strange tongue. When the islanders reached the compound, curious about the unanimous chirping, they found the lifeless body of Ezhuthassan lying beneath the thanni tree.

Kunjootty was busy with the wedding preparations when he heard the news. The pain that welled up was acute, as if an inseparable connection had been broken off forcefully.

He wondered whether Ezhuthassan had foreseen the impending tragedy. The way he had asked Kunjootty not to return; the way he had bid farewell the previous night . . .

Now he had no other recourse but to disobey the forbidding command and visit the house once more. As he pushed his boat into the river, his mother objected worriedly.

'Tomorrow being such an auspicious day, why go to such a dismal place today?'

An untimely death on the day before the wedding worried Eli, who always looked out for ill omens. But Kunjootty had to ignore that apprehension.

'I will come back immediately.'

'Then you undertake the confession in the church on your way. That will complete one wedding formality too.'

Kunjootty did not reply and steered the skiff to the opposite shore.

A large crowd thronged Ezhuthassan's house. Villagers, who had been afraid to take a peek till that day, wandered freely in the dark compound. In their midst, Ezhuthassan lay still with his eyes protruding hideously, blood dripping from the mouth, a broken neck.

'He slipped . . . was leaping from one tree to another!' Kunjootty heard someone whispering to another.

'He was wandering crazily all these days. And now, such an ill-fated death.'

'Today was the thirteenth day puja.'

'Where?'

'Kavilottu Temple. They had taken him along for the forty days puja at the Devi Temple.'

'Who?'

'Relatives. But he did not complete it. Ran away and returned home. Climbed up the tree to catch a bird. Slipped and fell to his death.'

'Horrible!'

The bright student of the village school looked again at the face of his first teacher. The one who had blessed him with Akshara, the non-perishing energy behind every learning, had now left the impermanent world. The strange migratory birds were no more to be seen. Perhaps they had arrived to take Ezhuthassan along. Having finished their mission, they might have returned.

Some of the villagers managed to bathe the corpse and cover it with white clothes. The strip of white cloth that tied the jaws and head together, and the rice strewn around the corpse, restricted Ezhuthassan. Some were still terrified that the old man might leap at them, remembering how they had teased him as 'Hanuman Kutty!'

The islanders volunteered to prepare a pyre for the teacher who had taught them their alphabets.

While Ezhuthassan burned to ashes in the southern corner of his yard, Kunjootty observed the situation dispassionately. He watched the bamboo grove in full bloom, the half-broken stalks, the scattered bamboo rice . . . a life was passing away.

The gossip was continuing near the bamboo grove.

'It is the curse of a woman, they say! That is why Hanuman never favoured him. There is no way out after committing such sins. In his hot-blooded youth, he had . . . a very young girl!' What more to say? Mother and sister died due to madness, and he ended up like this. God's decree!'

God's decree! A woman's curse!

Words had arrived to torture Kunjootty today.

A tumbledown family house nearby. An ancient, mould-ridden, palmyra manuscript. The precious secrets inside the manuscript would never see the light of the day again. The lifetime efforts of Ezhuthassan, investing his body, mind and soul, were all futile.

A sense of profound bleakness overwhelmed Kunjootty. The mortal world with its false solutions. The snares of curses that crept in from the past. And a woman's curse, from which there was no escape. He felt like laughing. In an instant, he felt like crying. But he stalled in the middle, unable to do either.

Kunjootty felt that Ezhuthassan was showing him the way to a certain place. Through the riverbank next to the bamboo grove, stepping across the wet grass, he started on a journey. Beyond the kiln where seashells were treated for extracting lime, there were sparsely populated isles. One such was the 'Panikkan Potta' where the low-caste people were cremated. Near that desolate place, on a piece of land abhorred by all, stood a decrepit hut. The thatch roof had withered away. It stood like an abominable refuse, chewed out by the hungry ghouls haunting that graveyard.

An emaciated old woman lay like a bundle of worn clothes on a cane cot in the porch.

Catching the shadows, she called out:

'Who is it?'

Kunjootty stood there, unsure of how to speak. It was a place he had long forgotten or had pretended to forget till that point in time. When he had succumbed to the urge to travel, he had not been sure of his course of action.

From the ramshackle hovel, a girl peeped out. She was pale and thin; her dress was shabby and tattered. Her eyes widened at the sight of the guest who had arrived at that untimely hour.

'From the other shore . . . Edappadathu Veedu!'

As she spoke the words with extreme hesitation, the woman's lips started trembling in agitation.

'Ku . . . njootty?'

The old woman was finding it hard to believe. Within the body refusing to move, something started stirring. Various seasons started passing through her as the wind, rain and mist. The seasonal changes the woman was experiencing, suddenly stopped, melting during a hot summer. It was during that summer she had lost Susanna.

'Why have you come? After ignoring us till now, why did you bother to come?'

Whatever was transpiring within her, came up to the surface and reflected spitefully in her eyes. The woman started breathing heavily due to the emotional upheaval. As Kunjootty stood lost for words, she breathed out:

'I have been wanting to see you! To ask you a question. What happened to my child? My mind says that you know the answer. Tell me if she is dead. At least I can ensure a requiem for her.'

'Amma, I!'

Kunjootty was sweating profusely in the summer heat enveloping him.

The old woman's words burned their way through Kunjootty's flesh and reached his bones. The accusation was scalpel sharp, leaving no means of escape. Kunjootty found his defences breached, and was allowed no time to don any armour.

'My body may be paralyzed but my mind will not lie to me! Tell me what happened to my daughter. Or else . . . or else . . . I shall.'

The old woman was screaming by now.

There was no place to hide. Not even a fig leaf to cover his stark nakedness.

Maybe one could trick a bag of bones, but to cheat the eternal spirit within was impossible.

Was that the reason why his mother had hailed from behind, interrupting his journey, and reminded him of a confession?

A true confession happened only while speaking truthfully before someone powerful enough to grant pardon or punishment.

Kunjootty had to keep the word given to his mother and also provide an answer to another mother. The long-drawn-out admission became the most traumatizing predicament he had faced till then. To reveal himself as the murderer of a beloved daughter to an aged mother on her death bed.

Where was he supposed to begin?

His voice affected by his intense remorse, Kunjootty searched for words. It was his first holy confession.

'I do not know what to say. I made a mistake . . .' A welter of words. His words stumbled and fell. 'On the lagoon . . . the wind was strong . . .'

A Sunday when everyone was at church, two young people sneaked away for a trip in the lagoon with their Qurbana debts in tow. The fear spreading as the boat heaved in the waves and winds. A scream that echoed till it touched the depths of death . . .

When the mind plummeted again into the unnerving turbulence, words and meanings parted ways and became lifeless.

Kunjootty was struggling to breathe. The palms of his hands, his feet, his thighs had dampened with perspiration. In utter devastation, Kunjootty slowly fell on his knees before the bedridden old woman and started whimpering.

'My sin . . . my sin!'

The woman was lamenting much more forcefully. A scream, stronger than the ones bygone, was trapped in her chest. Her veins stretched taut to the point of bursting. The eyes were enlarged, almost popping from their sockets. They blazed with a fire that could turn the man into ashes.

'You devil, you proved that you are of the same damned bloodline!' The words that emerged from her dried lips were fatal in impact. 'I could not even get a Qurbana conducted for her soul! You are the blasted son of the evil man who stole our house and land claiming unpaid debts! Do you know something? If we had not given up our property, your father would have . . . You would have been born in my womb, you sinner. If you have a son, he will continue this accursed legacy. May it never happen! May no more children be born in your damned family!'

The curse was enough to split his forehead in two, and Kunjootty acknowledged his own death. He stared in wonder as the incredible power of her words made the old woman's hitherto immobile hands and fingers quiver. Amassing all of her remaining will power, she reached out for the short wooden pestle lying on the plank nearby and smashed it against the head of the sinner kneeling before her.

'May you and your clan be damned forever!'

Kunjootty was aware only of the pestle striking his temple.

An explosion in the consciousness . . .

The last bit of strength ebbing away, like a cage bereft of the bird, the old woman fell back on her cot.

A girl's shriek could be heard.

The lagoon . . . the wind . . . the boat turning on its side . . . a woodpecker's chatter like an ominous omen of death.

Kikki . . . Kikki . . . Kikki . . .

Sandhyayam kujatashchapi daarvaghadasye

The cry of a sparrow-hawk in the evening is a bad omen

The journey towards death begins slowly when the mind's throbbing becomes feeble. A cypher, stacking many moments inside one moment. A state that transcends sight and hearing. Within the borders of insanity and sleep, through an accustomed path, through the undulations of darkness, no light, wrong again, through darkness, or perhaps light . . . rising, falling . . .

42

The Land Where the Sun Never Rises

A journey from the cloud canopies. A fledgling fire bird, waving its slender wings, started its exodus towards the earth where the sun had not yet risen.

It could see nothing in the darkness. Neither the one-legged tree nor the inhabitants therein. The fire bird was unaware of the malevolent vultures thirsty for her blood.

Soon the shuffling sounds approached her. A volt of vultures emanating the stench of carcasses, with eyes resembling smouldering embers, started interrogating her:

'Who are you?'

'I am the fire bird!'

'Why have you come here?'

'To see everything. The earth, the rivers, the flowers . . .'

The group cackled maliciously:

'In the land where the sun doesn't rise, how will you see the earth? How will you see the river? How will you see the flowers?'

As the little fire fledgling stood there, appalled and apprehensive, they edged closer.

'Let us show you, this is the earth!' Their claws sank into her tender head.

'Let us show you, these are flowers!' Flowers of blood bloomed on her delicate neck.

'Let us show you, these are rivers!' Their beaks pecked at her, and a river of blood spurted from her beautiful body.

Then the wake of vultures feasted together. A few feathers and bones were the only chaff they spat out.

Over the terrified and chilly contours of Potta Hill, an untimely star rose. The rays were streaming towards him, tantalizing enough for him to blink his eyes open. However, the sharp-edged light beams made the task difficult.

After a brief tussle with the eyelids, slowly, light and sight became congruent.

There was no fire bird. There was no one-legged tree or corpse-eating vultures. What remained were mild sounds. Someone was consoling him, with a gentle caress.

'Kunjootty . . . my son!'

A familiar voice.

On emerging from deep slumber to half-awakened consciousness, Amma became visible, like a faded picture. Wisps of grey hair fell on her forehead and tear drops sparkled in her aged eyes.

'Amma!'

Did he call out or was it just a longing? The yearnings were lying helplessly deep within his self. His body felt as if it was being stretched in multiple directions. Nozzles were stuck in numerous veins. An inverted bottle with a colourless liquid was hanging from a stand nearby. Through a syringe in his hand, the liquid was being injected into his bloodstream.

He must have overcome another death. Kunjootty felt that he had been suspended in a space between two islands of consciousness. A big bandage was around his head. There was a vague memory of something hard hitting him. The last sound he heard was the woodpecker's scream. How long was it since the connections to the universe had been snapped?

As Kunjootty tried to get up, the wound on his forehead started stinging badly. The train of thoughts was lost once more. When he struggled to recollect, memories became elusive. And words too slipped away.

Within the dimming vision, Kunjootty recognized his appan's familiar presence. There were other people with him. But he could not see Isaac anywhere. The eyes grew exhausted, searching in vain. Then a weight descended on his eyelids. Slowly, slowly, the descent began. Now as the momentum escalated, in order to escape, he desperately clutched at a black boat.

'Come on,' someone was inviting him.

'Who is it?'

White clothes, teary eyes.

Someone was wiping his tears with a white handkerchief.

'Valiyammachi!'

Listening to his call, Valiyammachi turned, and showed him the kerchief that had wiped tears from his eyes. It was full of blood.

'May you and your clan be damned forever!'

Panting heavily, Kunjootty forced his eyes open.

The harsh whiff of medicines met him once again. He held on to the hand that was gently stroking his chest. That hairy hand was not familiar to him. Whose was it?

He was astonished to see the man. Appan.

Zavarias was wiping the perspiration from his son's chest, neck, forehead . . .

Kunjootty felt a simmering hatred. The face that he never wished to see was right in front of him. He tried to avert his gaze and stared at the ceiling. They had come together after what seemed like lifetimes. The father, the son and a cold silence were alone in the room.

'Are you thirsty?' Zavarias asked.

Kunjootty felt desperate for a drink of water, but did not answer.

'Shall I give you some warm milk?'

Kunjootty lay motionless, his eyes unblinking. Even before he murmured an answer, Zavarias filled a glass with milk from a flask. Unable to assuage the unbearable thirst, Kunjootty surrendered.

He could have hated his appan forever. He had negotiated the very soul of a family in return for an old debt. A man who had tried to haggle over a poor woman's dignity, exploiting her poverty.

Kunjootty tried to remember at which juncture he became associated with the man. When had dark circles emerged underneath his eyes? How come the thick moustache looked so ancient and lifeless now? When had the wheezing begun, veins marked out the feeble muscles and the stentorian voice lost its harshness? Kunjootty had forgotten the last time he had hailed his father as 'Appa'. That affectionate address had long frozen in his chest. Even if it did manage to escape, the obdurately shut throat wouldn't let it out.

'Do not vex your mind any more!'

There was a special consideration in Zavarias's voice. The solicitude, which was at odds with his father's persona, disturbed Kunjootty unreasonably. Perhaps it was due to the advice of the doctor. Kunjootty wished that his father would desist from being open with him.

'Isaac . . . where is he?' he asked.

'He will come in the night. Then I will leave.'

There was nothing more to be said. A morose, lacklustre silence started gathering between them. As the discomfort stretched, Zavarias tried to chat about the latest gossip in the village. How the relatives of Ezhuthassan were fighting over his property, how a fire was seen burning on the branch of the thanni tree in the compound, how Kora almost lost his wits on seeing Ezhuthassan's ghost, how the fishermen caught the skeletons of a man and a dog in their nets, how the police took those remains to Koppan's home, how Unnicheera collapsed on seeing that . . .

Nothing seemed to touch Kunjootty deeply. The breeze from the backwaters was wafting by and he caught a whiff.

From within the forehead, an interminable, sharp pain throbbed. Had a nerve snapped in the fracas? Kunjootty closed his eyes exhaustedly.

A huge silence loomed overhead.

After some time, Zavarias called out gently:

'Kunjootty!'

His son opened his eyes and listened. Kunjootty could not remember the last time he had heard his father calling him by that name. From a man like Zavarias, who always called him as 'Eda' or 'You', this was unbelievable.

What happened next was beyond his wildest beliefs.

His father started sobbing, letting down all pretensions of toughness.

Something melted inside Kunjootty at that sight. From within him came a long-forgotten endearment.

'Appa!'

Zavarias could not stand it any longer. He blurted out thoughtlessly:

'How did you manage to hide so much within you, my child? Why didn't you tell us? If we had known earlier!'

Kunjootty lay stunned and speechless.

So it was not a dream.

All the sins that were written on the lines of his right palm, now stood revealed.

The earth must have rotated many times while he was deep asleep. How many days had passed since that incident? What had happened after that?

'It was all my fault! At a young age, when I had no wisdom, I ended up doing unforgivable things. I could not even have a proper conversation with you, my son. Now, I no longer have any idea how to help you.'

Kunjootty found himself incapable of enduring that deep atonement and lamentation.

'Don't cry like this . . . please don't cry!' He begged his father.

Zavarias was mumbling, hardly able to control himself.

'And now, how will you endure that news, my child?' His words broke as he struggled to breathe normally.

'What news?' Kunjootty asked apprehensively.

Zavarias was wresting with words now. He stood at the desolate crossroads, not knowing what to utter.

'When the wedding was called off . . . that girl . . . Lord!'

Grasping the horror hidden in those words, a frenzy seized Kunjootty. A poignant, moist look, back at the valley of the Potta Hill.

'Teresa, what happened to her?'

'That girl's fate!' Zavarias covered his face and wept, 'The news they heard was . . . of your death.'

Kunjootty felt that his nerves were stretched to bursting point.

Everything was clear to him now.

Nothing more was needed to fill in the blanks.

When the gossipmongers heard the latest story to add to the old one, they must have added oil to the blazing fire of their pernicious mockery. They must have hurried to highlight the accursed girl who killed off prospective bridegrooms. When the calamity struck her a second time on the eve of the wedding, the wretched young girl chose to end her role in the drama, determined not to be the cause of yet another death. She was beyond all accusations now.

'Oh God!'

Everything was a blur again. Kunjootty felt dizzy, nauseated. A chaotic state of mind where he could no longer distinguish between reality and fantasy.

Zavarias sat ruing his own words, staring anxiously at Kunjootty.

'I could not contain it within me, please forgive me. Do not let your mind get disturbed again!'

Under the veneer of toughness dwelled a grieving man, and Kunjootty gazed at him with much pity and great compassion.

'No, I will not.'

Kunjootty had to forget those moist eyes in order to keep his word. Shutting his eyes, he endeavoured to reach the pure consciousness where the illusions of the waking life did not intercede. However, he was ruthlessly pushed back from there.

'Jehovah's decision! Susanna's mother passed away. Now her younger sister is all alone.'

As Kunjootty flinched, the shock too much to bear, his father continued to speak.

'See, on thinking about it, something struck me. Will you listen to me, Kunjootty?'

'What?'

'I am asking because of my anxiety. How will that young girl live alone? Can you not offer her a life? Money and status . . . I realize their futility now.'

For one moment, Kunjootty found himself going still. Then he felt the old depression returning.

'Remorseful, are you?' he asked.

Zavarias sat with his head bowed down, wordless.

Kunjootty did not have the heart to needle his aged father again.

'I tried to save another recently,' he replied, 'Before the effect of that subsides, why venture into a new adventure? Appa, nobody can save anyone else.' Then softly, yet firmly, Kunjootty said, 'If you feel guilty, why don't you accept that girl as your unborn daughter, Appa?'

'Kunjootty!'

Kunjootty couldn't hate his father even a tiniest bit any longer.

Who dared to cast blame on whom?

When one examined the charter of sins, everyone was equal.

From the emotional centre of his consciousness, a spark of love surged into Kunjootty's hands. Clutching his father's tense hand with both of his own, Kunjootty held it close to the sinful beats of his own heart. As the hands found one another after ages of forgetfulness, Zavarias put his head on his son's chest and started heaving with sobs.

Kunjootty's remaining strength waned in that instance.

They were crying together for the first time.

43

The Sacrament of Penance

That night, for some reason, Isaac did not arrive to keep Kunjootty company. Zavarias had to keep watch on the patient.

The next morning, Chiriyankan and his French wife, Patricia, came to visit Kunjootty as he lay expecting Isaac.

'We are returning. Thought of seeing you before we left . . .'

Kunjootty was disconcerted on seeing the unexpected visitors. He had not attempted to meet them when he was in the isle. Now, meeting those who were bidding goodbye, whatever was interred seemed to poke up its head again.

'I heard that you were kind to my child!' Chiriyankan's words were redolent with gratitude and respect.

Kunjootty floundered on facing the new test. 'I . . . I failed to keep her safe!'

'Be consoled that it is all God's decree. What's decided for us, life or death, is not in our hands. The one who has given alms can always demand its return. We are going back to France tomorrow. We have cancelled Anita's ticket.'

Chiriyankan's voice never wobbled. Kunjootty recognized that the man was in touch with a great source of strength. His composure commanded respect.

'When will you come back?' Kunjootty asked politely.

'Never again, Kunjootty. There is nothing left to call us back here. It must have been the divine verdict. We are embarking on full-time evangelistic work from now. Haven't we received the benediction to be dedicated to the work without any encumbrances? We would like to express our gratitude for your affection towards our little girl.'

The French woman's eyes were mournful.

'*Merci pour tout* (Thank you for everything).'

'Before I leave, here is a line from the Holy Bible for you Kunjootty!' Chiriyankan said softly. 'Inscribe these words from the *Book of Exodus* in your mind forever: *But when they measured it with an omer, those who gathered much had nothing over, and those who gathered little had no shortage!*'

One by one, they were bidding farewell: leaving behind only the signboards of their journeys. Kunjootty lay inert in his bed, watching all those who were passing by. Maybe their discovery was true. Tomorrow, they might think it wrong. But they had escaped from the grappling of today. Let it be so always. Kunjootty closed his eyes and slipped into silence; yearning to forget most things and remember something else. The lonely road, the never-ending solitude, the mesmerizing nuances of the holy lines Chiriyankan had gifted him with. 'The Word' was splitting into colours, before merging back to form a single entity.

He must have lain like that for long, trying to immerse himself in that experience. When Kunjootty woke up from the reverie of life's connection with the Word, he saw that Isaac was by his side. Like a felon, he was sitting with his head bowed. Isaac looked devoid of energy and spirit, almost half-dead. Dishevelled, unkempt, with heavy eyelids and darkness around them caused by lack of sleep.

'When did you come?' Kunjootty asked gently.

'Some time ago. I did not want to wake you. How are you feeling now?'

'Good!' Kunjootty muttered, 'I was expecting you yesterday.'

'Could not come . . .' Isaac looked traumatized. He had the same grief-stricken look that Kunjootty had sighted on Zavarias's face. He knew that the anguish was connected with Teresa.

'Do not worry,' Kunjootty said with a marked resignation, 'Perhaps it was all destined like this!'

Isaac lost his control then.

'To think that I also played a part. Why did she have to? Why?'

Why indeed? Kunjootty reflected. Whatever it was, death was now a phenomenon that left him cold. There was no need to raise it to a stature that it did not deserve. Yet, he felt an inimical pleasure at Isaac's ill-timed contrition. He knew it was uncalled for and cruel but yet . . .

Both moved away from each other, marooned in their own silences. After some time, Isaac spoke, as if stumbling against an indefinable point in his sojourn.

'When it rained, it poured! All disasters occurred together . . . Have lost everything.'

Kunjootty discerned that it was not merely Teresa's tragedy that was plaguing Isaac. He felt apprehensive that his friend might collapse any moment in his agitation. He caught a whiff of liquor even amidst the pungent smell of medicines.

'What happened to you, Isaac?' Kunjootty scolded.

'I am defeated, Kunjootty. I have become a pauper overnight.'

'What do you mean?'

'They came in mobs and destroyed my shrimp farms. Tore all the barricades down!'

'Who?'

'The fishermen living near the lagoon. Even the ones who were part of my workforce betrayed me and joined their cohorts. I was in heavy debt for carrying out all the work, and in one night everything was demolished. On top of that rioting, murder, criminal case.'

Kunjootty lay listlessly, listening. A sense of detachment, as if something was happening somewhere. Who said that everything first happened in the imagination? If so, whose imagination formed the framework for all these events?

Isaac got lost in ruminations again. Then he returned penitently, to confess his own sins.

'I agree with what you said that day. The mind is a restless monkey that jumps from one thing to another without respite. A creature that gives no peace. Though it struck me at that point, I was too arrogant to admit to it. Some sort of meaningless ego. Today, I realize that my avarice, my ambition, they were pointless!'

If only he could get some time to sit idle, forgetting this universe. If only he could grieve a little at Isaac's plight. Nothing remained in the nest of dried-up emotions to be shared with this man. The mind was like a heap of ashes, all freshness extinguished long ago. Not even a smouldering ember to kindle a spark.

Let Isaac cry. Cry to himself. A kind word, a healing touch or a conciliatory word might further weaken the resilient embankments that held Isaac together.

As the brackish wind blew about the room, Kunjootty remembered the backwaters again. The livelihoods of many innocents depended on the rise and fall of the lagoon's moods. For them life meant stoic resolve while facing hunger. Yet they were undone by the cries of their starving children. When they saw that the new shrimp farm's barricades were the reason behind the hunger, they were forced to surround the enemy camp with weapons hidden in their traditional Irruttu Kuthi, the traditional skiffs called the impalers of darkness. The lagoon, whose waters were swollen with their perspiration, lay waiting for salvation through its own Bhagiratha. When they hacked away at the stubborn stone blockades, channels of water burst through, and soon, prawns and slushy mud joined the river.

A boat came speeding furiously. There were warnings issued using a loudspeaker:

'Disperse immediately.'

The fishermen did not heed that stricture.

'Don't try to scare us!'

As the fire leapt from one flambeau to another, laying bare the secret of the night lagoon, many stones, catapults and work implements were readied for the combat.

'Disperse immediately! This is an order!'

'No, we will not go away. This is our lagoon!'

One fisherman aimed his stone at the boat. Soon, many more stones and blazing torches started buzzing in the air. They surmised that the watch-guards would return empty-handed at their spunky fight.

All surmises and predictions went fatally wrong.

The first bullet was fired in the sky. Yet the natives did not back down; using their hand shovels as shields and twirling their

lances and spikes, the men defended themselves. A few fell in
the desperate upheaval that ensued. The wounded jumped into
the lagoon, screaming. They tried to swim, but many sacrificed
themselves to the lagoon.

The backwaters turned red after tasting blood.

The flambeaus dimmed and were snuffed out, one by
one. The orphaned skiffs, Irruttu Kuthi, floated on the river
surface whilst their masters lay dead in the depths. Something
unnamed, loathsome and terrifying seemed to encircle the
surroundings.

Kunjootty recollected that history was repeating itself.
Another echo of the battles in Potta Hill's valley. The ghastly
ending of hubris. Conflicts arising from ignorance. That was
behind everything.

However, the essence of the truth lay beyond their
understanding in some other plane. Since the men could not
see it with their eyes, they did not value it. Since they could
not hear it with their ears, they did not heed it. Since they
could neither taste, nor touch or smell the truth, they did not
comprehend it.

* * *

When he was alone, Kunjootty got up, troubled by his own
discovery. The debilitating pain from his wound was disregarded.
Taking up the incomplete *Book of Exodus*, Kunjootty stared at it
like a creature under examination. This was the book that had
ransacked his very life. The life breath of his ancestors stirred
within its spirit. As representatives of ill-fated lives, Ezhuthassan
and Koppan slept within its pages. The final farewell of Diwakar
Menon, who set off on a quest for truth, was inscribed inside.

The stories of Nandini who never returned, and Anita, who would never return, were caught therein. The story of the fire bird, whose saga started before everything else; the breeze over the backwaters, then time itself, oft forgotten while straddling everything, all of these lay scattered in the pages.

It was the height of stupidity that someone oblivious of the cause of creation attempted to bind down time in that manner. Let 'time', unyielding and unchanging, forgive him if it could. Shower mercy on all meaningless whims, and his ignorance. The great flow of exodus could never be caught in any book. As long as time existed, the exodus would continue. Not even a speck was free from that law.

Finally, Kunjootty discovered this with great torment:

The written book was just a dismal imitation of what was happening around. Why should one record the tribulations, merely to trigger repetitions?

In a moment when he felt mighty enough to cast out all falsehoods, Kunjootty passionately tore up the incomplete *Book of Exodus*.

Vertically. Horizontally.

Again, vertically. And then, horizontally.

Thus, time was divided. A throbbing universe reduced to fragments of paper . . . a prayerful offering for all the souls inside, for the river and time; strips of paper that embodied the relentless meditation of many years.

Gathering a fistful of the shredded paper, Kunjootty reverently touched his heart, before offering it to the river.

'This sacrificial food for the memory of my forebearers. For my Valiyammachi, who told me the story of the fire bird. For my Valiyappachan, whom I have never seen, who stays in my flowing blood forever.'

Again, another fistful of paper bits was submitted worshipfully to the flowing river.

'For those souls who lived and drowned in the pages of this creation—Murali, Nandini, Koppan, Diwakar Menon, Ezhuthassan, Anita . . . then . . .then . . .'

Another fistful, in holy remembrance of his beloved Potta Thuruthu, the isle that gave him his identity; and the wind, which remained part of the lagoon's last breath.

Yet there remained many more bits of paper. Kunjootty had no doubts about whom those were meant for. The most deserving recipient of the final salutation's flowers of ruin was the current of life itself—the deathless, nameless river.

Struggling to be impassive, Kunjootty gazed at the river that was hurrying with its portion of the sacrificial offerings towards the mouth of the sea. The holy remnants of the *Book of Exodus.* The ending of all dreams, all vices. The fairness of time.

The lagoon was coloured black now. The frolicking bits of time were coloured white. Some slivers of the scattered paper meandered in the wind, unsure of their destination. One small piece flew straight towards Kunjootty and stuck to his chest. He did not know from which part of his offerings this little speck had returned, from that belonging to his ancestors, the isle, or the river.

Kunjootty asked it plaintively:

'Why are you not going away?'

'Where?'

'To the flow . . . far away.'

'I cannot go anywhere. When everything ends, I shall remain.'

Kunjootty extracted the bit of paper carefully using his forefinger and thumb. He looked at it with unbridled eagerness.

One letter. Just one letter.

It was brimming with all the answers.

'0'

Emptiness. Everything was emptiness.

When everything that had been confined within started attacking him, Kunjootty burst into tears. He had loved that book so very dearly. So much of his life energy had been spent working on it.

After crying for a while, he felt calm.

It was as if a flickering light was floating about in his consciousness. A marvellous insight arrived in the procession of revelations:

What he had seen as emptiness was completeness.

Poornamadah, Poornamidam!

The recognition dawned that everything he had known had been complete. After the gargantuan effort of adding completeness to completeness, and subtracting completeness from completeness, the enigma of the completeness remained . . .

The nature of emptiness too was no different. After addition of emptiness to emptiness and deletion of emptiness from emptiness, emptiness alone remained.

If so, emptiness and completeness could not be diverse. If one actualized emptiness, one would know completeness. A state of emptying oneself, shedding the *Aham*, the ego. Then, one experienced completeness.

Heeding that revelation, Kunjootty began his exodus.

To whom should he bid goodbye? He searched all around him. A jungle crow looked at him intently, perched on the tip of the stationary China net.

Kunjootty did not bid farewell even to the creature.

The solitary journey to the consecrated ground for conducting the sacrament of penance, towards the valley of Potta Hill.

All the journeys of exodus inevitably reached the promised land where the ancestors rested. Over there, a graveyard where crosses sprouted lushly. On a neglected corner, where wild creepers ruled, was a fresh grave. The woman who killed her soul had no resting place in the front. Hidden far behind, in a pauper's grave, she was condemned to lie in agony.

There, Kunjootty had a debt to pay. The debt of a burning candle.

Epilogue

After the End . . .

At the end of a long journey, Kunjootty stood lost among black crosses, wild blooms with parched stems and luscious corpse-stench flowers. The day was snuffed away then and night came treading heavily over the valley.

Kunjootty did not want to return.

He wanted to stay as the companion to the darkness and the dark crosses; through deep penance, get rooted in that place and emerge as another cross amongst his forebearers. The satisfying denouement of the exodus.

He looked lovingly at each cross. Recognizing that each grave held his ancestors, Kunjootty lit up the candles one by one. At the desolate pauper's grave, having lit up three candles, he stood silently for a while.

A much-delayed kindling of light.

Om . . . Om . . . Om.

The church bells tolled, communicating their acceptance of his offerings.

Kunjootty walked towards the church, as if in a trance.

The gigantic front door was wide open as if waiting to welcome him. A cool, soothing breeze and the flickering life-flames of the melting candles. The Good Shepherd, accepting, both the tax collectors and the sinners, with open arms, into his heart's great benevolence. The Holy One, who went in search of the single missing lamb, leaving the other ninety-nine behind.

Like a lost lamb, Kunjootty knelt down before the Basilica. Then he devotedly traced the cross on his forehead; something he hadn't done for years. The Shepherd's eyes exuded serenity, compassion and sanctuary. His Holy wounds had the depth to absorb many more mortal sins of the world. And Kunjootty had mountainous amounts of sins to offer.

Kunjootty was not alone.

With his eyes raised to the heavens, seated very close to the altar, was a very old man. He had shrunk with age. A rosary was held tight in one hand, where a web of veins was visible. And a canticle was on his lips.

The occasion, when the veils that caused forgetfulness were removed, one by one.

Om apyayantu mamangani vak pranashcakshuh
shrotramatho balamindriyani cha sarvani sarvam
brahmaupanishadam . . .

May all my limbs—speech, breath, eyes, ears and other senses—
stay strong and fulfilled!
May they all be acting at the words of God!

A man who had been full of himself in his lusty, arrogant youth now stood forlorn in the depths of helplessness: counting the moments before death in the beads of his Holy Rosary, before sprouting up as another Cross.

Even Kunjootty, a mere mortal, felt a wave of compassion in his heart.

All those crosses blooming in the graveyard were once human beings. Yearning for much, leaving without anything, ending up as simple crosses. The rich man who built his mansions and the poor man who remained enslaved all his life, became adjacent crosses. Yet the living lot was diligent in inscribing addresses on the crosses. It would survive for a short interval of time. After one or two generations, there would be hardly anyone left who would recognize the crosses. When these men and women too would transform into crosses forgotten by time, they would embody the truth spoken in the Upanishads.

Innu Njan, Nale Nee.
Today, it is I; tomorrow it is you.

Behind the holy wounds of the Shepherd, Kunjootty caught sight of an open skylight. A lattice that opened to the path, life and truth. He could catch a glimpse of the Potta Hill. Like the stirring of a forgotten dream, a self-centered desire that refused to be suppressed.

Beyond that was the sacrificial ground of the fire bird that had been reborn in the deep sighs of Valiyammachi, and had lived in the tears of her grandson.

Those were not exaggerated fairy tales: the wailing procession of the scattered feathers or the desiccated, thirsty Chama Potta. The childhood obstinacy, insisting on an expedition to the

place, still remained strong. As another miracle, Kunjootty
recognized the return of his Valiyammachi, with her fragrances
of ksheerabala oil and dhanwantaram salve, to the land purified
by his Valiyappachan's blood.

'Little one!' The affectionate call.

'Valiyammachi!' The obedient response.

Amid both calls lay the path to the hill imprinted with
the footprints of Ramban with his filariasis-ridden left leg and
Pakeeri, with his sightless right eye. The final markings of
those who never returned, having embarked on a quest for the
fire bird's feathers.

'Little one.'

Hearing that call once more, Kunjootty gazed ardently at
the pinnacle of Potta Hill. In front of him was the Holy Mount
of the Commandments; and the wind that blew originated
from the Creator Himself. As the air, which transformed the
lifeless body into spirit, entered through his nose, Kunjootty
experienced the words of the Holy Bible merging in his blood
like a diksha mantra.

> 'But when they measured it with an omer, those who gathered
> much had nothing over, and those who gathered little had no
> shortage . . .'

Burnishing the words bright in his heart, for fulfilling the
unrealized prophecies written in the book that was torn apart,
following the path trodden by those who had walked before
him, Kunjootty began his exodus.

Scan QR code to access the
Penguin Random House India website